Magic Through The MIRROR

Thank you for ~~by~~ buying My book. 🙂

[signature]

Aria Raposo Trueman

Tellwell Talent
www.tellwell.ca

ISBN
978-0-2288-1483-2 (Hardcover)
978-0-2288-1482-5 (Paperback)
978-0-2288-1484-9 (eBook)

To my parents,
for your support and encouragement
throughout the entire process of writing,
editing, and publishing my first novel.
Thank you both for always believing
in me and for your love.
Also, I'm truly sorry for making you watch countless
hours of Dora reruns with me when I was much younger.
I sincerely apologize for making you endure that.

PROLOGUE

RACHEL FREE ANGEL

$\mathcal{I}$n a small village, a delightful little baby girl was born in the hospital and her cries echoed throughout the halls.

"Look at her," said Rebekah Free, the child's mother, delighted to stroke her baby's delicate curls. Rebekah had coffee-coloured eyes, long blond hair, and rosy cheeks.

"Our baby's gorgeous," said Rick Angel, the child's father. He had dark copper-coloured eyes, dark brown hair, and a large button-shaped nose. He wore his mining uniform.

"She has your eyes and cheeks," Rick said.

"And your nose and hair," Rebekah said. "What are we going to name her?" she questioned her husband.

"I'm not certain," he replied.

Rebekah looked down at the newborn baby girl she held tenderly in her arms. She gazed deeply into her little girl's eyes, noticing her small smile and her dark brown curls. Though a rather quick decision, she was one hundred per cent convinced she had the ultimately perfect name. "Our daughter's name is Rachel Free Angel."

"Rachel, sweetie, don't play with the oven," Rebekah told Rachel, scooping her lovely two-year-old daughter up into her arms.

"But why, Mommy?" Rachel asked in her baby-like voice.

"Because you could get hurt. Now go to Daddy; he's probably in the tree fort, okay?" Rebekah set Rachel down and showed her out the back door.

Rachel ran to the large oak tree that grew in the centre of the backyard. "Daddy!" she called up. There was no response. Next, she strolled onto a wooden plank that lay on the ground. This plank was fastened to a rope that led to an iron hook that was screwed into the wooden platform far up above her head. The end of the rope hung in front of her little face. When she tugged on the end of the rope, the board she stood on was mechanically pulled upwards. When she was high enough, she pushed on a wooden hatch diagonally above her head and pulled herself into the tree fort her father had built for her when he'd become a construction worker and quit his mining profession. About her were four walls; in one corner there was a staircase leading to the second and highest level of the wooden tree fort. Scattered all over the floor were Rachel's toys: small building blocks, several dolls, and a dollhouse.

"Daddy!" she called again, but there wasn't a reply to be heard. She ran to the staircase and to the second floor. On the second level was Rick, tightening loosened screws with his new screwdriver and humming to his favourite song, "Eye of the Tiger," and a bit too loudly, if Rachel had anything to say about it.

"Daddy!" Rachel beckoned once more. Rick turned around and Rachel jumped into his lap, his screwdriver almost puncturing her head.

"Hi, Rachel," Rick said, putting his screwdriver onto the floor and away from his daughter.

"Mommy's relaxing; want to come and join her?" Rachel asked as though it were the most important question in the complete universe.

Abruptly, they heard a scream that was too close for any type of comfort. Rick spun his head around towards the house and shouted in a concerned tone, "Rebekah!" He seized Rachel and got out of the tree fort as quickly as he possibly could.

"Mommy!" Rachel cried.

Their house was aflame. Through the window they saw Rebekah frantically struggling on the floor, trying to extinguish the flames spreading across her body. Rick and Rachel could see fire reaching the ceiling from the oven. Rick brought his daughter to the nearest house and pounded on the door.

Their retired neighbour, Ms. Richards, opened the door, unaware of the house fire next door. Before Ms. Richards could say anything, Rick put Rachel down, ran into their neighbour's residence, seized the closest telephone, and phoned the fire department, "Hello, yes this is a genuine crisis, house fire on Sunshine Drive, entire house ablaze, one victim indoors!" he shouted into the receiver.

"My, what's going on?" Ms. Richards asked, holding Rachel's hand as tears streamed down the child's cheeks.

"Our beloved home is burning and Rebekah is inside!" Rick explained.

"Oh my," Ms. Richards said.

Rick glanced out the window to see the inferno spreading to the other houses and the tree fort he'd worked so hard to create.

"Daddy, do you want to play with me?" a five-year-old Rachel proposed to her father.

"Sorry, not now, perhaps later," Rick returned from their alcohol-stained sofa. After Rebekah had died, Rick began to smoke ten times the amount he used to, and he now had an uncontrollable drinking obsession that caused him to be ill. Rachel and her father had moved into a small apartment that now reeked of beer. Rick was frequently in the hospital because of his illness. He practically never acknowledged Rachel; in truth, Rachel could only talk to a nearly destroyed doll by the name of Rose. She'd received the doll as a gift on her first birthday, and Rose had miraculously survived the fire. As for Rick, it was true beyond a doubt that he'd become a horrid parent without his late wife. Without Rebekah, he would die in the near future.

"Daddy," Rachel said, "could we maybe go to the park later?"

"Certainly, I promise," Rick said, though they both knew they weren't going to any park any time soon. Then suddenly, Rick passed out cold, a beer bottle in his hand. Rachel looked up at her father with sad eyes that were wet with tears; she feared what the future would bring and she couldn't help but consider the worst.

Over the next few months, Rick was regularly in the hospital. Since Rachel couldn't stay at their apartment on her own and there was nobody to look after her, she was forced to stay in the chair near her father's bedside. To pass the time, she would read fairy tales that she'd received on her first birthday without Rebekah. As she read, her fingers glided across the words and pictures. Slowly, tears trickled down her cheeks. The unfortunate truth that life was not a fairy tale and that not everybody gets a happy ending was slowly seeping in. Yet while she slept, dreams of a happy ending with her father would fill her subconscious and she couldn't help but smile. She dreamed of them going to Snow White's cottage, or flying around in *Neverland*, maybe even meeting Cinderella herself. When she awoke, she was back in her dreadful reality. She picked up one of her storybooks and read for a while.

Rick awoke suddenly and Rachel immediately put her book of *Cinderella* down with her pile of other books and looked at her father. "Daddy," she asked, "are you ever going to be better?"

"Of course, then we can have all the fun in the world," Rick replied, though they both knew that was a lie. That was probably one of the biggest lies Rick had ever told.

By the coming week, Rick was in the hospital once again.

The following day, Rick woke to cough up blood. Rachel immediately awoke in the seat by his bedside and called for a nurse. Three doctors rushed in and tried whatever they could to keep Rick alive, though it wasn't good enough because he died the next week.

Rachel became an orphan. None of her relatives desired anything to do with her so they concluded it would be best to put her in a boarding school and never see her again.

CHAPTER ONE

THE ACADEMY

"Now, everyone, what does a protractor help us do?" Ms. Glass asked her math class. She had curly blond hair, piercing green eyes, and thin glasses that sat on the edge of her nose. She wore a knee-length green dress with yellow felt flowers sewn in around her waist like a belt; she also wore bright red lipstick and shiny black shoes. One thing about her that most students learned the hard way was that she may have been beautiful, but she was most certainly not someone anyone would want to mess with.

A girl in the back of the class with light blond hair raised her hand.

"Samantha?" Ms. Glass asked.

"Um, well, Miss," Samantha sneezed quickly; her sneeze was so high-pitched it sounded more like a squeak. "A, um, protractor helps us calculate the measurement of an angle."

"Yes, Samantha," Ms. Glass said; Samantha smiled. "A protractor does help us measure an angle, as well as an acute angle, or an accurate angle. Does anyone else have anything to add?" Ms. Glass scanned the classroom and one student caught her eye: Rachel Free Angel, the worst student in the school, who thoroughly enjoyed taking naps during class. The teacher walked over to her student and bent down slightly. "Rachel," Ms. Glass said loudly into Rachel's ear. This was answered with a snore.

"Rachel Free Angel!" the teacher yelled. This woke Rachel and she almost knocked over her desk. Her dark brown hair had grown down a little past her shoulders and was still quite curly, her brown eyes were large, and her cheeks were now rosier. She wore the school uniform which consisted of a long-sleeved navy-blue shirt, a red plaid overall skirt, red stockings, and bright red shoes. In her ten years at the academy she had become a spiteful fifteen-year old whom the students and teachers resented.

"Who? What? Where? When? How?" Rachel asked quickly, her voice much deeper than it used to be.

"Well, Ms. Angel," Ms. Glass said, leaning away from her student. "Who? You are Rachel Free Angel, I am Ms. Laurie-Anne Glass, and the other students around us are your peers. What? You are attending a math class taught by me. Where? In class two four one, in Little Girls to Fine Women Learning Academy, on Lonely Dove street, in the United States, which is on planet Earth. When? At nine forty-five a.m. on Wednesday, the twelfth of May, year two thousand. How? Your family put you in this facility. You walked downstairs this morning to your first class, which should be at eight a.m. sharp and ends at nine a.m. sharp; you then walked into my class and fell asleep, taking a hopefully restful nap, which is quite disrespectful, considering I was talking. Is that right?"

"Yes, it is," Rachel said with a yawn. "But the real question is why were you teaching while I was sleeping, because some people here are trying to rest and not listen to your horrible and annoying voice? But, then again, you did answer all the questions, and I'm surprised because of how you're practically dumber than a donkey's bottom."

Ms. Glass breathed a large gust of air out of her nose and said, "Now, my questions. What were we talking about?"

"Something," Rachel said with another yawn.

"How many weeks of detention would you like?"

"None, if that's fine with you."

"What time did you fall asleep last night?"

"Can't remember."

"And do you find my lesson boring?"

"Yes, very much actually, and it would be *sooo* much better if you could just shut up."

"That's it!" Ms. Glass shouted at the top of her lungs as her face turned bright red. "For all of your disrespect, you will have three weeks — no, three months of detention!"

"So?" Rachel said.

"You're such a—" she started.

"A little angel?" Rachel interrupted. "Yes, I know, my name says so; it should be obvious. Oh right, I forgot, dummies like you couldn't possibly solve any type of riddle or problem, even if the answer was right in front of your face." Rachel batted her eyelashes overdramatically whilst the other students simply rolled their eyes.

"You're such a brat; I can't wait to retire," Ms. Glass said to herself.

"Oh, you're that old already? I only thought you were fifty; didn't know you were sixty or older," Rachel commented.

"To all the good students of this class, and our little brat, turn to page ten in your math books and silently read to yourself as I go to my desk and fill out detention slips for Ms. Angel." With that said, Ms. Glass turned on her heel and headed to her desk. Once their teacher was gone, some of the students sitting in front of Rachel turned to face her and shook their heads in disappointment, ashamed to have her in class. Rachel stuck her tongue out at them until they turned back around to read in silence.

Rachel looked at Ms. Glass to see if she was paying any attention to her; she wasn't, so Rachel continued her nap in peace.

The dream Rachel was having was strange; she was in a dark room full of candles. Suddenly, she rose above the ground and saw that the flame of each lit candle played a part in spelling two full words: *AVOID TEMPTATIONS.* Rachel looked at the words in wonder for a few moments before it changed into: *WAKE UP!* Then Rachel heard a familiar voice boom the same words the flames from the candles spelled. She jolted awake and saw Ms. Glass staring down on her.

"Yes?" Rachel asked, playing dumb.

"You were sleeping in my class again!" Ms. Glass said loudly.

"So?"

"Wouldn't want you to wake up in my class all alone while your peers were in their next ones."

"Class dismissed?" Rachel asked.

"You should try, Rachel," Ms. Glass said, her tone softening. "I can tell you have the potential for great things, so please try; it could help shape an amazing future for you. And keep the tone just not so impolite; it could help you win a bet. Of course, only when you're done school."

Rachel smiled. "Yes, Ms. Glass. So, when's my first week of detention? For three months, right?"

Her teacher shook her head. "Last warning, got it?"

"Got it," Rachel said, and then she walked out of her math teacher's classroom.

"You should at least try to stop napping in class, especially when the teacher is talking," Hannah Black said from beside Rachel.

"Were you waiting outside the class for me?" Rachel asked, partially creeped out.

"Maybe, but we always walk to third class together; it's tradition." Hannah had wavy blond hair, green eyes, and a sweet smile.

"It's so much easier for you. You're Ms. Glass' granddaughter; you're a legit teacher's pet!" Rachel said to her best and only friend.

"Doesn't mean I'm the top student," Hannah reprimanded.

"I wish this school were different," Rachel said with a heavy sigh that carried a large thought.

"Different how?"

"I don't know." She knew she was close to the answer, but she was still unsure.

"Well, it's not like you can really do anything about whatever it is you want to change. Well, unless it's the best idea the principal's ever heard."

"Actually, there's another school in the next town over, right?" Rachel asked randomly.

"Yeah, a boys' school, why?"

"What if — never mind."

"What?"

"I said never mind."

"Tell me, pretty please. Please, please, please!"

"Fine. What if I went to the boys' school?"

Hannah stopped. "W-w-what?" she said and fainted dead in her tracks.

CHAPTER TWO

RACHEL'S PLAN

*A*fter dragging Hannah to their dorm and waiting for what felt like forever for Hannah to come to, Rachel elaborated, "A fresh start: wouldn't it be great?"

"Rachel, you're my best friend; please stay," Hannah implored.

"But I hate it here!" Rachel reprimanded.

"I'll always be here to cheer you up!"

"But that isn't good enough. I don't want to be known as the worst student of this craphole."

"I can help you fix that!"

"I want to not be known. What I really want is a really fresh new start," Rachel said firmly. "Besides, I already have a wire transfer from my uncle to the principal of the boys' academy. My uncle signed everything without even looking at the details because he doesn't really care. The contract saying I can attend has been signed by him and a copy will be here later tonight. I just need to bring that with me and I'll have a new life."

Hannah knew she wouldn't be able to convince Rachel otherwise. "Fine, but you're forgetting something in your plan," Hannah said.

"What's that?"

"You can't just disappear."

Rachel knew exactly what to say. "That's where you come in."

"I'm in your plan?" Hannah asked fearfully.

"Yes. When I sneak out, you tell the teachers that I've been transferred to another school, and that I had to leave very late to get there by the early morning of Monday."

"W-when will you leave?" Hannah asked, looking at the floor beneath her feet.

"Sunday night at twelve a.m.," Rachel said.

"You've got an entire plan planned out?"

"Of course, because I am a genius."

"What time is it?" Hannah asked.

"Dinner time."

"Well, since it's dinner time, why don't we go to the dining hall, eat, then come back here and you can fully explain everything to me."

"Yeah, because I am starving," Rachel said and patted her belly.

They walked out of their dorm, down the stairs, and towards the dining hall. The line moved much less hurried than it usually did because two girls at the front of the line were arguing with the dinner ladies about the food quality.

After a full twenty minutes of impatient waiting, Rachel was at the front of the line, ready to order her food. The dinner ladies in front of her had pale skin and their eyes were lifeless, like the ones of a doll.

"Let me see, let me see, what shall please my huge appetite?" Rachel said, carefully observing the trays of food in front of her.

"Hurry up, Ms. Angel; there are plenty of people behind you if you're unaware," one of the dinner ladies said, already annoyed.

"It is rude to rush a person while she is thinking," Rachel said, wagging an overly dramatic finger at them. "I have been offended by the elderly! Scandalous!" The girls behind Rachel rolled their eyes.

"But," Rachel said, her voice back to normal as though she'd never made an outburst, "my hunger will be appeased with mashed potatoes, chicken, and a bowl of gravy, oh, and water."

The dinner lady put the food on a black tray that sat beside the food as Rachel walked over in front of the other dinner lady and waited for her meal. Once she got her hands on the tray of food, Rachel took it and went to a vacant table in the corner of the dining hall.

Hannah spotted Rachel and sat down beside her.

"Seriously?" Hannah said to Rachel.

"What? Do you see a teacher? I was never here!" Rachel said and dove underneath the table.

Hannah pulled her back up onto her chair. "No, it's just that you always eat the same thing."

"So?"

"You eat the same thing every time."

"Your point?" Rachel asked, using her fork to shove a piece of chicken into her mouth.

"First of all," Hannah said, "you should eat more healthily. Second of all, if you try new things, you might actually like them."

"Na, na, na," Rachel said, mouth full of food. "I eat what I want when I want and how I want."

Hannah sighed and continued eating, knowing she would never convince Rachel.

After a short and silent dinner, Rachel and Hannah went sluggishly back to their dorm and sat on their beds.

"Plan?" Hannah asked.

"Okay," Rachel replied. "On Sunday at twelve a.m., I cut off all my hair so I look like a boy." Hannah gasped like Rachel had suggested murder. "Then," Rachel continued, "I take off my stupid girl's uniform and wear the boy's outfit that I bought instead. I sneak downstairs, out the front doors, and towards my new life at the boys' school and sign myself in as... I need a name."

"Jack?" Hannah suggested. "Oh, I've always adored the name—"

"No," Rachel said sharply.

"Karl?"

"No."

"Benjamin? That name isn't bad, admit—"

"No."

"Bryce?"

"No, because I don't have a price, get it? Get it?"

Hannah stared at her blankly; Rachel dropped her smile and cleared her throat. "Any other suggestions?"

"Justin?" Hannah asked.

"Okay, that one I like. It sounds free, if you know what I mean."

"I don't," Hannah said.

"You're such a bummer," Rachel said. "Okay, Justin, Justin, aha! Justin Campridge!" Rachel smiled warmly at Hannah. "Thank you — for everything." She lay down on her bed and quickly fell into a deep sleep.

Just help Rachel, that's all I have to do, Hannah thought. *Just say she's gone to another school and had to leave late at night to get there on time.*

They both woke up to the ring of the bell at seven o'clock on the dot like every morning, and this particular morning was no different. Rachel threw on her uniform and ran as fast as she possibly could to the dining hall with Hannah behind her, as they did every morning. They both made it to the front of the line quickly because, as usual, every morning a person craves food. Every girl in the school would ask for almost anything and run away to a table to eat.

"Let me see, let me see," Rachel said. "What shall I choose to satisfy my hunger?"

The two dinner ladies rolled their eyes at Rachel; they were used to her dramatic phrases by now, but they were still annoyed by them and nothing in the world would change that.

"I will have one slice of French toast, one pancake, two waffles, three pieces of bacon, a bowl of maple syrup, and chocolate milk," Rachel said. "I mean if you are actually capable of doing such a task, that is."

The dinner ladies gave Rachel her food, and Rachel ran over to the same vacant table as the day before and impatiently awaited Hannah's arrival.

Hannah came to her a few seconds later carrying a tray with a plate with two pieces of lightly buttered toast, another with a single piece of bacon, and a large bowl of fruit.

"It's Thursday!" Hannah exclaimed randomly.

"So?" Rachel asked, taking a bite of her pancake with way too much maple syrup to be healthy in the slightest.

"Three more days until Sunday!"

"Shut up!"

"Why?" Hannah asked, looking around to see a few girls staring at her as though she had two heads.

"My secret plan won't be so much of a secret if you yell it out loud, in front of the whole school, not to mention," Rachel snapped.

"Sorry," Hannah apologized in a whisper.

The two girls ate the rest of their breakfast in silence.

After finishing their food, Rachel and Hannah hurried to their first class: science. They sat at random desks, took out their science books, and waited for the teacher.

Once all the seats were full, Ms. Marie walked in. She had straight long blond hair, full red lips, and crystal blue eyes. She wore a knee-long black dress, white gloves, and shiny black shoes. "Class," she said in an English accent, "today we will be focusing our utmost attention on the digestive tract." She picked up a piece of chalk and drew a quick sketch of what she would be teaching. "Could anyone tell me the first step of the digestive system?"

To everyone's surprise, Rachel's hand shot straight up.

"Yes, Rachel," Ms. Marie asked. "Can you tell me—"

"Actually," Rachel interrupted, "I have a question for you."

"Yes? Is it about—"

"No, not about stupid science," Rachel said coldly. "I just wanted to know why you have an accent."

"I have an accent because I'm from London. I grew up there; it is a wonderful place—"

"Okay, you can go back to your science," Rachel said with a snort.

Hannah's hand shot up.

"Uh, yes, Hannah?" Ms. Marie asked.

"Um, the digestive process starts with your mouth, then goes down your esophagus, which leads to your stomach, though at this point whatever you ate is chyme."

"Yes, very good, Hannah," Ms. Marie said. "And, everyone else, write this down in your notebooks."

Every student scribbled this down in their notebooks, except Rachel of course, who made a doodle of a boy she'd liked when she was three years old until he'd moved away and gone to a boarding school, never to be seen by her eyes again. Little did she know she wouldn't even get the slightest glimpse of him because of a gruesome reason.

Rachel raised her hand.

"Yes, Ms. Angel?" Ms. Marie said.

"May I use the bathroom?" Rachel asked.

"Sure, but not more than five minutes," the teacher warned.

"You got it," Rachel reassured Ms. Marie. Rachel stood up, grabbed her bag, and headed to the restroom with an evil smirk spread across her face. The truth was that she never actually used the bathroom during the day; she just made a huge mess.

When she arrived at the bathroom, Rachel took all the toilet paper from each stall and draped the paper over the stall walls as though they were streamers. She then took a large permanent marker and wrote the name of the person she hated the most on the walls and sinks. She finished off with cuss words before finally leaving and returning to her classroom just in time to hear the bell ring, signalling her next class.

"What did you do?" Hannah asked.

"What?" Rachel asked.

"Whenever you go to the bathroom with a smile on your face, coincidentally, the bathroom is a total mess," Hannah explained.

"Well," Rachel was about to explain but an announcement did so for her:

"Announcement for the girls' restroom," the intercom started. *"Toilet paper streamers and permanent marker. Elisha Bright, report to the office immediately."*

"Um, well, that said most of it," Rachel said with a shrug.

"Toilet paper streamers?" Hannah asked.

"And," Rachel whispered, "permanent marker with Elisha's name and some bad words."

"But seriously, why would you send Elisha to the principal's office?" Hannah asked as they walked.

"Because she deserved it," Rachel replied.

"Like the time she deserved honey in her hair while she was sleeping?"

"Precisely."

"Like the time you stole all her clothes and she had to run around in a towel for five hours, getting humiliated until you finally let up and returned her clothes, then got detention for a month?"

"The detention was totally worth it, and she deserved that, too."

"And the time you put three frogs in her bed?"

Rachel snickered.

"And the time you put yellow-painted worms in her spaghetti?"

"I honestly thought all her screaming would turn the school deaf, but it was still worth it. And she deserved that too."

"You're so lucky I'm your friend," Hannah said with a sigh.

"That's very true," Rachel said with a smile.

"What's our next class?"

"French, taught by Madame Chaise."

"Ugh," they groaned in perfect unison.

The two girls arrived at class four three two at the same time the other students did. They sat down at random desks and patiently awaited the presence of Madame Chaise. After a few minutes, she stepped into the full classroom.

She was a tall woman with a long nose and a face full of makeup. She wore thin glasses, a frilly pink dress, and casual black shoes. "Hello, class," she said in a French accent. "Today I will say French words that come to my mind. You will all repeat the word in French then translate it into English, got it?"

"Yes, Madame Chaise!" said every student except Rachel.

"*Table.*"

"*Table*, table," the students chorused.

"*Chien*, and that is?"

"*Chien*, dog."

"Good, *sourire*, this will be the last one before I give you some work—"

"BORING!" Rachel yelled, interrupting the teacher.

"Excuse me?" Madame Chaise said.

"I said BORING!" Rachel replied, raising her voice for the last word and putting her feet onto her desk.

"You will shut your mouth!" Madame Chaise yelled.

"Na, I'm good," Rachel said.

"One week of detention for disrespect, interruption, and well, put your feet down!"

"Whatever."

"Should I call your guardians?"

"Na thanks."

"That's it! Go to the office, IMMEDIATELY!"

"You can't make me," Rachel said with a yawn. "And do you mind keeping it down a bit, some people are trying to learn. And also, just a tip of beauty advice, you should do something about the nose."

Rachel was forcefully dragged on a chair by Madame Chaise to a corner of the classroom, though Rachel didn't mind at all.

Soon enough, the bell rang. The students of Madame Chaise's class exited the classroom. Rachel stayed back for a moment to leave behind a spiteful comment.

"Bye, Madame Nez-Longue," Rachel said and walked out of the class.

"That wasn't even conjugated correctly!" Madame Chaise shouted after her.

The seconds, minutes, and hours went by until it was noon on Saturday.

"Let me see, let me see, what shall satisfy me?" Rachel asked the dinner ladies like she did every day. "Hmm," she looked at all the food before finally knowing what she wanted. "I have decided!" she announced. "I will have a hamburger with lettuce, tomato, pickles, ketchup, mustard, and bacon with a side of fries!"

The dinner ladies gave Rachel her food. She was starting to walk to her table when she was suddenly confronted by a familiar face.

"What do you want, stupid mutt?" Rachel asked.

"You framed me; we both know it," Elisha said. She had curly black hair, a small and perfect button-shaped nose, and big innocent-looking eyes.

"Yeah, what she said, imbecilic jerk," Elizabeth Pinkie said from Elisha's right. She had shoulder-length dark brown hair that was brushed to perfection, green eyes, and a small but crooked nose.

"It's obvious: we can tell because you have guilt spread across your face like jam on a piece of toast, just like Daddy used to make me," Annabella Smith said from Elisha's left. She had curly hair the colour of gold, rosy cheeks, and big blue eyes that were deep like the ocean.

"Stay on topic," Elisha snapped.

"Oh, sorry, I just really loved the baked goods Daddy made for me," Annabella apologized.

"Well, you get the point: Rachel's not so much of an Angel," Elisha said.

"Whatever. It's not that big of a mess; just deal with it. Oh right, you're too much of a stuck-up baby to do anything," Rachel snapped. She walked around Elisha and her two sidekicks and continued her route to her usual table, but they followed.

"No," Elisha said. "I want revenge."

"Over a little prank? Jeez, woman, get a grip," Rachel said and continued to her table.

"I have to clean up toilet paper streamers!" Elisha roared.

"Were streamers in your childhood nightmares, because they aren't that bad. Or maybe you didn't have a good birthday party once? Was it because no one showed up? Sorry to break it to you, but that would just be natural when you're going to be there," Rachel said.

"It's your mess and I have to clean it! How is that fair?! Why is my life so sad and miserable?"

"No," Rachel said, turning on her heel to face Elisha. "You know what's sad? That you're a big baby and everyone has to put up with you; that's sad."

"Well, I don't care what you say because I'm a fabulous girl, and if I wanted to, I could easily win over one million beauty pageants without a problem. So, back on topic, what am I going to do to you? Well, for starters, I'm going to—"

"Get me in trouble?" Rachel asked mockingly; she stuck out her lip. *Tell your mommy?*

"No," Elisha said, furious. "This, humiliation." She put her hand underneath Rachel's tray and flicked it up, sending food down the top of Rachel's dress and in her hair.

As Rachel stood in shock, Elisha took advantage and dumped Elizabeth's tray of food over Rachel's head. She then did the same with Annabella's. "Look, everyone," Elisha called out. "Rachel's such a baby!"

Girls around the dining hall pointed at Rachel and laughed. "You little..." Rachel said with food in her uniform and hair while rage bubbled in her blood.

"Someone send her to—" Elisha didn't get to finish her sentence because Rachel took her fist and rammed it into Elisha's nose. She then took a random girl's tray of food and dumped it on Elisha's head, reversing the roles. The students around them laughed at Elisha, who had a nosebleed and whose cheeks were turning red with rage and embarrassment. Even Elizabeth and Annabella let out a few snickers.

"Don't just stand there!" Elisha yelled. "Get her!"

Before Elizabeth and Annabella could react, Rachel kicked them both in the stomach, sending them to the floor. Every girl in the hall clapped and Rachel bowed overdramatically, took a piece of bacon from the top of her uniform, and ate it proudly. She walked across the hall and waved as she did so. Rachel then hurried out of the dining hall and to her dorm.

As she sat on her bed, she tried to find the rest of her lunch in her dress.

She waited for Hannah who came back almost half an hour later.

"Hannah!" Rachel exclaimed happily.

"Yes?" Hannah asked.

"Can you please help me get everything out of my hair?"

"Sure, what are friends for?"

Rachel ran into the bathroom to wait for Hannah.

The bathroom Hannah and Rachel shared could only be described as enormous and shiny but slightly old. The bathtub was plain white porcelain, and the sink was the same.

Rachel leaned back and let all her hair rest in the sink. Hannah turned the water on and washed every crumb of food out of her friend's hair. She turned the tap around and the water stopped running. Hannah took a fluffy white towel off the rack and gave it to Rachel, who used it gratefully.

They left the bathroom and sat on their separate beds.

"Time?" Rachel asked.

"One p.m.," Hannah replied.

"Eleven more hours before my new life starts!"

"You can say that when it's three minutes away."

"Oh, says the one who got excited three days before."

Hannah cleared her throat. "So, since it's Sunday and there are no classes," she said.

"Oh God, please help me get through whatever is going to happen," Rachel whispered to herself.

"Want to go equestrian riding?"

"Say what?"

"Horseback riding," she clarified.

"Ugh," Rachel said and plastered herself across her bed.

"What, you've got somewhere better to be? With something better to do?"

"Today is the annual bacon-eating contest!"

"You actually want to go to that?" Hannah asked, partially disgusted. "It's only ten girls shoving food down their throats, and sometimes they choke!"

"Of course," Rachel said, making her bottom lip puff out and quiver while batting her eyelashes wantonly. "But, if you really don't want to come, I can go by my lonesome. Oh, the pain this causes me!"

"Oh, my poor dear," Hannah said sarcastically and put the back of her hand to her forehead. "I couldn't let you go on your own! That would be a tragedy!"

"Yay!" Rachel exclaimed, getting off of her bed, throwing her hands up into the air, and running out of their dorm. Hannah followed.

Rachel led Hannah to the dining hall where a long table able to fit ten people stood in the centre of the room. Large piles of bacon were lined up in front of each chair.

"Okay, stay here for a sec," Rachel said to Hannah and ran off to a clipboard-holding teacher. The teacher and Rachel exchanged a couple of words. Hannah saw her best friend sign the clipboard, which she now realized was for the list of the competitors' names. With this realization in her mind, Hannah's jaw dropped. She saw the teacher with the clipboard hand Rachel an outfit from a woven sack that sat beside her and with that, Rachel ran off to the nearest restroom. Hannah found the strength to close her mouth and look around the room where, surprisingly, a lot of students stood, waiting for the contest to begin. Hannah saw one person in particular. *Why would she show up?* Hannah wondered. She walked toward Elisha, but before she could say something, Rachel came out of nowhere and turned Hannah around to face her.

"Hi!" Rachel said happily. She now wore overalls, a white T-shirt, and brown boots, and she had her hair tied back.

Hannah forced her mind to forget she saw Elisha and focused on Rachel. "You never told me you were going to enter the contest!" she fussed.

"I don't say a lot of stuff to you," Rachel replied.

"Excuse me, contestants, please take a seat at the table," the teacher holding the clipboard said loudly enough for every girl in the dining hall to hear.

Eight girls wearing the same outfit as Rachel immediately shuffled through the crowd to find a seat. Hannah counted the girls at the table, including Rachel, coming up with nine.

"Look, everybody," Elisha called from somewhere in the crowd. "Rachel's in the contest! She's so fat and used to eating crap that she won't have a problem winning!"

Hannah turned her head toward the sound of Elisha's voice but couldn't spot her, though Rachel could find the runt in any crowd.

"At least I'm going to win, unlike you, Elisha!" Rachel shot.

"I've won lots of things," Elisha shot back. "But you're so dumb, how would you know? I mean, I've won first place at—"

"Being a dumbass!" Rachel yelled.

"At least I've won something, unlike you, Rachel not so much of an Angel!"

"I doubt that."

"Well, I'll win first place today!"

"At what?"

"Bacon-eating! And I'll make sure you get pushed all the way down to last place!" Elisha said.

"Yeah, sure," Rachel remarked. "You're so pencil-thin you wouldn't even get a participation award!"

"That's it!" Elisha screamed loudly enough for the whole school to hear. She stormed over to the teacher with the clipboard, signed her name onto the list of contestants, grabbed an outfit, and ran into the nearest unoccupied bathroom.

Rachel grinned and Hannah's jaw fell once more.

Three minutes later, Elisha came back wearing the same outfit as Rachel and the other girls. She sat at the last chair available, which was right next to Rachel.

"Three," the clipboard teacher said. "Two, one, and start eating!"

All of the girls sitting at the table instantly started swallowing as much unchewed bacon as their throats would permit without choking, eating like barbaric pigs rather than elegant girls. Even Elisha got competitive and at least tried to eat like the others.

After eight girls passed out, Rachel and Elisha were the last girls eating, devouring more and more as the seconds passed by.

Eventually, Rachel finished her pile just as Elisha collapsed to the floor, unconscious and stuffed to the max.

"Ms. Rachel Free Angel is the winner," the clipboard teacher announced. She pulled out a medal that was hiding underneath the papers on her clipboard and proudly gave it to Rachel. Rachel bowed and waved as though she were now a queen, and then she not so gracefully left the dining hall with Hannah.

"Time?" Rachel asked.

"Three thirty p.m.," Hannah replied.

"Nine hours to go!" Rachel said, making it sound as though it were the plainest thing in the world.

"Come on," Hannah said. "*Ninety* hours can go by fast if you're having fun."

"You should stop acting like you're my mom or something," Rachel noted.

Hannah pointed to herself. "Woman, I'm fifteen. I don't think I'm in any position to have kids, or be a parent."

Rachel laughed at the face Hannah was making.

"So, you want to go swimming?" Hannah asked.

"Sure."

The two girls changed into their swimsuits, taking turns using the dorm bathroom. Rachel's resembled a starry night sky while Hannah's looked like something you could buy for a Barbie doll. They wrapped towels around themselves and headed to the school pools that were open to anyone on the weekends, though they were usually completely empty. Once they got to the edge of the pool, Rachel threw off her flip-flops and towel and jumped into the water. She ended up screaming because of the ice-cold temperature. "Eek!" she shrieked. "Cold! Cold! Cold! Cold! Cold!"

"It can't possibly be that bad," Hannah said. She jumped in and ended up screaming ten octaves higher than Rachel. "Eek!" she yelled. "Why are these pools so cold?!"

"*It can't possibly be that bad*," Rachel mimicked with chattering teeth. "Guess again!" she tried her best to swim to the edge of the pool and made it there in almost two minutes, even though she hadn't been more than five feet away.

"Why don't you take the school's swimming lessons?" Hannah asked.

"Because I don't need them," Rachel snapped, shivering as she lifted herself up onto the ledge.

"One day you'll get caught in a current and no one will be able to save you," Hannah said grimly.

"That'll never happen because I don't go swimming in lakes or oceans. The only place I submerge my full body, and occasionally my head, in water, is in the bathtub. And I'm starting to think coming here was a waste; we can't swim in freezing cold water. And it's only May!"

"We just need to get used to it by swimming around a bit," Hannah suggested.

"Sure," Rachel said, using her hands to try to rub away her goosebumps.

"Look, there's an inflatable ball over there; we can play catch in the shallow end."

"Okay, I'll meet you there." Rachel got up onto her two feet and walked to the shallow end as Hannah swam, somehow bearing the cold. They met up at the end of the pool and Rachel hopped in. "So, we're just going to be playing with this thing for a couple of hours?"

"Yeah, and we can talk about school and stuff to make the time pass," Hannah said, grabbing the colourful beach ball that floated blissfully on the surface of the pool. "Catch!" she threw it at Rachel's face, causing Rachel to belly flop onto the water's surface; Hannah winced at the sound. Rachel slowly found the bottom of the pool beneath her two feet and stood up straight. She grabbed the ball that floated in front of her, calm as ever despite what had just happened.

"Oh, good thing you're okay," Hannah said and sighed relief, though her breath was cut short when Rachel yelled, *"PAAAAAYYYYY BAAAAACK!"* and threw the ball straight at Hannah. Luckily, she dodged it in time and it hit the wooden wall behind the pool, leaving a dent. Hannah looked at Rachel's extended arm.

They stared at each other's faces for a few moments before bursting into laughter.

Rachel calmed down enough to say a couple of words through her laughter, "You...get...it."

After Hannah retrieved the ball, she and Rachel played with it for a good two hours before deciding to get out and head back to their dorm.

"Seven more hours!" Rachel said.

"Horseback riding?" Hannah asked.

They wore riding pants, half chaps, and paddock boots and rode the most gorgeous horses they'd ever seen with pristine white coats and matching shining manes. However, as Rachel had expected, she got the most stubborn horse. When she yanked on his reins to stop, he kept walking; when he finally stopped and she wanted him to keep walking, he would stay put. Her horse continued this horrible behaviour, which aggravated Rachel so much she started cussing loudly and barbarically. Some of the horses actually tried to stick their heads in their bales of hay, unsuccessfully of course.

Rachel came back to the dorm missing a riding boot, surprisingly the only object she no longer had after being bucked off several times.

"Four more hours," one-booted Rachel said.

"Tennis?"

They played the sport until Rachel got hit so many times that she ended up breaking the racket in two with her bare hands.

"Two more hours," Rachel said blankly.

"Library?" Hannah suggested.

They came back only half an hour later because Rachel had yelled (whispering loudly as she put it) about how the books had horrible content, leaving her and Hannah on the *don't come to the library* list.

"An hour and a half," Rachel said, exhausted from her day out.

"Well, we can always—" Hannah started.

"No, stop right there. I am not doing something else that is suggested by you; I am going to take a long nap and you can wake me up at twelve," Rachel interrupted.

"I was going to suggest we could prank a random girl from the junior year. But if you don't want to, well, that's fine I guess."

"Whoa, who the heck are you, and what have you done to Hannah?" Rachel asked with a grin.

"I just want to prank someone, like you always do to Elisha, because this is the last hour or so I have with you. So, do you want to do it?" she asked, rubbing her hands together in an attempt to look menacing, but the results of that came up short; she looked like a little girl on a snowy winter night who'd forgotten her mittens inside and was trying to keep her hands warm.

"The kitchen's this way," Rachel whispered to Hannah.

"So, what are we doing exactly?" Hannah asked, eyeing the walls as though a teacher would just jump out and yell, "*Ha, ha! I got you! Detention for five months!*" Just the thought of it made her slightly regret coming here with Rachel.

"So, I'm thinking honey and maple syrup on the floor, so they get their bare feet all sticky; whipped cream hairdo; and we'll need string, cardboard, and water balloons, which I have in my wardrobe." She quickly turned to face Hannah. "Don't ask and don't repeat," she warned.

"Sounds like fun. And nobody will think about me being the culprit because I would never do anything so scandalous," Hannah said with a smile, all her regrets fading away into the depths of her soul.

"And no one can blame me 'cause I'll be gone," Rachel said happily. "No more detention or trouble. I'll be free from that, but first comes the prank."

Rachel waltzed into the kitchen with Hannah tiptoeing behind her. They grabbed the supplies Rachel had requested, carefully walked back to their dorm, took the cardboard and string they needed, and went to the dorms occupied by the younger generation of students.

"This one," Rachel said firmly, stopping in front of a random dorm.

"Good pick," Hannah said.

"Huh, why?" Rachel asked. Hannah pointed to the pink door sign that read: *This room is occupied by Adriana Bright, Carly Pinkie, and Lauren Smith.* And in smaller writing: *Those who enter this room without permission from these three girls will be reported and given detention, the length depending on how long you were in the room.*

"Pinkie, Smith, and Bright, I recognize those names," Rachel observed. "I only chose this one because there wasn't any sign of light underneath the door, but this, this is amazing!"

They quietly opened the door, careful so it wouldn't creak. Once the door was wide open, Rachel and Hannah saw three girls in their separate beds, all sleeping peacefully with not one single care in the world.

Hannah signalled for Rachel to start their prank.

Hannah started to pour honey and maple syrup on the floor, starting at the back of the room so she and Rachel would still be able to work without getting anything on themselves. Rachel slowly crept towards the three girls with her whipped cream can in hand, ready to give them new hairdos. She quickly sprayed the cream on the girls' foreheads and around their heads.

Hannah made a clucking noise from the back of her throat, telling Rachel they were ready for their biggest prank yet, Rachel nodded and took the water balloons to the bathroom and started filling them up. Hannah got the setup ready, making a string trigger so the piece of cardboard Rachel would put the water balloons on would bend down and the water balloons would come down on the girls' heads, drenching them. Rachel came with the balloons and put them on the piece of cardboard. Hannah finished with the syrup and honey and she and Rachel backed away, careful not to get the sticky substances on them.

Once they were out of the room, Hannah closed the door just enough for them to be able to peer inside.

"Now Little Miss Bright will get her foot creamed and drenched. This is going to be hilarious."

"But are we just supposed to wait here for who knows how long just to see their reaction?" Hannah asked.

"Oh, I can wake them up now," Rachel said.

"How?"

"This," she said and kicked the door.

Rachel and Hannah heard groans of exhaustion as one of the girls woke. "Hey, Carly," the girl said. "I heard something."

"Hmm?" the girl in the next bed said. "You're hearing things, Lauren; just go back to sleep."

Rachel kicked the door again for further persuasion.

"*What was that?*" Carly asked.

"Told you so," Lauren said. "Adriana, wake up; we hear unusual noises."

"Hmmm," the third girl said. "I don't hear anything; just go back to sleep."

Rachel kicked the door a third time.

"Um," Adriana said, "maybe we should go check it out."

Rachel and Hannah looked at each other with identical smirks across their faces, ready to hold in their laughter. They heard the three girls slowly climb out of their beds and step onto the slimy and disgusting surface.

"Eek!" Lauren shrieked.

"Oh. My. God," Carly said.

"Who on Earth did this?" Adriana asked.

Rachel and Hannah bit their fists to hold in their laughter so the trio wouldn't hear them. They listened to the three girls groaning in high-pitched tones.

The door opened towards them and Adriana, Lauren, and Carly walked closer to the string, not knowing what they were walking into. Soon enough, the trio of girls tripped on the string and the water balloons fell onto their heads, drenching them. Rachel and Hannah ran to their dorm as fast as they possibly could, though, for one of the first times in history, Rachel was behind Hannah. They ran into their dorm and collapsed onto their beds in laughter.

"That was hilarious!" Hannah said.

"That is what I always feel," Rachel said happily through her laughter.

"It's amazing."

CHAPTER THREE

PLAN IN ACTION

" 𝒯 ime," Rachel said.

"Eleven thirty," Hannah replied.

"Thirty minutes."

"Yeah, I'm really going to miss you. Promise me one day we'll meet up and still be friends."

"Promise, and I'll miss you, too," Rachel grunted. "I can't believe I just said something so sentimental. Anyway, I might regret this, but bring me the scissors."

"Okay," Hannah said. "But remember, to a girl like me, this is considered a crime, like the level of murder."

Rachel rolled her eyes as though Hannah had insinuated petting sheep was heinous.

From her drawer, Hannah took out a pair of scissors, slowly, as if they were a deadly weapon. She gulped. "You ready?" she asked.

"I was born ready. Now, Hannah Black, cut my hair off."

After fifteen long minutes, Hannah had managed to cut off almost two inches.

"Hannah," Rachel said, annoyed, "give me the damn scissors." Hannah slowly closed the scissors and sluggishly extended her arms to give them to Rachel—

Rachel snatched them out of her hands. Quickly, she cut all of her hair off until she could have been mistaken for a boy if she weren't wearing the school uniform. She put the scissors on her night table, grabbed the boy's outfit she'd bought several days before, and went into the washroom.

Once the door was closed, Hannah fell to her knees and looked at Rachel's hair littered all over the floor. A single tear escaped her eye, knowing how much she would miss her friend. She took some of the hair and tucked it under the books on her nightstand, and the rest she put in the garbage. She wiped the tears away from her eyes and sat patiently on the bed, waiting for Rachel, promising herself she would make her last moments with Rachel the best.

Rachel came out of the washroom wearing skin-tight beige breeches, a white dress shirt, a plaid knitted sweater, a golf hat that matched the sweater, and shiny black shoes. "Okay," Rachel said with a confident nod. "I'm ready to go."

Hannah ran up to Rachel and hugged her tightly for a whole minute, almost crushing her friend's ribs.

Rachel smiled weakly as she took a step back. "Goodbye, Hannah." Then she turned around and walked away, out of Hannah's life. Rachel went out the door and gently closed it behind her, barely making a sound.

Once the door was fully closed, Hannah crumpled down to her knees and cried; she cried until she thought her eyes would slide out of their sockets.

Rachel made her way down to the school's front door, undid the lock, and ran outside in the direction she knew the school was in, mostly because of the signs she saw.

"GOODBYE, STUPID SCHOOL!" she yelled as she ran in the night, her permission slip in her pocket.

After a whole seven hours of switching between running and walking, she started to jog, then walk, and then she finally saw the boys' school ahead. "There it is," she said to herself, "at last." After a short rest to watch the sun rise above the school's towers, she knocked on the front door and was brought into her new life.

"Hello, Justin Campridge," the principal said. He had piercing green eyes; greying chestnut brown hair, beard, and thick mustache; and light wrinkles. "I'm Sir Robert Evergreen, though students and people in general call me Sir Evergreen. Anyway, I got the wire transfer from ye uncle, Nathaniel; I just need the permission slip which ye should have."

Rachel sat in a chair in front of the principal's dark wood desk. The office was relatively small, and the large furniture made it feel even tinier. On either side of the desk were two large filing cabinets, presumably with the records and paperwork for every student. Behind the desk was a door, though she knew she wouldn't be allowed to go through this door. The door gave one an instantaneous feeling of being inferior and not allowed past the door frame without war. Rachel ignored the room's characteristics, took out the permission slip from her pocket, and handed it over.

Sir Evergreen quickly looked it over, and with a firm nod, he stood up and put it in the filing cabinet to Rachel's right. As he did so, Rachel told the lie as to why her uncle wasn't here, "Um, my uncle Nathaniel can't be here to meet you in person because he has a crucial meeting today. Which is why I had to be the one to give you the signed paperwork."

"Give him my regards. But anyway, I'll get a boy to give ye an outfit," Sir Evergreen said, stepping back to his seat behind the large desk. He cleared his throat, "Leonardo Dash!" he yelled. Without warning, a boy with dark brown hair and dreamy hazel eyes dashed into the room, stopping before the desk and saluting.

"Yes Sir, Evergreen Sir!" the boy said obediently.

Sir Evergreen leaned close to Rachel and said, "That's what ye say when I call y'all." He cleared his throat again, "Leonardo, get a uniform for Sir Justin Campridge immediately."

"Affirmative, Sir Evergreen, Sir!" Leonardo said and signalled for Rachel to follow him out of the office, which she did.

"Where are your parents from?" Leonardo asked Rachel once they were out of earshot, now loosened up thanks to no longer being in the presence of the headmaster.

"Texas," she said.

"Cool. My parents are from Italy. I don't have an accent because I was born here, in the United States, but my name's obviously Italian," he said. "You can call me Leo, or Lee Lo. That's what my family and close friends call me, anyway."

"Seriously?" Rachel asked. "Lee Lo?"

"Yep, the first thing my siblings called me, and they still do, then my parents started, and now it's just one of my nicknames," Leo said.

"Okay," Rachel looked down. "I don't actually have siblings,"

"Well, consider yourself lucky, because they are hell—"

"Consider *yourself* lucky that you have family that actually cares for you."

Leo said nothing in return to that.

They turned a corner and arrived at a door that had a sign nailed onto it: *School Uniforms.*

"What size are you?" Leo asked, walking into the room full of uniforms.

"Sixteen," Rachel said immediately.

Leo looked through the uniforms hanging against the wall until he found her size. He handed it to her and led Rachel farther down the hallway.

"Here," Leo said, pointing to another door with a sign, once again nailed into the wood, that read: *Changeroom.*

"Thanks," Rachel said and walked into the changeroom.

"Shoot," Leo said suddenly.

"What?" Rachel asked, poking her head out of the changeroom.

"I forgot the shoes; I'll be right back." With that, Leo ran back in the direction of the uniform room.

Rachel shrugged, closed the door, and started undressing. Unfortunately, she forgot one very slim but crucial detail: lock the door.

Leo came back with a shiny pair of shoes in hand, and, without thinking, he opened the door to give them to her. "Here are the shoes—" He stopped because of what he saw: Justin, who wasn't actually a boy, but a girl. A girl half undressed. He dropped the shoes in shock and ran out of the room, slamming the door behind him and leaning on the wood, breathing heavily.

Rachel heard the shoes drop, but when she turned around, the door was closed again and no one was to be seen. It was mostly a guess, but she knew what had happened.

"So," Leo said through the closed door, trying not to be awkward, "you're a girl?"

"Uh, yes," Rachel said. She finished putting on the rest of her uniform once she figured out what Leo had witnessed. She now knew she'd need to explain everything thoroughly. She marched out of the changeroom and looked Leo dead in the eye. "Look, don't tell anyone about today, got it? This is something I need; I can't be kicked out," Rachel warned.

"Okay," Leo said, his eyes slightly wide with fear.

"So, promise me you'll never tell a soul about this," she threatened.

"Promise," he said.

CHAPTER FOUR

SECRET SAFE

"But why, though?" Leo asked Rachel. "Because I want a new start. You wouldn't understand, but if you had known me for a while, then you might've."

"I actually get it," Leo said.

"No, you don't," Rachel said, looking at the floor.

Leo could tell he'd touched upon a sore subject and let it go. He quickly asked, "So, how old are you?"

Rachel almost jumped at his suddenness, though she subconsciously thanked him. "Um…" She quickly returned to her fiery self and said, "Hey, you do know it is rude to ask a girl her age, but I'm fifteen."

"Well, if you're fifteen, why are you so flat-chested?"

"Excuse me!" Rachel said loudly. "It's not my fault I'm not like most girls!" She slapped him across the face, leaving a red handprint on his cheek. She pouted and stuck out her lip. "First you walk in on me changing, then you ask my age, and now you ask why my chest doesn't look like the chests of most girls my age. What's wrong with you?!"

"S-s-sorry," Leo said, rubbing his pink cheek. "But what's your real name?"

"Rachel Free Angel, you gonna criticize that too?"

Leo's jaw fell down to his chest.

"Rude," Rachel muttered.

"No, it's just that, mega coincidence, I've always wanted a little sister named Rachel."

"You're just saying that."

"No, seriously."

"Nope, not true, no way in hell with hell-blazing donuts are you serious."

"Do I have a reason to lie?"

"I'm a new student who knows nothing about this school, who barely knows you, and who just slapped you across the face. You kinda do," Rachel noted.

He frowned. "I am telling the truth. I would always tell my mom that I would like a younger sister," Leo said. "But instead, I got a lousy brother named Joshua, then I got two more stupid buttheaded brothers named Jay and Logan."

"How old are they, your brothers?" Rachel asked.

"Oh, well, Joshua was born when I was five, so he would be eleven," Leo thought aloud. "Jay was born when Joshua was three, so he's eight, and Logan was born when Jay was two. So, he's six. Yeah, Joshua's eleven, Jay's eight, and Logan's six. And thankfully none of them go to this school."

"When did you first come to this school?" Rachel asked.

"Um... when I was thirteen, about." Leo looked at Rachel. "We should go to Sir Evergreen's office to have you fill out the paperwork to properly enroll here. And to see which dorm you'll be in, which will hopefully not be mine."

Leo didn't understand why, but as soon as Rachel had confirmed she was a girl, he'd had this weird feeling in his stomach like butterflies madly flying around. What was it? That question was stuck solid in his mind, though he didn't know why. Maybe he liked her? Perhaps that was why he could feel his cheeks burn pink when he looked her directly in the eye, though to his relief, Rachel didn't notice because she'd slapped him. She just thought it was the mark she'd left.

"Um..." Leo said. "We should flow— I mean snow —no — blow — I mean *go* to Sir Evergreen's office now." He started speed walking away from Rachel and down the hallway.

Rachel thought it was peculiar that he'd just walk off, though she decided it would be best if she kept her mouth shut for once, figuring he needed to be left alone.

I'm such a moronasaurus! Leo thought to himself. *She probably thinks I have word issues!* Images of Rachel finding about his crush on her flashed through his mind and he stopped cold, causing Rachel to bump into him.

"Hey," Rachel said and shoved him forward. "Keep moving."

Leo's heart did cartwheels until they soon arrived at Sir Evergreen's office. They immediately walked inside.

"Sir Evergreen, Sir," Leo said. "Justin needs to fill out the paperwork about himself to officially be enrolled in this school."

"What?" Sir Evergreen asked. "Oh, um, yes, here ye go, Justin." Sir Evergreen gave Rachel two pieces of paper with personal questions on it.

"Pen," Rachel said. Leo grabbed a random pen from Sir Evergreen's desk and gave it to Rachel, who smiled at him. Again, Leo felt his cheeks turn red; he scratched his nose to cover the pink.

"Um," he said, trying to avoid awkward tension. "What room will she be in?"

"She?" Sir Evergreen asked.

Leo's eyes grew wide and Rachel's head shot up, glaring at him, just daring him to screw this up. "Oh, did I say she?" Leo said. "I must've accidentally said it wrong. What room will *he* be in?"

"Um…" Sir Evergreen said, "Room six six three."

Rachel almost gasped and caught so much air in her throat that she choked.

"Is something the matter?" Leo asked, not noticing he was putting Rachel on the spot.

"Oh, yeah, fine," Rachel said. "Just choked on a wee bit of air." Not exactly a full lie, just not the exact truth either. She went back to her paperwork and finished filling it out. "Um, here," she said and gave it to her headmaster, who looked it over thoroughly before giving it a satisfied nod and placing it in one of his two filing cabinets.

"Sir Evergreen," Leo said, "which room will Justin be in again, I forgot?"

"Room six six three," Rachel and Sir Evergreen chimed in perfect unison.

Leo turned snow white. "That's the number of *my* dorm," he said.

"Leonardo," the schoolmaster said, completely ignoring what Leo had announced, "you are to take off a day of schooling to show Justin around, understood?"

Leo nodded and he and Rachel walked out of the office.

"How many beds are there?" Rachel asked as soon as the door had closed behind them.

"Um…" Leo said, not looking very promising. He cleared his throat and almost finished in a whisper, "Two, but the mattress is missing on the one that I don't sleep in, so Sir Evergreen will have to order the mattress for the other one, so kind of one."

Rachel fainted on the spot. Luckily, nobody was there to witness it, except for Leo, who picked her up and carried her into his dorm, gently putting her on his, and now also her, bed. He locked the door and sat on the floor in wait.

Rachel woke up almost an hour later. "I didn't do it!" she said once she sat up. Leo looked at her as though she had two heads. "What?" she asked.

"So," Leo said, trying to break the newborn silence. "We could split the bed—"

"No," Rachel said immediately after he said the word *bed*. "I am *not* sleeping with a *boy* at age *fifteen*," Rachel reprimanded before jumping out of bed.

"Fine, I'll sleep on the floor," Leo decided.

"Now you're making me feel bad!" she scolded.

"Well I'm being a stupid gentleman, so don't complain."

"I know you secretly want the bed, whether you'll admit it or not," she snapped. They had a short staring contest; Leo won. "Fine," Rachel said and swallowed whatever it was that came up. "We could," cough, "you know," another cough, "maybe, share," two coughs, she sped through the last words, "share the bed."

"That's exactly what I said!"

"But I said it better."

"Yeah, okay, Miss Cough-Cough."

"Shut up and deal with it."

"Well, this is going to be awkward."

"Oh, shut up, and if anything," she tried to find the right words for it, "*overly awkward* happens, just, completely forget about it, got it?"

"Overly awkward?"

"I meant if something I *do not* want to happen happens, just... forget about it."

They spent the rest of the day in their dorm with Leo explaining to Rachel the school schedules and whatnot.

The sun descended on the horizon as the day came to an end. Leo let Rachel borrow some pajamas that he had in his closet from two years before. Why hadn't he gotten rid of them? Not even Leo himself knew.

"Okay," Rachel said, rubbing her tired eyes. "You'll sleep on *that* side, and I'll sleep on *this* side."

Leo nodded. "Fine by me," he said and climbed into his side of the bed. He lay on his side as Rachel scooted farther and farther away from him like he had the plague, which was completely fine by Leo. Both yawned for a little while but otherwise fell asleep in no time.

Leo woke to see Rachel nuzzled up against his chest. He let out a quick gasp and slowly dragged himself away, though he ended up falling on the floor. "Dang it," he said to himself and rubbed his head.

"Mommy," he heard Rachel say to herself. "No, they'll be here to save you. Mom!" She woke with a bloodcurdling scream. Forgetting Leo was in the room, she curled up into a little ball and cried to herself as Leo stayed on the floor.

"It's all my fault," Rachel sobbed.

Leo slowly got up and put the sheets and comforter over Rachel's shoulders. "It's okay," he said in a comforting tone.

"Leo!" Rachel said, sitting up. "Uh, you see…"

"Sleep," Leo said and gently pushed her back down. "We have no school today; sleep."

Last night, Leo would've done almost anything to get Rachel put in another room, considering her snappy attitude and the way she treated him, but now he actually felt *sorry* for her. Sure, he didn't know exactly why she'd been crying, but whatever it was, he knew if he helped her enough, he would eventually make her feel better.

Leo went to the bathroom and got changed into his uniform. By the time he finished deciding on one hairstyle,

Rachel was still asleep in her little ball. He sighed and went to the dining hall, where he ate a huge stack of pancakes. After returning his plate to the dirty pile of dishes and apologizing to a boy he'd accidentally hit on his way out, he returned to his dorm, wondering if Rachel was still asleep. Leo opened the door to his dorm to see the bed vacant. "Rachel?" he asked. He looked around and saw steam pouring out from underneath the bathroom door. He knocked; there was no reply. He opened the door out of instinct, and his jaw dropped so low it almost touched his chest; Rachel was in the bath, with bubbles all the way up to her neck. *His* earbuds were in her ears, leading to *his* MP3, and she was humming to *his* favourite song, which was "Bye Bye Bye."

Rachel was enjoying her bath when she felt someone's gaze on her. She turned and screamed, "Get out!"

Leo quickly ran out of the bathroom and slammed the door behind him.

"How long were you here for?!" Rachel yelled.

"Um," Leo said, "two seconds." *Well, we're off to a good start,* he thought. *She totally doesn't think I'm some creep, totally not, not.*

"You're such a creep!" he heard Rachel yell.

Called it, he thought. Leo heard water splash. "Probably my precious MP3," he whispered to himself.

That wasn't the case, however. Rachel had just gotten out of the bath, pulled out the plug so the water would go down the drain, and carefully put Leo's MP3 and earbuds on the counter, under her clothes. She grabbed a towel off the rack, threw it around herself, and stormed out of the bathroom.

"Look," she said, grabbing Leo's shirt collar, even though he was taller. Her other hand held her towel up. Leo turned bright red.

"Sorry?" Leo asked.

"*Sorry?!*" Rachel said loudly. "You *never* walk in on someone while they're in the bathroom. No matter what! Understood?" Her hand softened and so did the threatening expression across her face. "Sorry, I-I should go." She turned to go back into the bathroom—

Leo grabbed her free hand; Rachel turned around.

"Why were you saying it was *all your fault?*" he asked.

Rachel flashed back to the memory of her mother burning in her house. She remembered that she'd been the one who had been playing with the stove. She was the one who was fully responsible for her own mother's death. "Nothing," she said quickly.

"No," Leo said, seizing her wrist. "It wasn't *nothing*, and you'll tell me."

"I can't," Rachel said as tears started running down her cheeks. "I-I did something horrible. I can't." She ripped her hand free from his grip and ran into the bathroom, shutting the door behind her.

Leo heard Rachel let herself fall to the floor and cry. Slowly, he walked away and plopped himself onto his bed. He never understood girls and their moods; well, the only girls he ever saw were the ones his age who lived near his house, but he'd never understood why they'd just randomly be rude. He probably never would.

"Stupid Leo," Rachel muttered to herself as she put on her school uniform. "Stupid boys who don't understand anything." She furiously tried to tie her tie but time after time it turned into a bow. She took it in her hands and stormed out of the bathroom. "Leo!" she said. "Tie this stupid thing or I'll *kick you where it hurts*, and I won't hesitate."

Leo gulped and quickly had the tie in his hands. He fastened it around her collar and finished tying it perfectly.

"I don't get how guys can tie this thing," Rachel said, holding the tie up and looking at it thoroughly.

"Oh, and," Leo said, "sorry about before; I shouldn't have come in."

"Yeah, damn right you shouldn't have," Rachel said. Her eyes looked up into his with wonder spreading into the brown of each iris. "Did someone tell you to apologize to me?" she asked. "Because nobody has ever said *sorry* to me without being forced to."

"No," Leo said with a grin. "Nothing like that."

Rachel raised an eyebrow. "Well," she said, reaching into her pocket and pulling out his MP3 and earbuds, "here you go."

"Thanks," Leo said and put them in his pocket.

"And," Rachel said, preparing to do one of the things she'd never done in her entire life, "sorry," she said quickly. She cleared her throat. "So, what's first class going to be?"

"No school today," Leo said. "Today's Tuesday."

"You get Tuesdays off or something?" she asked.

"No," Leo said. "We just get one day off every week. This week it's Tuesday, next week it's Wednesday, then Thursday, Friday, Monday, and the cycle continues. Goes like that all year 'round."

"I wish the girls' school had been like that."

"So," he said, "what do you want to do? Tour of the school? Meet my friends? Or prank someone?"

"First of all, this is my clean slate; second, you have friends?" She saw Leo's mad face and added, "Jeez, I was kidding; stop taking everything so seriously."

"So, which one?" Leo asked firmly.

"Tour of the school, *s'il vous plaît*," Rachel said.

"Is that French?" he asked.

"Yes, I took French in school," she said.

"Cool, now, let's go." He headed out of the dorm with Rachel behind him. "Okay," he said, turning to face Rachel. "This is the first floor, north tower, there are three other towers, four total, north, south, east, and west, each has five floors."

They walked down the hallway to a pair of double doors. Leo pushed them open and continued walking with Rachel on his tail. "These are the bathrooms," he gestured to a plain grey door.

"That's one way to be discovered," Rachel said with a judgmental snort.

"You snort?" he asked.

"I am not a girly-girl," she noted.

Leo took that in. He showed her the rest of the school and named everything they saw.

"Hey, look, it's Leonardo, the big baby," said a boy that walked in front of them, blocking their path. He had black hair and brown eyes. Two boys were on either side of him.

"That's Zachary Seam," Leo whispered into Rachel's ear.

"Speak up, Chicken Little," said the boy from Zachary's left. He had blond hair and green eyes.

"That's Alexander Page," Leo said to Rachel.

"Come on, speak up," said the boy from Zachary's right. He had brown hair and blue eyes.

"And that's Victor Williams," Leo explained. "Together they make one of the scariest group of boys this school's ever had."

"Nicely put, Lee Lo what's his face," Zachary said.

"Stop talking to him like that," Rachel said loudly, making her voice slightly deeper to sound like a boy. She took a step forward. She then realized she was much shorter than these three students; she was a little girl compared to them. Rachel quickly swallowed whatever came up because it was too late; she was going to have to face them.

"Oh, look, we have a new student with the weak little face of a girl," Alexander said.

"Yeah, Alex, what's she going to do? Lecture us? — Ah!" Victor's words quickly turned into a series of screams, groans, and grunts because Rachel had slapped his face so hard, blood dripped from his cheek. She'd also punched him in the stomach and kneed him in the groin. He fell to the floor, clutching his stomach.

"That was only a warning," Rachel threatened.

"Yeah, a pathetic one," Alex said. He stepped forward and shoved Rachel backwards into Leo, who caught her. Quickly back on her feet, she punched Alex in the nose and kicked him in the stomach.

Victor was still groaning on the floor when Alex joined him. "He's unnaturally strong, Vic," Alex said.

"Be careful, Zach!" Vic warned Zachary.

"You idiotic weaklings!" Zach said. He stepped forward and seized Rachel by the throat, raising her a foot above the ground. "This is what happens when people like you try to be strong," Zach said to Rachel who was violently kicking the air around her. She coughed as Zach squeezed her neck harder.

"Stop it!" Leo finally said, finding his voice at last. "This has gone far enough!"

His words were pointless because Zach's full attention was on Rachel.

Rachel looked around. What could she use to get of this mess, away from this psychopath? Suddenly, a smart, risky idea showed itself into her mind. She immediately agreed with herself that this would probably be one of the easiest ways to escape. She flipped one of her legs over the arm that held her, doing it as fast as she physically could so Zach wouldn't have any chance to react. She quickly threw over the rest of her body and landed behind him.

Zach, not wanting to break his arm, let go of Rachel and she ran to Leo's side.

"Now remember," Rachel said with a bloody mouth, "that was only a warning."

"Come on, let's go," Zach said, walking away with Vic and Alex limping behind him.

Once the scariest boys of the school were out of sight, Leo exclaimed, "That was amazing; how did you beat them like that?"

"Thanks—" Rachel covered her mouth because she felt blood crawling up the back of her throat.

"We should go back to our dorm," Leo suggested and Rachel nodded.

Once they got back to their dorm, Rachel spat out all the blood from her mouth into the toilet as Leo looked through a medical book, trying to find out how he could help Rachel. "Oh," he said finally, "just swallow."

Rachel closed her mouth and swallowed the blood.

"Or at least that's reasonable," Leo whispered to himself, though Rachel heard and her eyes grew wide. "Um... better?" he asked.

Rachel eyes went back to normal and she nodded. Then she went from good to horrible as more blood came and she threw up. Leo winced at the sight.

After a few minutes, Rachel stopped vomiting.

"Are you okay?" Leo asked. She slowly nodded.

Rachel sluggishly got back up onto her feet, a little wobbly because of the loss of blood. She walked over to the wardrobe, pulled out a spare uniform, went back into the bathroom, and closed the door behind her.

Leo just watched the door close, waiting to hear it lock, which it didn't. He jumped off the bed and took out a book that was underneath the mattress. The cover read: *What to do when you like a Girl*. Leo's father had given it to him as a birthday present. He didn't know why he still had it; he'd always thought it was the stupidest present anyone could ask for, though he never even asked for it at all. And who on Earth would sell such a book? He flipped it to the first page, read a couple of lines, and exclaimed, "This is crap!"

"What?" Rachel asked from the bathroom.

"Nothing," Leo said quickly. "Almost done?"

"Yeah," she replied and Leo threw his book back under the bed just as Rachel walked out of the bathroom.

"Want to go swimming?" Leo asked, getting up off of the floor.

"Leo," Rachel said and shook her head, "I am a girl, and this is a school for boys. Think about that for a second."

"Tennis?" he asked.

"No, one time one of those stupid balls got me in the stomach and I promised myself I'd never play the sport again."

"Soccer?"

"No," she said immediately.

"Marketplace?" Leo asked.

"Sure, but I have no money."

"I can lend you some money."

"Okay, but don't complain about being poor afterwards. Wait a second, you said there was a money system, right? You know, yesterday, when you were explaining everything to me. So, we need to go to Sir Evergreen and get some money. Hannah would've advised it!"

"Hannah?" Leo asked.

"Oh," Rachel's smile turned upside down, "she was my only friend at my old school. Though it's weird because we were total opposites. She was this perfect role model, never in trouble, and I was nothing but trouble."

"Well, no more time to waste," Leo said. "To Sir Evergreen's office!" Leo marched out of the dorm and

Rachel followed. They walked down the hallways to their headmaster's office, walking side by side.

She really is cute, Leo thought, glancing at Rachel. *Strong and pretty.* He looked at Rachel's big brown eyes, lopsided smile, and rosy cheeks. He smiled. Rachel caught him smiling at her and he instantly diverted his gaze forward. They walked in awkward silence until Leo finally broke the thick tension. "So, what were you talking about in your sleep?"

Rachel stopped cold. "Oh, um, nothing."

"Crying and saying it was all your fault doesn't seem like nothing to me," he said.

"Well, I'll tell you eventually, just not now," she said, knowing she probably wouldn't fulfill that promise.

"You will," Leo said.

They walked into Sir Evergreen's office but stopped as soon as they stepped through the door frame; they heard something graceful, like a—

"Is that the sound of a harp?" Rachel asked.

"I think so," Leo said. The noise stopped.

"Maybe it's coming from back there," Rachel said, pointing to the door behind the schoolmaster's desk.

"No," Leo said. "That room's off-limits!"

"Sourpuss," Rachel said. She walked around the desk and put her hand around the doorknob. "Do you dare me?" she asked.

"No," Leo said, but against his wishes, Rachel turned the doorknob and walked inside.

"Whoa," Leo heard her say. He knew he shouldn't go inside, or anywhere behind the desk for that matter, but he simply couldn't help it. Leo cautiously walked around the desk and inside the room, letting out a quick gasp. Against one wall was a mirror the size of a doorway, and against the opposite wall were six huge brown woven sacks filled with what felt and sounded like gold coins. The mirror had glass so clear it looked like water. Attached to the top was a chalkboard with the words *Snow White* written on it.

"Why do you think Sir Evergreen has gold coins? Aren't those things only in fables or something?" Leo asked Rachel.

"Why do you think I have the answer?" Rachel snapped. Suddenly, the mirror started to ripple like when you drop a stone into a lake.

Through the rippled mirror came a foot, then another.

"Quickly, behind the bags!" Rachel said and she and Leo jumped behind the sacks, poking their heads out to see what would happen next.

Sir Evergreen walked out of the mirror, looking younger than before. He erased the words *Snow White* from the chalkboard and returned to his office, shutting the door behind him.

Rachel and Leo walked out from behind the bags of coins and thoroughly examined the mirror. Rachel placed her hand on the glass. It was solid. She even pounded on it, but her hand didn't go through. Leo rubbed his eyes over and over again, trying to deny what had happened, though neither could deny a thing they'd just witnessed: a man walking through a mirror.

"Am I dreaming this up?" he asked.

Rachel slapped him hard across his face.

"Ow!" Leo said as quietly as he could. "What was that for?"

"You wanted to know if you were dreaming," Rachel said with a shrug.

"Well, I know I'm not dreaming."

"That's for sure," Rachel whispered with a quiet snort.

CHAPTER FIVE

MAGIC MIRROR

"**W**hat is this?" Leo asked.

"Magic mirror?" Rachel suggested.

"Magic doesn't exist," he said coldly.

"A man just walked out of a mirror; of course magic exists!" she argued.

"Shh!" Leo said, covering Rachel's mouth with his hand. Rachel licked his hand and he quickly withdrew.

"We can't get out or we'll get caught," she noted as Leo furiously wiped his hand on his pants.

"We should," Leo smelled his hand before continuing, "just wait for him to come back and go inside the mirror, then we make a mad dash and leave."

"Good idea," Rachel said and she snickered quietly.

They sat behind the bags of gold coins and waited. The seconds turned to minutes, the minutes turned to hours, and the hours multiplied until it had been four hours since they first entered the room. It felt as though they were frozen in time.

Sir Evergreen finally (finally!) came back holding a small brown bag. He wrote the words *Sleeping Beauty* with a piece of chalk he kept beside the chalkboard, gently placed his hand on the glass, waited for it to ripple, and walked through.

"Let's go!" Rachel said. She and Leo got up, their joints cracking in all sorts of areas, and ran out of the room and office, their heads spinning with questions.

They started walking toward their dorm.

"We should go back there sometime," Leo said.

"What?!" Rachel said loudly, turning to face him. "We can't go back there!"

"And why is that?"

"We almost got caught!"

"We did not," Leo objected. "And dinner's in an hour."

"I know," Rachel said. The rest of the walk to their dorm was walked in silence.

"What do you think Sir Evergreen does with the mirror?" Leo asked, opening the door to their dorm.

"How should I know?" Rachel asked, closing the door behind them.

Leo shrugged, taking a seat on the edge of the bed.

"Hey, do you have a notebook I can borrow?" Rachel asked, sitting beside him.

"No," Leo said. "But I could buy you one in the market."

"Thanks," Rachel said and gratefully used his shoulder as her pillow, happy to have a friend.

"Leo," Rachel said.

"Yes?" Leo asked.

"Do your parents love you?" she questioned.

"Yeah," he replied.

"Do you think they'd care if you died?"

"Pretty sure."

"Do you think they'd get rid of you if they could?" she asked as a tear rolled smoothly down her cheek.

"Hopefully not," he said. Leo unexpectedly felt a tear fall onto the skin of his arm. "Rachel, are you *crying?*"

"My family doesn't care for me," Rachel said, ignoring Leo. "My family wouldn't care if I died, and they already got rid of me. In fact, my parents both died when I was young. My relatives are the ones who don't want anything to do with me. They shipped me off to the girls' school, not wanting to ever see me again. Actually, my parents died and it's all my fault." More tears fell onto Leo's arm. "I have nobody to go home to, not even a home to go to."

"Rachel," Leo said, hearing her light sniffles. He remembered when she'd said it had been all her fault. He wondered what she'd meant and hoped now he would finally know.

"All my fault," Rachel said, her sniffles growing louder.

"What do you mean? Can you please tell me?" Leo asked.

"You wouldn't like me anymore," she said.

"I'll always like you."

Rachel turned and looked into his eyes. "What if I told you that I'm the cause of my parents' deaths? What if I told you what happened? Nobody knows, not even my relatives. They thought it was all just bad luck. It never was. That's just what they thought, though it wasn't that! They never knew the truth, and they never will!"

"You can tell me, Rachel," Leo said.

"But you have to promise you won't tell anybody!"

"I promise."

"Fine." Rachel took a deep breath, exhaled, and dried her tears. "My mother's name was Rebekah Free. One day, when I was two, I was playing with the stove; she told me to go outside to play with my father. We heard a scream—"

she choked on her breath. "We ran out of the tree fort and saw my mom on fire in our home. We couldn't save her. Instead of focusing on me, my father turned to alcohol for comfort. About six or seven bottles of beer a day, always in the hospital, always drunk. He died by the time I was five. And all that was my fault!" Tears poured down her face. "Nobody knows, and nobody ever will; it's been my deepest and darkest secret for my entire life!" She broke down into sobs and cried into Leo's chest, who wrapped his arms around her.

"But it wasn't your fault; you didn't know any better," Leo said.

"But it was; it was all my fault!" Rachel cried louder. "I shouldn't have, but I was just so stupid!"

"Toddlers don't know what they're doing," he protested.

"Really?!" Rachel said, looking up. "Well, if all toddlers are like that, how are there still parents in this world?! How many children do you know who *killed* their own parents?!" She continued crying into his chest and soaking his uniform for another five minutes before eventually drying her tears. "Where did you say we could get a notebook?" she asked.

Leo was surprised she could change the subject so easily. "Um, we would have to go into town. We will take a bus. There's a little shop that I used to go to all the time, just to read some books and stuff on the weekends, then I'd come back at the end of the day. I would enjoy myself a lot."

"Can we go before dinner?" Rachel asked.

"Yeah, I just need to bring some money; my parents send me a lot every month—" his cheeks turned red with shame. "Sorry."

"It's okay, now let's go."

They walked out of their dorm and to the exit of the school. Leo and Rachel peacefully walked out of the school, the door closing automatically behind them, and started walking toward the bus station.

Once they arrived, Leo bought two bus tickets to *Brandy's Books* with the money he'd brought.

When the bus came, they almost literally jumped onto the bus and took one of the free seats in the back, sitting side by side.

Rachel looked at the town through the window, smiling at the peaceful sight.

Leo smiled at how happy Rachel was, considering she had been crying her eyes out not even twenty minutes before.

It took them a good, silent ten minutes to get to *Brandy's Books*. Rachel and Leo walked into the small bookshop that looked like it was pulled out of a fairy tale. Rachel immediately asked the man at the front counter, "Where can I find the notebooks?" before the shopkeeper could even ask what she wanted.

"Uh, the last aisle," the shopkeeper said. "Oh, and no running."

Leo and Rachel walked to the back of the shop to see dozens of books on the shelves. After two minutes of pure concentration, Rachel decided. "That one," she said confidently, pointing to a notebook that had a hardcover wrapped in leather with a magnetic strap going around it, doing an elegant job of keeping it shut. "Nineteen ninety-nine," Rachel said, turning to Leo.

"I got that," he said. Rachel took the notebook off the shelf and brought it to the front counter, where Leo paid for it.

"What a nice couple of kids you are," the shopkeeper said.

"What?" Rachel asked, looking around to see if there were any more customers in the bookstore. "Us? Oh, we're not a couple. Not at all, we're just friends," she said quickly, not realizing he didn't mean what she thought. She grabbed Leo's wrist and her new notebook and ran out of the shop to the bus station where Leo paid for the tickets to get back to the school.

The tension between Rachel and Leo was so thick it could be cut with a knife, with difficulty, until Rachel said, "So, have you thought about going through the mirror?"

"No, I dropped that idea because you were right: we could get caught so easily."

"Okay, good thing none of us were thinking of that," Rachel said.

Leo turned his head toward Rachel so quickly he heard a small *crack*. "Wait, were you thinking of going through the mirror?"

Rachel's cheeks turned from a little rosy to strawberry red. "No, why would you think of something so preposterous?!"

Leo leaned slightly away from Rachel, worried she might punch him in the nose if he continued. "Never mind," he peeped. The rest of the time it took them to get to the boys' academy could be described perfectly with two words: complete silence.

When they got back to their dorm, Rachel hid the book in her pillowcase as Leo used the bathroom. They went to the dining hall and got in line for dinner. Rachel had expected a huge of a selection of food as she had experienced at the girls' school, but her expectations came to an abrupt halt when she saw the only food there was: mashed potatoes and gravy. Though at least it looked good. The dinner *men* served Rachel her food and she headed to the table Leo was sitting at, although, unfortunately, it was not a subtle journey. Zach stepped in her way, blocking her path.

"Move," Rachel said, craning her neck up to look him in the eye.

"Na thanks," Zach said and *accidentally* dumped her tray of food on her chest. Rachel froze, remembering that Elisha had done the same to her at one point to get revenge on Rachel for framing her. Zach punched her food-drenched face and she collapsed from the impact. He snickered to himself before walking away.

Leo turned to see what had caused the noise and saw Rachel unconscious on the floor. Zach was walking away from her. "Quick, get the nurse!" he hollered.

The students who'd watched everything ran out of the dining hall immediately. Meanwhile, Leo scooped up Rachel in his arms and joined the running students, grunting because of Rachel's weight.

When Leo finally reached the medical room, he gently put Rachel on the cot and shooed all the other students out, especially the one who asked why he got to stay. After he got the door locked, which took more effort than one would think, he sat on a chair near the bed Rachel was lying in.

The nurse, who was a girl in her twenties with auburn hair and green eyes, took off Rachel's suit jacket because of all the food.

"Is she going to be alright?" Leo asked. "Is she seriously injured?"

"*She?*" the nurse asked.

"I-I-I meant he! He, he, he!" Leo said instantly.

"Well, nothing's wrong with him, and he'll be alright; he just banged his head a bit," the nurse said, examining Rachel closely.

"So, she's perfectly fine?" Leo asked.

"Yes, though *he's* going to have to stay the night," the nurse said, giving Leo a peculiar look.

Leo slumped slightly.

"You may leave now, Leonardo. Justin will be just fine."

Leo wanted to stay but knew if he did it'd end up awkward. He walked out of the medical room and down the hallway.

After about five minutes, a deep and masculine voice said from behind Leo, "We know your little secret."

Leo turned around to come face to face with Zach, Vic, and Alex. "And what would that be?" Leo asked, attempting to play dumb.

"That Justin is a girl," Zach said.

"How do you know?"

"Ha! I told you boys he'd admit it!" Zach said. "Actually, little Leo, we weren't one hundred per cent sure, though we knew that you always get straight to the point."

"You share a room, the two of you, correct?" Alex asked.

"Yes, that would be valid," Leo said.

"And you only have one bed, right?" Vic asked.

"Yes, that would also be correct."

"And you're how old?" Zach asked as he, Vic, and Alex started circling him like sharks around their prey.

"Sixteen," Leo said. "Same age as you three."

"Too bad you're short; it makes you look closer to thirteen," Alex said.

"I'm as tall as you," Leo shot. "Or are your eyes as bad as your personality?"

"Why you," Alex said, though before he could do anything about it, Vic stepped in to ask,

"And how old is she?"

"Fifteen."

"Are you her boyfriend or something?" Zach asked, ready to humiliate Leo.

Leo knew what Zach was doing, just as much as he knew his name. So, instead of letting Zach get his way as usual, he decided to flip the tables around and for once be more powerful than the three jerks circling him. "Matter of fact, I *am* her boyfriend. *Jealous?*" *Crap*, Leo thought, remembering that he was much weaker than Zach, Vic, and Alex and that he'd just lied. But he was still on a roll and decided that trying to stop himself would be as pointless as stopping a train. "Actually," he said, "we've slept with each other since she first came to this school, and every time she wakes up in my arms." Another lie slipped out of Leo.

"Is that so?" Zach asked, his confidence starting to stumble.

"Yes, in fact, she kissed me yesterday!" Leo said. "Meanwhile you're still single, and will be forever. Actually, I'd bet my life that if you went into a room with all the girls in the world, none of them would even acknowledge you for more than a second."

"Really, she kissed you?" Alex asked, half shocked.

"Where?" Vic asked.

"Oh, wouldn't you like to know," Leo said with a smirk.

Zach snorted. "Ridiculous lies!" he said and ran off, Alex and Vic behind him, trying to keep up.

It was a little late, but Leo realized what he'd done and knew he would need to tell Rachel before she found out herself and went on a rampage or the boys told everybody in the school. He then remembered that she was in the medical room and figured his emergency could wait for the next morning. He finished the walk back to his dorm. As soon as his body made contact with the bed, he fell into a deep sleep.

The morning sun came up with a glowing splendour that awoke Leo. He jumped out of bed; he was still in his uniform. What time was it? *Did I sleep the rest of yesterday?* he wondered. The memory of Rachel in the infirmary struck him like lightning. He ran to the door to the hallway, but before he could open it, Rachel walked in wearing new pajamas.

"Hi," Leo said. He stared awkwardly at Rachel, wondering how she'd gotten blue pajamas. "Where did you get the pajamas?" he asked.

"Nurse," Rachel said casually. "Hey, um, Leo, you know the mirror?"

"Yeah, why?" he asked.

"I want to go back inside, like the room from the office, and, well, maybe, go inside the mirror," she said.

"What?!"

"Come on, don't you have curiosity bubbling in your veins, thirsting for knowledge? Okay, that was cheesy crap; I guess school did do something to me."

"I don't want to go inside the mirror; it could be dangerous," Leo said. However, he knew that, deep, deep, deep... deep down, Rachel was right: he *did* want to go back, and into the mirror. He did want to know what would happen. Would he evaporate? Explode? Or maybe turn to dust? Either way, he wanted to know; the curiosity would eat him alive.

"You have guilt on your face," Rachel noted, then she added, "Enjoy the dorm; I'm going to eat some breakfast!" She was about to leave the dorm—

"Pajamas, genius," Leo said.

"Shut up," Rachel said. She took out another spare uniform from the closet, and then she went into the bathroom to change.

Leo yawned when the door shut, wondering why he was tired.

Rachel came out of the bathroom a few minutes later, trying to tie her tie. "Seriously, how do guys tie this thing?"

"Want help?" Leo asked.

"No, because I... got it!" She secured it and it looked like a huge knot. "Or not," she said, untying it. "Let me try this again." She placed the tie the way it was supposed to be with her thumb and index finger. "Now give me a stapler; I'mma staple this thing the way it's supposed to be!"

Leo slapped a palm against his face. He then went up to Rachel, slapped his hand down on hers, and made *her* tie it. "There," he said.

Rachel blinked twice before running out the dorm, yelling, "Bye!"

Leo shrugged, closed the door, and belly-flopped onto his bed — ouch! His face hit something hard. He rubbed his hand against the pillow and felt the shape of a book. Leo reached inside the pillowcase and pulled out the book he'd bought for Rachel the previous day. He could smell ink from the inside. Leo opened the book to the first page but quickly slammed it shut; it was probably personal, but, then again, Rachel was certainly not a girly-girl. He slowly opened it back up to the first page and started reading Rachel's elegant writing:

Dear Free Diary,

That is so Rachel, Leo thought before he continued reading.

I just wanted to say that I found a magic mirror! I'm not crazy; I promise. I'm not writing this in an asylum, I'm just saying I found a magic mirror that belongs to my schoolmaster! This is EPIC! I don't know how you're reading this, or why, or even when, but this is my diary so you're not supposed to be, but why would I lie? Whatever, moving on. I went into the headmaster's office (by the way, I call him Sir Evercrap; I just naturally dislike him. I don't know why; I just do. Anyway, his actual name is Sir Evergreen.) Soooo, I was actually with someone else, Leonardo, my friend-ish. We went to the office to ask Sir Evergreen for some money because I gave him extra when I enrolled in the boys' school, but we encountered a surprise. I wanted to find out what it was but Leo was all like "No, we're not allowed to go there blah blah blah..." I obviously didn't listen to him. I went into a secret room behind Sir Evercrap's desk and found the magic mirror, then Leo came after me and he witnessed the mirror. It looks like your average door-sized mirror, except there's a chalkboard on the top where you can write where you want to go. But, the secret of the day is that tomorrow in the morning I'm going to say that I'm going to breakfast (I'll say that to Leo) but actually go into the mirror. That's all for today.

Rachel Free Angel ^_^

Leo was shocked. The only thing his mind could focus on was whether he should stop Rachel or go with her. He put the book back in the pillowcase and ran out of the dorm as fast as his legs could carry him until he came to a screeching halt in front of Sir Evergreen's office. He looked inside through the crack of the door and saw nothing but an empty office… perfect. He opened the door and walked inside. He didn't see any sign of Rachel. He grunted in frustration and ran into the room with the magic mirror.

"What are you doing here?" Rachel asked, walking out from behind one of the brown sacks. "I thought you were Sir Evergreen."

Leo looked at the mirror and saw the words *Snow White* on the chalkboard. "I'm not letting you go inside the mirror," Leo said, standing in front of the mirror.

"Well, I'm going through that mirror; watch me," Rachel said. She grabbed Leo by the arm and swung him into the sacks of gold coins. "Goodbye, Leo!" she said and jumped into the mirror, back first. The last she saw was Leo lunge out and try to grab her hand — too late, Rachel was out of his reach.

"Rachel!" Leo yelled and jumped in headfirst after her.

CHAPTER SIX

A FAIRY TALE PRINCE

Rachel looked around; she was in some type of galaxy. There was a dark blue sky blurred in shades of pink and purple with billions of stars making a beautiful sight. She looked around a little more and realized she was falling straight toward the ground. Under her was a gorgeous palace that looked like it was from a fairy tale; then again, this was a fairy tale. The palace was a sandy beige colour, with coral-coloured turrets. She fell to the ground with a *thud* and didn't feel any pain whatsoever. Rachel saw a beautiful courtyard around her. There were many flower beds containing many sorts of flowers, though mostly roses and tulips.

"Where am I?" she asked herself.

Her train of thought was interrupted by a scream that had a recognizable sound to it. She looked up and saw Leo falling; she moved over and Leo face-planted into the ground next to her, still screaming.

"Leo," Rachel said and gave him a nudge. He stopped screaming and slowly opened his eyes one at a time.

"Whoa," Leo said as he took in the sight.

"I know," Rachel said.

"Wait, where are we and how do we get back?" he asked.

"Uh, I don't exactly know," she said quietly.

Leo was so mad at Rachel he pushed her back, though he didn't realize there was a pond directly behind her! She fell in and Leo couldn't even see her silhouette.

"Rachel?" Leo asked. "Rachel!" He poked his head into the water, expecting to see fish or the sand or something you'd find underwater; instead, he saw Sir Evergreen's off-limits room with Rachel on the floor, looking confused. She looked up at Leo and anger washed over her face.

"You jerk!" she yelled and hit him. She then pushed him back through the mirror and jumped in.

"Okay," Rachel said to Leo, climbing up onto the shore. "This is our way back home. So, until I want to go back because I clearly can, I'm going to explore." Leo grunted in annoyance. "And right now," Rachel continued, "I want to visit that palace!"

"Rachel," Leo said, though Rachel was already at the palace doors.

"Come on," Rachel urged him.

Leo groaned at her ignorance and joined her at the huge doors. Rachel kicked one of the two doors instead of knocking as you would normally do, hurting her toe in the process.

The door opened to reveal a young and beautiful woman.

"Hello," the woman said in a singsong. She had hair black as ebony, skin pale as snow, and lips red as blood. She wore a simple beige dress with shiny black wooden shoes.

"Hey," Rachel said and waved awkwardly, knowing she was looking at *the* Princess Snow White.

"Sup," Leo said.

"W-who are you and what are you wearing?" Snow White asked.

"I'm Rachel — Justin, I said Justin, my name is Justin," Rachel said.

"Leonardo," Leo said. "And you are?"

"Princess Snow White," she said.

"Well," Rachel said, "we come in peace."

"Yeah, totally," Leo said.

"Don't worry, I won't hurt you, and come in," Snow White said as she opened the door fully to let them inside.

The palace was just as beautiful on the inside as it was on the outside. A gorgeous marble floor stretched beneath their feet, ten white crystal chandeliers hung from the ceiling, and painted on the ceiling were crowns the colour of gold.

"Whoa," Rachel said, her voice echoing off the walls.

"If you think this is grand you must see the ballroom," Snow White said happily with a smile.

A beautiful woman who was obviously much older than Snow White walked towards them. She had a cold gaze, a permanent scowl, and a black braid slung over her shoulder. She wore a big gold dress, black gloves, and matching black shoes. "Snow White," the woman said sharply. By her tone of voice, you could tell she wasn't in any position to lose a fight. "What are these peasants doing here?"

"Leonardo, Justin, this is my stepmother, Queen Evelyn Pureheart," Snow White said, though her stepmother didn't care that she'd introduced her.

"I can introduce myself," the queen snapped. "And I prefer it if people just called me Queen Evelyn."

Leo and Rachel bowed; they knew their fairy tales.

"And what are they doing inside my palace?" Evelyn asked.

"They were at the door, so I invited them inside," Snow White explained.

"So, you think it's fine to invite just anyone inside *my* palace?" Evelyn said, raising her voice.

"S-sorry," Snow White apologized.

"It will not happen again, understood?"

"Of course."

"Good, now get them out of here." With that said, Queen Evelyn stormed off, her footsteps echoing throughout the main hall.

"I'm sorry, but you should go," Snow White said. "Though maybe you could come to one of the inclusive balls, then you may see the ballroom."

"Yes, we can see ourselves out," Rachel said and led Leo out of the palace.

"We need to get clothes, proper clothes," Rachel said once the doors closed behind them.

"Do you have any money on you that I'm unaware of?" Leo asked.

"No, but the pond does," Rachel said. She started running, and once she got to the edge of the pool, she jumped in. Leo followed, though more calmly.

Leo landed on something that wasn't the bottom; he looked down to see Rachel. "Sorry!" he said and immediately got off of her.

Rachel gave him a mean look before jumping back onto her feet and filling her pockets up with gold coins. Leo started doing the same, keeping a safe distance from Rachel.

Once their pockets were full, Rachel and Leo jumped back through the mirror. This time, instead of falling, they appeared in front of the pond, though they didn't notice. They followed wooden signs to town.

"Here's the plan," Rachel said to Leo when they were on the outskirts of a little town. "We'll go to some stores, buy some decent clothes, and meet up at the pond in about three hours."

"Got it," Leo agreed.

"See you later, alligator," Rachel said.

"In a while, crocodile," Leo said.

They both parted and went into the town to go on a shopping spree.

Leo found a little tailor shop where he tried on fifteen different suits before deciding he wanted something more casual.

Rachel found a small shop selling adorable shoes and plain brown dresses with white aprons. She tried on four different dresses, which were practically all the same, before deciding to buy all four of them.

"How many for all of them?" Rachel asked the shopkeeper.

"Four pieces," the old shopkeeper said. Rachel paid her and left the shop.

"I could use some more underwear," she mumbled to herself.

Leo came across a shop with casual clothes where he bought a brown pair of pants, a white shirt, black shoes, and a brown vest. He figured it had been around two and a half hours, so he explored the town before heading back to the pond.

Rachel was wearing one of her four outfits when she arrived at the pond to see Leo laying on his back, wearing a common fairy tale outfit. A piece of straw was in his mouth as he watched the clouds.

Rachel set down her bag of clothes, lay down next to Leo, and watched the clouds float by with him.

"That's a cat," Rachel said, pointing to a cloud.

"No, it's a dog," Leo argued.

"Wait, no it's a squirrel."

"A rabbit."

"A shark."

"A dwarf."

"A bear," Rachel said, squinting.

"Oh yeah, definitely a bear," Leo agreed.

They sat up, sighed with happiness, and faced each other.

"Leo," Rachel said, "I want to visit the seven dwarves."

"What?" Leo asked. "You can't be serious; how are we even supposed to find—" He was interrupted by the sound of heavy breathing and running. Rachel and Leo turned their heads to see Snow White running away from her home palace. Rachel's eyes lit up with an idea, and she got up and ran as fast as she could to keep up with Snow White.

"Hey, Snow White," Rachel said to the running princess, who slowed to a stop once she heard her name. "Where are you going?" Rachel continued, playing dumb.

"My stepmother wishes me dead; the huntsman is chasing after me. He let me get a head start from inside the palace, though he'll be outside very soon!" Snow White said, fear in her voice.

"Well, run behind the palace; there's a village there. Just go down the path and you'll find it. You can live there freely for the rest of your life," Rachel said.

"Oh, thank you!" Snow White said and ran toward the castle.

Leo made his way up to Rachel. "What did you say to her?" he asked.

"To go in the village that we went to," Rachel said. "And that's the direction the dwarves' house is in." Rachel started speed walking in the direction Snow White was going, Leo reluctantly following behind her.

After almost half an hour, Rachel exclaimed to Leo, "I can see it!"

Leo squinted his eyes and saw a comforting cottage through the trees.

They ran up to the front door and knocked without any reply. Leo opened the wooden door and Rachel walked inside, taking in the sight. "Hey," she said to Leo as he closed the door. "Do you think if we went to sleep in their beds, they'd find us?"

"Doesn't Snow White do the dishes before going to bed?" Leo asked, eyeing the kitchen where you could see nothing but dirty dishes piled up in the sink.

"They'll have to go to bed eventually, so they'll find us then, and I'm tired. And according to the movie, the stairs should be in the corner of the living room or something."

"Didn't the movie come out in 1937?" Leo asked.

"Yeah, by Walt Disney. Boy, if only he had a magic mirror," Rachel joked. "But yeah, I watched the movie when I was six. Me and Hannah would play it on our little T.V.; we would watch it on her birthday every year."

"What did you watch for your birthday?" Leo asked.

"Well, when I was a kid, like from around six to twelve years old, I would watch the movie called *The Aristocats*. Then on my thirteenth birthday, I found *Alice in Wonderland*, and then that was my favourite movie of all time — still is, actually."

"When *is* your birthday?" Leo asked.

"Hmm," Rachel said, "I can't really remember. I know it'll come back to me soon, though. Now I'll go sleep." She ran upstairs to the dwarves' room, just like she'd remembered from the movie. She opened the door at the top of the wooden steps to reveal a bedroom with seven little beds. If you lay down on them all sideways, the seven beds would be just a tad bit bigger than the bed size anyone would have in their bedroom. Rachel felt the beds, making sure this wasn't a dream and she'd suddenly wake up before she got a happily ever after.

Leo came upstairs to see Rachel already asleep on the dwarves' beds. He smiled at her blissful expression before curling up in the blankets on the floor.

The seven dwarves came home after a hard day of work. One of the seven little men was about to go have a nap when he saw a girl lying on the beds and a boy on the floor, cuddled up in a little ball on top of some extra blankets. The dwarf screamed and every other little man in the house came rushing upstairs to see what all the commotion was about.

Rachel woke to a series of gasps, whispers, and yells. "Hmm?" she said, rubbing her eyes. Her memory returned and she remembered that she was in the dwarves' house, in *Snow White*, and she was waiting for the seven men to wake her up. "Oh, hello," she said, trying to play a perfect princess. "I'm sorry; I didn't know this cottage belonged to anyone. Could you forgive me?" Rachel's smile warmed the dwarves' hearts.

"What's up?" Leo asked, waking up. With his face shown to their eyes, the little men scowled.

"Oh, he's my friend, Leo; he was accompanying me when we got lost in the woods," Rachel lied. "We found this place and couldn't help but fall asleep. I do hope you can find it in your hearts to forgive us."

"Oh, of course," one of the seven dwarves said as he yawned.

"Would you like to stay here for a little while?" a second dwarf asked as he adjusted his small glasses.

"Yes," Rachel said happily.

Leo looked around, wondering what had happened while he was asleep.

"Though the boy must go," a third dwarf said with a scowl on his face.

"Well, no Leo, no me," Rachel said and crossed her arms.

"I guess it wouldn't hurt to have him around," a fourth said while blushing uncontrollably.

"Well, men," a fifth dwarf said and sneezed. "You heard her; he must stay." Another sneeze.

Every other dwarf nodded his head in agreement, though some looked hesitant.

Leo and Rachel stayed at the cottage for a week. One day, while Rachel was picking flowers in the field in front of the dwarves' cottage, a petal flew away from her bouquet and, without her noticing, was blown down her throat. She started coughing because of the plant stuck in her windpipe; unfortunately, Leo couldn't hear her muffled cries for help. She coughed until she drew breath no more and fell to the ground, looking beautiful with the bouquet in her hand.

Luckily, a prince nearby had heard her wheezing and coughs. When he saw her lying on the ground in the field of colourful flowers, he couldn't help but stare in awe as he approached her. He kneeled down and checked her pulse: it was slow, too slow for any type of comfort. He inhaled every fibre of air he could fit in his mouth and breathed into the sleeping girl's mouth. Rachel's eyes flew open and she sat up face to face with a prince who was everything a fairy tale prince should be: charming, handsome, and with a twinkle of kindness in his eye. The prince slowly got back up to his feet, still holding eye contact with the girl he'd just saved.

"My name is Prince Silas," the prince said as Rachel steadied her balance on her two legs. "And you are?" he asked.

"Rachel, Rachel Free Angel," Rachel said.

"You can call me Silas," Prince Silas told Rachel.

"Yeah, just call me Rachel," she said.

"Would you like me to come here every day to see you and bring you to my private beach? It is beautiful, though no beauty compares to yours," he said. Silas picked Rachel up and kissed her passionately, certainly long but loving nonetheless.

"Why don't I take you to my castle?" Silas asked, putting her down.

"I would love to, but," Rachel choked on her breath, "I can't stay here forever. I'll have to go soon, in just a few more weeks or less." Her prince was saddened by this.

"Well," Silas said, "I will make this time together be the best few weeks of my life."

"But if you love me, then you'll be all sad and stuff when I leave."

"Too late, I love you already," Silas said and pecked her on the cheek. "And you'll always be my first love, my top priority."

Leo had been on his way to check on Rachel when he saw some random prince seduce her in no time. He wanted to kick that prince where he knew it would hurt like hell, but he didn't; he just stayed on the porch of the cottage, emotionally frozen in a sea of sadness.

"I'll come here every day at noon just to see your pretty smile, so promise you won't let anything get you down, okay?" Silas said to Rachel, who nodded with a smile.

"No problem," Rachel said. Silas ran off into the forest where he'd come from, though to Rachel it looked like he was running in circles around her because of how light she felt. Suddenly, her prince snuck up behind her, spun her around, and kissed her one last time. When they parted, the face she saw wasn't the one Rachel had expected. It wasn't Silas holding her close to him; instead, it was Leo.

"Get away from me!" Rachel screamed, pushing Leo away from her. "What's wrong with you?!"

Leo instantly felt guilty. "Um," was all he managed. Before he could say anything else, Rachel ran into the dwarves' cottage with tears in her eyes, feeling betrayed by the one she called a friend. Once she managed to get to the bathroom, she locked the door and fell to the floor, a flood of tears flowing down her cheeks. She had found someone she loved, and Leo, the one she called a friend-ish, had toyed with her feelings when she'd felt so happy.

"Rachel," she heard Leo knock on the door.

"G-g-go away!" Rachel cried.

"I'm sorry," he apologized.

"I d-don't need to hear it!" she sniffled. She heard Leo walk away, cursing himself as he went.

After almost an hour of feeling sorry for herself, she realized that it really wasn't that much of a big deal. She left the bathroom in search of Leo, who apparently wasn't in the kitchen, living room, or other bathroom. Instead, he was in the bedroom, his face in a pillow, tilting his head up to breathe in air every ten seconds.

"Leo," Rachel said.

"Yeah?" Leo asked, his voice slightly muffled.

"It's okay," she assured.

"No, it's not okay." Leo looked up, and when he saw her eyes were pink and puffy from crying, he only became angrier with himself. "The reason you were crying was me, wasn't it?"

"Well, yes, but it was just a meaningless kiss, right?" she said.

"Yeah, but you were crying," he argued.

"And I overreacted."

Leo stayed silent, not knowing what to say.

"But why?" Rachel asked.

Leo sat up, ran over to Rachel, grabbed her shoulders, and looked her in the eye. "Rachel, I kissed you because I—"

"We're home!" the dwarves said in unison. Rachel and Leo heard the front door open and close.

"We'll get back to this," Rachel said, her eyes back to normal. "Whether it's in this world or not." She then headed out of the bedroom, ready to greet the seven dwarves. Leo sighed in relief. His secret was still safe, at least for now.

"Hello, Happy, Bashful, Sneezy, Doc, Sleepy, Dopey, and Grumpy," Rachel said. She hugged each dwarf as she said his name, having to bend down to do so.

"I'm going to bed," Sleepy said with a yawn. Bashful blushed for no apparent reason. Dopey smiled and waved at Rachel. Sneezy sneezed repeatedly without being able to get a sentence out.

"How was your day, Miss Rachel?" Happy asked blissfully, not a care in the world.

"Amazing," Rachel replied.

"Were you safe?" Doc asked, looking concerned.

"Safe as air," Rachel said.

"What's for dinner?" Grumpy asked with a scowl so low the corners of his mouth almost touched his chin.

"I will cook," Doc said.

"Cook what?" Grumpy asked.

"Chicken, mashed potatoes, stuffing, and gravy," Doc answered like it were a fact.

"Whatever," Grumpy said.

"I can help," Rachel volunteered.

Leo and Rachel, mostly Rachel, absolutely loved the upcoming thirteen days; each morning and evening Silas would come by the dwarves' cottage and spend at least an hour with Rachel.

"I'll miss you," Rachel said to Silas on her last day in *Snow White*.

"I'll miss you more," Silas added on.

"But I may be able to come back here for short visits every once in a while," Rachel said.

"Really?" Silas asked.

"Really," Rachel assured.

Silas kissed Rachel goodbye and walked out of the field with a bounce in his step. He knew he'd see the one he loved once again, and he was willing to wait. Once he was out of sight, Rachel fell to the ground and cried, knowing that she may not actually be able to come here ever again.

"Rachel," Leo called from the dwarves' cottage porch. Rachel stayed on the ground. Leo left the cottage, came toward Rachel, and hugged her in comfort.

"You can come back whenever you want," Leo said.

"But I don't want to leave this place at all," she cried.

"We have to go back to our world; people will start wondering where we've gone," Leo reminded her. "Sir Evergreen could come here at any time; it was reckless to stay here for this long. We don't know what could happen!"

"I don't care! Nobody in that world gave a crap about me, but in this world somebody does," Rachel said while drying her tears. "Silas does. Silas cares about me."

Leo wanted to say that she was wrong; he cared about her, more than Silas ever could, but it wasn't the right time and place to mention it. Maybe one day he'd have the courage to tell her how he felt, but for now those feelings were to be kept deep down within his soul. And maybe, if he was lucky, she'd love him, too.

CHAPTER SEVEN

HOME

"Come on," Leo urged. "We'll leave a note then head on toward the lake."

"When can we come back?" Rachel asked.

"Another time, not that long from now," Leo replied. He helped her up to her feet and they started walking toward the cottage. Leo kindly opened the door to let Rachel walk inside.

"I'll get paper and quill with ink from the bedroom to write the letter," Rachel decided as the door shut behind Leo. And so she did. She marched up the stairs to the bedroom, took what she needed, and went to the kitchen table to write a goodbye letter. Rachel tapped the feather against her chin before finally forming the right words in her head. This was hard with Leo hovering over her. She scribbled down a legible note and passed it to Leo, warning him not to touch the ink because it was fresh from the pen and not dried yet. Leo read it:

To: The Seven Dwarves (Happy, Doc, Grumpy, Dopey, Sneezy, Bashful, and Sleepy)

From: Rachel Free Angel

These have been the happiest, best-spent weeks of my entire fifteen years of life, but I must go home now. I will come back to see all of you, not exactly soon, but I will, and that's a promise. I'll forever miss Happy and his cheerfulness, Doc and his wisdom, Grumpy and his attitude, Dopey and his silent smiles, Sneezy and his forever-lasting cold, Bashful and his blushing cheeks, and last but most certainly not least, I'll miss Sleepy and his laziness. Thank you, the seven of you, for your hospitality; it was very appreciated, more than words could ever describe.

Goodbye,

Your Friend
Rachel Free Angel

"That's fantastic!" Leo said. He put the note on the table for all the dwarves to see as Rachel headed to the door. Leo caught up with Rachel and they started walking toward the pond in front of Snow White's palace. Once they had safely arrived, they both threw in their belongings they'd bought in the fairy tale before cannonballing into the water. They appeared on the floor in Sir Evergreen's secret room.

"Did you forget anything?" Leo asked Rachel.

"No," Rachel said, gesturing to her sack of clothes.

"We need to change into our uniforms," Leo said with a heavy sigh.

Rachel looked at him, confused for a moment before an expression of realization poured down her face. "No," Rachel said once she realized what Leo was implying. "No way in Hell, Heaven, or on planet Earth am I changing in front of you, and what if Sir Evergreen comes in?"

"Well, we can't exactly waltz around the school not wearing our uniforms," he noted.

"I hate it when you're right, now turn around," she grouched.

They finished in the room and headed back to their dorm, Rachel telling onlooking students they'd gone shopping for fun.

"They don't seem to notice that we were gone for two weeks," Rachel whispered to Leo.

"Maybe they're too stunned to react?" Leo suggested. Rachel shook her head, knowing it was more than that.

They opened the door to their dorm and sat on their bed, side by side, after throwing their bags of clothes in the corner.

"What day is it?" Rachel asked.

"I have my flip phone so I can check," Leo said. He got up, Rachel's gaze following his every move. He took his phone from the first drawer of his nightstand, flipped it open, and let a shocked expression crawl onto his face.

"What?" Rachel asked, waiting in suspense.

"The day we left was June twentieth, year two thousand, right?" he asked.

"Yeah, so? What about it?"

"It says June twentieth," Leo said, looking up at Rachel.

"What? But that's impossible; we were in the mirror for two *weeks*!" Rachel protested, not believing him.

"I beg to differ,"

"So, what you're saying is that whenever someone goes inside the mirror, time just freezes?"

"Pretty much," Leo said.

"So, does that mean that we've been frozen in time several times before?" Rachel asked.

"I guess, but at least now we know what'll happen," Leo said with a forced laugh.

"Just, wow," Rachel said, laughing with him.

"It's still morning," Leo said.

"Want to get breakfast?" Rachel asked. They went downstairs, got their food, and went to a vacant table that reminded Rachel of the girls' school.

"Can we go back soon?" Rachel asked Leo, excitement burning in her eyes like the dancing flames of a fire.

"Where?" Leo asked, attempting to play dumb.

"Through the mirror, silly," Rachel said.

"Shh!" Leo snapped.

"Okay, jeez," Rachel whispered. "But what's really bugging me is not knowing why Sir Evergreen has the magic mirror in the first place."

Leo thought about this. "Probably a gift," he decided and continued to eat his breakfast. "But if you want to sneak through the mirror and Sir Evergreen's actually there, you'll need a list of excuses." He swallowed a chunk of pancake.

"I can make a long list in the notebook you bought me, and thanks, by the way."

I thought that was your diary, Leo thought.

"But where could we go next?" Rachel asked, even though she hadn't yet touched her food. "*Oz, Neverland, Narnia*? No, not *Narnia*, it's too, well *Narnia*, maybe once we really get the hang of it, but not yet. Though we could go to Neverland; I don't have a problem with that. Maybe Rapunzel, Sleeping Beauty, or is her name Aurora? We could always go into *Cinderella*, yeah, *Cinderella*; could we go there next?"

"Sshh!" Leo snapped and covered Rachel's mouth with his hand, getting licked in return. "Sure, sure," he continued, wiping his hand on his pants. "Of course we can visit your Aunt Ella."

"Aunt Ella?" Rachel asked.

Leo eyed the boys around them as a signal; Rachel understood. "Well, I'm going back to the dorm," Rachel said, leaving her tray full of food on the table in front of Leo and heading out of the dining hall.

"What were you and your girlfriend talking about?" Zach said mockingly from behind Leo, who jumped in surprise.

Leo pulled himself together enough so he could reply, "None of your business."

"Doesn't mean we can't make it our business," Vic said from Zach's left.

"No, you can't," Leo argued.

"I wouldn't be running my mouth like that if I were you," Zach said.

"You don't scare me," Leo said.

"Doesn't mean we can't make you. And also, do you mind telling us where your girlfriend went?" Alex said from Zach's right.

"I'm not telling you," Leo said.

"Come on, tell us; would it really hurt?" Vic said.

"Leave me alone," Leo snapped.

"Just tell us where she is," Alex said.

"No."

"Come on, just tell us where she is," the trio said in unison.

"In the bathrooms?" Vic asked.

Leo kept his mouth shut.

"In the workshop?" Alex asked.

He didn't let a word slip.

"In your dorm? Well, it belongs to the both of you," Zach asked. Leo glanced back at him, wondering how he'd have known. "Ah," Zach said, knowing he was right by Leo's reaction. "Which dorm?"

"Not telling," Leo said.

Zach, Vic, and Alex looked at each other and identical evil smirks were painted across their faces. Zach pulled Leo out of the dining hall by the ear with Alex and Vic walking behind him. They brought him past the library and Sir Evergreen's office to a dark and vacant hallway.

"Make him tell us," Zach instructed Vic and Alex.

Vic grabbed Leo by the collar and pushed him against the wall with extreme force. Alex joined and punched Leo in the face. Vic kneed him in the groin and Alex kicked him in the shin. For the finishing touch, Vic pinched Leo's cheek hard.

"Stop it!" Leo said loudly.

"I don't think so. Keep going, boys," Zach said, and then Alex and Vic continued beating Leo up.

At this point, Leo had a bloody nose, a red cheek, and a bruise on the knee. It wasn't too bad, though it hurt every time he was hit, kicked, or punched.

"So, which room?" Zach said, and then Vic and Alex let go of Leo.

"Room four, south tower," Leo lied.

"I expected that much sooner," Zach said, and then he led Vic and Alex away to room four of the south tower. Leo ran away before the trio found out that he was lying and decided they should beat him up some more.

"Rachel?" Leo asked, opening the door to his dorm.

"Yeah?" Rachel asked, writing in her notebook.

"Where did you say you wanted to go?" he asked. Rachel smiled.

After Leo had freshened himself up from his fight, and after he had held Rachel back so she wouldn't go beat Vic,

Alex, and Zach to death, they started walking toward the office.

"Okay, my excuse if Sir Evergreen is there is that I was sick," Rachel said to Leo as they walked. "And you had to accompany me so I wouldn't collapse or do anything severe."

"But wouldn't we have to go to the medical room, not the office?" Leo asked, and Rachel frowned.

"Well, we could say that I've lost my— what do boys find precious?" she asked.

Other than the girls we love? Leo thought. He cleared his throat. "Maybe something they've had their entire life; that would be pretty precious to me."

"Could I say that I lost a gold ring my mother had given to me?"

"Yeah, that would be a good reason to come to the office."

They arrived at the office and opened the door; the room was empty as always.

"Seriously, how irresponsible is this guy?" Rachel asked, shaking her head from side to side. They walked past the desk, opened the door, and walked into the room with the mirror.

Rachel took a piece of chalk from beside the chalkboard and wrote *Cinderella* before placing her hand on the glass. She watched it ripple and jumped inside; Leo reluctantly jumped in after her.

CHAPTER EIGHT

CINDERELLA

They were in the middle of a bright blue sky, then they fell to the ground.

"Ouch!" Rachel said as she hit the ground with a *thump*. Leo landed beside her.

In front of them was a beautiful grey brick mansion with tall towers that seemed to touch the sky, scraping the setting sun. There were rose bushes on either side of the path leading to the house.

"Where do you think the portal is this time?" Leo asked.

"My guess is the bushes," Rachel said and got up.

"Rachel, what if it's not the bushes? You could get stung by bees or get all scratched," Leo said, trying to talk Rachel into being reasonable.

"Only one way to find out." With those confident words came a confident jump of stupidity.

"Rachel, you idiot!" Leo yelled and ran to the rose bushes, though Rachel wasn't there. Leo cleared his throat and looked around, thinking that he was lucky Rachel didn't hear him call her an idiot. She came back a moment later without a scratch on her body.

"Through the bushes," she said. "Though we need money." She jumped back through the bushes and Leo followed.

"Stuff as many gold coins wherever you can, got it?" Rachel instructed Leo, who gaped at her as she stuffed gold coins in her pockets and down her shirt and pants.

"Why so many?" Leo asked.

"Because I want to go to each ball that the prince hosts; you know, those balls where he wants to find a bride," Rachel explained.

"I thought there was only one," Leo said, scrunching up his face as if he smelled something foul.

"That was in the movie. In the original fairy tale, there are three balls — just saying."

"And how would you know this?"

"Because I had this type of fairy tale class learning thing in the girls' school; don't ask," she explained.

"Why do they have that?" he asked.

"Hey, I said no questions," Rachel shot, looking overweight with coins. She looked down at herself and started emptying her pockets, only keeping what was necessary. "Oh, and fun fact," she said. "Did you know that in the original *Cinderella* the two stepsisters try to cut off their toes to fit their feet in the glass slipper? And it wasn't even a fairy godmother who gave Cinderella her dress; it was a tree growing near her late mother's grave."

"Now I see why they didn't tell the original story," Leo said.

They finished filling their pockets with a suitable amount of gold coins before heading back through the mirror.

"Where can the market be?" Rachel asked, looking around them.

"Maybe there'll be a sign on a road pointing to where it is?" Leo suggested.

"Yeah, maybe," Rachel said. They walked down the pathway, away from Cinderella's mansion instead of towards it. They took a turn onto the main road and quickly found a sign with letters carved into it: **MARKETPLACE DOWN THIS ROAD.** Rachel and Leo walked down the road, seeing the occasional carriage pulled by a horse with the passengers inside giving them bewildered looks in response to the clothes they wore. They eventually came to the outskirts of a little town. The tiny houses were made with red brick and hay roofs, the classic fairy tale home. A pole was beside the pathway leading into the small town with several signs, either pointing right or left, with the names of shops on them. Rachel and Leo decided it would be best to go to the shop called *Everyday Clothing.* They turned right and started making their way to a cute shop almost on the other side of town. Some stores they saw were populated, some were nearly vacant, others were just in between.

"This place is just so perfect!" Rachel said, her hands pressed against her cheeks.

Leo raised an eyebrow, "Well, you do remember that this is actually a fairy tale."

"Yeah, but it's just so perfect! Isn't it?" she said, gesturing around them at the townspeople and shops.

"Yeah, I guess," he said unenthusiastically.

They arrived at a shop with casual clothes.

"Are you sure?" Leo asked Rachel.

"Well, maybe that one?" Rachel proposed, pointing to a tiny store named *True Toppers* with more clothes that were obviously cheaper, though they looked about the same quality.

"Yep, that looks good," Leo said with a thumbs up.

"Cheapskate," Rachel muttered under her breath.

They walked into the shop and were bewildered by the sight of all the clothes everywhere. Pants were hanging from the ceiling, dresses were hanging above the front counter, hats of all shapes and sizes were randomly placed around the store, and shirts of all kinds filled in the empty spaces between everything else. All the clothes were organized, although they looked very unorganized; half the store displayed clothes for women or little girls, and the rest of the shop displayed clothes for men and younger boys. On the girls' side of the shop, Rachel noticed how many dresses there were with white aprons — almost every single one a different size than the other. On the boys' side of the shop, Leo noticed how many pairs of pants there were compared to the number of shirts, and he was almost appalled by the sight.

"May I help you?" a man said, walking towards them from the back of the store. He had a long mustache, greasy black hair, and kind blue eyes that shone like crystals. He wore an everyday outfit for the fairy tale world, which was just your average plain brown pants, a beige top, and wooden shoes.

"Um, yes," Leo said. "We would like to buy some casual clothes."

"Marcus," a feminine voice hollered from the back of the shop, obviously listening in on them. "You take care of the boy and I'll take care of the other one."

"Liliane, where are you?" Marcus called.

"In the dressing room!" she called back.

"Are you trying on our clothing again?"

"No, I just need to organize them!"

"Organize how?"

"Some customers left the garments they didn't want in the changeroom so I have to put them back where they belong!"

"Hurry up, then!" Marcus yelled.

Rachel and Leo saw at the back of the shop two barely visible doors open and a woman emerge, carrying at least fifty pounds worth of clothes.

"Marcus, help me!" Liliane yelled. Marcus walked calmly toward her and took half of the clothes, and then they quickly put the garments back in their place.

After they finished, Liliane came over to Rachel and Leo and said, "So, what did you folks come here for?" Liliane had greasy black hair tied back into a loose hair bun, clear blue eyes, and pale skin. She wore a plain brown dress with a white apron and black shoes. As a matter of fact, she could have easily been mistaken for Marcus had she cut her hair, grown a mustache, and worn Marcus' outfit.

"We just needed some clothes," Rachel said.

"Oh, honey pie, just come along with me," Liliane said. She took Rachel by the hand and led her deep into the female side of the shop.

"Come with me," Marcus said to Leo and led him to the opposite side of the store.

"What is your gender exactly?" Liliane whispered to Rachel. "We need to ask if we're uncertain."

"I'm a girl," Rachel replied. "I know the clothing looks contradictory."

"Well then, what would you like?" Liliane asked Rachel.

"Just a brown dress, a white apron, and black shoes," Rachel said.

Liliane took out a measuring tape from somewhere underneath her dress. Nodding her head, she measured around Rachel's waist, neck, arms, legs, and even her nose, muttering something about how she would rub it in Marcus' face that most girls had a nose bigger than his.

"I'll bring you three selections of what size you most probably are," Liliane said, and she suddenly dashed off all over the store to take everything she needed.

"What would you like?" Marcus asked Leo.

"Just something casual," Leo replied. Marcus took measurements around Leo's shoulders, hips, and nose, muttering to himself how he'd rub it in Liliane's face that most boys had a nose the same size as him and his wasn't small for his age.

Marcus then dashed away from Leo to get everything he needed. He practically shoved Leo in the changeroom with the clothes and waited impatiently for him to come out, asking if he was done yet every five seconds.

Leo came out five minutes later wearing an outfit of plain brown pants, a beige shirt in the perfect size, a brown vest, and black shoes.

"How does it fit?" Marcus asked.

"Good, I'll take it," Leo said.

"That'll be five gold coins."

"So, are you and Marcus siblings?" Rachel asked as she tried on one of the three outfits Liliane had given her.

"Unfortunately," Liliane said with a scoff. "You know my life was perfectly perfect until he came into it."

Rachel cleared her throat. "How old are you?" she asked, changing the subject.

"Twenty, and Marcus is only sixteen."

"Do you like him?"

"Marcus? No, of course not! He's loud, obnoxious, annoying, idiotic, and well, *him*!"

"Heard that!" Marcus yelled from the front of the shop.

"It's true!" Liliane shot back.

"So, how long have you been working here?" Rachel asked.

"Since I was about thirteen, so seven years for me now, and Marcus started working here when he was thirteen. I worked here for four years on my own, and it was great. So anyway, how does it fit?"

Rachel walked out of the changeroom wearing one of the three outfits Liliane had given her to try on. "I'll take them all," Rachel said.

"That'll be seven gold coins," Liliane said. She and Rachel went to the front counter and saw Leo and Marcus. The siblings shared a fair number of death stares before returning their focus to their clients.

"So, for her it's seven," Liliane said, eyeing Marcus.

"For him it was five," Marcus said, ignoring Liliane's existence.

"Total of twelve gold coins," Liliane said to her customers. Leo pulled out thirteen from his pocket and gave them to Liliane, the extra coin for her kindness. "Oh, do you have a sack?" Leo asked.

"What? Why?" Marcus asked.

"Because I would like one," he said.

"Okay." Marcus went to the back of the store and came back in no time at all with a sack. "Here," he said, giving the bag to Leo, who put his uniform inside; he then held it open for Rachel who put her uniform inside.

"Thank you," Leo and Rachel said together as they headed out of the store.

Not even five minutes down the street, Rachel and Leo heard an old woman yell, "Look, everyone!"

Every townsperson gathered around the old woman, and for some reason, so did Rachel and Leo. The woman was in front of a poster made of parchment which read:

Royal Balls

The Prince of Agommestay is hosting three royal balls.
At the balls, the prince plans to find his bride.
Every maiden in the land is requested
to attend at least one ball.

The dates and times are as follows:

August twenty-first at nineteen
o'clock to twenty-two o'clock
August twenty-second at twenty
o'clock to twenty-three o'clock
August twenty-third at twenty-one o'clock to Midnight

Please come wearing formal attire suitable for a ball.
If not, entry will be strictly prohibited.

Hope to see you there!

"What day is it here?" Rachel asked.

"I don't know," Leo answered. "Maybe we could ask someone?" And so that's precisely what they did.

"Excuse me, Miss," Rachel said to the closest woman. "What day is it?"

The woman turned around and said, "Today's the twentieth."

"Thank you," Rachel said with a smile. She led Leo away from the crowd. "Depending on the story we enter, the time of the year can be completely different! Anyway, the first ball's tomorrow!" she exclaimed excitedly, shaking Leo. "That means we have to go shopping again! I mean what are we going to wear to a *ball*, these?"

"Okay, first of all, like heck I'm going to a ball," Leo said.

"Well, of course. I must attend at least one, and who else will distract Cinderella from the ball?" she said.

"Let me guess," he said. "You're going to sabotage this story, too?"

"Obviously. This is going to be one of the best nights of my life."

"But what am I going to do while you buy whatever it is you need?"

"What are you talking about? You're coming with me."

"What?!" Leo asked, mortified.

"It won't be torture; besides, I should know, I *love* shopping," Rachel said, and then she pressed his nose like a button.

They spent the rest of their day going from store to store, with Rachel trying on a dozen different dresses at each establishment. She kept asking Leo for his honest opinion, though he couldn't care less about any of it.

Finally, Rachel had found her perfect gown. She also bought many *needed* accessories. Her dress was dark blue with specks of white to make it look like the night sky. By the end of the day, they were done shopping. They ate at a nice restaurant and found a cheap hotel to sleep in. The following day, Rachel bought a pair of elegant shoes to match her dress. She headed to the shop she had the dress saved in; Leo came with her, of course. She put on her dress and went to the hairdresser where she had her hair lengthened with a spell and done up gorgeously. Leo tried his best to keep his jaw from dropping in awe. They then went to a makeover shop where Rachel had blush added to her cheeks, red lipstick put onto her lips, and her eyelashes curled.

They then went to a fountain where Rachel and Leo sat by their lonesome.

"So, how do I look?" Rachel asked Leo at one point. "You haven't said anything for a while."

Well, for starters, you look gorgeous, second— Leo thought then cleared his throat and said, "You look pretty good."

"Well, I don't know if that's a good thing or a bad thing, but are you ready to distract Cinderella?" she said.

"Yep," he said before giving her a confused look. "Wait, *how* am I supposed to distract her?"

Rachel grinned like an evil cat.

Leo's eyes widened. "No! No way! That's going too far!"

Rachel kept her grin.

"No! You can't!" Leo said.

"Come on, Lee Lo," she said. "Cinderella's lonely; she needs a boyfriend."

"No way!"

"Please, for me?"

Leo looked at her with clenched teeth for a few moments, but he couldn't resist helping her. "Fine," he said and looked away, frustrated with himself for giving in. "But what am I supposed to do about the tree?"

"I don't know. Chop it down or something; you figure it out," Rachel said. She squinted at the clock tower in front of the castle where she'd attend the ball, looking perfect.

"I'll just keep her away from the tree," Leo decided.

"It's seven o'clock," Rachel said.

"What? *Go!*" Leo said.

"I'll wait for seven thirty," she said.

"Why the heck are you going to do that?!" Leo said.

"Oh, dear idiot," Rachel said, "haven't you read or watched *Cinderella*? Cinderella was late to the ball, and I'm going to be exactly like her. Then I'm going to dance with the prince, socialize, and enjoy myself, just like the princess did. And she got a perfect happily ever after, and so will I, in at least one story. But you need to go to her, now!"

With his orders given, Leo dashed to the mansion where the portal was, ready to pretend to love the girl he was about to meet.

Half an hour later, Rachel walked up the steps to the castle, taking in the sight. The guards let her in through the grand castle doors where she found her way to the ballroom.

Rachel knew she was the last girl to arrive at the ball because the ballroom was full of other girls wearing gorgeous ball gowns, just like hers, and there was almost no more room on the dance floor. She walked toward the crowd gracefully, and every prince, princess, king, and queen turned to look at her.

The prince, who was bowing to two girls wearing big red ball gowns, glanced up at Rachel before continuing his conversation with the two girls. One of the two girls had red hair so dark it almost looked purple; the second had green hair that was such a dark shade it seemed to be black. Behind them was an elderly lady with greying brown hair done up in a stylish do. Rachel knew without a doubt in her mind that these were the two stepsisters and stepmother Cinderella had to deal with her entire life. Apparently, while watching the prince, stepsisters, and stepmother, Rachel lost her balance and fell forward onto the marble floor. Every person in the room turned their heads toward her and Rachel's big brown eyes started filling up with tears.

The prince looked away from the stepsisters and, seeing Rachel on the floor, ran to her aid. "Are you alright?" the prince asked Rachel.

"Um, yes your highness," Rachel said, not used to someone being genuinely worried for her. The prince took Rachel's hand and helped her up to her feet. The orchestra in the corner started to play a soft love song.

"Would you let me have this dance?" the prince asked Rachel, putting his hand out for her to take.

"Yes," Rachel replied as he took her hand in his. They slowly danced, though it was mostly Rachel apologizing for stepping on the prince's toes.

"What's your name?" Rachel eventually asked.

"Jonathan Edward Agommestay," the prince said. "And yours?"

"Rachel Free Angel," Rachel said. "And do you have a nickname or something? Because calling you Jonathan every time I see you will eventually get old."

"John or Johnny," Jonathan said.

"I like Johnny; it's more casual," Rachel decided, finally getting the hang of dancing.

"Johnny it is," he said.

"What else do you want to do?" Leo asked Cinderella.

"Maybe a kind of question game, to get to know each other a bit more," Cinderella suggested. She had bright blue eyes, a kind smile and heart, and flowing, long blond hair. She wore an ash-covered brown dress and white apron, black shoes, and a bandana made out of blue cloth. Some mice followed her around; they were also ash-covered.

From what Leo knew so far, Cinderella's stepmother made her clean the fireplace and sleep there as well.

"Sure," Leo said.

"Okay," Cinderella said. "Why did you come here?"

"Well, I was passing by and I saw the beautiful roses. I love flowers," Leo lied. "So, I wanted to ask the flower-owners where they got them. Anyway, my turn: do you love your stepsisters and stepmother?"

"Yes, very much," Cinderella said.

"But why?" he asked. "And where are they?"

"They are at the ball the prince is hosting to find a bride; you must've heard of it. Though they forbade me from going. I know they aren't very fond of me, and they call me Cinderella, even though my name is actually Ella, but they're the only family I have left," she replied.

"But don't they make you sad?"

"Yes, they make me very sad, but I might as well make the most of what I have, don't you think? You never know what life could throw at you. I mean, tomorrow I could wake up and they'd love me."

"How did you become so positive?" Leo asked. "I mean, if you ask me, your life kind of sucks."

"Well, once I realized that my life couldn't exactly get better, I decided that I shouldn't waste my life sulking around. I should be happy that I have clothes and a roof over my head."

Leo sighed; she was right about it all. "What time is it?" he asked.

"Nine forty-five," Cinderella said.

"I should go," Leo said.

"Will you be here tomorrow?" she asked.

"Sure," he replied, and Cinderella smiled. Leo ran out of the house to the castle so he could see Rachel.

"You'll be here tomorrow?" Johnny asked Rachel.

"Yes, of course," Rachel replied. Johnny smiled in happiness and let her go. Rachel walked down the castle steps to see Leo waiting for her. She jumped the last four steps, almost breaking her shoe's heel.

"It was spectacular!" Rachel told Leo.

"Really?" Leo asked Rachel as though she were a tiny child. They walked to a nearby fountain and sat on the ledge.

"Oh, and Jonathan, he was just wonderful!" Rachel exclaimed. "We danced across the ballroom floor so gracefully and so perfectly, everyone couldn't help but stare in awe! Oh, it was just amazing!"

"Can't we just find a place to sleep?" Leo asked in frustration, turning towards Rachel. She stopped talking and looked at him in shock. "I've had enough of you just talking about your stupid fairy tale adventures and pleasures; I couldn't care less!" He turned back to his facing forward seated position. "I mean, you don't have to rub it in. I get it, you had a good time, but just shut up! I don't need to hear it!" He turned back to Rachel to see tears flowing down her cheeks; Leo instantly felt guilty. "Rachel."

"I can't believe you," Rachel said, and she stormed off, away from Leo.

"I'm such a moronasaurus," Leo said to himself. He got up and ran after Rachel, though she'd already gotten a head start. "Rachel, I'm sorry, I didn't mean to!" he called after her, though Rachel didn't even slightly glance back at him. She was frustrated with his lack of patience and compassion. She eventually came to a dead end and turned around, ready to run in a different direction, only to come face to face with Leo.

"I'm sorry," Leo apologized.

"For crushing my happiness under your boot of being an ass? Well, sorry ain't gonna cut it," Rachel snapped, drying her tears.

"I'm sorry," Leo tried again.

"I told you: sorry isn't going to cut it. You need a bigger pair of scissors for this one," she said.

"I'll let you have all the money my parents send me for the next six months," Leo said, taking a step forward.

"What do you think I am? Some sort of heartless money-loving person?!" she yelled.

"Um, all the bed to yourself?" He took another step forward.

"It's not like you have some sort of contagious disease or something!"

"My darkest secret?" He took another step.

"You know what? Forget it!" Rachel yelled and shoved Leo away from her. "Just forget all about it! Just forget! Forget! Forget! Forget! That'll be your big pair of scissors! Just forget about it all!"

Leo looked at her like she'd suggested something wrong.

"Don't look at me like that," Rachel said with a heavy sigh. "Let's just sleep here, in this stupid alleyway. Doesn't bother me at all." She sat down on the ground and Leo sat down beside her. "Goodnight, dummy," she said softly.

"Goodnight," Leo said. He turned to smile at Rachel before she fell asleep, but he found she was already snoring.

Morning came and Rachel and Leo woke up to the sun's morning glow.

"What time is it?" Rachel asked Leo, still leaning against him with her eyes closed.

"Look at the big damn clock tower in front of you," Leo said, squinting at the sun's light.

"But my eyes are closed," she argued.

"Open them," he said. She did, one at a time, slowly.

"Eleven o'clock," Rachel said, squinting her eyes to differentiate the small hand from the bigger one. "Huh, I can sleep in."

"Rachel," Leo said.

"Yeah?" she asked.

"You had friends at your old school, right?" he asked her.

"Should I feel offended?"

"No, but you did, right?"

"Yes, one." Rachel looked away from Leo to avoid his eyes.

"Who?"

"Hannah Black," she said and quickly wiped her eyes.

"Was she a good friend?" Leo asked.

"Yes, she was my absolute best and only friend. When I told her about my idea to change schools, she, being the perfect friend, agreed because she only wanted me to be happy. But a new start meant a new life, and a new life meant new, and that would mean no more Hannah." Rachel burst into tears before she said the rest. "I miss h-her so m-much!" she buried her face into Leo's shoulder and continued crying.

"Sorry I asked," Leo apologized, patting Rachel's back. "I, too, had a friend that I miss dearly,"

"She was the only one in the entire world who liked me at all. Even my relatives despised my guts, but she was so nice, even though I wanted nothing to do with her at first, because I was forced to go to the girls' school. She was the only one in her dorm so they put me in with her. I remember everything about that day, even the little paint stain on the kid uniform Hannah wore," she cried.

"Let it out," Leo said.

Rachel cried and cried until she thought her eyes would slip out of their sockets because of all the tears. "Do you want to go home?" Leo asked her. Rachel looked up at him. Her makeup was running down her cheeks with her tears but she managed to nod. "But before we do that, you should probably get all that stuff off your face." Rachel laughed a little at his comment. They left the fountain and went to a washroom where Rachel washed her face thoroughly. Rachel walked out of the washroom and waited patiently for Leo, who came out of the men's washroom not that long after her. They were about to jump into the portal when Rachel remembered.

"What about Jonathan?" she said to Leo.

"He's just a fairy tale character," Leo said.

"So is Silas, but you're right. I guess Jonathan *is* just a fairy tale character, nothing more," she said.

"And what about Silas?" Leo argued.

"He's more than a fairy tale character that some person invented; he's special."

"Saying that makes you sound weird, like asylum-level weird."

Rachel turned and slapped Leo across the face. "There is nothing wrong with me," she snapped and walked towards the mansion.

"Ow," Leo murmured to himself before following her; he felt a twinge of guilt for leaving Cinderella but knew that she would forget about it; she was very strong-hearted.

They came to the rose bushes in front of Cinderella's mansion and Rachel dove in with Leo on her tail. They fell onto the floor of Sir Evergreen's office where Rachel erased the word **Cinderella** and wrote **Snow White**. Rachel placed her hand on the glass before jumping in and Leo came in immediately after.

CHAPTER NINE

BACK TO SNOW WHITE

$\mathcal{R}$achel and Leo appeared near the dwarves' cottage where someone Rachel recognized stood; she smiled in delight.

"Hi Silas!" Rachel said happily as her prince lifted her off the ground and twirled her around.

"I missed you," Silas said. Leo tried to sneak away into the dwarves' cottage but was caught by Silas' eye. "Who's he?" the prince asked, a scowl replacing his smile.

"Oh," Rachel said as Silas put her back onto solid ground. "He's just my travelling partner."

"Oh," Silas said, thinking nothing more of the matter and regaining his smile. "How long are you here for? And how did you just appear like that?"

"Well, how did we just appear? That's magic. And we'll be here for about two days. Is that a sunset?"

"Hmm?" Silas looked behind and him and saw the sun starting to descend. "Yes, it's just starting; actually, would you like to watch it from a beautiful place with me?"

"Yes, I'd love to," Rachel exclaimed. "But first I have to say hello to the dwarves." She left Silas and Leo in the field and went inside the dwarves' cottage to give her regards to her seven little friends.

Once he heard the door shut, Silas' smile evaporated again. "Leave her alone," he threatened.

"What do you mean?" Leo asked, obviously puzzled.

"It's obvious you like her. Here's a little note of advice: Rachel would never love someone who is as much of a lowlife as you, so back off. And also, once she's finished with her voyages, I will marry her, and I won't let a stupid mutt like you get in my way."

"You can have her, but the only lowlife here is you."

"I thought I told you that a stupid mutt like yourself should just buzz off, or are you a dumb little mutt? Well, are you, shorty?"

"I said you can have her, and quit calling me names because a person who calls someone names is a little—"

"Hey, guys!" Rachel said, walking out the front door. Silas' cheerful expression came back almost instantaneously.

"Come on, or we'll miss the best part of the sunset," the prince said. He took Rachel by the hand and led her away from Leo, who was practically breathing fire.

"You're wrong, Silas," Leo said once they were out of sight. "She's mine, and nothing you do will prevent that from happening."

Silas led Rachel to a sandy beach. Side by side, they sat on the flawless sand. There was no another person in sight for as long as the eye could see.

"It's beautiful," Rachel said in shock.

"Well, that's how I feel about you. Just seeing your big brown eyes and your beautiful smile — it's all so blissful," Silas said, lacing his fingers through her hair, still long from the last fairy tale sabotage. Rachel blushed at the wave of compliments. They watched the sun fully set and looked at the stars in the dark sky, the glowing moon shining down on them.

"Hey, Silas," Rachel said.

"Yes, my love?" Silas answered.

"Do you ever wonder if the stars are actually alive? Like, what if they knew they shone? Or do they not have any chances to see themselves? Do you ever wonder about that?" she said.

"I've actually never really thought about it. Maybe they don't know that they shine; they're just beautiful, accepting all the attention like they deserve it. I guess they wonder where the glow is coming from, and then they turn to the star beside them and see that that's what was causing the light. Then the stars just do that, every day and every night, never knowing that they are the ones who shine down on us," he answered.

"Yeah, maybe that is the way they are, just unbeknownst to their beauty. Never knowing that they are one and the same as the other stars."

"But imagine how boring it must be for them, just staying in the sky, doing nothing, all day, all night," Silas said. Rachel laughed.

"It's late; I should probably get back to the dwarves' cottage," she said with a yawn.

"Yeah," he said. They helped each other up to their feet and the prince led his future princess back to the dwarves' cottage.

"Thank you," Rachel said, walking up the steps to the cottage front door.

"No problem," Silas said. He pecked her on the cheek before heading off toward the forest. Rachel let herself lean against the door, feeling light and warm inside her heart. She breathed slowly before deciding to head into the cottage. Rachel went into the dwarves' bedroom and, not caring that she was still in her dress and shoes, lay down onto one of the beds and fell into a deep sleep, just like a princess.

"Rachel!" Leo yelled from the kitchen as the sun's glow shone through the cottage's windows. "Get up!"

Rachel lazily opened her eyes one at a time. She begrudgingly got out of bed and went to the kitchen to see why Leo was waking her up early, or at least she thought it was early. "What?" Rachel asked, half-asleep,

"Somebody's outside," Leo said, pointing out the kitchen window. Rachel looked at what he was pointing at and saw Silas standing in the flower field.

"What?!" Rachel asked, suddenly fully awake. "He can't see me like this; look at my hair!"

Leo rolled his eyes, "Well, why don't you go get ready?" he said unenthusiastically.

Rachel ran upstairs and made herself presentable. She then rushed back downstairs with her hair brushed beautifully and tied back into a ponytail. She should've won a gold medal for how fast she'd been.

Rachel walked out the front door to Silas. "Hello," she said.

"Hey, Rachel," Silas said.

Leo watched everything from the window as jealousy bubbled in the pit of his stomach. He turned away from the window and stormed off, not wanting to hurt his heart any more than it already was. Silas noticed this, despite the sun shining in the window, and smiled mischievously.

"What are you doing here so early?" Rachel asked.

"It takes a while to get to my place, so I figured we'd better get going," Silas said, grinning.

"You want me to come over to your castle?" Rachel asked, pointing to herself.

"Are you against that idea?" Silas said, leaning towards her.

"No, of course not! Why would I be?" she said.

"Well, since you want to go," he said, "we should start heading to my carriage now." The prince led Rachel to a white and gold carriage that would be pulled by five horses. Four of the five horses were white with bright silver manes, tails the same colour, and sky-blue eyes. While these horses looked like they could represent light itself, the horse at the front was dark as night. It had a black coat, mane, and tail, and dark brown eyes, easily representing the dark shadows. Sitting at the front of the carriage was a coachman holding the gold-coloured reins. For the dark horse, the reins and bridle were black. The coachman wore white clothes with silver lining; he also wore black boots that seemed to have a little bit too much of a heel in Rachel's opinion.

"What's up with the black horse?" Rachel asked.

"Actually, I never really thought about it that much, but I'll ask once we get to the castle," Silas said.

"You do know their names, or haven't you really thought about it that much?" she teased.

"Well," he said, a smug look on his face, "the black one's name is Midnight, naturally. The white one closest to the carriage on the right is Starlight. The one beside Starlight is Silver, behind Silver is Twinkle, and the last one's name is Bright."

"How do you remember all of that?"

"They've always been placed in the same order since I was just a little kid, so it was only hard to remember over a decade ago."

"Cool," she said, stroking Midnight's mane.

Silas took her hand and brought her into the carriage, which was just as beautiful on the inside as it was on the outside.

"Go!" Silas hollered and the carriage started racing down the dirt road.

"Do you think your parents will like me?" Rachel asked anxiously, looking Silas in the eye.

"Yes, of course; why would you even think of worrying over such a petty matter?" he asked.

"Are you sure?" she asked, sounding obsessive.

"Yes. One hundred per cent sure," he replied, holding her hand in his.

"How are you so sure?"

"Because they are my parents. There is no need to elaborate on that. I know that they will adore you, and if not yet, soon enough."

Rachel became silent and looked out the carriage window. She'd expected to see huge trees soaring up to the sky; instead, she saw a large village with cute cottage like houses. She looked from an angle, with the side of her face pressed against the window, to see more. She gasped at what she saw and Silas smiled. Past the village was an unmistakable castle that looked like it was drawn by a professional artist and brought to life, but then again, this was a fairy tale. The tower tops and roof were a vibrant royal blue, standing out against the beige bricks and looking somehow flawless. The drawbridge was lowered over a clear moat with little goldfish swimming around happily, as if showing off where they lived. From the top of the towers, blowing in the wind, were yellow flags with what looked like roses sewn into them, looking perfect.

"Do you like it?" Silas asked.

"You live there?" Rachel asked in disbelief; her voice was high-pitched because of her amazement.

"Well, I am the prince, aren't I?" Silas said, looking out the window with her.

Citizens around them smiled and waved at them, recognizing the royal carriage. Rachel waved back with a huge smile spread across her face, so happy to be having the time of her life.

"Don't pay too much attention to them," Silas whispered in her ear.

"How could you not?" Rachel asked. The carriage was pulled onto the castle grounds and the drawbridge was put back to how it was before.

"I can't believe this is happening!" Rachel said.

The coachman opened the carriage door and let the prince and Rachel exit the cramped space. They went to the castle door and walked inside.

CHAPTER TEN

THE KING AND QUEEN

"And this is the throne room," Silas said, pushing open two large oak doors. He was giving Rachel a tour of the castle. The throne room was huge with a bright red carpet rolled across the floor to the two thrones, which were occupied by a king and a queen who wore gorgeous crowns. One of the two thrones had blue cushioning while the other had red cushioning and was slightly smaller.

"Hello, Mother, Father," Silas said, stepping aside so his parents could see Rachel, who waved awkwardly.

"Hello dear, who may you be?" the queen asked. She had crystal blue eyes, a small nose, and long hair almost as dark as ebony. With her makeup she looked even prettier than she would've without.

"Uh, I um, well…" was all Rachel could manage to say.

"She will be my future bride, wife, and queen," Silas said.

"What is her full name?" the king asked. He had the same facial structure as Silas, green eyes, and brown hair.

Rachel swallowed whatever came up. She was obviously so nervous she could barely manage to say her name.

"Rachel Free Angel, Queen," she said with a bow.

"Oh, how beautiful; isn't it a beautiful name, huh Peter?" the queen said.

"Rachel," Silas said, "these are my parents: Queen Clarissa and King Peter."

"Nice to meet you, Queen Clarissa and King Peter," Rachel said, bowing much more than she should have.

"When do you expect to be married?" King Peter asked with a stern expression.

"Uh, well," Silas trailed off, looking at Rachel for help.

"Ya see," Rachel trailed off just as Silas had.

"Rachel, would you mind leaving the room for just a second?" Silas whispered into Rachel's ear.

"Uh, sure," Rachel said, surprised by the request. "May I use the bathroom?" she asked the king and queen.

"Sure, down the hallway, fifth door on your left; you simply can't miss it," Queen Clarissa said.

Rachel bowed another time before rushing off to the restroom.

"Mother, Father," Silas said to his parents, "I haven't proposed to Rachel yet, but I am planning to propose tomorrow," he explained.

"You do plan to take her somewhere nice, don't you?" King Peter asked.

"Of course, when the sun hits the water on my beach," the prince said.

"Good, now don't screw this up," Queen Clarissa warned. "She seems nice, that girl; you wouldn't want to make her hate you."

"Gee thanks, Mom," Silas said and rolled his eyes.

"Yes, do not screw this up," King Peter said.

"Good, show us the ring," Clarissa said.

Silas stared at them blankly.

"You don't have the ring?!" Peter roared.

"I'm going to get one today," Silas whimpered. "I promise."

At that exact moment, Rachel walked back into the throne room. "Hey," she said.

"Rachel, would you like to stay for lunch?" Silas asked her.

"Okay, but not too much; I'm not really a heavy eater," Rachel lied.

"Sure, let me take you to the kitchen; you can choose whatever you want to eat," Silas said. He took Rachel by the hand and led her out of the throne room.

Once the doors were shut, Clarissa asked, "So, I'm guessing she isn't royalty?"

"I suppose not," Peter said. "I mean look at what the girl was wearing? I thought our son would choose someone more appropriate for the throne, but he's made a huge mistake."

"Imagine what everyone else is going to think; they'll be so disappointed in us for letting him choose her," she said, slowly shaking her head from side to side.

"Such a disappointment," he said. They both sighed with dismay.

"Maybe just chicken with mashed potatoes and gravy?" Rachel told the chef.

"That's all?" Silas asked.

"Sorry, I'm just not that hungry, and this is a little bit more than I usually have," Rachel said.

"It's fine. I'm just used to seeing people ask for so much food. I shouldn't have said anything," Silas apologized.

"Well, um, what are you going to have?" Rachel asked.

"Yes, I'll tell the chef that." He asked the chef for a salad and the same thing that Rachel was having. "Bring it to the table once you're done preparing it," he instructed.

Rachel and Silas left the chef and went to a long table with over a dozen chairs. They sat down, facing each other as the chef brought their food.

"So, when could I meet your parents?" Silas asked Rachel, not knowing this was a sore topic.

"I'm afraid you can't," Rachel said, looking at her food.

"Why not?" he asked.

"Well you could, I mean if you died and went to heaven," she replied.

"Oh, dear God, I'm so sorry; I didn't mean to," Silas apologized.

"It's alright. It all happened before I turned six, so there isn't any pain anymore."

"But where have you been living all this time? Oh, silly me, you've been living with the dwarves."

"Well, at the moment at least. Actually, the place where me and Leo are from is like a whole other world," Rachel explained.

Silas let go of the subject and started eating his food, as did Rachel.

"This is fantastic!" Rachel exclaimed after she swallowed her third bite.

"Yeah, this food is made by the best chefs in the kingdom," Silas said.

"Can I take them home with me?" she joked.

"So, where are you from exactly?" he asked, more serious.

"Well, like I said, it's like a whole other world."

"Why won't you tell me?"

"Wow, this food is really good," she tried to change the subject.

"Tell me," he demanded.

"Look, I can't tell you. Maybe soon, but not now. Why can't you just understand that?!" With that said out loud, Rachel stormed off. Silas stood up, pushing his chair back. He tried to run after her but he heard the doors slam shut and it hit him that he'd pushed her too hard.

Rachel ran as tears streamed down her face all the way to the dwarves' cottage. She stormed passed Leo, ran into her bedroom, and splattered herself across the bed, burying her face in the pillow.

"Rachel," Leo said, gently knocking on the door Rachel had slammed.

"What?" Rachel asked.

"Can I come in?" Leo asked. Before she could reply, he opened the door and sat on the edge of the bed. "What's wrong?" he asked.

"Hmm, hum huuum hum hum," Rachel replied, her voice muffled by the pillow her face was buried in.

"What?" Leo asked. "Rachel, I can't hear a damn thing you're saying."

Rachel craned her neck up, though she still was not looking at Leo. "Can I tell Silas about our world? Like where we're from?" she asked.

"No, are you crazy?" Leo rejected this idea immediately.

"But he'll keep asking me about it, and if I don't answer his question soon, he'll stop loving me!"

She burst into tears and buried her face back into the pillow.

"Rachel," Leo said, trying to comfort her, and failing terribly.

"Hum hoo!" Rachel screamed.

Leo rolled his eyes at her attempt to speak. "Fine," he said, not thinking straight with all Rachel's muffled screaming as she tried to make him feel bad. "You can tell him."

"There, that one right there," Silas told the shopkeeper of the ring shop, who was pointing at a selection of rings. One by one, Silas declared if he would buy it or not. The shopkeeper, knowing who Silas was, held his tongue kept and his disrespectful comments inside, not wanting to upset a person who could have him executed with a snap of his fingers. "Yes, that one over there," Silas said, pointing to a gorgeous ring with small rubies and gems.

The shopkeeper took the ring out of the glass case, put it in a small navy-blue ring box, and gave it to Silas.

"And how much would that be?" Silas asked.

"It's free of charge for those of royal blood," the shopkeeper said.

"No," Silas said. He put a small bag full of gold coins onto the front counter before taking the ring box and leaving the shop.

"Okay, I'll tell him about everything, like the mirror, Earth, and everything else, right?" Rachel asked Leo.

"Yes, you can. Besides, I know that even if I tell you not to, you'll still do it anyway," Leo said.

Someone knocked on the front door. Rachel turned to Leo. "Who do you think it is?" she asked.

"How should I know?" Leo asked.

Rachel walked down the stairs, opened the doors, and saw the one person she didn't want to see at that moment. "Silas, hi," she said through clenched teeth. This was probably the only time in her life she didn't want to see him.

"Is everything alright?" Silas asked. "I apologize about lunch." He was about to say more but Leo stepped in front of Rachel.

"Go home," Leo said.

"You have no right to speak to me in that manner," Silas said, staring Leo down.

"What are you going to do about it?" Leo asked, stepping forward.

"Why you…"

"Too scared to step forward? Hmm, well, you can always go back to wherever the hell you came from. But from the looks of you, I bet you were adopted by royalty only so they would look like they weren't heartless people who didn't care about hopeless pieces of crap like you!"

"And I bet your mother is signing the papers to disown you!"

"Well, you don't deserve anything you have because you're so stupid, once you fully own any of it, everyone will want you dead for using it all poorly."

"Well, your face looks like it's been in the trash and was smashed to pieces!" Silas yelled.

"I'm not a damn mirror!" Leo shot back.

"You're right, you're not, because with me standing in front of you, you'd actually look good, but you still look like your own ugly self! And nobody will ever love you, not even your own mother! And I'd bet my life on the fact that you've brainwashed Rachel to bring you along, and I know for sure that that's true because no person in their right mind would choose to spend more than a split second with you!"

"You know what? You sound confident with those words, so why don't you come and actually fight me?!" Leo yelled.

"Fine!" Silas replied.

"THAT'S IT!" Rachel screamed. She stepped in between Silas and Leo. "Why are you fighting?! You haven't even known each other for more than an hour!"

"You're right," Silas said. "I apologize, fellow common boy."

"Sorry," Leo said. "Fellow spoiled son of a—"

"Leo, please," Rachel said.

Leo sighed in frustration. "Sorry, fellow prince."

"Okay, now it's time for you two to properly meet," she said. "Leo, this is Silas; Silas, this is Leo. Shake hands the both of you." Surprisingly, they did; they shook hands before Leo went back into the dwarves' cottage and up the stairs. "So," Rachel said, closing the door. "Why did you come here today?"

"To see you, of course."

"You saw me at lunch," Rachel noted.

"And the sun is about to set," Silas added.

"Yes," Rachel said, wondering what he was getting at.

"Would you like to come to my beach?" he asked. "I brought my carriage so we wouldn't have to walk."

"Sure," she answered. Silas led her away from the cottage and to the same carriage he'd brought earlier that day. They walked in and the carriage sped off in the direction of Silas' beach almost instantaneously.

"I have something to tell you," Rachel said, looking at her fingers as they fidgeted with one another.

"Sure, I'm all ears," Silas said.

"Where do I start?" She cleared her throat and quickly added, "I'm from a different dimension."

"What?" Silas asked.

"I swear it's the truth; I wouldn't lie to you!" she exclaimed.

"No, I didn't hear you," he explained.

"I'm from a different dimension," Rachel said, now quiet.

"Did you hit your head?" Silas asked.

"No, it's all the true truth! There's this mirror and then there's a lake and a chalkboard where you can write where you want to go! And—"

"And I think we can talk about this a little bit later; I mean, we're at the beach already." He gestured out the window at the water view. The sand was a beautiful peach because of the sun's glimmering light. The ocean water was so clear you could see the smallest shell from thirty feet above the surface. And the sunset was shining in yellows, oranges, and pinks, its light being reflected on the ocean.

"That's beautiful!" Rachel exclaimed, opening the carriage door.

"It's my private beach," Silas noted.

"Too bad I can't go swimming in this." She spread her arms out so Silas would notice her pink dress.

"Well, we can always walk," he said.

"Sure, I guess," Rachel said, and they did. They walked along the water's edge, their fingers intertwined. "Silas," Rachel said after a while.

"Yeah?" Silas asked.

"Do you actually love me? Or is this just some sort of sick charade?"

"Rachel, I love you, and I have loved you since the very first day we met. Why wouldn't I love you?"

"I don't know," Rachel said, looking at the sand beneath her feet.

Silas stepped out in front of Rachel, went down onto one knee, and presented the ring he'd bought especially for her. Rachel gasped in delight and surprise. "Rachel," Silas said, opening the ring box, "will you make me the happiest man alive and be my wife?"

"Yes!" Rachel exclaimed happily. "Oh my God, yes, yes, yes!" Silas smiled as he put the ring on her finger.

"And we'll get married as soon as you've finished with your voyages," the prince said, getting back up onto his feet.

"Yeah, of course, and I only have a few voyages left!" she said.

"Would you like to come to my castle for dinner?" he asked.

"Sure," she replied. They ran back to the carriage, hopped in, and rode off to the castle. They arrived at nightfall.

"Mother, Father," Silas called, "I proposed to Rachel on the beach."

"They knew?" Rachel asked.

"Maybe," he said playfully. Rachel punched his shoulder lightly.

Clarissa walked into the dining room and asked, "What is it?"

"I proposed to Rachel today!" Silas exclaimed as though he'd won the Olympics.

"Oh, how — um, lovely," Clarissa said with hesitation.

"Is there a problem with me?" Rachel asked. "You seem hesitant."

"No, not exactly, anyway," Clarissa said, forgetting she had to think about her words before saying them.

"I should go." Rachel stood up and pushed her chair back.

"No Rachel, you don't have to!" Silas pleaded.

"Goodness, sorry if I said something to offend you," Clarissa apologized. "Please stay,"

"Do you really want me to stay?" Rachel asked, her snappy attitude kicking in. "Or is it just that you don't want to dirty your image by hating on someone you just met? Hmm, which is it?"

Clarissa was appalled by this outburst.

Rachel's eyes grew wide. "Oh my God, I'm so sorry; I didn't mean to." She quickly bowed before standing straight up, her cheeks burning red.

"It's okay; besides, you'll be our future queen, and someone with the attitude to stand up like that, well, that's what our kingdom needs nowadays," Clarissa said, smiling lopsidedly.

"Um, I'll leave right after dinner," Rachel said, her cheeks returning to their normal amount of rosiness. "But I won't be back for at least another two months."

"Yes, you have the voyages you have to go on," Silas said, understanding her cause. "When I was a child, my biological mother would travel all the time. Before she'd leave, she would say it was super important as she was on peace missions to support the kingdom — turns out she was seeing another man. Then my father married Clarissa."

"I never knew," Rachel said.

"Yes, I remember it very clearly," he said through clenched teeth. "Then, not more than a week after her return, she was executed. She looked a lot like me, actually." Silas chuckled. "I had nightmares for weeks because of how my mother resembled me. I actually saw her at the execution, so seeing her head being chopped off by a guillotine was kind of scary."

"How did they find out about the truth behind her voyages?" Rachel asked, not being able to help her curiosity.

"My father went on some voyages, too, when I was young, not many; don't know why I mentioned that. Anyway, it's not the point. So my mother thought he'd be on a voyage when she left. My father received a letter that was only supposed to be seen by my mother. But it was a love letter, saying how much the man my mother was seeing missed her. My father was furious; he sent out a guard to find my mother to validate his suspicions, and boy did they discover a lot. Though when my mother came back, she acted completely natural, because she was carrying a child. My father was about to pull the order to have her executed when he fell and got amnesia; my mother took the letter he had on his nightstand and burned it in the fire immediately. Thankfully, my father's injuries were only minor, but the guards were so focused on his injuries, they completely forgot about what they'd learned about my mother. Once my father fully recovered, he was back to his duties as king and blah blah blah. My mother said the child she was carrying was his; this was three months after her last voyage. My parents were about to announce the child to the kingdom when my mother was called out on another voyage, then everything came back to the guards. They told my father, and once my mother came back, she was executed shortly after the baby was born."

"Where's the baby now?" Rachel asked.

"I was told the baby was stillborn," the prince replied.

"Sorry I asked," Rachel said. "But um, I promise I'm not doing any of that." She then thought about how she was going through fairy tales with Leo, changing each fairy tale so she could have never-ending Happily Ever Afters. But what she shared with other princes was never true love, not like the love she shared with Silas.

Silas laughed a little, and then he suggested, "Rachel, how about after dinner you get fitted for your wedding dress? That would be fine with you, *right, Mother?*"

"Yes, yes, I suppose," Clarissa said.

"Okay, well then, what's for dinner?" Rachel asked.

"Five-course meal," Silas said. "Appetizer of mushroom caps, potato and leek soup, citrus salad, steak with rice and optional vegetables for the main meal, and for dessert we have either cheesecake, not recommended by me, or chocolate fudge cake."

"Bring it on!" Rachel said cheerfully, sitting back down.

As soon as Clarissa sat down, dinner was served. The meal had the perfect amount of herbs to enrich the natural flavours. As the juicy steak was set down in front of them, it was obviously medium-well; however, Rachel couldn't care about that fact at the moment. She just ate with her stomach feeling fuller and fuller as she went. When dessert arrived, Rachel couldn't help but gawk at the delicious-looking chocolate fudge cake. It was layered perfectly with chocolate frosting between each layer. The top had sprinkled fudge on top of the black icing. Silas smiled at Rachel's happy smile as she dug into her cake. "This is so good!" she said.

"It is quite delicious," Clarissa said from the other side of the table.

"Mother," Silas asked Clarissa, "where's Father?"

"He won't be joining us this evening," the queen replied.

"Why?" he asked.

"It's because of me," Rachel said, putting her fork and knife diagonally on her empty plate. "But I just wonder why."

"Rachel, it's not because of you," Silas assured. "*Right, Mother?*"

"Actually, it is because of you," Clarissa said.

"Not helping," Silas mouthed to his mother.

"I knew it, Silas: your parents don't like me," Rachel said quietly.

"It's not that we don't like you," Clarissa said. "It's just that you don't have royal blood coursing through your veins."

"Well, do you and the king even feel comfortable with me marrying Silas?" Rachel asked.

"Rachel, please don't," Silas said.

"We're fine with it, as long as Silas is happy. It's the least I can do, considering how I just stepped into his life when he wasn't even ten. Besides, I know that before long, Peter will love you like a daughter."

"Well, I guess I'll go get my dress fitted," Rachel said, the happiness coming back to her.

"Sure, *Sally! Come over here!*" Silas hollered.

A young maid no older than thirteen ran into the dining room and stopped directly in front of Silas. She had bright red lips, happy green eyes, blond hair tied back in a messy bun, and blond bangs that were curled so they wouldn't hang over her eyes. She wore a knee-length black dress with white lace around the edges and a white apron tied around her waist; she also wore shiny black shoes, white socks, and white gloves. "Yes, Prince Silas?" she asked.

"My future queen needs to get sized so you can have a wedding dress tailored for her in three months' time," Silas instructed. Rachel waved awkwardly, feeling overexposed.

"Come with me," Sally said and started heading out of the dining hall. Rachel got up and followed the young maid. They walked down several hallways until they came to a large room.

"You have to take off your dress," Sally said as though it were the most casual thing in the world.

"What?" Rachel asked, shocked.

Sally took a measuring tape off a desk with a mirror and stood still expectantly.

"Can you at least help me take off my dress?"

Sally helped, and Rachel stood on a podium in the middle of the dressing room only wearing her stockings and undergarments. Her face was bright red with embarrassment. Sally took measurements around Rachel's stomach, waist, and chest, taking notes on a piece of parchment.

"Can I put my dress back on?" Rachel asked.

"Sure, besides, who would want to look at you half-naked?" Sally said. Her eyes grew wide, remembering she was only a maid and Rachel could have her fired. "Oh my God, I wasn't thinking; please forgive me, future queen!" She bowed repeatedly.

"It's fine," Rachel said and quickly put her dress and shoes back on.

"Um, how do you want the dress to look?" Sally asked.

"Let's see," Rachel said, thinking of the wedding dress she'd always wanted. "It has to have lacy edging, and I want it to really poof out from the waist down." Sally wrote notes.

"Any other requests?" the maid asked.

"I want it to be sleeveless and collarless, maybe some white gloves that end at my elbows and start halfway up my finger, with gold edging. And white shoes with a one-inch heel."

Sally wrote it all down, her smile never fading. "That's all?" she asked. Rachel nodded.

The future queen left her future home and headed to the forest. When she was on the outskirts of town, someone grabbed her by the arm and pulled her into a small house. It was dark so Rachel couldn't see anything around her.

"From the castle, eh? A runaway princess, eh?" A high-pitched, raspy voice said from somewhere in the darkness.

Rachel stayed quiet.

"You mute, eh?" the voice continued.

"No, I am not," Rachel said. "Nor am I a princess or a runaway."

"But did you come from the castle?"

Rachel pursed her lips together tightly, knowing she'd said too much. She could've just stuck with being mute.

Without any indication, a candle was lit on the opposite side of the room. Then another candle was lit, and another, until the room was glowing from the amount of candlelight. Rachel winced at the sudden lighting, but when her eyes adjusted, she jumped back because of what she saw: the nightmare-inducing creepy face in front of her. Rachel screamed.

"Zip it, child," the creature snapped, no longer in a playful mood. The creature had pea-green skin, two horns protruding from the sides of his head like a bull, green warts sprouting from every possible location, and blood-red eyes.

"W-who are you?" Rachel asked, terrified.

"My name is Girben, the goblin," the being said.

"What do you want with me?" Rachel asked, frozen in place because of her fear.

"Hmm," Girben said delightedly. "Well, there is one thing we could use you for."

"*We?*" Rachel asked, afraid of what would happen.

"*Night!* I have your dinner here!" Girben called. A boy with dead black hair, cold black eyes, and ghostly pale skin walked towards them.

"What the—" Rachel started; she stopped talking when Night stretched his mouth into an open smile. Rachel could barely breathe, for two of Night's teeth were deadly sharp.

"H-h-he's a v-vampire," Rachel stuttered.

"Yes, I am; I am indeed," Night said, walking towards Rachel at a slow but threatening pace.

Rachel wanted to kick Night in the stomach and run away, but she was frozen in her tracks. She eventually found some strength and backed into the wall. Night kept moving towards her.

"Enjoy your meal," Girben said and walked away from Rachel and Night.

"Will do," Night said, closing in on Rachel.

"I won't let you drink my blood!" Rachel screamed; she was about to throw some punches when Night took her wrists and pinned her to the wall. Rachel's eyes grew wide with fear as Night came in closer. "S-s-stop!" she pleaded.

Ignoring her, Night buried his vampire fangs in her neck and she let out a bloodcurdling scream. Rachel could feel herself get dizzier the more blood Night took; she felt her blood drip down her neck. Would this be the way she died? By loss of blood? Rachel was mad at herself for getting into this situation; now she was going to die so stupidly! "Stop!" she screamed. "I'm not going to die at your hands! This is just so stupid!" She tried to loosen Night's grip around her wrists but was unsuccessful.

Suddenly, a man holding a large stick ran into the small house and hit Night and Girben on their heads until they lay on the floor, unconscious. Rachel covered her eyes with her hands and sat on the floor.

"It's okay now," a familiar voice said.

"Who is it?" Rachel asked, her voice still muffled by her hands.

"Leo."

"Leo?" Rachel looked up. "Leo!" she jumped up from the ground and hugged Leo tightly. "How did you find me?" she asked.

"You screamed," Leo said as though it were obvious, which it was. "But we should go now. Are you alright?"

"I'll be alright."

Once they were away from the danger and in the dwarves' cottage, Rachel became a chatterbox. "And then Silas proposed!" Rachel exclaimed.

Leo looked at her. "What did you say to him?"

"Yes, obviously. Then after that, I ate the best meal I'll ever have, and afterward I got my dress sized and designed; it'll be ready in time for the wedding."

"Well, that's great. Do you feel up to travelling? Your neck looks like it was bitten. Was one of the guys I knocked out a vampire?"

"I'm fairly sure," Rachel said reluctantly as she stroked her neck gently. "What do you think that means for me?"

"Well, perhaps what happens in a fairy tale stays in a fairy tale and we should just move on," Leo suggested.

"You're probably right," she agreed. "How about we just think about our travels for now?"

"Well, where do you want to go next?" Leo asked, trying to change the subject.

"*Sleeping Beauty*," Rachel decided. "We can pack tonight and leave at dawn."

"I won't argue," Leo agreed. "Let's start packing. But how's your neck?"

Rachel rubbed her fingers over the two wounds in her flesh and sighed. "It'll heal in a couple of days; don't worry."

They went upstairs and packed. Once they concluded their packing, their bodies made contact with their beds and they fell into a blissful sleep.

The sun rose up to the height of the clouds and Rachel and Leo woke with it. They grabbed what they'd packed the night before and ran to the door, meeting in the front hall at the same time. They walked to Snow White's palace and jumped into the pond, falling into Sir Evergreen's secret room. Rachel erased **Snow White** and replaced it with **Sleeping Beauty** on the chalkboard. Rachel and Leo each placed one of their hands on the mirror before they jumped through the rippling glass, bringing their luggage with them.

CHAPTER ELEVEN

A SLEEPING PRINCESS

They fell in front of a large palace covered in vines and all sorts of different varieties of plants.

"It's Sleeping Beauty's castle!" Rachel said happily.

"And how are you going to make the prince love you this time? Throw the princess out a window?" Leo said sarcastically.

"It's not a bad idea," she said. Leo's jaw dropped. "But I have a better one."

"Which is?" he asked.

"You're strong, right?"

"Why do you ask?"

"You're capable of lifting up a teenage girl, right?"

"No way, I am not stealing her!"

"Hurry," Rachel said, ignoring Leo's objections. "The prince will be here soon, and could you *pleeeeeease* do it?"

"I don't have a choice, do I?" Leo asked.

"Nope, now come on," she said. "There has to be a front door somewhere around here."

They did four laps around the castle before finally finding a huge set of dark wooden doors. Rachel pushed lightly on the doors and they creaked open; the sound was deafening. Rachel took a step on the marble tiled floor and heard the *clank* echo throughout the castle. Leo joined her inside and the doors shut behind them. Leo and Rachel then began searching for the famous sleeping princess.

After over half an hour of searching, Rachel found the highest tower of the entire establishment, and after trekking the steep flight of stairs, she looked upon one of the most famous princesses in fairy tale history.

Leo looked all over the castle, seeing passed out servants, maids, and royal family members. On the walls were portraits of the royal family members, though one caught his eye more than the others. It was a portrait of a beautiful maiden with hair the colour of gold, leaf-green eyes, and a bright smile that could make anyone smile.

"Leo!" he heard Rachel scream. Leo followed the sound of her voice and eventually was at the bedside of the same maiden he'd seen in the portrait.

"Come on," Rachel said. "Carry her away."

Leo did as Rachel wanted and carried the light princess out of the castle. He had no trouble carrying her down the stairs because of how little she weighed. "This is proof you need to eat," Leo muttered. "Seriously, how was she able to stand after waking up? She was asleep for one hundred years without any food; how is she not dead?"

Rachel climbed into Sleeping Beauty's bed and closed her eyes, pretending to sleep.

Leo, instead of relaxing in a bed after all he'd done to save Rachel, was carrying a sleeping princess who was somehow still alive out of her own castle and into the surrounding forest. He made his way to the shore of a lake and rested the famous princess on the sand.

"Sorry," Leo apologized. "But you can't do anything to make me stop." He headed back to the castle, knowing he'd done what he had to. As he walked back to the castle, he thought of how Rachel swooned over fairy tale princes, how she manipulated each story for a happy ending over and over again. He thought of how she never even considered how he felt, that she never even had the slightest thought of staying in their world with him. These thoughts led him to realize that he was in fact jealous of these fictional characters. Leo wished desperately that he had Rachel's courage, so he could stand up to her and give her a piece of his mind, but alas, he couldn't yell or speak badly to her, it would crush his soul if he did.

Leo came to a tree stump and decided to rest there for a while to let him calm down.

On the outskirts of the forest, a handsome and daring prince stood, ready for the adventure of his life. He'd been sent on a journey to find *the forgotten castle* and wake the people of the kingdom. In reward, he was promised to be married to the sleeping princess. He'd heard that the famous princess could be found in the tallest tower of the castle. Once he succeeded, he'd be crowned king and could ban his parents from his castle, have children, murder his wife, pretend to be sad, and rule as the selfish prince he was. He found the front doors and entered the castle. Next, he found the tallest tower, or at least he thought it was the tallest tower. The selfish prince ran up the flight of stairs, ready to put on the most important act of his life. He found Rachel in the bed. "You're supposedly supposed to kiss her and she awakes," the prince said to himself. He did so and Rachel fluttered her eyes open, knowing this was her cue.

"Hello," Rachel said.

"Are you the sleeping princess?" the prince asked, cutting to the chase.

"Yes," Rachel lied.

"I heard you muttering something in your sleep about a man named Evergreen?" he asked.

It was true; Rachel had been muttering about her headmaster, unaware of speaking her thoughts out loud.

"The weird thing," the prince continued, "is that my father, King George, owes one billion gold coins to a man named Evergreen. Evergreen calls himself *Sir* Evergreen, though."

"Does he have white hair, a mustache, and a beard?" she asked.

"I believe so."

"Before I have a complete meltdown, what's your name?"

"Prince William Elgar, but you may call me Will," the prince said. "And you are?"

"Princess Rachel Free Angel, but you may call me Rachel," she said.

"Would you like to come to my castle? Upon arrival, you could meet my parents," Will suggested.

"Of course. After all, you are the one who woke me after a long— how long has it been?" Rachel asked, playing dumb.

"One hundred years," Will replied.

"Oh my," Rachel feigned shock. "How are the people?"

"They were sleeping when I got here," he answered.

"The sorceress put a curse on this castle and the people who worked here so when I pricked my finger, everyone would fall asleep, and once I was awakened, my people would have to wait six more years until they could finally be awake. Or at least that's what I was told on my sixteenth birthday before I did the stupidest thing I've ever done," she said.

"Well, I don't hold a grudge, considering that if you'd never done that, I wouldn't be here right now."

"Well, I guess that's true."

Will helped her out of bed and carried her out of the castle. Rachel pretended to be horrified at the sight of the workers and royal family sleeping in random places, looking dead. When Rachel wasn't looking, Will had an evil smirk spread across his face, knowing he would soon have it all. During the time it took Will to get Rachel out of the castle, they didn't speak a word.

The prince helped his future queen mount a black horse with a black mane and dark eyes. He hopped on in front of her. "Hold my waist," he instructed. Rachel did so and the horse bolted away from the ivy-covered castle. Will pointed out landmarks to Rachel, making sure he was acting polite so she wouldn't suspect a thing.

After almost an hour, they arrived at a shiny, majestic, and, surprisingly, dull, extremely dull castle. The entire thing was painted in a boring beige. When Will looked back at Rachel, she tried her best to fake a smile. The prince, who saw right through that fake smile, said, "I know it's not much to look at, but the inside is nice."

He let the horse go once he and Rachel were off and it immediately bolted away from them.

"Um," Rachel said, confused.

"It's okay, he'll find his way back to the stables," Will assured. He then led Rachel inside and she let out a gasp of surprise. A blood-red carpet was laid out underneath their feet, portraits of past rulers marked the walls, and at the end of the carpeted hallway were two thrones where the king and queen sat.

"Oh, Will," the queen said happily. "You brought over a guest; oh, how nice!"

"Mother," Will said, "you're humiliating me."

"He's right, Michelle," the king agreed. "Calm down."

"Anyway," Will said, changing the topic. He turned to Rachel. "These are my parents: Queen Michelle and King Edward Elgar the fourth."

"Yes, that's us," Michelle said loudly. "The king and queen of the middle kingdom."

"Mother, please!" Will said.

"Sorry," the queen apologized, now almost in a whisper.

"Michelle, what's done is done," Edward said.

"Um," Will said, unsure if he should talk.

"Go ahead, Will," Edward said.

Will cleared his throat, "Mother, Father, this is Rachel, the sleeping princess."

"But where's her crown?" Michelle asked.

Rachel didn't know how she could've answered the question, so she fluttered her eyes closed and fell back onto Will, pretending to have fainted.

"Oh, my," Michelle said.

"It's okay, I got her," Will said. He scooped Rachel up into his arms and carried her into a spare room. He gently put her onto the soft bed and sat in the chair in the corner of the room.

Rachel decided she would stay *fainted* for another five minutes so nobody in the castle would get suspicious. Once she thought it had been roughly five full minutes, she fluttered her eyes back open and sat straight up. "Who? What? Where? When? How?" she asked.

"Rachel!" Will exclaimed, and he hugged Rachel tightly.

"Okay, okay," Rachel said.

"Thank goodness you're alright," Will said, not meaning a word he said.

"Yeah, could I ask you a couple of questions, though?" Rachel asked.

"Sure, anything, ask away," Will answered.

"You said something about a man named Sir Evergreen. Who is he?" she asked.

"He's an evil man who goes to the evilest witches he can find and trades gold coins for potions," he answered.

"What type of potions?"

"Youth potions, memory loss potions, beauty potions, and more."

"I need to go," Rachel said. She jumped out of the bed, ran out of the room, and down the stairs, passing the throne room.

"Thank goodness you're alright," Michelle said. "You had us worried sick — *where are you going?!*"

Rachel ignored her; she just kept her pace steady and bolted out of the castle and towards Sleeping Beauty's castle. "Leo!" she yelled once she was in the forest around the castle. "Leonardo!"

Leo walked out from behind one of the trees. "Yep," he said casually.

"We need to find the portal to go back home!" Rachel said, slowing to a stop.

"Why?" he asked.

"Don't ask; just help me find it!" she snapped.

"I already found it twenty minutes ago."

"Great, where is it?"

"It's the lake near the location where I put the real princess," Leo said.

"Okay, let's go."

Leo led Rachel to the lake shore where he'd disposed of the actual princess, who still lay asleep.

"*In* the lake?" Rachel asked.

"Yeah," Leo replied.

"Okay. I'll go through the mirror first, change into our uniforms, and then come out of there. Then you go in and do the same," she decided.

"Okay."

"Wait for me here," Rachel said before jumping into the lake.

CHAPTER TWELVE

EXPOSED

Once they both finished changing, they peeked out the door to make sure nobody was in the office. It was vacant as usual. They ran out of the room and office, leaving their sacks of clothes behind the huge bags of coins, out of view. Leo led Rachel back to their dorm because she'd forgotten how to get there.

"Okay, why did we have to leave so abruptly?" Leo asked, closing the door behind Rachel as she sat on their bed.

"Sir Evergreen, he collects potions in the worlds!" Rachel proclaimed.

"That's why he has the magic mirror in the first place," Leo said, putting the pieces together.

"Yeah, he collects youth potions, beauty potions, and memory loss potions," she said.

"He uses the youth potions to stay young," he said.

"He uses the memory potions on the students who graduate so they don't wonder why he's still alive."

"And the beauty potions, well, I'm not exactly sure, but I don't think I want to know or guess."

"What time is it?" Rachel asked.

"I don't know," Leo said, feeling lazy. "But I'm going to take a nap."

"Me too—" Rachel stopped herself. "Never mind, I'm not sleeping with you again."

"Whatever," he said and instantly fell asleep once his body made contact with the bed.

Rachel poked Leo's cheek to make sure he was fully asleep before she pulled out her notebook and started writing:

> Honestly, I'm starting to think that Leo's getting jealous of Silas. But why would he? Leo doesn't like me, right? But at least I know he'll never read this journal, or at least hopefully not. Anyway, I know 99.999% that Leo doesn't like me, and if he does, well, that 0.001% has arisen, but there ain't anything he can do about it; I'm getting married in less than three months to Prince Silas from Snow White! He was the first prince I met, and the first thing he did was save my life — honestly, he's just nicest prince I've met so far. I know it may seem ridiculous, swooning over the first prince I meet, but he has a great personality and he's so very kind as well. But I should go before Leo wakes up; I'll write again tomorrow.

Rachel closed the notebook, put it back under the bed, took Leo's flip phone, and checked the time.

"Eight o'clock," she said to herself. She put the phone back on Leo's nightstand before shaking him awake. "Leo!" she yelled.

"Huh? What?" Leo asked, waking up.

"We have classes," Rachel said loudly.

"You've been here for a while now and haven't gone to classes *once*. Can't you just let me sleep for a little while?" he asked.

"Well, you shouldn't be tired; it's the middle of the day," Rachel said. "And I haven't gone to classes because I've been *busy*. So, let's go now because I'm not busy at the moment."

"Wait," Leo said. "Your hair; it's still long."

"Huh?" Rachel asked. "Oh, yeah, thank God no one was in the hallways while we were coming here." She grabbed a clump of her hair. "Do you have any scissors?"

"Yeah, in my nightstand," Leo said. He begrudgingly got out of bed and gave Rachel his pair of scissors.

"Here we go," she said. Rachel took the scissors and cut her hair so it was just the way it had been before she got her magical hair extensions. She made sure all the hair she cut off fell into the garbage can before finally handing Leo his scissors. "Okay, *now* let's go," she said, her hands on her hips. She looked at Leo to see him asleep in bed. "You're so stubborn!" Rachel said loudly and pushed Leo out of bed. He hit the floor with a *thud* before jumping to his feet.

"*What the heck, Rachel!*" Leo said loudly. "I was taking a nap!"

"Well, it's time for class," Rachel argued.

"Doesn't mean you have to push me out of bed," he shot.

"Well, how else was I supposed to wake you up?" she shot back.

"You figure it out!"

"Whatever! We're going to class, NOW! So *you* figure out what class we have at this time and take me there, or are you so useless you can't even do that?"

"I have to check my phone!"

"Hurry it up!"

"Shut up!" Leo checked his phone. "And we have math, is that a problem for you? Huh, Miss Priss?"

"I am not a priss!" Rachel yelled. "A priss is a stuck up little—"

"Just shut up for once!" he said.

Rachel stood up on the bed and kicked Leo in the back, making him fall. "A priss wouldn't have done that," she said.

"Are you trying to kill me?!" he asked, standing back up and attempting to rub his sore back with his hand.

"No, but we should go to class already, so come on, mush!"

"Am I a dog now?"

"No, but you should hurry the heck up!"

"Fine!" Leo led Rachel to their classroom that was already halfway through the class. The students were taught by a man with auburn hair and brown eyes. Leo and Rachel walked into the classroom awkwardly, interrupting the lesson. Rachel looked at her peers and noticed that Zach, Vic, and Alex were sitting directly behind the two free seats. She almost choked on her despair.

"Sir Bellsnap," Leo said. "Here's the new transfer student."

"Hello Sir, Bellsnap Sir," Rachel said, putting her hand in a saluting position.

"Nice and cooperative," Sir Bellsnap said. "What's your name?"

"Justin Campridge, Sir," she lied.

"Okay, Justin," the teacher said. "Sit in front of Zachary over there."

"Yes, Sir," Rachel said, her saluted hand falling back to her side helplessly. She sluggishly sat down in the seat and Leo sat where he usually did; beside Rachel.

"Okay, I'm going to review what we were doing so Leo and Justin can get a hold on what we'll be doing," Sir Bellsnap said. "So, Leo and Justin, take out your textbooks and turn to page one hundred and read that text; it finishes at page one hundred and three. Read that like the rest of the class is doing. Once you've concluded your reading, you'll come to my desk and I'll give you a worksheet that you need to fill out. Use the information that you read to help you. Understood?"

The students nodded along before getting down to work. Rachel took out the textbook that was in her desk and flipped it open to page one hundred.

"So, what's up, *girly?*" Zach asked from behind Rachel, his warm breath sending a shiver down her spine. She tensed up when he addressed her by *girly*.

"Nothing, leave me alone; I've got better things to do than talk to an idiot like you," Rachel said.

"Why, *girly?*" Zach said, knowing he was bugging her.

"Shut up, and why are you calling me girly?" she asked.

"Because I know your secret," he replied.

"And what would that be?"

"You're a girl, and my buds and I are going to let that little secret leak all over the entire school. Or the physical exam will, but either way, no more secret."

"What physical exam?"

"The one next week. Didn't Lee Lo what's-his-face tell you?"

"No," Rachel said, already planning to make Leo tell her.

"Well, it's mandatory; just try not to faint as you did in the dining hall, you know, like a girl," Zach said, ticking Rachel off.

The truth was that Rachel *did* feel like fainting, but she forced herself to keep her cool. She finished reading the text, not hearing another whisper from Zach, and went to Sir Bellsnap's desk.

"Well, Justin, you're one of the first students to come to my desk," Sir Bellsnap said. "Well done. Here you go." He handed her a worksheet with over a dozen questions on it. Rachel took it calmly, went back to her desk, and started filling it out soon as she was seated.

Rachel finished writing the last word of her last sentence just as the bell rang.

"Class dismissed," Sir Bellsnap said.

The students gave Sir Bellsnap their worksheets before filing out of the classroom.

"Hey Rachel," Leo said to her once they were out of the classroom.

"Hi," Rachel said. "What's next class?"

"Uh, I'm not sure," he replied.

"Didn't you hear?" a nearby student said to them, obviously an eavesdropper, but it was apparent that he hadn't been listening for long. "Sir Evergreen is going to call everyone to the gym."

"Why?" Rachel asked.

"I don't know," the student replied before walking away.

"What a nosy brat," Leo muttered.

"Do you think he was lying?" she asked from the side of her mouth.

"Why would he?" he replied.

"Yeah, I guess you're right."

"*All students report to the assembly hall,*" a voice that obviously belonged to Sir Evergreen said over the intercom. "*This assembly is mandatory.*"

"Well, it wasn't the gym," Leo said.

At the assembly, Sir Evergreen stood on the stage with a microphone in hand, constantly adjusting his tie, that is until he realized every student was seated. He cleared his throat. "Now, students, I will be telling you about our physical exam."

Murmurs spread across the assembly hall.

"I will be telling you the rules and what to expect."

Every student sighed in boredom. Most of the boys there sighed, remembering this exact same speech from the year before.

"So, the physical exam will be on June twenty-eighth. The younger students will have their exam first, then we will move up until the twelfth grade."

A student in the middle of the audience raised his hand.

"Yes?" Sir Evergreen said as if he meant, '*What the heck do you want? Can't you plainly see that I'm in the middle of a speech, you stupid imbecilic pig-like creature?*'

"Why are we having another physical exam this year?" the student asked.

"Simple," Sir Evergreen said. "We have recruited many other students since then. Now, moving on to the rules, you have to come; it's completely mandatory. As for what to expect, my daughter will be making sure you're a male, so she'll—"

Leo covered Rachel's ears for the rest of the speech, though Rachel didn't mind at all.

"And also," Sir Evergreen said, concluding his speech, "it's lunchtime, so enjoy that. And the number of physical education classes will increase because it will be healthier. Good day to you all."

The students filed out of the assembly hall with half headed to their dorms, including Rachel and Leo.

"So why didn't you tell me about the exam?" Rachel asked.

"Well, I didn't realize that many people had joined the school in the past seven months," Leo answered.

"But why do they have it in the first place?" she said.

"Just to make sure there aren't people like *you*," he replied.

"I guess that's a good point."

"But everything about you, you're just-just-just-"

"Just what?"

"Just not a boy."

"Yeah," Rachel said, chuckling. "You've seen proof of that." She cleared her throat. "Forget I said that."

"Well, I would've eventually found out, even without seeing you — you know, what I saw," Leo said.

"Really, how would you have figured it out?" she asked, intrigued.

"You don't act like a boy, at all," he noted.

"Who am I supposed to act like? You? That would be horrible! Because if I acted like you, I'd have zero friends, and that's just for starters."

"Okay, ouch."

"Anyway, can we go to *Rapunzel* next?"

"Not yet. I want to stay in reality for a little while."

Rachel stuck out her tongue at him. "Boo you," she said.

"Don't act like a brat, and let's go to lunch," he said.

"You're the brat here," Rachel muttered. "And I want to take a nap."

"You kicked me out of bed just so you can have it!" Leo exclaimed, appalled.

"Basically," she said with a shrug.

"Well, then you take half of the bed and I'll take the other half."

"No, no way in hell. And I changed my mind. I'm hungry."

"Make up your mind!"

"I don't really want to listen to what you have to say."

She exited their dorm and headed to the dining hall. Leo grunted in annoyance before following. At the dining hall, Rachel received strange looks from the other students.

"Do you know why they're looking at you like that?" Leo asked Rachel.

"I don't know—" Rachel thought on it for a moment. "*Zachary!*" She immediately took off towards Zach, who sat with Alex and Vic. Leo immediately ran after her, knowing that at one point he'd have to restrain her. Eventually, Rachel got tired of Leo following her and told him to back off and get them some lunch so he left her and got in line. Rachel made it to Zach's table and slammed her hand down in front of him, almost cracking the wooden table.

"Oh, well, isn't it the girl," Zach said.

"You told people, didn't you!" Rachel yelled.

"Why are you blaming me for stuff? I didn't do anything," he said with a devilish smile.

"You evil son of a—" she said.

"Now, now, no need for name calling."

"You told everyone I was a girl!" she yelled. "Didn't you! You just couldn't keep your damn mouth shut! Oh right, your mouth is too big and stupid to do anything except blabber!"

Leo turned at the noise, knowing Rachel had lost her temper. He knew he should've been there. He'd known it all along. He wanted to yell at Rachel to stop but it was too late.

Zach shook his head. "Now *you're* the one who can't do anything except blabber. Should've kept your mouth shut."

"No, no, no, no, no, no," Rachel said, trying to take back what she'd said. "You made me, no, no, no." She tried to block out the truth, but with everyone's gaze on her, she couldn't do anything. "You made me," she whispered, falling to her knees.

"No, I didn't," Zach said. "All I did was sit back and watch; you did all the talking for me." He kicked Rachel in the chest and she went flying to the other end of the dining hall, smacking into the wall. Leo instantaneously ran to her side.

"Rachel!" he said. "God, are you alright?!" He looked up at Zach, Alex, and Vic, who were smirking evilly. Rachel opened her eyes, ignoring the pain. She got up like a warrior and charged Zach, only for him to kick her again, though in the stomach this time. Again, Rachel smashed into the wall, getting a nosebleed.

"Want us to take care of her?" Alex asked.

"Yes, I shouldn't waste my time on a filthy piece of rat crap like her. And she doesn't even have a good feminine form; there's no good point in wasting my time on her," Zach said, feeling cocky.

"We'll be done with her in no time flat," Vic said. He and Alex walked over to Rachel, who lay in Leo's arms, her eyes barely open.

"Everyone out!" Zach roared. "Or else you're next!" Every student obeyed and soon enough, the dining hall was filled with only Zach, Alex, Vic, Leo, and Rachel. Even the dinner men had hidden in the kitchen, shutting the doors behind them.

"I'll make some room so you can go all out on her," Zach said. He then shoved all the tables to one end of the dining hall, making an empty space.

"Rachel," Leo said, tapping the side of Rachel's face.

"Leo?" Rachel asked quietly.

"How cute," Zach said as he shoved all the chairs where the tables were and sat on one. "You two could play the lead roles in a cheesy love movie."

"Shut up! You good for nothing jerk!" Leo yelled. "This is serious!"

"Back off of her," Alex said, grabbing Rachel by the neck and tearing her from Leo's grip.

"Stop!" Leo screamed. He was about to charge Alex when Vic restrained him.

"Thanks, Vic," Alex said.

"Hey, just don't kill her before I get a shot at torturing her," Vic said with a wink.

"You got it."

"No!" Leo yelled.

"Entertain me, boys," Zach said. "And Little Miss Girl, make sure to scream in pain. It would be much more amusing if you did so."

Rachel finally found enough strength to open her eyes. "What the—" she didn't get to finish because Alex punched her hard in the face. He let go, letting her get smashed into the wall for the third time. Rachel barely had time to cough before Alex came running towards her, finishing off with a kick to the stomach.

"Stop!" Leo yelled as Rachel let out a scream in pain.

Tears stung at Rachel's eyes, though she urged them to evaporate.

"Very entertaining," Zach said. "Continue. Oh, and Rachel, don't try to swallow the blood; I mean come on, we all know that's what you're doing. Besides, a little blood on the floor isn't that bad; we could just say you fell and got a bloody nose, *right*? But I won't judge if you just spit out the blood right now. You would look like some type of animal, but hey, this is a boys' school after all."

Rachel swallowed the blood that crawled up the back of her throat for the third time, not listening to Zach. She painfully got up to her hands and knees and coughed, though her efforts were for nothing because Alex kicked her in the back and she fell right back to the floor. The blood she swallowed made her feel nauseous like she would either faint or hurl.

"Stop!" Leo screamed. "Leave her alone!"

Rachel turned to Leo with a smile. "It's fine; I can handle it. Besides, they don't know what I'm capable of." This note took Leo by surprise and he didn't know what to say next.

Or at least he didn't know what to say until Alex started running at full speed towards Rachel. "Watch out!" he yelled.

Rachel turned back to the fight and raised her foot to the level of Alex's head.

Alex, who was running too fast to stop, smashed his face into Rachel's shoe. "What the—"

Rachel let the foot that gave Alex a bloody nose fall back to the floor and quickly used her other foot to swing at him. Alex, pain surging through him, didn't have time to avoid getting kicked in his side and falling to the floor.

Rachel looked at Leo. "Told you," she said softly before she fell to her knees and coughed.

"Rachel!" Leo yelled as drops of Rachel's blood dripped onto the floor. She gritted her teeth and kicked Vic in the groin.

"Why you," Vic said, now on his knees. Leo ran to Rachel's side just as she collapsed because of the loss of blood.

"Rachel," Leo said. "Wake up, Rachel."

"Leo?" Rachel asked softly, slowly opening her eyes.

"Yeah, I'm here, Rachel," he said. She smiled as her eyes closed. "Rachel!" Leo yelled as he checked her pulse "You murderers!" he yelled at Zach, Alex, and Vic.

He sat up, awake in his dorm bedroom, Rachel by his bedside. "What the?"

"You're finally awake," Rachel said. "You passed out after Vic knocked you out."

"Why did he knock me out?" he asked.

"You were trying to escape from him," she answered.

"Why?"

"Because Alex started fighting me. But obviously, I beat him, and now he's twitching on the floor with Vic. And I had to put all the chairs and tables back."

"It's funny that you say that so casually."

"What? He's not strong enough to beat me. And I know that."

"I guess," Leo said with a shrug.

"Hey, can you go check to see if Sir Evergreen's office is empty?" Rachel asked.

"Sure," he replied. Leo left their dorm, closing the door softly behind him.

"Everyone knows," Rachel said quietly to herself, remembering the outburst she'd made in the dining hall. Tears started running down her cheeks as she climbed onto the bed and buried her face into her pillow. "Why don't problems just go away?!" she cried to herself.

"Because they don't," a cold voice said from the doorway.

Rachel sat up and turned around to see Zach. "What do you want?" she asked, the anger showing in her facial expression.

"Oh, that expression on your face is so priceless," Zach said. "And problems don't disappear, no matter how much you want them to."

"Just shut up!" Rachel yelled. "Shut up! Shut up! SHUT UP!"

"Well, that just proves you have a big mouth, and everybody knows the bigger the mouth, the harder it is to shut up. Looks like that's the reason you had your little outburst today. For starters, you jumped to conclusions. The students were just giving you looks because your hair looked nice and you just *assumed* I'd blabbered so you yelled at me, not considering the chance that I didn't say anything. And now you expect your problems to just simply disappear. Seriously, grow up already. And are you waiting for Leo to wipe away your tears? I mean, I wouldn't blame you; he has been taking care of you for a while now, about a week. Looks like you've already gotten used to it. Well, that's what happens when there's a spoiled brat around."

Rachel wiped away her tears immediately.

"There you go," Zach said, spreading out his arms in front of him. "You did something on your own; you know that's the first step to growing up. Just take another fifty steps and you might reach the level of a five-year-old. Another thousand and you might actually reach ten years old. Maybe a billion more steps and you'll finally reach fifteen. But that's just a *maybe*, so it probably won't happen."

Rachel felt the tears start rolling down her cheeks again.

"Oh no, did that hit a sore spot?" Zach asked.

Rachel remembered her childhood of tragedies. She stormed out of bed and marched up to Zach.

"What are you going to do? Hmm?" he asked mockingly. "You're face to face with me; what are you going to do—"

Rachel grabbed his head and pulled him into a kiss.

Leo walked back to his dorm, ready to tell Rachel that Sir Evergreen was in his office for once, then he saw Zach kissing Rachel. Steam was practically shooting from Leo's ears.

Rachel waited for Zach's defences to fall before she made her move: she punched Zach in the gut, kicked him in the shin, and let him fall to the ground.

"Um, hi, Rachel," Leo said, cautiously walking towards her.

"Hi, Leo," Rachel said.

"So, um, what happened exactly?" he asked, glancing at Zach who would twitch every other second.

"Oh, I just beat up this horrible kisser," she replied, gesturing to Zach. "But I don't know how he found our dorm."

"He probably followed me or you here one day."

"I guess. Well, now I have a nickname for him," Rachel said, grinning.

"What?" Leo asked.

"Emotionally unavailable stalker," she said proudly.

"That's actually perfect," he said.

"Of course it's perfect. Anyway, is Sir Evergreen's office empty?"

"No, he's inside for once."

"Bummer, but let's go and see if we can get him to leave."

"I won't argue. But first we need to deal with the stalker," he pointed to Zach, limp on the floor of their room.

Rachel quickly nodded and together they took him to the other end of the hallway, Rachel carrying him by his arms and Leo by his ankles.

They left Zach propped up against the wall and walked down the hallway to Sir Evergreen's office, not saying a word.

Rachel pushed open the door to the headmaster's office.

"Ah, Justin, just the boy I wanted to see," Sir Evergreen said from behind his desk.

"Yes Sir, Evergreen Sir," Rachel said, her hand in salute.

"Good job with that, Justin," Sir Evergreen said. Rachel put her hand down. "So, the reason I wanted to talk to ye is just to inform ye that your physical exam will take place two days from now."

Every sign of colour drained from Rachel's face. "Why is that?" she asked.

"Because I've been hearing some rumours lately that ye be a girl. And well, this school's policy strictly prohibits any girls from enrolling. I trust that ye be a boy, but just to double check," he said.

"O-okay," she said.

"Well, I should be going to the medical clinic now; they said I would need to be there soon to check the medical equipment." Sir Evergreen left the office and closed the door behind him, not thinking that his loyal students would ever consider going behind his desk.

As soon as the door closed, Rachel let out a sound from the back of her throat that was one-half groan, one-fourth grunt, one-third sigh, and one-fifth yelp.

"Are you alright?" Leo asked.

"Yeah, I'll be fine," Rachel said in a non-intentionally high-pitched tone. "We should probably get to Rapunzel pretty soon so I can have a little bit of freedom before the stupid exam."

"Okay, I guess that'll be fine with me," Leo said, and then he muttered, "Not like I have any choice."

They went to the room in the back and Rachel wrote **Rapunzel** on the blank chalkboard.

CHAPTER THIRTEEN

RAPUNZEL RAPUNZEL LET DOWN YOUR HAIR

$\mathscr{R}$achel and Leo fell in front of the tallest tower they'd ever seen in their lives. It stretched up towards the sky. Each brick looked like it was over a hundred years old, and the ones nearer to the bottom were caked in moss. They craned their necks to see a window roughly the size of a door, though they had to squint to properly to see the wooden frame around the window.

"This really puts things into perspective," Leo said. "I mean, before this, I thought burglars might have a *tiny* chance of breaking and entering, but, for starters, I don't think it's really possible to break or enter into this tower."

"I need to get up there," Rachel said, not having listened to a word Leo had just said.

"What? I just said it was impossible to get up there," Leo argued.

"You're forgetting about the princess on the inside," Rachel noted. She cleared her throat and shouted with all the strength in her lungs, "RAPUNZEL! RAPUNZEL! LET DOWN YOUR FREAKISHLY LONG HAIR!"

Leo immediately covered his ears after the first word, afraid his ears would bleed or he would go deaf.

On cue, long locks of hair the colour of gold were thrown out the window. Rachel smiled at Leo, grabbed on to the hair, and started pulling herself up. When she was a quarter way up, Leo started doing the same.

After a while of relentless climbing, Rachel swung her leg over the window ledge and walked into the tower. Leo attempted to do the same but fell on his face. Rachel looked at the girl in front of them, noticing her grass-green eyes, freckled rosy cheeks, and small button nose. She appeared to be around Rachel's age.

"Who are you?" the girl in front of Rachel asked fearfully, slowly stepping back as she pulled her hair back into the tower.

"I'm Rachel," Rachel said.

"But your hair," the girl asked in bewilderment.

"I'm not a boy!" Rachel said, already annoyed.

"Well, I apologize for her," Leo said, standing in front of Rachel.

"I thought you were on the floor," Rachel said spitefully.

"I got up from the floor because I am capable of doing so," Leo said before turning his focus back to the girl. "Anyway, don't mind her. I'm Leonardo Dash, but you can call me Leo."

Rachel looked around the tower, checking to see if there was anything she could use to cut off Rapunzel's long hair. Eventually, she spotted what she'd need. "Unfortunately, you won't be seeing us for very long," Rachel said.

Rapunzel looked at her, confused. "What do you mean?"

Without losing a second, and ignoring Rapunzel's question, Rachel lunged out from behind Leo, grabbed the knife she'd spotted on the floor, and cut off Rapunzel's long hair.

"What did you do?" Rapunzel asked, horrified.

"I cut off your hair. You should at least be smart enough to know that," Rachel said casually. "Oh, Leo, could you tie all her hair to the inside of the windowsill, on the top? Then maybe take Rapunzel out of my sight, and you know, let her *be free.*"

"Sure," Leo said. He walked around the tower, looking for something he could use to properly support Rapunzel's hair. While he did so, Rachel looked Rapunzel up and down.

"So, you're the princess, eh?" Rachel said, her face very judgmental.

"W-what do you mean?" Rapunzel asked. "I live here with my mother; we aren't of royal blood."

"Oh right, I forgot. One, this is the old-fashioned storybook version; and two, you aren't from Walt Disney's version. Dang, it really sucks that you aren't the actual princess."

"What do you mean?" Rapunzel asked.

"Oh, and you don't have your trusty frying pan like in the movie either," Rachel continued. "Damn, this sucks. Hey Leo, are you done with that yet?"

"Almost, just need to make sure it's secure," Leo replied, adjusting Rapunzel's hair to the windowsill.

"Could you hurry it up a bit?" Rachel asked.

"Do you want me to end up falling to my death?" Leo asked.

"Jeez, I was just asking," she apologized.

"Well, it was offensive," he said.

"Sorry, I promise I won't say anything like that again — *Hey you, not-princess, don't run away!*" Rachel started chasing after Rapunzel, who was running away from her and Leo.

Leo rolled his eyes and continued attaching Rapunzel's hair to the window. Once he knew that Rapunzel's hair was tied firmly enough to hold two teenagers' weight, he called for Rachel. She came back with Rapunzel slung over her shoulder.

"She's not some type of blanket," Leo noted as his left eye twitched with annoyance.

"How else am I supposed to carry her?" Rachel asked.

Leo shrugged. "Anyway," he said, "Rapunzel's hair is attached to the window firmly enough for me and Rapunzel to climb down now."

"Great," Rachel said. She put Rapunzel down and crossed her arms, looking at the famous fairy tale character from head to toe.

Just as Leo picked Rapunzel up and was about to leave the tower, Rachel said, "*Wait!*"

Leo turned around and asked, "What?"

"I want her dress," Rachel said.

Leo rolled his eyes and put Rapunzel down. "Wouldn't she have a lot more dresses?"

"But I like that one a lot," Rachel said.

"B-but *I* like this one a lot. I just got it a couple of days ago," Rapunzel said meekly.

"Does it look like I care?" Rachel asked.

"But—" Rapunzel tried.

"No, I want that dress." Rachel grabbed Rapunzel by the back of her dress and brought her to the prisoner-in-her-own-home's bedroom where she forced the dress off of the Fairy Tale character.

Leo heard Rapunzel yell in protest and Rachel yell right back.

As Rachel put on Rapunzel's dress, the fictional character whined about how unfortunate and unfair this was while putting on a plain grey dress.

"Oh my God, shut up!" Rachel yelled. "Would you rather me throw you out the window and let you fall to your death?!"

Rapunzel slowly shook her head, drying the few tears she'd shed.

"Good, now you can leave and be free." Rachel grabbed Rapunzel by the ear and dragged her out of the fairy tale character's bedroom and back to Leo. "Here," she said and pushed Rapunzel over to him.

"Okay, I'll see you in a little while," Leo said. He picked up Rapunzel, grabbed onto her hair, and started climbing down to the ground.

"Okay, now let's see what the witch who lives here has that I can use," Rachel said to herself.

Rachel looked around the tower until she found a secret room with spell books, cauldrons of different sizes, and everything else a witch would need. She picked up the spell book on top of the largest cauldron in the room and opened it to the table of contents, looking for something that sounded like the spell she'd need. "Let's see," she mumbled to herself. "There's got to be a spell on how to have long hair."

She eventually found that the table of contents was useless; it was all written in strange writing. "Screw it," Rachel said to herself. She threw the spell book across the room and grabbed another. She opened it, but had zero luck finding anything. "Damn it!" Rachel went through several more spell books, with each ultimately being thrown across the room. She opened the last one in the pile and opened it. "Why are these all written in strange lettering?!" she yelled. Rachel threw it across the room and it landed in a cauldron, making a loud echoing noise, or at least that's what Rachel expected to hear when she saw it fly into the cauldron. Instead, it sounded as though it'd hit leather, or perhaps another book. "Huh?" she asked herself. Rachel crawled across the floor and looked into the cauldron to see the spell book on top of another. "Yes!" she said to herself. She reached into the cauldron and pulled out the second spell book. She flipped it open to the first page and started reading the table of contents. "It's readable!" Rachel exclaimed. She put her finger on the first title and smoothly slid her finger down the page as she read, eventually stopping on one specific series of words: **Hair Growth - page 92**. Rachel immediately started flipping the pages of the spell book, looking down at the page numbers every twenty pages. "Eighty-nine, ninety, ninety-one, and ninety-two." She put her finger on the first word and started reading at a fast pace:

Hair Growth - 92

For your hair to grow fast, follow the following instructions:
1. **Collect a strand of your hair**
2. **Put it in a cauldron**
3. **Put the cauldron over a fire**
4. **Add lily tea to your hair**
5. **Let the ingredients boil for two minutes**
6. **Mix until bright green**
7. **Dip the ends of your hair into the mixture**
8. **Say: Grow forever, stay strong, make bonds**
9. **Enjoy**

Notes on potion: Any slight changes in the recipe can affect the outcome greatly, for better or for worse.

"Okay," Rachel said to herself. "Pretty simple. Let's go make my hair grow." She looked around. "Oh right, I'm alone," she sighed. "Damn that's sad." Rachel grabbed a fairly small cauldron and went to find the kitchen in the tower, hoping that there would be a fireplace.

"How the heck is this thing so heavy?" Rachel asked, halfway up the flight of stairs that would hopefully lead to the kitchen.

Rachel stepped onto the solid floor and saw a huge kitchen with a table in the centre, a fireplace against the wall, and a window beside the stove. She loved the look of the kitchen. "Okay," she said to herself. "Pretty simple, considering the fireplace already has a fire." She brought the small cauldron to the fireplace and hung it on the hook above the crackling flames, her shoulders feeling relieved. "Now for that tea." Rachel looked at all of the pots filled with mysterious liquids before she decided that she'd smell each substance to see if one of their scents reminded her of lily tea. Once she finished checking every pot that was on top of the counter, she started opening up the cupboards and looking for other containers containing a liquid, smelling each one.

Rachel stood back up after a full ten minutes of searching. She wasn't empty-handed. She held a note that had clearly been written by Rapunzel's evil stepmother:

> Dear daughter of mine, make sure that you have your daily dose of hair growth. I know you remember how, so just have a cup of that. And for the ingredient a strand of hair you can just rip one apart for less difficulty. Make sure you don't disappoint dear old mother.
>
> Mummy Dearest
> Love you sweetie,
> Even though I'm much prettier.

"Jeez," Rachel said to herself, putting the note back where she'd found it. "Just no shame in that woman. Though Rapunzel could be prettier..." she trailed off, seeing the note slide underneath the wooden wall behind all the other pots. Rachel took every pot out of the cabinet and tugged at the wood behind them. Surprisingly, the wood slid out to reveal another pot. "Jackpot," Rachel said, hoping she was correct. She took it out and gave it a thorough sniff.

"God," Rachel said, coughing at the heavy scent. "It smells like Hannah's lily tea perfume." She put the pot down away from her. "Jackpot indeed."

Rachel got up and took the pot with her to the cauldron where she poured every drop of the lily tea into it. "Damn, how easy can this get?" she asked herself. Rachel looked around, remembering she was alone, high above the ground, and no one could hear her. "Well, I'm talking to myself like I always do; I really need to stop talking to myself. Starting now!" she continued working on the potion she'd need to grow her hair in silence.

Rachel took the pot containing the lily tea and poured it into the cauldron, though the whiff of it flew into her face and she sneezed into the tea. "I hope that doesn't interfere," she said, forgetting entirely about her oath to never talk to herself again.

Rachel looked around the kitchen to find something to mix the lily tea with. She clawed at the utensils in some drawers. In other drawers, she cursed in shock at the number of spider webs.

After a dreadful time of searching, Rachel went back to the cauldron hanging above the fire with a large wooden spoon. She pulled out a strand of her hair and dropped it in. "Now just need to mix until it turns bright green," Rachel said to herself. She held her breath as she mixed the ingredients together.

Once the substance in the cauldron turned green, Rachel threw the spoon across the kitchen and it landed in the sink with a *clank*. She stuck out her lip and pouted in the quiet tower, "Why is it that I only do things great when nobody's around?"

Rachel eyed the potion in the cauldron and wondered why the colour was a dull green instead of being bright like it should've been. She pushed the question away from her mind and somehow managed to dip the ends of her short hair into the liquid. Rachel then said the enchantment needed: "*Grow forever, stay strong, make bonds.*"

Practically instantaneously, Rachel's hair started growing longer and longer by the second, not stopping until it reached the same length as Rapunzel's. "Looks like my little sneeze didn't interfere with anything," she said to herself, though she spoke too soon. Something else started to change and her eyes grew wide as the change spread down her hair...

Leo had just needed to put Rapunzel down and give her a little nudge for her to run off faster than a cheetah. "That was easy," he said to himself.

Leo took the few steps back to the tower and climbed up the gold-coloured hair. After an hour of climbing, Leo swung his legs over the window ledge and fell onto the floor of Rapunzel's tower. As he got up onto his feet, he heard a bloodcurdling scream from somewhere in the tower. "Rachel!" he yelled and bolted towards the sound. The screams continued and got louder as Leo came closer. He ran up a flight of stairs to the kitchen and saw Rachel on the floor, screaming. "Rachel!" Leo yelled and immediately sat down next to her. That's when he noticed that her hair wasn't brown; instead, it was *blond*. "What happened?" he asked.

"I-I made a potion to make my hair grow," she sniffled. "It was a spell in a-a spell book. But I sneezed by accident and it c-completely changed the effects. And now my hair is b-b-b-b-b-" she breathed in from her mouth. "IT'S BLOND!" she screamed.

Leo rolled his eyes and stood back up. "Seriously?" he asked. "That's why you screamed bloody murder?"

Rachel looked up at him with tearful eyes. "It could've turned maybe red, or perhaps, I don't know, black, or something else, but it turned BLOND! I HATE BLOND!"

"It's not the end of the world," Leo said, rolling his eyes.

"BLOND!" Rachel yelled, as though this proved her point.

"Get a grip," he muttered under his breath.

"I heard that!" she said loudly as she dried her tears. "And you should go; Rapunzel's prince is coming soon."

"Great, bye—"

"Wait, *first* you have to help me put all of Rapunzel's hair in a drawer or cupboard or something," she said after drying her pointless tears. "*Then* you can leave."

Leo sighed his disapproval, which Rachel ignored.

They walked in tranquility to the tower's window.

"So how are we going to do this?" Rachel asked.

"I don't know," Leo said, not caring at all.

Rachel saw how much he wasn't interested in helping her so she decided to throw out a punch with her words, "Okay, I have an idea. You hang on to the hair, just outside the window, and then I take some huge scissors and cut the hair and let you fall to your death; how about that?"

"What did you say?!" Leo turned in the stairwell and came to face with Rachel, who knew he'd do this. She had her fist ready and immediately threw a very physical punch at his face, causing him to go tumbling down the wooden steps.

"Leo!" Rachel yelled, not meaning for him to fall. She ran down the remaining steps and saw Leo, face planted into the floor. "I'm sorry," she said, sounding sincere. "I didn't mean to make you fall. I just wanted to fake punch you and make you trip a bit." Leo grunted his disapproval. Rachel held out her hand for him to take; he did. Rachel smiled, then he shot up to his feet and with practically inhuman force flung her across the room in one swift motion.

"Oops," Leo said, sounding unapologetic. "I didn't mean to hurt you; are you alright?" Leo walked up to Rachel.

"Who the heck said I was hurt?" Rachel shot and slowly got back up to her feet.

"It's obvious that you're hurt," he said.

Rachel grinned crookedly at his words. She charged at him, though just before she rammed into him, she aimed her fist at his stomach and hit him harder than he would be able to describe.

Leo grunted in pain.

"Now come on," Rachel said, holding out her hand for him. "Let's take care of Rapunzel's freakishly long hair." She smiled at him warmly and Leo couldn't help but smile back; the pain in his stomach was suddenly gone. He took her hand and she hoisted him up to his feet. They finished the walk to the door-sized window and started pulling Rapunzel's hair into the tower, which took some effort. At one point, Rachel looked out the window to make sure the fairy tale character's hair wasn't endless.

Eventually, the deed of somehow managing to put Rapunzel's hair in a closet and closing the doors was done and Rachel wiped sweat from her forehead. "That took effort," she said to Leo.

"Okay," Leo said. "Am I supposed to go somewhere so I don't *interrupt* your meeting with the prince?"

"Yes," Rachel said. She went back to the door-sized window, Leo behind her like always.

Rachel looked out the beautiful window as Leo climbed down her hair, to the ground far... far below. She looked at the countryside, the rolling hills, the bright green trees, the forest around her, the blur of the wheat field far in the distance. She paid special attention to the nearby lake, or at least it looked pretty close, and the last thing she saw was Leo waving goodbye before he ran into the forest. Rachel stayed at the window for another ten minutes before she sat on the floor in silence and waited to feel a tug on her long hair that was hanging along the tower's wall, reaching only a foot above the ground.

Just as she was on the brink of sleep, Rachel felt a tug on her hair that snapped her back to full attention. She peeked over the windowsill and saw a man climbing her blond hair. Rachel gasped and ducked back down, out of view.

Eventually, two hands grasped the windowsill. Rachel crawled away so he wouldn't end up on top of her. The man pulled himself up and through the window, his feet gracefully touching the tiled floor.

"Hello!" Rachel said and stood up almost as tall as the man who'd just entered the tower.

"Aye, God!" the man said and stumbled back, almost falling out of the tower, though luckily Rachel grabbed him by the shirt collar and pulled him back so he stood straight.

"Who are you?" the man asked.

"Rachel Free Angel," Rachel said, smiling. "And you are?"

"John Smittens," the man replied. "Where'd you get the rope?"

"Huh?" she asked. "What rope?"

"The one outside the tower, against the wall..." he trailed off, realizing that the *rope* outside was hair and that this hair belonged to the girl in front of him. "Dear God," he said and fainted.

"Seriously?" Rachel asked, looking at John's unconscious body on the floor. She took him by the arm and dragged him to the kitchen, wincing each time his head hit a step of the high staircase. Rachel then managed to get him onto one of the many chairs and tied him up with the last seven feet of her hair that she'd pulled back inside. Rachel went to the kitchen, got some sweets, and came back to her captive. She waited for him to wake up.

John woke with an unsettling jolt. "How long was I out for?" he asked.

"About ten minutes, not long," Rachel replied. She stood up, putting down the chocolate cupcake with blue frosting and sprinkles, and started unravelling the hair that was keeping John to the chair.

"You have *really* long hair," John said in awe.

"I've never cut it," Rachel lied.

"What was your name again?" John asked.

"Trixy," she answered with a lie. "But you can call me Trix."

"Okay," John said, thinking about the name she had said was hers before he was unconscious. He brushed the thought out of his mind and returned his focus back to the girl in front of him.

"*Rachel!*" a voice hollered from outside the window. "*Let down your hair!*"

"Leo," Rachel said quietly.

"Who?" John asked, still feeling drowsy and unable to pay attention to details.

"Oh," she said, "he's my um, he's my — *I'll be right back*." Rachel ran to the tower's window and looked down at the grass far below where she saw Leo, calling her name.

"SHUT UP!" she yelled down at him before she threw her hair out the window for Leo to climb.

Before long, Leo pulled himself over the window ledge and onto the floor.

"What the heck are you doing here?" Rachel asked immediately.

"I was hungry," Leo replied quietly.

"Oh my God, couldn't you have eaten some poisonous berries or something?" she said spitefully.

"But wouldn't I die?" he asked.

"Exactly," she snapped.

"Don't have to be so harsh," he whispered. "So is the dude here?"

"Yes, so you can leave—"

"Who's he?" John asked from behind Rachel. She turned around and cursed him for coming downstairs.

He had the cupcake in his hands, half eaten.

"Oh, he's — he's *Ricardo*, my um—" Rachel tried.

"*Husband*," Leo said without thinking.

Rachel turned to Leo so sharply her heels almost cracked and gave him a death glare. Then she returned her expression back to happy and slowly turned back around to John. "Yes," she said through a clenched jaw and gritted teeth. "*Ricardo* over here is my," she coughed, "my *husband*."

"Well, I'll just need to stay the night, then I'll be out of your lives by daylight," John said. "And you can continue your happy lives of marriage."

Rachel forced a smiled at John's comment. "That's *great*!" she said, forcing her voice to sound delighted. "But before anything else, I just need to have a *private discussion* with my *dear husband*." She grabbed Leo's hand and pulled him aside. "You make yourself at home," she called back as she continued walking away with Leo, who gulped in fear of what the very near future held.

Rachel brought Leo into a room and closed the door behind them. "Leo," she said, her left eye already starting to twitch with irritation. "Why, just help me understand this. Why on Earth, or on any planet of any of the dimensions there are, would you lie and say that you were my *HUSBAND*?!"

"It was just the first thing that came to my mind," Leo said, his voice shaking like a cowering dog's yelps for help.

"Is that how you think of us? As a *couple*? As *lovers*? You already know about Silas, that I'm going to be married to him within two or three months. You cannot love me. Love some other girl, any other girl for that matter. But you can't like me, especially not after I get married to Silas, *got it?*"

"Um..." Leo trailed off, avoiding eye contact with Rachel.

"Sorry," she said, realizing how ridiculous she sounded. "I overreacted like I always do; it was just the first thing that came to your mind."

Phew, Leo thought. *Safe for now.*

"I'm going to go see where John went, maybe show him a room that he can sleep in," Rachel said and walked out of the room, closing the door behind her.

Leo watched the door rebound with momentum and slowly rock back and forth before he too decided that he should leave the room as well.

"So, John," Rachel said to her guest-ish.

"Yes?" John asked.

"Do you know anything of a man named Robert Evergreen?" she asked.

"Yes, of course, he's one of the most wanted criminals in the world," he replied as though she should know.

"For what?"

"He stole the king's crown, melted it, turned it into a ring, and sold it for over one million gold coins."

"Oh, dear God," Rachel said, taking a seat on the door-sized windowsill. She looked out at the setting sun and quickly changed the subject. "Oh, look, the sun's setting. I should show you to a room that you may stay in." Rachel led him to the first spare room she could find. She apologized each time she entered the wrong room, saying that there were many other rooms that she got confused all the time. Afterward, she went back to Leo.

"What's up?" Leo said.

"Oh, nothing much. I just learned that *Evergreen's a wanted thief.*"

"What?" Leo asked. "But he's so... so... so, just so..."

"Old," Rachel finished for him.

"Exactly," he said.

"But seriously, John says he's the most wanted thief in the world! We *have to* stop him as soon as possible!" she said

"*Have to?*"

"Okay, we *should* stop Evergreen."

"And how exactly do we plan on doing that?"

"After John leaves tomorrow, we go back to our world, though before that I cut my hair again, then we capture Evergreen, bring him to *Snow White*, and have him locked up for good! Then I'll get married, have kids, and maybe grandkids too, oh, and perhaps great-grandkids, then I'll die peacefully, and afterward I'll be put in a glass coffin like dear old Snow White with a golden plaque and roses, emeralds, rubies, diamonds, and other jewels, and then I'll be put in the throne room to be admired forever!"

"You have everything all planned out, don't you?" Leo asked with a snort.

"Yeah, so?" Rachel asked. "I'm a futuristic planner. Wait, how about before we capture Evergreen we just finish up our travels?"

"I don't have a choice, do I?" he asked unenthusiastically.

"Oh, come on, exploring fairy tales is fun for you, too; admit it!" she said, lightly punching his shoulder.

"I'm tired."

"I'm pretty sure that other than John's bedroom there's only one other room with a bed," Rachel noted and groaned in frustration. "Why does this always happen to us?!"

"Come on, am I really that bad?" Leo asked.

"Yes!" Rachel said. "I'm sleeping on the floor!"

"Is there something wrong with me?" he asked.

"No, I just don't want things to end up awkward," she answered.

"It won't be because we know that we're just friends, nothing more, and there's nothing awkward about being friends if you ask me. And if anything *awkward* happens, we know that we didn't have another option."

"Fine," Rachel said, glaring at him. "Though before we go to bed, I'm changing into a nightgown, so don't come into Rapunzel's bedroom; we've already been through that once. We don't need history repeating itself, right?" She walked away from Leo and into Rapunzel's bedroom where she changed into a beautiful light blue nightgown that hung down to her knees. "You can come in now, Leo!" she called as she sat on the bed's edge. Leo walked into the bedroom soon enough and listened to Rachel's instructions about how he was going to sleep.

"Now, last and most important thing," Rachel said firmly. "You sleep on the left side of the bed and I'll sleep on the right side, got it?"

"Yeah. Whatever," Leo replied.

Rachel tucked herself in on the right side of the bed. Leo did the same though on the left side. Leo let himself get comfortable in the middle of his side as Rachel scooted away from him farther and farther until she was just on the edge of the mattress.

"You act like I have a disease or something," Leo said.

"Oh hush," Rachel snapped, holding on to the nightstand so she wouldn't fall off the bed.

"Hey Rachel," Leo said after a while of silence.

"Hmm?" Rachel asked, letting her eyes close and almost falling asleep.

"Do you like me?" he asked.

Rachel fell asleep before he could finish his question.

"I mean I know you're in love with Silas; you're going to marry him in a couple of months. I'm happy for you, though I don't think that Silas will make you as happy as I could. But he beat me to you, fair and square, even if I hate that fact with all my might."

Rachel was in a deep sleep now.

"But I-I," Leo said, his voice cracking, "I love you!" Then he heard a snore. "Rachel?" he asked. Leo then realized that Rachel was asleep so he sighed with sadness and felt that it would be best if he got his rest as well.

Rachel awoke in Leo's arms, underneath him, though on *his* side of the bed. "L-L-Leo," Rachel stuttered, a shocked expression across her face.

"What?" Leo asked, his eyes still closed.

"Things are awkward," she said. "*Very awkward.*"

"What are you talking about?" he asked. "I'm just hugging my pillow like I always do,"

"Okay," Rachel said. "First of all, that is definitely weird and not something a sixteen-year-old should do; second of

all, you're not hugging your pillow: *you're hugging me!*
And it is not *comfortable!*"

Leo immediately opened his eyes and fell off the bed
in shock.

"*Leo!*" Rachel said and instantaneously looked over
the bedside.

Leo looked up at Rachel's worried expression and
frowned. "Sorry," he apologized.

Rachel breathed in a deep breath and slowly exhaled
out her nose. "It's okay," she said. "It wasn't your fault."

"If you say so, but no matter what I do, whenever you're
around, I keep screwing everything up."

"Why are you thinking like that? It makes you sound
like you love me or something."

Leo quickly looked up at her, eyes wide. "What the heck
are you talking about? Of course I don't love you."

"I mean, I am the only girl you've known on a personal
level since you were what? Thirteen?"

"Shut up," Leo muttered, getting up off the floor.

"Embarrassed?" Rachel said, sitting up and crossing her
legs and arms. "Well, I'm sorry for being smart."

"No, you're not being smart because I don't love you.
Give me one reason why I would love a brat like you? Come
on, tell me."

"I don't know what guys like! I was just thinking that
maybe — never mind, forget it." Rachel looked at his
burning cheeks. "But why are you blushing?"

Leo quickly turned around in one swift motion.
"Enough about me and your stupid nonsense; don't you
have something embarrassing about your life from before
I knew you?"

"Nope," she said confidently. "I have no regrets, but
I have a bunch of stories. Anyone else who was in my

shoes would be burning red with humiliation — no, not humiliation, just regret."

Leo waited a long while for her to elaborate. She didn't.

"When you say something like that, you're supposed to explain what you mean," he said.

"Oh," Rachel said. "Well, this story is my absolute favourite time at the girl's school. Actually, I'll tell you another one after this.

"Okay, so first off, this one was really recent."

Leo sat on the bed, in front of her, intrigued.

"So, it was in math class," Rachel continued. "My teacher, Ms. Glass, caught me napping."

"You were *napping* in *class*?" Leo asked, appalled.

"Oh, for crying out loud, stop acting like Hannah. So anyway, she caught me napping during her," she cleared her throat, "*precious class time.* Then she asked me a bunch of questions like, for the first one, what was she talking about? I just decided, *Today I'm going to be a smart aleck.* So, I decided to answer her question with one word: something. Then she asked me a couple more questions: How much detention would you like? I replied nothing. She then questioned what time I'd gone to bed; I obviously answered that I couldn't remember. Then, here's the last and best one, well, the one with sass: she asked if I found her lesson boring. I said yes, very much, and then I told her to shut up. I actually didn't get detention for that. But her reaction — you should've seen it — was *priceless!* Her face was so red I genuinely thought her head was about to explode!" Rachel said, laughing at the memory.

"You were a horrible student," he noted.

"Awww, thank you," she said with a smile. "Well, I'll go let John leave, then make a potion to turn my hair back to dark brown, then cut it to an average girl's length, find the portal with you, and get us home. Then face my physical exam, then throw Sir Evergreen into Silas' prison, or dungeon, or whatever, but before that, I have to finish my travels. Okay, I'll see you later." Rachel walked out of the room, her long hair trailing behind her.

"She talks a lot," Leo said when the door closed.

Rachel walked to the window and threw out her long hair. Her locks swung down and came to a calm stop, one foot above the unrealistic grass, which seemed to be straight from an illustration in a storybook with delicate brush strokes against a canvas.

"Hi," John said, walking towards her.

"Hey, ready to go?" Rachel asked.

"Yeah, but first," he replied. Then, in a quick and swift motion, John leaned so close to Rachel that their noses almost touched.

"J-John," Rachel stuttered, surprised. She tried to back away but John held his grip on her arms, tightly.

"Have you ever heard of vampires?" he asked.

"Yes, why?" she questioned frantically.

"Well," John said, his mouth stretching into an open grin. "Did you know their breath can cause someone to fall asleep with only just one whiff?"

"W-why are you telling me this?"

"Because I figured you should know why you pass out."

Then Rachel saw it: deadly sharp fangs in John's mouth. "You-you're a *vampire*?"

"Goodnight," John said. He breathed in and let out a gust of air through his mouth.

The last thing Rachel smelled was a fresh minty scent before everything around her turned to nothingness.

Leo walked out of the room to see Rachel collapse into John's arms, so gracefully she looked like an actual angel.

The reality of the scene hit him and rage blasted through his blood. "What the heck do you think you're doing?"

John let go of Rachel and let her fall to the floor with a *thud.*

"What did you do to her?" Leo yelled.

"Oh, nothing much. She's just a bit unconscious, that's all; besides, she did talk a lot. It really is nice to have some silence—"

"Shut up! She doesn't deserve this!"

John laughed, showing Leo that he was a vampire.

"Y-you're a vampire?" Leo asked, shaking his head from side to side.

"You're not going to yell at me anymore?" John asked mockingly.

Leo fell to his knees and looked at John with betrayal shining in his eyes.

"Honestly, humans have always been so pathetic," the vampire said. "Well, now that you're on your knees, I guess that means you won't attack me when I taste her blood."

Leo's wide eyes became wider as John bent down, gently holding Rachel's head up as he sank his teeth into her neck. As John gulped down Rachel's blood, some of it gracefully slid down her pale neck.

"Stop!" Leo screamed, still frozen in shock. "If you take too much she'll die!"

John ignored everything Leo had to say.

Suddenly, a small girl with long black hair and bright blue eyes jumped over the windowsill. "Hello, brother," she said. "Is she the one who we're drinking from today?"

John looked up and let Rachel's head fall to his lap. "Carla!" he said with a bloody smile. "Do you want some? Soon that human over there will overcome his shock; I can hold him off while you drink."

"Okay," Carla said. Her skin was as pale as a dead person's, her eyes may have been bright but they were cold as ice, and her empty smile showed that she hated the world as it was. She wore an elegant black dress that was tight around her chest and waist with a high collar. She also wore a black and blue barrette that pulled her locks away from her face.

John let Rachel onto the cold floor and stood as Carla walked over to the bloody girl who was around two years older than she was.

"What a pretty face," Carla said, looking at Rachel's closed eyes, blond hair, and button nose. "I wonder what she'll look like when she's all bloody and dead. I hope she tastes good."

"She does, for sure," John said, licking his blood-covered lips.

Leo immediately shot to his feet as Carla bent down and licked the dripping blood from Rachel's neck. "Don't *ever* talk about the woman I love that way," he said with fury in his voice.

"One dollar," John said, calm as ever.

Carla looked up, her facial expression like one of a mad little girl. "That's because you knew for sure that he'd snap out of it! Stop making bets that you know you'll win!" she yelled.

"Just keep drinking." John waved her off like a pesky fly.

Leo suddenly charged John, planning on tackling him, only to be dodged. He came close to falling out the window before swiftly turning on his heel to see John's face inches away from his own. The vampire threw a punch but Leo dodged it then ran away to the kitchen.

"Like a cowering dog, tail between his legs," John said. "Such a child." he turned around and saw Rachel almost whiter than snow. "*Hey, I was going to have some!*"

Carla looked up with red eyes and blood on her lips. "I'm sorry; she just tasted so heavenly that I couldn't help it."

John frowned at her.

Something behind John caught Carla's eye and she yelled, "John, behind you!"

John turned too late. Leo hit him hard in the back of the head with a frying pan that he had found in the depths of the kitchen. John fell to the ground, unconscious.

"Brother!" Carla yelled.

Leo looked at the young vampire with eyes full of fury. "Let her go," he demanded.

Carla let Rachel fall to the floor, eyeing John's lifeless body. "Vampire's screech!" she roared. Leo looked at her for a moment before she opened her mouth and let out the loudest, most bloodcurdling scream ever heard by his ears. Leo could feel his ears start to bleed, as well as his nose. Pain surged through his body, the sound waves overpowering him. He collapsed to his knees and cried out in pain, cursing the entire vampire race. Carla stopped her screeching, said sorry to John, and jumped out the window.

Leo looked up in surprise. Quickly drying the blood from his ears and nose, he ran to Rachel's side and tapped the side of her face. It took her a couple of moments, but before long, she was standing on her two feet, looking around. "What happened to John?" she asked.

"Oh, nothing much," Leo said. "He just tried to kill us, so yeah, basically normal."

Rachel face-palmed. "We get into way too much trouble for people our age, and we're just trying to have fun. Seriously, this is unfair." She eyed John's unconscious body. "Anyway, I'm going to go get changed in Rapunzel's room, so don't come inside. We don't want history repeating itself, now, do we?"

"It's fine, besides," Leo said with a grin, "who would want to see you change anyway?"

"Should I be relieved or offended?" she asked.

"Both," he replied with a shrug.

Rachel raised an eyebrow before going into Rapunzel's bedroom and choosing a frilly purple dress.

Leo took his frying pan and banged John in the head several times before Rachel poked her head out of Rapunzel's bedroom, wondering what all the noise was about. "What are you doing?" she asked.

"Making this vampire go through pain!" Leo said, and he smashed John's head again.

"For crying out loud, you have put him through enough pain!" Rachel said, wanting the horrid noise to stop.

"But I want to put him out of his misery!" Leo said and hit the vampire again.

"*You're trying to kill him?!*" Rachel yelled.

"He tried to kill you," Leo reasoned.

"That doesn't give you the right to murder someone! And if you're going to kill him, you might as well throw him out the window."

"Great idea; will do," Leo said, and he started to lift John up from the ground.

"No, that was a joke!" Rachel said immediately, her eyes wide.

"It was still a good idea," Leo muttered.

"But whatever you do, don't come in here." She slammed the door shut and got changed. Rachel fumbled through a couple of drawers before finding a small diamond tiara. After trying it on and looking in the mirror above Rapunzel's dresser, she gasped in surprise at what she saw. "I-I look beautiful," she rasped.

Rachel quickly threw the tiara across the room, watching it shatter when it hit the stone wall; she didn't want to see herself in any sort of tiara or crown other than the one that would prove her love to Silas. She looked through the fictional character's drawers a little more and found some makeup. She looked at it for a couple of moments before deciding to put some on: a little rouge on her cheeks, some baby pink on her eyelids, and some hot red lipstick on her lips. She examined her face closely in the mirror before deciding that she looked fine. Rachel walked out of the room and saw Leo gaping at her like a toad, eyes wide, mouth seemingly wired shut.

Leo snapped out of his trance and gestured for Rachel to say whatever she needed to say.

"Um," Rachel said, not knowing how to snap the silence, "how do I look?"

Leo stared at the revealing dress and cleared his throat quickly. "You look great; maybe you should just put on, like, a necklace or something."

Rachel looked down at her bare neck and upper-chest and turned on her heel, her cheeks flushing red. "Creep," she whispered, before clearing her throat and saying, "A necklace would get caught in my hair, but if it bothers you that much—" she looked back at Leo.

"*No!*" Leo said, stepping forward; he stopped himself mid-step. "I mean, you look great in this dress, I really like it."

Rachel stared blankly at him for a moment before adding, "Well, I have a plan." She pulled her dress up a bit before continuing. "So, I turn my hair back to brown, let you out the window, cut it so it's about halfway down my back, jump out the window, and you'll have to catch me." She looked him dead in the eye. "And if I die, I will kill you."

"Uh, okay," Leo said, not knowing how he was supposed to process that. "So, can I leave now?"

"No, you're helping me with my hair," Rachel answered.

"Do I have a choice?" he asked.

"Never," she replied, walking away from him and into the room where she'd found the spell book. "Come on!" she called to Leo, who sighed before following Rachel, making sure not to step on her hair or any spell books.

Rachel looked through the spell book where she'd found the spell to grow her hair. "Okay," she said. "We need a chocolate chip — God, this is making me hungry. We'll also need a strand of my hair and a drop of water. Then boil it in a cauldron, then afterwards dip the tips of my hair in, then baboom! My hair is brown again; my hair is *saved*!"

"Not too hard," Leo said.

"That's what I thought last time, but if anything interferes it can ruin everything, so I need you to take another cauldron, bring it to the kitchen upstairs, and switch the cauldrons. After, bring the already used cauldron that's down here now."

"You said cauldron three times," Leo said to himself.

"That's not the point!" Rachel roared.

"Jeez, I was just saying," he said.

"Whatever, just do what I said," she ordered.

"But where—"

"The cauldron's behind the painting of a woman with black and gold hair wearing a blue dress," Rachel said, knowing what he was going to say. She left him in the room and started walking to the kitchen.

Leo quickly found the portrait of a stern woman with all the characteristics Rachel had described. He looked behind the painting and found over a dozen cauldrons. He chose one at random and brought it to Rachel, who had the other cauldron in the large sink and was holding the ingredients needed. Leo hung the cauldron on the iron hook above the sizzling flames and let Rachel put all the ingredients inside. Leo helped her with the strand of hair, making sure the entire piece was inside the cauldron.

"Okay," Rachel said, wiping her hands on her thighs. "Now we just have to mix it until it becomes a light pink colour, like the one in baby clothes stores."

"Okay, happy mixing," Leo said, and he started walking away from her.

"Not so fast," Rachel snapped and grabbed him by the collar. "*You're* mixing it; I'm exhausted."

"You're going to bed?" he asked.

"No, I'm just going to stand back and do nothing, as usual." She shrugged.

"Seriously?"

"Do you think I'm kidding?"

Leo searched Rachel's face for an indication of a joke but found nothing. His shoulders slumped and he sulked over to the cabinets. He retrieved a spoon and went back to the cauldron.

"You don't have to look like it's the end of the world," Rachel said, and then she gave Leo a light shove, pushing him toward the cauldron.

"My arms hurt from bringing the cauldron up here," he argued.

"Well, *buddy*, I had to carry that bigger one over there up the stairs, and move it out of the way for the *smaller* cauldron that *you* brought up, so I had to move the *bigger* one *twice*. Who do you think has it worse?"

Leo pursed his lips and stirred the liquid in the cauldron in silence.

At one point, Rachel looked at the potion and saw it turn into a baby pink. "Okay, stop," she said.

Leo took the spoon out of the cauldron, threw it in the sink behind him, and lay down on the floor, splaying his arms out cactus-style. "My arms feel like they're going to fall off!" he rasped.

"Don't guys work out? Like an abnormal amount?" she asked.

"When do I have the time to work out? Between classes? And get my suit soaked in sweat?" he said.

"Whose idea was it to have suits as uniforms?" Rachel asked, stepping over Leo's limbs and taking the cauldron off the iron hook.

"The first principal, Sir Evergreen's grandfather, though it was probably Sir Evergreen himself, and they haven't changed the uniform at all in over one hundred years." He saw Rachel's disbelieving expression as she put the cauldron on the counter. "Okay, they modified it a bit."

"The girls' school uniforms are modified every five years; they used to be ankle-length bright yellow dresses." She cringed at the memory. "With white stockings and black shoes, and your hair had to be curled. Then it was modified to basically the same thing except the yellow dress was knee-length, and now it's a blue skirt, white stockings, a white blouse, a blue tie that Hannah would always tie for me, and black leather gloves, but the best part is that they do not care what you do with your hair." Rachel started to pull her hair closer to her and found the tips after a short while.

"You're so lucky," Leo muttered.

"Well, imagine being five years old and wearing a long *yellow* dress," she snapped.

"Imagine being — wait, you went to an academy at age five?" he asked. "And haven't seen anyone from the outside world since?"

"Didn't I tell you? My parents died by the time I was five and my relatives didn't want anything to do with me, so they sent me to the girls' school, they even paid the school extra so I could stay there during the summer, and I have seen the *outside world* during field trips."

"And how many field trips have you been on?"

"About two per year, so twenty times. But I did go into the marketplace every once in a while, when I could convince Hannah to let me borrow some buckaroos."

"That's it?" Leo asked, flabbergasted. "For the boys' school there's about one field trip per month, but your family has to pay for it."

Rachel frowned as she dipped the tips of her hair in the baby pink potion. "That sucks. My relatives, as I said, don't want anything to do with me, so I would do whatever it is you do when you don't go on field trips."

"You stay at school and count the minutes," he replied.

"That is sad," she said to herself. Rachel looked down at her hair as it changed from blond back to its original brown. "My hair's normal again!" she exclaimed. "*Now* you can leave."

Leo slowly got up from the cold hard floor and followed Rachel to the window.

"Okay," Rachel said. "Remember, don't let me die."

Leo rolled his eyes at her.

"I'm serious," she said.

"I know not to let you die; *that's* why I'm rolling my eyes," he snapped.

"Sorry, just wanted to make that clear." Rachel threw her hair out the window and watched Leo climb down.

Once he was safely on the ground, Leo looked up and saw Rachel walk away from the window, her hair being pulled into the tower.

Rachel walked up the narrow flight of stairs into the kitchen, took a knife, and cut her hair so it was only halfway down her back. Running quickly back to the window, a wave of unease washed over her as she saw Leo extend his arms.

"Well," she said to herself, "nothing to it but to do it." Rachel climbed up onto the windowsill and jumped, her eyes tightly closed and her hands holding down her dress so Leo wouldn't see anything he'd seen before.

After what felt like an eternity, Rachel felt someone's warm embrace hold her tightly. Opening one eye at a time, she saw Leo holding her close to his chest. Even though Rachel usually hated being in physical contact with Leo, she felt like she could cozy up to him and stay there forever, safe. Rachel stopped smiling like a lunatic and snapped back to her usual self. "You didn't let me die!" she exclaimed happily, sounding surprised.

Leo looked offended. "Did you want me to let you die?" he asked.

"No," she squeaked.

"I found the portal."

"Where?" Rachel asked.

"The tower's walls," Leo replied, carrying her closer to the tower.

"Leo," she said.

"Yes," he answered.

"You can put me down now."

"Oh, yeah, of course, sorry." Leo put Rachel down.

"Okay, here's the plan," Rachel said. "Once we get back to our world, we go straight into the next story."

"Which is?" Leo asked fearfully.

"*Wonderland*," Rachel said, smiling like the Cheshire cat. She backed into the tower wall and Leo followed her carefully.

They stepped into Sir Evergreen's office. Rachel erased the name of the previous title and wrote **Wonderland**. She grabbed Leo by the arm and pulled him into the mirror after watching it ripple.

CHAPTER FOURTEEN

DOWN THE RABBIT HOLE

*R*achel and Leo fell onto a large courtyard with bright green grass, white roses everywhere, and one very large tree with thick branches.

Rachel noticed the setting from Walt Disney's 1951 film, *Alice in Wonderland*. She smiled in delight and nudged Leo. "We should see a White Rabbit in a waistcoat about now," Rachel said.

Right on cue, they saw a White Rabbit wearing a royal blue waistcoat. Holding a gold-coloured pocket watch, the rabbit ran past them and into some rose bushes close behind Rachel and Leo.

"Come on," Rachel urged. She ran after the White Rabbit and Leo came after her.

They followed the mammal through the courtyard to a small pond with stone steps across the water like a walkway. Rachel and Leo followed the rabbit across the pond. While hopping from stone to stone, they heard the animal saying to himself frantically, "I'm so late, oh dear, so very late indeed."

After a long while of chasing the rabbit to his rabbit hole and being patient enough to not scream at him to shut up and stop saying he was late, because they got the point, Rachel and Leo came to a halt in front of the hole in the ground.

"Are you ready to face a world of craziness?" Rachel asked.

"I think having you in my life is insane, so yeah, I'm ready," Leo replied with a sly smile.

Rachel smiled back at him before jumping into the rabbit hole.

"One day, in a long time, I'll tell her why I did this," he said to himself before jumping into the hole after Rachel.

After a few minutes of falling, Rachel started to see wardrobes magically attached to the dirt wall. As she descended, the rabbit hole became wider and wider. Before long she saw other pieces of furniture in the dirt wall such as beds, desks, random drawers, and many more items. She looked up and saw no sign of Leo. Beside her was a rocking chair, so she decided to sit in wait for Leo.

Before long, Leo passed by Rachel and she slid herself out of the chair to float down alongside him.

"How long do you think this will take?" he asked.

"A couple more minutes?" Rachel looked down. "Or now."

Leo looked down as well and saw a black and white tiled floor. They slowly floated down and their feet met the floor, Rachel's shoes clinking against the polished tiles.

"Okay," Rachel said. "I have a plan."

"Of course you do," Leo said under his breath; luckily, Rachel didn't hear what he'd said.

"We need to grab the key on the table, shrink down to mice size, and go through the small door," she explained.

"Then we can see Hapsolum, the Cheshire Cat, the Mad Hatter, and everything else there is to *Wonderland*!"

"You do know that you sound like one of those crazy fangirls?" he pointed out.

"Oh, shut it. What would you know about girls? Huh? You haven't seen girls in over three years; well, until me."

"I've been in town."

"I meant on a personal level!"

"Whatever. Is that the key? The one on the table?"

Rachel turned and saw a gold key on the table; she walked towards it and picked it up. "It's so small," she noted.

"So, do we just put it in front of the small door that we're supposed to go through?" he asked.

"Yes," Rachel replied with a scoff. "Of course."

"You weren't thinking of doing that, were you?" Leo asked, crossing his arms.

Rachel gave him a death stare before she took the key and put it on the floor. "And there should be a vial with the shrink-a-roo potion in it."

"*Shrink-a-roo?*" he asked.

"Shut up," she muttered, looking underneath the table.

"It's right there." From the table, Leo took a vial with a cork stopper that contained a glittery purple liquid.

Rachel stood straight up and grabbed it from his hands. "I knew that."

"So, are you going to drink it first?"

"Yes, because you'd probably forget that I'd need some," she snapped, and then she popped off the cork. Rachel swallowed some and put it on the table. "It actually tastes pretty good, like a marble cake." She looked down at herself and added, "But it doesn't work."

"Yes, it does," Leo said.

Rachel then noticed that her dress was getting looser and looser and her shoes were getting bigger and bigger. With her shrinking hands, she held her dress up as Leo watched her get smaller. Before a minute passed, Rachel was the size of a flower, looking for an opening in her dress so she could breathe.

"Rachel?" Leo asked in a concerned tone. He watched a bump in Rachel's dress move around and finally saw her small head poke out of the neck hole.

"I'm so small," she squeaked.

Leo burst into laughter at how her voice sounded. "Oh my God, Rachel," he said in between laughs.

"What?" Rachel asked, oblivious.

"Your voice!"

"What do you mean?" Rachel listened to her voice and covered her mouth with her hands. "*My voice!*" she shrieked. Leo laughed even more. Rachel looked up at him. "Well, why don't you have some? Then you'll be a hypocrite! Let's see how you'll like it!" she squeaked out aggressively.

"Fine," Leo said. He gulped down a bit of the potion and started to shrink just as Rachel had. In a few moments, Leo was the size of a flower, just as Rachel was.

"Speak!" Rachel demanded.

"Hello," Leo said, his voice just as high as Rachel's. "My voice!"

"Ha!" Rachel yelled. "Who's laughing now?" She let out a laugh that sounded forced and Leo cringed at the sound.

"Where's the key?"

"Over there," Rachel said and pointed to the gold key that she'd dropped, not too far away from her. "And look over there! There's the small door!" She pointed to a small door that was now the proper size for her.

"We don't have any clothes," Leo said, sitting down.

All the colour drained from Rachel's face as she sat down in her pile of clothes and pulled the collar lining up to her neck. "T-turn around," she stuttered.

"Fine," Leo said, and he let his bare back face her.

Slowly, Rachel got up and walked over to the key. She glanced back at Leo to make sure he wasn't watching her. She grabbed the gold key, ran over to the small door, and unlocked it. "I'll be back in a little while; stay here," Rachel said.

"I ain't going anywhere," Leo assured.

Rachel glanced over her shoulder at him one last time before rushing out the door and into a world of insanity.

The first of many things she walked into was, what seemed to her, a forest of mushrooms, all of which towered over her. Some were polka-dotted, some were striped, and others were multicoloured. "Whoa," she whispered to herself as she walked about, looking at every strange creature and object carefully, wondering either what it was or why it was in that certain place. After what felt like three minutes, she came upon a natural garden with all sorts of different flowers. Just as she had expected, each flower had a face. The flowers were a few inches taller than Rachel.

"Oh, look," a rose said when she noticed Rachel. "A human by the looks of it," the flower added.

"But she's so small, and she doesn't seem to have any clothes on," a daisy said, looking carefully at Rachel.

"And she looks rather in the dumps," a red tulip quipped.

"Maybe a song sung by the dandelions would help," a dandelion said.

A petunia laughed. "Oh goodness, no; a song sung by the gorgeous petunias would most certainly help her more than anything ever could."

"No!" the daisy shouted. "Everyone, calm down." Every flower looked at her in silence; even Rachel acknowledged what the daisy had to say. The daisy cleared its throat. If you are wondering why, don't; this is *Wonderland*, for crying out loud, "I propose," the daisy said, looking around with her eyes wide open, "that the daisies sing a song for this young maiden."

"Are you kidding me?" the rose yelled, outraged. "Like you could ever sing; look at you, you're just a daisy!"

"You and the daisies, *sing*?!" the petunia roared, laughing. "As if that could happen anywhere other than a world of craziness."

Something suddenly struck Rachel like lightning: *did these flowers not know that this world was practically the definition of insanity?* She looked back at the flowers to see them still bickering. "How about this?" she said. "I listen to all of you sing a song," Rachel proposed, smiling.

The flowers in the garden stared blankly at her for a moment before they all burst into laughter: uncontrollable, loud, irritatingly annoying laughter. Rachel looked at them, confused.

"You think we'll actually do something together?" the petunia asked between laughs.

"She's bonkers!" the dandelion said, laughing.

"Most certainly off her rocker!" the petunia added.

"She must be related to the Mad Hatter!" the daisy giggled.

"No, no," the tulip said, wiping away tears of laughter. "She's even worse than him."

"She's crazy!" the rose said.

Rachel scowled at what they had to say.

"Completely insane!" the petunia howled.

"A psycho!" the tulip laughed.

"No, a psychological mess!" the rose corrected, still laughing.

"And you know what all of you are?" Rachel yelled.

"Beautiful and talented flowers, isn't it obvious?" the petunia said.

"No, you're all just a bunch of nasty weeds!"

"How dare you," the dandelion said, appalled.

"You all heard me. You're all nothing but a bunch of nasty weeds! You're all nasty, talentless, ugly weeds that are a waste of time and space!" Rachel screeched. "And once I'm back to my regular size, I'll come back here and pick you all out of the ground and burn you in a fire!" With that threat fired at the flowers, Rachel stormed off, scowling.

"My, she is such a grumpy thing," Rachel heard the rose say. She grunted in annoyance and got as far away from the flowers as she possibly could. Before ten minutes had passed, she came along an old woman folding many clothes. Beside the woman were three baskets, each filled to the brim with folded clothing; on her other side were five other baskets filled up to the top with bunched up clothes, waiting to be folded.

"Hello," Rachel said, waving awkwardly.

"Hello, child," the old woman said, not looking at Rachel.

It slowly dawned on Rachel that this woman was regular-sized to her, so the clothes-folding woman must be shrunken also.

Rachel quickly pushed the thought away and continued. "Could I borrow some clothes?" She pointed at the basket of folded clothes.

"Sure, dear," the old woman said, still not looking up at Rachel, who was of course completely bare, trying to cover herself. She slowly inched towards the basket of folded clothes and picked out clothing for herself and Leo. For her, she picked out undergarments and a square dance dress with elbow-length sleeves, ruffled at the ends. For Leo, she picked out a simple white shirt, brown overalls, and white socks. Rachel spotted some shoes next to the basket. "May I take some shoes as well?" Rachel asked the old woman.

"Sure, dear," the woman replied blankly.

Rachel took polished black shoes for herself and brown boots for Leo. "Thank you," Rachel said as she put on the clothing she'd picked out for herself.

"No problem, dear," the old woman said, still not looking at Rachel.

In no time, Rachel walked back through the flower garden, ignoring their complaints about her.

Before she walked through the small door, Rachel turned back to the flowers. "Just you wait!" she yelled. Having shot that, she ran through the door and slammed it behind her, almost breaking the wood by the impact. "Those stupid flowers will burn in hell," Rachel said.

"Sup," Leo said casually.

"I got you some clothes," she noted.

"Gimme," he demanded.

Rachel threw the clothes at his head and turned around as he got dressed.

"So," Leo said as he put on his last shoe. "We go to see Mister Caterpillar, then Mister Kitty-Kitty, and then the Mad what's his name, right?"

Rachel glared at him, looking rather offended. "It's Hapsolum, the Cheshire Cat, and the Mad Hatter," she snapped.

Leo took a step back for his own protection. "So, can we go now?" he asked fearfully.

"Yes," Rachel replied through gritted teeth. She marched off towards the door. Leo walked up to her. Just before she opened the door, Rachel turned on her heel and her nose was an inch from his. Leo could feel his cheeks burn red. "Oh," she said, "and one last thing: *don't* listen to the flowers," she commanded.

"But why?" he asked.

"Don't ask; just ignore the flowers."

They walked out the door in silence and Leo stared in awe at the world around them.

"The flower patch is coming up," Rachel warned. "Remember, don't listen to a word they say."

"Okay?" Leo asked, staring at her as if she were a dinosaur, not comprehending why she was acting this way all of a sudden.

Rachel pushed some leaves out of their way and on either side of them were dozens of flowers: dandelions, roses, tulips, petunias, daisies, and many, many more.

"Oh look, it's the one who threatened to burn us in a fire," a rose said.

Every other flower looked at Rachel and they burst into loud howls.

"Remember what this little one with hair on her head said?" the petunia asked through her laughter.

"That we're nasty weeds!" the daisy howled.

"You did?" Leo whispered to Rachel.

"They are," Rachel shot.

The pair made it out of the flower patch and were soon in what seemed like a forest of mushrooms.

At one point, Rachel smelled something peculiar. "Do you smell that?" she asked Leo.

"It smells a bit like, like-*what in the world?*" Leo said.

Rachel followed his gaze to see a blue caterpillar on a blue spotted mushroom, smoking from a hookah. He was rather obese, even for a caterpillar, and his antennae were wrapped around the top of his head like a turban. The caterpillar blew smoke rings into the air before smoking again.

"Hello," Rachel said, waving awkwardly and stepping forward.

"*Who* are you?" Hapsolum asked.

"I'm Rachel and this is Leo," Rachel answered.

"*What* are you?" the caterpillar questioned.

"We're human," she replied.

"*Where* are you?"

"Right here with you."

"*What* do you want?"

"To talk to you, Sir."

"Rachel," Leo whispered, "this guy's drunk; there's no point talking to him like this."

Rachel nodded along to what he had to say. "You're right; there *is* no point talking to him this way," she said.

"Exactly," he said.

"So, to talk to him I'll have to get down to *his* level," Rachel said confidently.

"No, Rachel, that's not what I meant!" Leo tried.

It was too late, for Rachel was already sitting comfortably next to Hapsolum. "May I?" she asked the blue caterpillar.

"Why not?" Hapsolum said as he handed his hookah over to her. "Enjoy," he said.

Rachel breathed in as much as she could before blowing out smoke rings. She repeated the process until her eyelids dropped down and she could feel her sanity loosen.

"The Mad Hatter is here but not," Rachel said.

"He lies at tea time in the forest," Hapsolum said.

"Forest lie where?" she asked.

"Next to not here," he replied.

"Not here is not where?"

"'Tis not here."

"What 'tis not here?"

"White Queen's forest of whiteness."

"Castle next to not here?" Rachel asked.

"Precisely," Hapsolum replied.

"I understand completely," Rachel said and hopped off the mushroom. "Thank you, Hapsolum."

"What in the heck?" Leo asked.

Rachel picked off two parts from the mushroom: one from the right and another from the left. She put them both in a pocket on her dress. She looked at Leo. "We just need to go to the White Queen's castle; the forest is right next to it," she explained.

"And where is the castle exactly?" he asked.

Rachel was about to speak when no words came. "One second," she said and hopped back onto the mushroom. She asked Hapsolum for the hookah again and she smoked a couple of rings before they continued their confusing conversation.

Leo sat down against the mushroom. "This is going to take a while," he said, and then he let himself take a small nap.

After a long while of what seemed like forever, Rachel hopped off of the mushroom once again and pulled Leo up to his feet. "Okay," she said. "We just need to go *that* way for a while and we'll eventually make it there." She took a step in the direction she'd just pointed in but collapsed once her foot touched the ground.

"Rachel!" Leo yelped. He ran to her aid but she helped herself up.

"I'm fine," she said, waving him off as if he were a pesky fly. "Just a wee bit tired." Rachel yawned and took another step with the same result as before.

"Rachel, you're drunk; let me help you," Leo assured.

"No, I'm *fiiine*," Rachel said, waving him off again as her words slurred.

Leo rolled his eyes as Rachel attempted to stand up again, though this time she fell unconscious into Leo's waiting arms.

"Well, too bad for you," Leo said, and he picked her up fully, one arm under her knees and the other supporting her back.

A long hour of walking passed before Rachel opened her eyes and saw the horizon moving on its own. She stared at it peculiarly before realizing that Leo was carrying her. "Put me down! Put me down! Put me down!" she yelled, hitting his chest.

"Fine," Leo said, and then he dropped her like a hot stone.

"Not like that," Rachel grunted, rubbing her hurting backside. "And where did you take us?" she asked, slowly getting up.

"To the forest, which is right beside us."

Rachel looked behind her and gasped at the trees towering far above her head. "Good thing I brought my mushroom pieces," she said, and she pulled out the two mushroom pieces she'd ripped off. "One of them will make me smaller, and the other bigger," Rachel said, inspecting the two. "But the question is which," she said.

"Can't we just go into the forest, find the dude, and then we decide?" Leo asked.

"I guess," Rachel said. "What are we waiting for?"

"You," he said before running off into the forest.

"Hey!" Rachel yelled and chased after him.

The two of them ran and ran until they couldn't bear the pain in their legs and they had to rest.

"I think we're here," Leo said in between heavy pants, leaning against a tree.

"How do you figure?" Rachel asked, breathing just as heavily.

"Look," he said and pointed to a table far above them with many chairs. On one of the chairs, a rather colourful chair, for that matter, sat a man. He had skin paler than the lightest of snow, his hair was a deep red, and his eyes matched the green leaves of the forest perfectly. He wore a colourful suit with a big bow tie, and a large dark green hat with a pink ribbon that matched his bow tie.

"Leo," Rachel gasped, clutching his arm. "It's the Mad Hatter!" she exclaimed.

Sitting alongside the Mad Hatter was a small adorable white mouse with beady black eyes who wore a velvet puff-sleeved shirt on top of a white blouse, complemented by a brown belt. He held a sword that had a strawberry pierced on the end.

Beside the mouse was a large grey rabbit with one of his ears bent down and his eyes twitching as though he'd just had too much caffeine. He wore a dark brown vest and held a teacup, but neither Rachel nor Leo knew if the ceramic dish contained any liquid at all.

"I need to go talk to them," Rachel said and pulled out her mushroom pieces once again. "Nothing to it but to do it," she mumbled to herself. She took one of the pieces at random and smudged it into her clothing and afterward took a small bite. Before many moments passed, she was back to her regular size.

"My turn," Leo said. Rachel gave him part of the mushroom piece before putting it back into her dress pocket. Leo did the same as she did and was back to his regular size.

"You stay here, and I'm going to have some fun," Rachel said, and then she pushed Leo back a bit so he was completely out of view. "Stay," she commanded. Leo raised his hands up in defeat and sat down on a tree stump.

Rachel turned around and skipped into the clearing.

"Oh look!" the Mad Hatter said. "A guest!" he clapped his hands happily. "Come and sit."

"No room," the grey rabbit said sternly, his left eye twitching even more. He suddenly picked up a spoon and examined it. "Spoon," he said, tilting his head.

"Who's she?" the beady-eyed mouse asked rudely. Without any warning, he kicked off the nibbled strawberry and pointed his sword at her face. "I don't like her."

"*May* I sit here?" Rachel asked fearfully.

"Of course!" the Mad Hatter said. "We just love guests!" He suddenly climbed onto the table and walked towards Rachel, breaking a teacup and squashing a piece of cake on his way.

"No room!" the rabbit said, throwing the spoon at Rachel's head; luckily, she ducked, and the spoon flew into the nearby bushes.

"Come on," the Mad Hatter said and offered his hand to Rachel.

Hesitantly, Rachel took the hand of the craziest man and walked with him to his chair. He helped her down onto solid ground and pulled over a cushioned stool for Rachel to sit on; she did and felt it was rather comfortable.

"Tarrant!" the mouse yelled. "Tell her to leave!"

"She's not doing anything wrong," the Mad Hatter argued. The mouse and Tarrant had a staring contest and the Mad Hatter won. The small mouse sighed in defeat and looked at Rachel with a forced smile.

"What's your name?"

"Hannah," Rachel lied.

"That's not it," the Mad Hatter said, somehow sensing her lie.

Rachel flushed pink and immediately told him the correct answer. "Rachel, sorry, my name is Rachel."

"Yes, that's it," Tarrant said, feeling the truth in her voice.

"Well," the mouse said, breaking the tension, "since we have plenty of cake, would you like some?"

"I would, if it isn't a problem," Rachel said with a large smile.

Leo watched from afar, looking at Rachel smile as she took a bite of cake and a sip of tea. "Why can't *I* make her this happy?" he asked himself. An idea suddenly struck him. "I know how to see if she cares about me!" he said. "If she does care, she'll come looking for me!" Leo ran off in a random direction, thinking this was a good idea...

"I should go now," Rachel said, patting her belly, feeling as though she'd gained at least five pounds. "I have a friend waiting for me."

"We'll be here if you ever want cake!" the Mad Hatter said, and then he waved at her as she walked off.

Rachel came to the tree stump where she'd left Leo but he was nowhere to be found. "Leo?" she called. "Leo!" Rachel continuously called his name, hoping for any sort of response, but when the echoes of her voice faded out, all that could be heard were some animals rustling in the bushes and the Mad Hatter's tea party. She was starting to get worried. "Leo!" she yelled once more. "Leo! If this is a sort of sick joke, as soon as I see you, I'll kick your butt, and I would say the other word for that but there might be children in this forest!"

Rachel looked around a bit more. She tried calling Leo's name again, but the result was the same as before. She heard rustling and turned on her heel to realize that she didn't recognize anything. Rachel tried calling Leo's name again, but when silence followed, she gave into defeat, sat on the ground, and let tears slide down her cheeks. She was lost, she was all alone, and she didn't want her habit of talking to herself when she was by herself to get worse. Rachel sobbed for a small while before she heard someone call her name.

"Rachel!"

She sat up straight and looked around. "Who's there?" she asked loudly.

"Help, Rachel!" the voice continued frantically.

"Leo?" Rachel screamed. "Is that you?"

"Yes, please help!" Leo shouted.

"Where are you?" she demanded.

"On the outskirts of the forest!" he replied.

"Why?"

"The Queen of Hearts is ordering her soldiers to capture me!"

"I'm coming!" Rachel yelled and bolted in the direction Leo's voice had come from.

"No!" Leo shouted in protest. "They'll capture you too!"

"I don't care!" she hollered, tears streaming down her face as she ran. When she saw light through the thick trees, Rachel jumped over a bush and finally made it out of the forest. In the distance she saw walking cards holding spears. She squinted to get a better view and saw the figure of a boy around her age. "Leo!" she screamed and ran in his direction. Rachel nearly twisted her ankle when she landed after jumping over the White Rabbit. She watched as soldiers tried to shove Leo into a carriage, though she saw he was fighting them with every ounce of strength he could muster.

"Let Leo go!" Rachel yelled as she made her way to him. Every soldier present turned and she then realized there were at least fifty of them. Suddenly, Rachel regretted ignoring Leo's warning.

"Who is this?" a loud and obnoxious voice boomed. The card soldiers parted to reveal a thin woman with a large heart-shaped head and bright red hair. The woman wore a black dress with a bunch of red hearts sewn on, bright red gloves, and ruby red shoes.

"I am Rachel Free Angel, and who are you? Miss Big Head?" Rachel mocked, not showing the slightest bit of fear.

"Seize her!" the woman raged. "Nobody disrespects the Queen of Hearts!"

Rachel snorted before the soldiers could touch her.

"Problem?" the queen asked.

"Oh, nothing," Rachel said. "I was just wondering if your name is the Queen of Hearts because you don't have one and you just wanted to lie to the public."

"And mute her!" the woman roared.

Two card soldiers grabbed hold of her arms as two others took a strip of white cloth and wrapped it tightly around her head and over her mouth, preventing her from speaking. The two soldiers holding her arms shoved her next to Leo.

"Let Rachel go!" Leo yelled.

"Silence him as well," the queen said.

"I think this is your fault!" Rachel yelled into her gag, though all Leo heard was, "Hum sink kiss hum sure fall!"

"What?" Leo tried but Rachel misunderstood it for, "Swat?"

They quickly gave up on the idea of communication, and before long, the soldiers tightened their grip on their arms and pushed them closer to the carriage.

"They can be dragged behind!" the queen said, the echoes of her voice resounding through the trees.

Rachel looked at the Queen of Hearts with rage bubbling in her eyes.

The queen noticed Rachel's anger and laughed evilly.

The card soldiers took a thick rope and, against Leo and Rachel's will, tied it around their waists and attached them to the back of the carriage.

"I've had enough of this!" Rachel roared into her gag. This time, Leo understood and wondered what she was going to do.

Rachel took out the unbitten piece of mushroom and took a crumb's worth of it into her mouth, forgetting to smudge it into her clothes. Before she was completely shrunk, she grabbed the other piece of mushroom and gave it to Leo. "Keep it safe," she whispered. Leo could understand because the gag loosened around her, as did her clothing. Before much time had passed, she was the size of a flower. Rachel jumped into the palm of Leo's hand and his cheeks burned red at the sight. "Throw me!" Rachel demanded. She then noticed that Leo was in shock at seeing her completely bare. "Oh, for crying out loud, Leo!" she yelled up at him.

Leo snapped out of his trance and immediately rejected the idea.

The Queen of Hearts noticed Rachel's change of size and boomed, "Get her!"

"Throw me now!" Rachel screamed.

"Hand over the girl," a card soldier said to Leo.

"Now, Leo!" she yelled.

"Give her to me."

"Now!"

"Now!"

"Leo! Throw me as hard as you can!" Rachel yelled.

"Give her to me now, boy!" the card soldier demanded.

Quickly, Leo pushed the gag down so it was no longer covering his mouth. "Never!" he roared, and then he threw

Rachel, who screamed in regret as she soared far above the trees.

"Now why did you do that?" the card soldier asked.

"Because I love her!" Leo snapped.

"Go get the girl," the Queen of Hearts demanded of her soldiers. "And as for you, boy, OFF WITH YOUR HEEEEEEEEAAAAADDDDD!"

The soldiers abandoned the carriage and ran in the direction Leo had thrown Rachel.

Leo gulped in fear for two reasons: his safety and Rachel's.

Rachel was most certainly not enjoying herself, but instead of feeling scared of where she would land, she had all her emotions frozen into anger. She was angry at Leo for getting them into this mess. As she started plummeting closer to the ground, she started screaming again. As Rachel felt the wind rush past her, it sent shivers from her neck down to her tailbone repeatedly. In the distance she saw a long table that looked very familiar: a small white dot, a large grey blur, and a person with frizzy red hair. Rachel smiled as she realized where she would fall and let gravity pull her down. Rachel opened her eyes at the last moment to see cake a foot away from her face; instinctively, she covered her face with her arms and fell head first into the cake, her feet sticking out.

"My, my," Rachel heard the Mad Hatter say. "What has fallen into my cake?" She felt a tug as Tarrant pulled her out of the cake. "Oh my, indeed," the man said as he saw pieces of frosted cake fall from Rachel's bare skin. The Mad Hatter pulled out a piece of cloth and wrapped it around Rachel, who held it around herself. Tarrant took a teacup and filled it with warm water. "Here," he said, and he put Rachel in the teacup. Rachel moaned delightfully as the pieces of cake floated away from her body and the warm water made contact with her bare skin. She looked at the Mad Hatter and gestured to the cake-full teacup. Tarrant nodded in understanding, and then he took out another teacup and filled it with warm water. He covered his eyes, as did the white mouse and grey rabbit. Rachel quickly climbed out of the teacup, whose water was now a chocolate brown because of the cake, and then she slowly let herself sink into the other cup. The icing left her hair and it disintegrated in the water. She felt the warm water make her skin turn a light pink. The Mad Hatter moved his hands from his face and squinted at Rachel's small head. "Rachel, is that you?" he asked.

Rachel nodded slowly.

"What are you doing here?"

"The Queen of Hearts has my friend, and she is holding him captive."

"*Bloody bighead*," the Mad Hatter said as he turned even paler than before, if that were possible.

"Yes, her, and she has her army out for me!" Rachel said worriedly.

Suddenly, the grey rabbit's ears perked up. The Mad Hatter saw this and his eyes grew even wider. "Drink this," Tarrant said without warning. From his pocket, he pulled out a small glass vial containing a clear liquid and pressed it to her lips, forcing Rachel to drink it. She swallowed the liquid instinctively and shrank to the size of a thumb. The Mad Hatter picked her up and put her in an empty teapot, though with the severity of the situation didn't let Rachel smirk at the similarities to the "Alice In Wonderland" movie.

Card soldiers emerged through the trees. "Have you seen a small girl?" one of the many cards asked.

"Why?" the Mad Hatter asked, putting the teapot with little Rachel down onto his lap.

"The queen is looking for her," the same card replied.

"Sorry, haven't seen any girls today," Tarrant said with a fake smile.

"Let's go," another card soldier said and they all ran off. The Mad Hatter sighed in relief and put the teapot back onto the table. He opened the lid slightly before seeing a flash of bare skin and slamming the lid back down. "Pardon," he said. Tarrant ever so slightly opened the lid once more and grabbed a piece of spare fabric from one of his many pockets. Rather quickly, he stitched the sides together, trimmed the edges a bit, added a small bow, and gave it back to Rachel.

Rachel put on the small dress and saw that it fit her perfectly. She knocked on the inside of the teapot and the Mad Hatter opened it. He pulled her out and placed her on the table.

"Rather nice, if you ask me," Tarrant said, smiling for real.

"It's beautiful," Rachel said, sliding her hands across the lacy fabric that was so delicate she was afraid even the smallest twig could rip it from her body. "I need you to take me to a flower garden," she demanded, looking up at the Mad Hatter.

"The one with talking flowers who make you want to burn them and listen to their screams for hours?"

Rachel nodded; she understood completely.

"Well let's go," Tarrant said happily. He looked at the white mouse and grey rabbit. "Leave at least a third of the tea and food for me," he said before putting Rachel behind the ribbon of his hat and walking away from the long table.

CHAPTER FIFTEEN

SHINING KNIGHTS

After several hours of walking, Rachel and the Mad Hatter made it to the flower garden.

"Perfect," Rachel said. "You can put me down."

Tarrant put her down on the ground and started walking away.

Rachel walked through the flower garden, trying to ignore the flowers' insults.

"She's even smaller than before!" the rose said and burst into cackles. The other flowers soon laughed along with the rose and Rachel quickly started speed walking through the mushroom forest towards the small door. She slammed the door shut and breathed heavily. Rachel had sworn to them that she'd kill them; now, she was promising herself.

Rachel brushed the thought aside and ran towards the small cake in a glass box. As expected, it was in front of the table. In black frosting letters on the white cake were the words: Eat Me. She ate a bit of it. She rubbed a part of it into her clothes, hoping her clothing would grow with her; she did like this dress. Rachel started to grow with her dress and was soon back to her regular size. She wondered where the portal could be? It had to be in this room; she could feel it. Rachel pushed her hand on every large door, seeing if any one of them could be the portal; she came up without result. "Maybe the table?" she said after she'd tried the walls in between the doors and every separate floor tile. Rachel slowly pushed her hand onto the table leg and it felt as though the wood was melting around her wrist. She smiled and dove head first through the table leg, falling onto the floor of Sir Evergreen's secret room. Rachel quickly got up to her feet, erased the word **Wonderland**, and replaced it with **Snow White**. Without a moment to lose, she placed her hand on the mirror's glass, jumped through the mirror, and fell into Silas' world. She needed help if she was going to save Leo.

Rachel appeared dead centre in the middle of the sky — okay, not *exactly* dead centre, but to her it looked like it. She quickly looked down and saw a familiar castle. By squinting her eyes, she realized it was Silas' castle. She gasped and she started to fall down to the courtyard; surprisingly, there was a person walking in the flower gardens. Gravity pulled Rachel towards the person in the courtyard at full speed.

Rachel screamed as she fell, knowing that even if she did hit the ground, it wouldn't hurt. She was one hundred feet above the courtyard and the person in the gardens started to look familiar. "Silas?!" Rachel yelled.

The person in the courtyard looked up and gasped. "Rachel?!" Silas shouted.

Rachel was now fifty feet above the ground.

Silas ran to the spot where he knew Rachel would land, and he extended his arms, ready to catch her. Meanwhile, Rachel used her hands to hold down her dress so Silas wouldn't see what Leo already had. She was now twenty-five feet above the ground that was not so far down below.

Rachel closed her eyes. She remembered when she'd jumped from Rapunzel's tower, she'd trusted Leo, a *friend*. Now she was falling and knew it wouldn't hurt, but she couldn't shake the feeling that if this *were* deadly, Silas, the man she would *marry*, would end up missing her. Rachel instantly felt like slapping herself for thinking such things and kicked the feeling aside.

Silas caught her and let Rachel down soon after. "What are you doing here?" he asked. "And how did you get that high into the sky?"

Rachel looked at him seriously. "I can answer all your questions later, but right now I need an army of a hundred men willing to fight under a woman's control without hesitation."

For a moment, Silas looked flustered, but he quickly regained composure. With a firm nod of his head, he led Rachel into his castle. He took her through many hallways and several doors before leading her down a narrow staircase with cold stone steps and into a large room with many bare-chested men. Rachel stared at the floor.

One man in particular noticed Rachel and walked towards her. He had wavy blond hair, green eyes, and a bronze tan. He wore black tights underneath the bottom half of a suit of armour. "What's your name?" the knight asked in a French accent.

"Rachel Free Angel," Rachel replied quickly, not making eye contact with him. "And you are?"

"I," the knight said, putting a hand over his heart, "am Jacques Snicket, one of the most dashing, bravest knights there are in this glorious world."

Rachel looked up at him and gave him a friendly smile. Jacques took a step forward.

"Yes, Jacques," Silas said. "This is Rachel, my *fiancée*." Jacques took a step back. "Rachel," Silas said, facing her.

Rachel looked up at him. "Pick whoever you want to help you."

"You should choose," Rachel said, smiling lovingly. "You've known them longer than I have."

"Okay," Silas said, turning away from her and clasping his hands together. He quickly scanned the room before naming many knights. "Peter, Jacob, Liam," he called. Rachel waited as he called at least ninety more knights, leaving half the room uncalled. Silas turned to her. "These are the strongest knights in the kingdom," he said, gesturing to the knights who'd stepped forward.

Rachel noticed one among the many uncalled knights wearing a full suit of armour. He sat in the corner of the room, not making a sound.

"I want that soldier as well," Rachel said, pointing to the soldier in the corner.

"But that soldier hasn't even said *one* word to me or any of my knights since we first saw him, and he never takes off his suit of armour—" Silas tried.

"I don't care," Rachel reprimanded.

The prince sighed in defeat. "Hey, you in the corner, you're fighting too!" Silas called.

The knight walked over to them, his armour clanking loudly with each step.

"Now," Silas said, "you will all follow the command of this woman beside me. For this battle, you take orders from the future queen; do not disappoint me."

"Yes, Sir!" the knights all said in unison, except for the silent soldier, who went and sat back in his corner.

"Are you coming?" Rachel asked Silas.

"I can't; I've got a wedding to plan," the prince said, and then he kissed Rachel passionately on the forehead. "Good luck; oh, and don't get killed — we can't have a wedding without the bride, now, can we?"

"I love you, too," Rachel said with a smile. "And don't worry; I'll have the knights back in less than a week."

"Promise?" he asked.

"Promise," she confirmed.

Silas cleared his throat and spoke aloud. "All knights in this room, you will obey every command given to you by Rachel Free Angel, and not doubt a word she says!"

"Understood!" the knights all said together, except the knight in the corner.

While the knights were busy putting on their armour, Rachel and Silas were able to have a full conversation about their wedding and who'd they'd invite.

"Now go, my Princess," Silas said.

"I'll see you soon," Rachel said. She and Silas shared a kiss before they broke apart and Rachel led the soldiers away from the castle to the portal.

"Dance again!" the Queen of Hearts yelled at Leo who was dancing in front of her large throne with a scowl painted across his face. He'd been forced to wear a revolting red and black jester outfit that was awfully tight for any sort of comfort. For the last hour, Leo had been praying that Rachel would come to save him; she cared about him enough to do that, right?

"Faster!" the queen roared as Leo continuously tried to dance the way the other jester had told him to. Sweat trickled down his neck to his back. "More! Or do you want your execution to be in a day instead of a week?!"

Suddenly, the White Rabbit that Rachel and Leo had followed into *Wonderland* hopped into the room. "Your Majesty!" he cried.

"What is it?!" the Queen of Hearts yelled, turning her head sharply towards the animal. Leo came to a stop, breathing heavily.

"Soldiers led by a woman are coming to the castle!" the rabbit yelped.

"Send our army to defeat them," the queen said, and then she waved the rabbit off.

Leo smiled hopefully.

"Did I say you could stop dancing?" the Queen of Hearts asked.

Leo immediately continued the weird dance.

Meanwhile, Rachel led Silas' army to the castle. They had thankfully fallen from the sky instead of being transported directly into the room of doors. Her prince had let her borrow one of his suits of armour so she would be safe; he simply couldn't bear the thought of losing her. She had her helmet tucked underneath her arm while her other hand held the slick shining sword with a tight grip. Rachel marched forward as sweat dripped off her chin; walking in a heavy suit of armour was more tiring than she'd thought it'd be.

As she neared the Queen of Hearts' castle, Rachel slowed to a firm halt. She took a deep breath before turning to the soldiers behind her. "Okay," she whispered to herself before she spoke loud enough for the very last soldier to hear. "The queen of this castle knows we're coming; she will surely send out her army of cards. Now, I don't know a lot about fighting or war or any *soldier stuff*, but what I do know is that you need to all help each other survive through this entire battle, fight strongly, and never give up, now and forever!" Rachel raised her sword as her voice echoed around herself and the soldiers. She looked back at the soldiers with a cocky grin. "And that's an order! Understood?"

"Understood!" the soldiers roared in unison, courage surging through them.

Rachel's cocky grin grew wider as she turned and marched through the courtyard. Once they came to the drawbridge, Rachel yelled, "Open the door, you ugly, annoying mutt!"

Slowly, the drawbridge was lowered and many card soldiers emerged, each holding a spear and solid helmet. Rachel tried her best to keep a straight face and not laugh at how ridiculous her opponent's army looked.

Managing to turn around, Rachel raised her sword once more, this time much higher, and then she roared, as loud as a lion, "CHARGE!" She turned as fast as a cheetah, and then she and her army charged the castle at full speed.

For a while all you could hear was the clanking of metal on metal, cries of pain, and the dreadful sound of blood splattering against the cool ground.

When the battle was over, card stock, human limbs, and weapons were all you could see on the ground for miles around.

"Now come out, you coward!" Rachel raged towards the castle, holding in the urge to vomit at the sight of all the bodies. Unfortunately, no soldier other than she had survived that she knew of.

Before much time had passed, the Queen of Hearts herself stepped out of the castle and marched towards Rachel, not even wincing at the sight of all the dead bodies.

"Give Leo back!" Rachel yelled.

"Why?" the queen mocked. "Do you love him?"

Rachel was shocked at the question, so shocked that it took her a few moments to answer. "Of course not!" she said as if she were talking to a close friend who was teasing her. "Why would you say that? Because I *need* to save him? No, you're sick; how did you come up with that?"

The Queen of Hearts shrugged. "But why waste your time on him?" she took a step forward.

Rachel was revolted by the queen's thinking process, mostly because of the question she'd asked.

"Well?" the queen asked, taking another step towards her.

Rachel was about to answer but something far behind the queen caught Rachel's attention. It was Leo, and he was sneaking out of the castle. He caught her gaze and signalled for her to continue talking to the Queen of Hearts.

"You're right," Rachel said. "I don't really need him; I just keep him around as a slave. But why do *you* want him?"

"What the bloody hell are you talking about?" the queen asked, taking a step back in shock. "He's my dancing boy."

"Let me get this straight," Rachel said. "He's *your* dancing boy; does that mean you dance *with* him?"

"No!" the queen shot.

Leo ran into the forest nearby.

"Well, I really should be going," Rachel said, turning around. "Wouldn't want your dancing boy to escape, now, would you?"

"Goodbye," the Queen of Hearts said. "I hope to never see you again." With that said, she stormed off into her castle.

Rachel turned back and remembered all the bodies that lay lifeless behind her. She said a quick prayer for them all before rushing off into the forest where Leo had gone. Though she did not know this, Rachel was being followed.

"Leo!" Rachel called out.

"Who are you calling?" someone said from behind Rachel.

Rachel was so surprised she jumped and turned at lightning speed.

"Sorry, did I frighten you?" the soldier who'd never spoken a word asked.

"Yeah, a bit," Rachel said.

"Sorry," the soldier said, and he bowed.

"Take off your helmet," she ordered suddenly.

The soldier jerked his body upwards in shock at the request. "What?" he asked.

"I told you to take off your helmet," she repeated.

Reluctantly, the soldier removed his helmet, and long flowing locks fell out.

Rachel was surprised to see beautiful brown eyes, olive skin, and luscious pink lips.

"You're a *girl*?" Rachel asked, gawking.

"Yes," the soldier said. "Surprised?"

"Yes, but hey, you prove my point that girls can be much better than boys. Oh, and congratulations on surviving,"

"Thank you," the girl said.

"What's your name?"

"Mulan," she replied.

Rachel's jaw fell once more.

"What?"

"Oh, nothing; it's just that you share the same name of someone I knew," she lied, recalling the movie of this very name she'd watched as a small child.

"Hey, Rachel!" Leo said, coming out from behind a bush.

Rachel turned. Once she saw Leo wearing a jester's outfit, she burst into loud howls, as did Mulan.

"What are you wearing?" Rachel asked between cackles.

Leo looked away, fuming red. "The queen made me," he said firmly.

Rachel continued laughing for a while before she heaved in deep breaths and looked at him. Mulan calmed down as well.

"Sorry, we should head back to the room," Rachel said. "Your clothes are there."

"Yeah, so come on," Leo said grumpily, and he marched ahead, his tight jester outfit making Rachel snicker.

"That's the wrong way," Rachel said, looking in the opposite direction.

Leo turned around, his cheeks beet-red. "Well, then lead the way, *princess!*" he fumed. Rachel smiled at him before she turned around and led them in the other direction. Before much time was able to pass, they were at the flower garden.

At the sight of Rachel at her full size, the dandelion screamed and the other flowers quickly saw why their friend was terrified. They screamed in fear. The rose added to this racket by announcing, "The crazy woman is back!"

Leo and Mulan looked at Rachel for an explanation, but all she did in return was roll her eyes. She stepped forward, stomping on the flowers and twisting her ankle back and forth, crushing each petal and stem. "Enjoy hell!" she yelled at them.

Mulan and Leo were mortified by this sight.

"Who's laughing now?" Rachel muttered before turning back to Leo and Mulan. "Let's go." She led them to the small door. "Here we go."

"We're supposed to go through that door?" Mulan asked skeptically.

"Yeah, but don't worry. I have something to shrink us, but remember to rub it into your clothes," Rachel said, smiling.

Mulan wasn't comforted by this, just even more confused.

"Do you still have it, Leo?" Rachel asked.

"Yeah," Leo said, knowing exactly what she was talking about. He stuck his hand into a pocket of his jester's outfit and pulled out the small chunk of mushroom Rachel had given to him.

"Okay," Rachel said. She took the mushroom chunk from Leo and broke it into three equal pieces. "Here," She gave Leo and Mulan each a piece and kept one for herself. They each smudged a bit of the mushroom into their clothing and ate the rest. At once, they all shrank down to the size of a flower.

"I'm small!" Mulan shrieked, her voice a tiny squeak. Rachel chuckled at her reaction.

"Remember, that's what you said," Leo whispered to her. She playfully punched his shoulder.

"Now let's go!" Rachel said, and she marched through the door. Leo gestured for Mulan to follow and they both entered the room of doors after Rachel, closing the small door behind them.

Rachel led them to the small piece of cake which was missing a small chunk from her last time here.

"Now, do the same with this as you did with the mushroom," Rachel instructed. The three of them rubbed part of the cake they held into their clothing and ate the rest. This time, instead of shrinking, they grew back to their regular size.

"Perfect!" Rachel said, looking down at her suit of armour. "Then the portal is through the table."

"I'll come in a little while after you guys," Leo said, pointing to his jester outfit.

"Okay," Rachel said. "Come on, Mulan." She got on all fours and crawled through the table leg's smooth surface, Mulan crawling behind her.

Rachel tumbled onto the floor and Mulan fell on top of her. Slowly, they got up off the ground and waited patiently for Leo.

Soon after, Leo fell through the mirror and landed flat onto his face. Slowly, he got up to his feet and brushed the dust off his school uniform.

"Follow me," Rachel said. She quickly changed the word on the chalkboard from **Wonderland** to **Snow White** before placing her hand on the glass and diving head first into the glossy mirror.

Mulan looked at Leo.

"We don't have to *dive*," Leo said before walking backward through the mirror, still facing the brave soldier. After he disappeared, Mulan jumped through the mirror.

The trio appeared in front of Silas' castle. Rachel made a mental note that the mirror would decide to let you fall from the sky at random. There was no predicting. The next time she went through the mirror, she'd just simply appear in front of a random place.

"Okay, Mulan," Rachel said. "This is your stop. Tell Silas that all the other soldiers died fighting and none of their deaths will be in vain, and also that I'll see him in a little while."

"Understood," Mulan said, and she rushed into the castle.

Rachel and Leo walked together to the lake in front of Snow White's large palace.

"Where are we going to go now?" Leo asked.

Rachel took a deep breath before replying, "We'll stay at the academy for a little while longer."

"What?" Leo exclaimed. "But what about Zach, Vic, Alex, and Sir Evergreen, not to mention the physical exam?"

"I know, I know," Rachel said, closing her eyes and massaging her temples. "But I need a little bit of real life in my system."

"But—" he tried to protest.

"And I also need you to help me find something out."

CHAPTER SIXTEEN

TANGLED IN LIES

$\mathcal{H}$annah had told every person who'd asked her about Rachel's sudden disappearance the same thing, over and over again: that Rachel had left in the middle of the night to get to a new school. Even though she knew nobody in the whole school believed her, what other explanation could there be?

For some unknown reason, Elisha now targeted Hannah, and only Hannah.

"So, where's not an angel?" Elisha asked Hannah in the dining hall.

"As I've said many times, she transferred schools!" Hannah roared, as loud as a lion.

"Oh my," Elisha said. "You sure don't know how to calm down—" she never got the chance to finish her sentence because Hannah punched her in the nose with every bit of strength she had. Elisha fell to the floor with a bloody nose.

Girls from around the dining hall crowded around them, eager to see what would happen next. The girls around Hannah and Elisha were entertained because without another second to lose, Elisha shot up to her feet and kicked Hannah in the stomach, causing her to cough up a small amount of blood. Quickly, Hannah grabbed Elisha by her shirt collar and kneed her in the stomach over and over again until blood came out of Elisha's mouth like a waterfall.

"Someone get the nurse!" a girl in the crowd yelled.

"This is what you get!" Hannah shouted. "Every time you said something to Rachel, she was hurting inside, every time, but she made sure never to show any signs of it!" Hannah lifted Elisha above the ground by the collar. "Words hurt! You should know that by this age! You should! Words can hurt as much as you're hurting right now! You should know all of this, everything I'm telling you!"

"I never did anything to Rachel!" Elisha yelled, a tear rolling smoothly down her cheek. "She did everything to me! All I did was react the way I did so I wouldn't look weak! All I wanted was to be known and loved! That's it!" Tears were now escaping her eyes, dripping off her chin.

"Really?" Hannah asked, squinting her eyes.

"Yes, I swear!" she cried.

"Sure?"

"*Yes!* Every time, all I ever did was react!"

"How can I trust you?"

"You don't have to trust me; just believe me."

CHAPTER SEVENTEEN

FACING THE TRUTH

"Excuse me?" Leo asked Rachel.

"Look, there's this guy I liked as a kid," Rachel repeated for the fifth time. "He went to the boys' academy and I never saw him again. All I want is your help to find out what happened to him."

"Sure," he said.

"Really?" she asked. "You don't want anything in return?"

"Only your smile."

"What?"

"Nothing," Leo said quickly. "But before we go back to the academy, you need to cut your hair again."

"Yeah," Rachel said. "I guess we'll have to make a quick stop at the dwarves' cottage."

They walked to the dwarves' cottage, Rachel leading the way.

Leo decided that he didn't like the silence and decided to cut it with a question he'd been wondering for a while. "Rachel, why do you want to go through the stories? I mean, I know it's fun for you, and it is for me as well, but what's the real point to it all?"

Rachel stopped walking and turned around to face him. She said, "I came to the boys' academy for a new start; I explained that to you when you found out I was a girl."

"Well, I already know that," he said plainly.

"Let me finish," she snapped. "I came to the boys' school for a new start, and I intend to keep that goal. When I found out about the mirror, I swear my heart skipped a beat, maybe even two. Who wouldn't want to find the perfect fairy tale to live in? That's why I keep dragging you through these classic stories with me, for your fun and my destiny."

"But you're already engaged to Silas—"

"You never know when *you* could find something better than what you already have," she said.

Leo was left speechless. She was going through these fairy tales partially for *him*, the dork who liked her, even though she didn't know that yet. He'd been thinking of himself as a burden on her, like shackles, but instead she truly cared for him, even though it wasn't as more than a friend. His heart fluttered as he thought about this.

Rachel was the one who opened the front door and told Leo to stay put at the door, even though she really shouldn't have…

"I'll go to the kitchen and cut my hair," Rachel said before running into the kitchen, behind the wall so Leo couldn't see her.

Leo started to whistle a cheerful tune but was cut off by an ear-splitting scream. "Rachel!" he yelled and ran into the kitchen. By the time he took in the scene, his jaw had dropped and his eyes had doubled in size. Rachel was suspended in the air by what looked like a lightning bolt, though purple. It was wrapped around her neck and the beam of bright light was shooting from and old bony finger belonging to a hunchbacked person underneath a thick black cloak. Rachel and Leo both knew without a doubt in their mind that this person was Snow White's wicked stepmother turned into an old hag, though every trace of her former beauty was gone.

Leo soon heard the evil stepmother chanting some type of curse; the last words he grasped were, *"Bring havoc."* After the incantation was set, Rachel's eyes started to glow like searchlights. Her veins glowed such a bright gold it was almost blinding, like looking at the sun.

Leo ran towards Rachel, not caring if the stepmother hurt him. "Snap out of it!" he yelled at her.

Rachel flinched slightly; fortunately, Leo noticed this.

"Shut it, child!" the witch snapped.

"Rachel, go back to your normal self!" Leo yelled again, ignoring the witch's warnings. "We need to go through fairy tales together!"

Rachel flinched again, though this time it was more noticeable.

"I thought I told you to shut up!" the witch shouted at Leo, who didn't listen to a word she had to say.

"Remember Silas, Hannah, your parents!" he continued. "Remember everyone you care for!"

She flinched again, though this time it was her hand moving up to her neck, before her arm snapped back to her side.

"Remember *me*!" Leo yelled at the very top of his lungs.

"I thought I told you to shut—"

The witch didn't continue her phrase because Rachel had ripped the magical light from her neck and it shocked the witch so hard, she stumbled backwards and almost toppled over.

Rachel turned back to normal and Leo, as always, was there to catch her.

"Leo," Rachel said thankfully, "thank you."

"Not so fast, deary," the witch said. She pointed her old finger at Rachel who was instantly knocked out. "As for you," she pointed at Leo, "don't piss her off." The old hag left the cottage cackling while Leo held Rachel, staring out the door where the witch had been, utterly confused. He pushed the thoughts aside and let Rachel's head rest in his lap, though something was off about her. It wasn't her appearance; it was something deeper. Leo leaned down and squinted his eyes, trying to discern what the difference was. His face was so close to hers their noses touched.

Suddenly, Rachel eyes shot open, and without losing any time, she sat straight up, her head knocking into Leo's. They got away from each other quickly and clutched their foreheads in pain, groaning.

"What the heck, Rachel?" Leo asked.

"Ugh," Rachel moaned. "What the heck happened?"

"You mean you don't remember?" he asked worriedly.

"What?" Rachel asked. "Did you do something disgusting to me while I was out?"

"No!" he reprimanded her immediately. "And besides, you were not even out for a minute."

"Whatever, what happened?" she asked.

Leo decided he would save the events of today for another story; besides, maybe the witch was just bluffing and nothing would happen. He didn't want to worry her, and this could make a good story for later on. "Oh, nothing," he said. "You just hit your head and blacked out."

"Okay, well, time to cut off my hair!" Rachel said cheerfully. She launched up to her feet, as if forgetting about the pain in her forehead, and started shuffling through the drawers and cabinets.

Leo smiled happily at how oblivious and blissful she was, forgetting the pain in his own head as well.

Rachel eventually found a sharp pair of scissors, and she asked Leo to cut off her long brown hair so it looked just like it had before. He actually did a surprisingly good job. As Leo put the scissors away, Rachel took all her hair and dumped it into the barrel that the dwarves used to put all their trash. She knew this barrel was just for garbage because she'd once made the mistake of dumping her leftovers into their laundry basket, which was made of steel.

They left the cottage and headed back to the lake in front of Snow White's palace.

At the lake's shore, Rachel suddenly remembered something. "I forgot my school uniform in *Wonderland*," she blanched.

"It's okay, for two reasons: one, it's probably the middle of the day back at school, so people are either in classes or at lunch, or just in their dorms, lounging around, and Sir Evergreen is on his lunch break, so he's out of the academy; two, you can run."

"I can't believe you," Rachel said, putting the palm of her hand to her forehead.

"What?" Leo asked.

"Nothing," Rachel said. Without warning, she suddenly grabbed Leo by the hand and jumped into the lake, pulling him in with her.

They tumbled through the mirror into Sir Evergreen's room and onto the floor.

Leo heard the door handle start to open so he grabbed Rachel by the waist and pinned her to the wall, behind one of the sacks of coins, covering her mouth with his hand. He leaned close to her because the sack of gold coins was being tilted towards them from the swift motion.

Rachel wanted to slap Leo across the face for the awkward position they were in but knew that if she did, the sound of her hand hitting his face would be much more than loud enough for Sir Evergreen to notice them.

The door handle turned more and Sir Evergreen walked in. Leo leaned closer to Rachel, his chest touching hers, not wanting their evil headmaster to see them. Rachel felt her cheeks burn red from the contact.

Sir Evergreen placed his hand on the glass and walked into the mirror, not stopping to check if there were words on the chalkboard or not.

When Sir Evergreen was fully gone, Rachel immediately shoved Leo off of her. "What the heck, Leo?" she demanded.

"I'm sorry," he said, his arms in the air as though she were a police officer.

"You'd better be!" Rachel said loudly as she repeatedly slapped Leo across the face.

"I am, I am!" Leo tried.

Rachel grabbed him by the shirt collar and pulled him close to her. "Never again will you press yourself against me," she warned.

"Wait," Leo said, pushing her off of him. "How are we not frozen?"

Realization was shown on Rachel's face as she took that in. "I-I don't know how this is possible. But we really don't have time for that right now," she said.

"Right, we need to find out about that guy you were talking about earlier, I know."

"But I think that can wait for a couple of days. Let's just head over to our dorm for now," she said.

"Sure, besides, I want to see what it looks like to be frozen in time," he agreed.

"Wouldn't it just be the students in the same position they were in before, but just not moving?"

Leo pursed his lips before walking out of the room. Rachel smiled, content with herself, before following him.

Through the halls were students of all ages, each going to either lunch or their next class. Rachel and Leo found Vic, Alex, and Zach in front of the dining hall, leaning against the solid wall.

Leo and Rachel stared at the trio for a moment before they looked back at each other with identical smirks spread across their faces. Leo ran to the dorm and got his phone as Rachel stuck Zach's finger up Vic's nose, placed Alex's hand on Zach's buttocks, and inserted Vic's hand in Zach's pocket. As for their faces, Rachel took the corners of their mouths with her index fingers and turned their scowls into large, open grins. For their feet, she desperately wanted to test their flexibility. She took Zach's right leg and rested his ankle on Vic's shoulder. She did the same to Vic and Alex, by putting Vic's ankle on Zach's shoulder and Alex's ankle on Vic's shoulder. She laughed hysterically at her creation.

Leo returned with his phone. After several minutes of laughing alongside Rachel, he took a picture and used an unidentified account to send it to every student in the school.

Leo and Rachel laughed all the way back to their dorm.

"I can trust you to do any sort of prank!" Leo laughed on their bed, Rachel beside him.

"You know, I did that a lot for most of my life, ever since I turned seven. That was the year I gave up on being a good child, up until I got here," Rachel said.

"You did that sort of stuff to people for *eight* years?" he asked.

"Yep, and I enjoyed every person's reaction," she said. "Anyway, I'm going to get changed into a spare uniform. I remember I sneaked one into here in the middle of the night around a week ago." Rachel got up and walked over to their wardrobe. She opened one of the doors, took out a uniform, and brought it into the bathroom to change into.

Leo watched as the door closed; he heard it lock with a *click*. He sighed and lay back onto the soft comforter, not caring he was messing up what Rachel had '*worked so hard on to create*' as she'd put it when she was done.

Rachel soon walked out of the bathroom to see Leo lying down on the bed that she'd worked so hard to make. The comforter was now completely wrinkled and a pillow lay on the floor.

"Leo!" Rachel screamed. She dropped the clothes she'd changed from and ran over to him. "What the heck! This was my creation! Hannah usually did this; I always watched her! I did it for probably the second time in my entire life and you *ruined* it!"

Leo looked up to see Rachel, furious and yelling at him. "Chill out, it was just a bedspread; we can put it back to the way it was before without any real effort."

"How could you?!" she roared. "I tried three times to get it like this!"

"Sorry," he said, thinking she was definitely overreacting.

Rachel was about to lecture Leo but was interrupted by the intercom: "Justin Campridge, please report to the office, now," Sir Evergreen said.

"I guess he's back," Rachel said. "Too bad, though; we could've had the entire place to ourselves."

"Are you going to go?" Leo asked her, getting straight to the point.

"I don't think I have a choice," she replied with a shrug.

"Well, let's go," he said, about to step out the door.

"Leo, you're not coming."

"But why?"

"I don't want you in my messes, not now or ever," Rachel said.

"But what if Sir Evergreen does something to you?" Leo asked, worried.

"I can take care of myself, Leo, and besides, it was *my* choice to come here in the first place, not yours." She walked out of the dorm.

Leo watched as the door slammed behind her. He waited a few minutes before he opened the door himself and started running after her.

Rachel slowly opened the door to Sir Evergreen's office and it closed behind her.

"Hello," Sir Evergreen said from behind his desk, looking younger.

"Hello, Sir Evergreen," Rachel returned. "Why did you want me here?"

"Just to tell ye that yer physical exam has been moved to today," her headmaster replied casually.

Rachel gulped loudly, though Sir Evergreen didn't seem to notice. "What time will it be at?" she asked.

"In about twenty minutes," he said.

Rachel choked on a combination of air and saliva.

Sir Evergreen looked up at the sight, "Aye! Justin, ye alright?"

Rachel swallowed her saliva and nodded, "Yes," she croaked.

"Okay, ye have to go to the auditorium; it's all set up."

Leo stepped into the office; Rachel and Sir Evergreen jumped at his sudden appearance. "Sir Evergreen, Sir," Leo said, "is it okay if I go to the physical exam with her — I mean him?"

"Uh, I don't know why, but I don't see why not," Sir Evergreen replied.

"Thank you, Sir," Leo said, and he bowed.

Rachel stormed out of the office.

"What be his problem?" the headmaster asked.

"I'll go fix it!" Leo said and ran after Rachel.

Rachel ran to her and Leo's dorm, ran into their bathroom, slammed the door behind her, and locked it.

Leo came after her and tried to open the door, but then he realized it was locked. "Rachel," he said, frustrated, as if she were a disobedient child he was supposed to look after.

"Go away!" he heard her yell.

"You can't storm off like that!" he yelled back.

"Well, I just did! And don't yell at me!"

"Make me!" he yelled back.

"Shut up!" Rachel yelled more quietly than before.

"Come out here and make me!" Leo yelled, much louder than his earlier demand.

Rachel shoved opened the door, the wood cracking slightly on impact. She then punched Leo in the nose, making him bleed.

Leo didn't react to the blow much, though he pushed Rachel back into the bathroom. Her body stumbled back and she tripped on her own feet, smacking her head on the wall. The curtain rod fell on her head with a loud *bong*.

It took him a moment, but he realized what he'd done and he ran to Rachel's side. "Rachel, crap, I'm sorry, please tell me you're fine," he said stupidly, as if not knowing the damage he'd caused.

Slowly, Rachel rose up to her feet, Leo helping her.

"Thank God you're al—" Leo stepped back in shock at what he saw was happening: his fear of what could've happened after the incident in the dwarves' cottage.

Rachel's veins glowed like they had in the cottage; her hair grew waist-long for some reason, and it floated behind her like a cape; and instead of the school uniform, murky blue water flowed down from her chest to her ankles, were it magically stopped. She also wore gloves, though instead of fabric, her gloves were made of frost crawling up from her fingertips to her elbows. On her head lay a diamond tiara; on her feet were shoes made of ice with a three-inch heel. Laying coolly on her neck was a necklace of fire, though it was not burning her skin or spreading. Three rings of ivy were on the index finger, middle finger, and ring finger of each of her hands. The last details Leo noticed were two huge purple diamond earrings, though they were obviously fake.

"R-R-Rachel?" Leo asked, terrified. He backed away from her.

"*You really shouldn't have hurt me!*" Rachel said loudly, though her voice was different. It was commanding yet soft, like a siren's, but either way, this voice was *not* Rachel's.

She opened her palms and spread out her arms. In her right hand appeared a ball of flames, while in her other hand there was a ball of icy spikes. Rachel extended her right arm back, about to severely hurt Leo. She started to grin wickedly. "*Goodbye,*" she said.

"No!" Rachel yelled, though in her own voice this time.

"Rachel?" Leo asked.

"Stop it," Rachel tried. Her face continuously went back and forth from evil to her own self, her eyes dimming and lighting back up, her hair shrinking back into her scalp and re-growing, over and over.

"I will never hurt Leo!" the true Rachel said.

"*Stop this foolishness; he could reveal your secret any time he damn pleases,*" the fake Rachel reasoned.

"No, Leo's my best friend!" she reprimanded.

"*What about Hannah?*" she tried.

"Leo is practically just as important!"

"*Practically?*"

"Second place, right after the person who's been with me for nine years — that is really worth something!"

"Rachel?" Leo asked.

"I will never intentionally hurt Leo!" the real Rachel roared.

Leo rolled his eyes at that last comment, knowing that wasn't true and that she meant not kill him intentionally. Rachel's hair returned back to the way it was before she had turned into some type of sorceress. Her eyes dimmed back to brown, her facial expression went dull. The water evaporated, everything that was fire was put out, her jewellery disappeared, and she fell to the bed, unconscious. She was now wearing the school uniform, though the uniform was quickly turning to ashes. Without much time to react, Leo threw the sheet over her almost bare body, covering every inch of her from her toes to her neck.

After about two minutes or so, Rachel sat straight up; she quickly noticed her state and pulled the sheet up to her nose. "What happened?" she asked.

"You don't remember?" Leo said, surprised, leaning down to make sure it was really her.

"No," Rachel said, leaning into the bed away from Leo.

"Well, for starters, you tried to kill me," he said as though it were the plainest thing in the world.

"Why?" she asked. Suddenly, her eyes grew twice in size. "The physical exam!" she exclaimed loudly. She was about to hop out of the bed when she remembered she was butt naked. She felt light tingling on her shoulder, she turned to see the windows wide open, and her big eyes grew bigger. "Leo!" she said loudly, her voice cracking.

He saw the windows and he calmly walked over to them and closed the curtains, the light dimmed at the coverage. Leo turned around to see Rachel's cheeks a deep shade of red, her index fingers rubbing her temples whilst her upper arms held up the bed sheets and comforter. "The physical exam; I'm gonna get kicked out," she said. "They're going to find out everything."

"Rachel," Leo said, looking away from her. "Don't get mad, okay?"

Rachel looked up at him. "Yes?" she asked.

"So, in *Snow White*, I came across this village one day while you were out with Silas; there was a magic shop. I knew about the physical exam, so I asked the shopkeeper for a mind-controlling kind of potion thing. You can make people believe the lies you tell, and here it is," he said and pulled out a vial from the top drawer of his nightstand that contained a pasty silver liquid.

"*Now* you tell me?" Rachel asked, surprised that Leo, Leo of all people, was able to get his hands on such a powerful thing. "How long does it last for?"

"Yeah, sorry about that," Leo apologized and tossed the vial over to her. "I'm not sure, I would assume an hour?"

"Thanks," Rachel said as she caught the vial. She stared at the liquid for a few moments. "Here we go," she said, and then she popped off the cork with her thumb. Rachel gulped down the potion and felt a low burning sensation in the pit of her stomach. She dropped the vial onto the stone floor and Leo heard it crack; he turned to see Rachel clutching her throat.

Rachel had one eye closed from the pain and the left corner of her mouth raised; she was obviously trying to keep her mouth shut. As this unknown pain surged through Rachel's body, she felt her mind change slightly. Her throat closed up for several moments, as if preparing for the lies. The pain left her throat and travelled down to the pit of her stomach before it finally faded away.

"Rachel, are you alright?" Leo asked pointlessly.

Rachel looked up at him and found the strength to reply, "Do I look fine to you?"

"The shopkeeper told me there might be some pain, but not this much," he said, running his fingers through his hair and tightening his grip, pulling each strand in stress.

"Did he say how long it would last?" she asked.

"He said the pain would only last about twenty seconds."

"I guess that explains why it's going away."

"Yeah, and when it's fully gone there wouldn't be any pain left," Leo noted.

"It's almost gone," Rachel's eyes widened at the sound of her voice. "My voice," she gasped.

Leo stopped thinking and looked straight at her shocked expression. "Huh?" he asked.

"It's deep," she said, her hands over her mouth.

"Your voice is naturally unnaturally deep, there really isn't much of a difference."

"Don't you hear it? I sound like a-a-a…" she paused for a second. "I sound like a *you*."

"You sound like yourself."

"My voice is abnormally deep." She reconsidered her words, and added, "Even for my standards."

"Do we really have time for this?" he asked. "And it's just your subconscious playing the role of a boy."

"Good point," Rachel said. "But I can't believe it; I can make people think I'm a *you*."

"Could you please stop saying that?"

"Fine," Rachel said, and she gave him a death glare.

"I'll get you a uniform," Leo said. He ran over to the wardrobe and grabbed a suit at random. Leo walked back over to Rachel and gave her the uniform.

"Won't you turn around?" Rachel said, snatching the uniform from his hands. Leo obeyed and Rachel scrambled out of the bed and ran into the bathroom like a spooked cat, locking the door behind her. "Thanks, Leo," Rachel said, her bare back leaning against the door.

"Thanks for not killing me, I guess," Leo returned. "But Zach might want to try to, um, kind of prove to the school that you're a girl."

"Seriously?" Rachel asked. "He's so stuck up."

"I know," Leo said. "You almost done?"

"Yeah," Rachel said and walked out of the bathroom. She stood on her tiptoes for some reason, almost Leo's height. "Let's see how much of a good actor I'll be," she said.

"We have a couple minutes until the physical exam," Leo said. "If we run, we can make it in no time. Good thing our dorm is on the first floor."

Rachel walked back into the bathroom and was back out again not long after, holding up the undone tie. "Could you please," she said.

Leo didn't need her to say much more; he took the tie and tied it perfectly.

"Now let's go!" Rachel said and ran out of their dorm, Leo hot on her trail. They ran down the long hallways and took many turns, with Leo telling Rachel where to go. They made it to the auditorium. Rachel opened the doors and walked in; Leo waited patiently outside for her, or at least that's what they would hope for. In front of the doors, waiting for the two of them, were Zach, Vic, and Alex. Each had their arms crossed with matching grins painted across their smug faces.

"What do you want?" Rachel asked.

"Nothing much; we just wanted your permission before we told every boy attending this place that you're a girl," Zach said.

Rachel snorted and pushed past them with her usual strength, grabbing Leo's arm and pulling him along with her.

"Aren't you gonna kiss for good luck?" Zach asked.

Rachel turned sharply. "What would give you satanic brats that idea?" she asked.

"Your lover boy told us that's what you do," he replied with a shrug. "You don't?"

Rachel turned to Leo. "What the heck did you say?"

"You have to go for your exam," Leo said, and then he pushed Rachel through the doors. "I can deal with these delusional guys."

"Leo—" Rachel tried.

"Come on, you need to go," he said and closed the doors behind her. "Good luck!"

Leo turned back around to see Zach chuckling to himself. "You two are very amusing."

CHAPTER EIGHTEEN

TRUTH? WHAT'S THAT?

"Why would I believe a word you say?" Hannah asked, still suspending Elisha in the air.

"You just have to!" Elisha pleaded, struggling for air. "Please!"

Slowly, Hannah recognized the plea for mercy in Elisha's expression and she softened her grip. "We're going to my dorm and you're going to explain everything," she ordered.

Elisha nodded.

Hannah dropped Elisha and she gasped for air, clutching her throat.

"Hurry up," Hannah said, and she started walking away. Elisha quickly got up to her feet and chased after the blond up to her dorm.

"Sit," Hannah instructed, pointing to Rachel's old bed. Elisha obeyed as Hannah sat on her own bed, arms crossed. "Now tell me why I should believe you," Hannah demanded.

"Look, I'm really not asking you to believe me; I'll just tell you something huge about Rachel's and my past," Elisha said. "So, it started when we were two years old; this is where our story begins. She'd just moved there and I was the only child there her age. Our parents wanted us to play with each other, for friendship reasons, I guess.

"We would play at each other's houses and have sleepovers and all of that fun childhood stuff," she said, smiling at the blissful memory. "Or at least that was until *he* came along," Elisha scowled. "He ruined everything we had: our friendship, our happiness together, and everything else that made our lives happy. Rachel started ignoring me, playing with him all the time, even sleeping over! I was so hurt, so upset, and so *betrayed*. She just left me to the side like some piece of worthless trash, all because of him. Though eventually," she smiled, "he left us. I never saw him again; he went to some academy. Rachel was a little sad but she started playing with me again. But by being too eager to rebuild our friendship that I missed so much, I ruined my chance. One day, when we were playing at the lake, our parents were talking and walking towards us; we'd run ahead because we were so excited to play together again.

"Rachel was talking about how much she missed him, how much she'd love to see him one more time. It was so obvious she loved him. I hated that. I snapped at what she said. I quickly replied, looking at the sand underneath the clear water, 'But isn't it amazing that he's finally gone? Now we can play together again, just us.' She was furious at that. She now understood that I envied her time with him. She was so mad that she threw a chunk of sand at me; part of it flew into my mouth. The taste was so bitter, like the way I'd felt for that long, lonely year she'd spent with him. That was all it took for us to fight each other like complete savages. We pulled at each other's hair, chunks of our locks flowing in the water downstream. She threw another chunk of sand at my head, though it went into my eye and I couldn't see out of it. Letting out a yell of rage that our parents somehow didn't notice, I strangled Rachel, tripped her, and held her under water for a while. My right eye was stinging so painfully, like my raging emotions. I cried so much. Luckily, Rachel bit my wrist, and in shock, I let go of her. She ran back to her parents and I wasn't allowed to play with her. I was grounded and almost went to an asylum for attempted murder. The authorities thought I was a psychopath with serious brain malfunctions, and in a way, they weren't wrong. My mother sent me to a therapist where I talked about my issues; she even sent me to another asylum for a couple years. I missed my parents and brother so much while I was there. I was all alone, and each night I cried in regret and sadness.

"When I was finally let out, I learned that a year back Rachel had been sent to this academy. My mother asked if I wanted to go to this place or another, though I could tell she was skeptical about sending me to the same place as the girl I tried to kill. I chose to come here and I was so happy when I saw Rachel, playing with you, having a good life. I ran up to her and hugged her so tightly. I'd let go of the past and thought she had to, but she hadn't. I was so lonely, like in the asylum. I remembered what my brother had told me, that I'd always have him, but I didn't have him, or my parents, or any friends. All I had was Rachel's hatred towards me. So, in anger, I lied to everyone and said Rachel had done all those horrible things to me. Everyone believed me because Rachel immediately reacted, as though I'd told everyone her deepest secret. And since that day, we've been going back and forth, bickering, fighting, hating, all because of something I brought upon myself. And if I hadn't been so selfish, none of that would've happened in the first place,"

Hannah covered her mouth with her hands, back to her regular caring self. "That is so tragic," she gasped.

"Well, she hates me eternally now," Elisha said.

CHAPTER NINETEEN

PHYSICAL EXAM

"Aye boy, good to see ye," Sir Evergreen said to Rachel, patting her shoulder. "Go behind the curtain; Lucy's waiting for ye. She'll be making sure ye be a male."

Rachel nodded and stepped behind the not very secure-looking blue curtain draping down from the ceiling. Behind the curtain were many futuristic-looking computers. Sitting behind one was a woman around the age of twenty-eight.

"Are you Lucy?" Rachel asked, forcing her voice to be deeper than usual.

"Yes," the woman said, looking at her with a kind smile. "And ye be?"

Rachel noticed that she had the same sort of accent as Sir Evergreen. "Uh, I'm Justin Campridge."

Lucy typed in Rachel's false name and nodded approval. "Now, let's get started—"

"Wait, before you start," Rachel said, cutting her off, "why do you work here?"

"Well, I guess my father didn't really have the time to hire someone he didn't know," Lucy said simply.

"Who's your father?"

"Sir Evergreen," Lucy said.

Rachel blanched. "But who's your mother?"

"I honestly don't know. She left us before I was old enough to remember her, but I have two older sisters, they both have their own lives now, and here I am, working for my father."

"Well, let's get started," Rachel said, clasping her hands together.

"Okay," Lucy said, smiling.

"She's going to be discovered sooner or later, or better yet, now," Zach said to Leo.

Leo chuckled lightly to himself. "No, she won't," he said.

"Yes, she will," Zach argued. "Girls and boys are very different, in case you were unaware."

"Oh, I know that."

"Are you mocking my intelligence?"

"That would be very difficult," Leo said, softening.

Zach looked confused. "And why is that?"

"Because there wouldn't be anything to mock, duh."

"Why you," Zach clenched his hand into a tight fist.

"What happened to your point of her being discovered?" Leo asked, glaring at Zach.

"She is going to be discovered," Zach said firmly. "And stop being so optimistic; it makes me sick."

"Well, you just made me want to be a tonne more optimistic, so you'd better get a doctor who can actually stand your face."

Zach was about to punch Leo in the gut when Rachel jogged out of the auditorium, smirking widely.

"How did it go?" Leo asked.

"It went great!" Rachel replied. "I passed!"

Zach's, Vic's, and Alex's jaws dropped at the sound of this.

"But how?" Zach asked.

Rachel walked up to him and pressed his nose with her index finger as though it were a button. "Magic," she said.

"I don't believe this crap; you're coming with me," Zach said. In a swift motion, he flung Rachel over his shoulder.

"What the—" Rachel realized what had happened. "Put me down! Put me down! Put me down!" she said loudly, slamming her fists on his back and kicking the air around her feet wildly. Zach ignored all of her fighting and whistled for Alex and Vic, who quickly rushed to his side like two minions.

"We're going to my dorm," Zach said.

"Put me down!" Rachel roared. Images of the three boys *thoroughly examining her* flashed through her mind and sent shivers up and down her spine. Then there was Hannah standing in her mind. Sweet, innocent Hannah who she missed so dearly. Everything they had worked towards in their lives was together, at school. Rachel didn't even know why she was thinking of Hannah at a time like this but she let the memories sink in, each one more precious than the last.

The day she met Hannah, on Rachel's first day at the girls' academy, Rachel was scraping dirt from the bottom of her shoe when Hannah sat down beside her. "Hey, can I sit here with you?" was what Hannah had said, on that fateful day. Rachel scoffed at her and continued rubbing the dirt off her shoes with the sharp stick. "You're quiet, aren't you?" Hannah asked her. Rachel shot her a death glare and went back to her shoes, though in aggravation, her hand slipped and the stick pierced her skin, drawing blood. "That looks like it hurts," Hannah had said, all worried.

Rachel had glared at Hannah. "It's all your fault that I probably have an infection now," she snapped.

Hannah had looked at her feet for a moment, sad, before she asked, "How about I take you to the office?" And she did. The office staff had sent them off to the infirmary, Hannah holding Rachel's dirty hand all the way.

"Why are you doing this?" Rachel had asked Hannah. "Nobody likes me."

Hannah had just smiled at her happily and said, "Well, I guess I'm the only one who likes you."

Rachel remembered her own reaction to that comment and how emotional she'd gotten. Her eyes had swelled and she cried, so happy to have a true friend at last. "So, let's be friends," Rachel had suggested through her happy tears.

She remembered that every time she did something horrible to Elisha, Hannah had talked to the teachers and somehow managed to get Rachel out of trouble.

Oh, Rachel missed Hannah so much. Tears started flowing down her cheeks at all of her memories, then she suddenly snapped back to reality. "Why are you doing this?" she asked Zach.

"I have nothing better to do," Zach said, brushing her off.

Hearing that simple, merciless answer come out of Zach without a second thought, she took her foot and rammed it into his groin, making him yell out many curse words in pain. He let her go.

As she stood in front of the three boys she hated so much, Rachel felt herself lose control over her normal self. "You," she said as she felt the potion leave her body, "are the worst beings I've ever known!" she said.

"So?" Zach asked. "What are you going to do about it?"

Rachel let out a bloodcurdling scream and she turned into the sorceress of the spirit possessing her soul.

"What's going on?" Alex asked, terrified.

"What happened to her?" Vic asked, petrified.

"How?" Zach asked, awestruck.

"Look at what you've done!" Leo yelled, standing in front of the trio. "You guys really do always find a way to screw things up, don't you?"

Under regular circumstances, Zach would have asked Vic and Alex to beat Leo up, but he couldn't even reply. Rachel simply pointed a finger at him and ivy shot up from the floor, the thorny vines tangling around him and pulling him to the cold tiles. Next, she pointed to Alex and a ring of fire grew around him, its flames coming closer and closer to his clothing. Finally, she pointed her ringed finger at Vic, and before he had the chance to run, a huge block of ice formed around his legs.

"Rachel!" Leo yelled. "Stop it!"

Rachel's glowing eyes flickered before they dimmed and she returned back to normal. She fell and Leo caught her before running to their shared dorm.

Meanwhile, the ice around Vic's feet turned to thick steam and soon evaporated. The fire around Alex quickly dissipated. The vines tangled around Zach and fell to the ground like dead snakes before they slithered back into the ground and the tiles magically repaired themselves, each crack that wasn't there before being sealed. The boys looked at each other, utterly confused.

Leo threw open the door to his and Rachel's dorm, and then he threw her onto the bed, quickly putting the comforter over her. He breathed heavily from the long run while carrying a girl only one year younger than him. "Phew, that was close," he said to himself, leaning against the wall.

Suddenly, Rachel sat straight up, the sheet up to her neck. "What happened?" she asked.

"You turned into a full sorceress at the auditorium, and whenever you do that, your clothes disintegrate," Leo answered.

Rachel's cheeks burned red. "Did you see anything—"

"God, no, thank the Lord," he said quickly, still heaving in deep breaths. "Like you said a little while back, we don't want history repeating itself."

"Doesn't the sorceress only take over when I get mad?" Rachel's eyes opened wider when she remembered who was at the auditorium's large doors. "They know?" she asked.

"Who?" Leo asked. "Vic, Alex, and Zach? Yeah, they know about your messed up all-powerful side."

Rachel bit her lip. "She was right," she whispered. "I guess it's really biting me now."

Leo looked at her. "Who?" he asked.

"Hannah," she replied. "A couple of years ago, she told me that I'd need to learn to control my temper; she was right."

"Did she give you any other helpful tips?"

"I know I'll remember them when I disobey her *life tips*."

"But if they *do* tell someone, who will believe them?" Leo asked, returning to the main topic.

Rachel brightened. "Especially since they came out unscathed," she said. "Now turn around; I need to get another uniform."

"That's another reason you need to control your temper," Leo said. "You keep wasting my uniforms."

"Twice," she clarified. "Not that often."

"So, we're going to *Neverland*, right?" Leo asked Rachel as they walked down the hallways.

"Yep, you got it, Lee Lo," Rachel replied.

As they turned a corner, Zach, Vic, and Alex stepped in front of them.

Rachel rolled her eyes in annoyance. "I swear, could you guys just leave us alone?" she asked.

"Don't speak to us, you *monster,*" Zach sneered.

Rachel was taken aback by this hateful comment, one that she'd heard so many times at the girls' academy from Elisha, Elizabeth, Annabella, and every other girl she'd gotten into a fight with. Each had called her a monster for standing up for herself. Today, this stung more, for this academy was supposed to be her new start, with every trace of the past gone. She choked on her breath, tears about to spill.

"She is not a monster," Leo said stepping forward. Rachel's eyes shot up to him, remembering that she was not alone in this big academy. "You're the monsters here, the *only* monsters in this entire academy," he said, taking another step forward.

Rachel wiped her wet eyes and smiled largely, so big her cheeks hurt. She'd never been alone; she should've known this from the moment she first met Hannah. She'd always had at least one person who truly cared for her. She saw Leo and Zach about to clash—

"Leo," Rachel said, her confidence far above the clouds, "leave this to me."

Leo looked surprised, for not even a minute ago, she had looked like the scared little girl she'd been when her mother died with eyes wet, bones shaking. But now he saw what he should've seen before: a powerful, not evil, and in full control girl. He stepped back and let Rachel take his spotlight. As she stepped forward, Zach took a scared step back towards his minions.

"Scared, are you?" Rachel asked, smirking. "Come on, fight me."

"Sure thing, sorceress," Zach said, clenching his hands into tight fists.

"But, Zach, she could become a sorceress again," Alex warned.

"Yes, she could," Zach said, not looking at Alex. "But we have physical proof."

"What proof?" Vic asked.

"Our broken bones, perhaps, maybe even large open wounds, huge scarring gashes, blood on the walls, floor, and perhaps ceiling. We have all the proof we need to send this demon into jail for a couple of months, then Lee Lo what's his face won't have a protector." Alex and Vic looked at each other and identical grins spread across their faces.

"Fine," Rachel said. "If it's a fight you want, it's a fight you'll get. But if I hurt you, sorceress or not, I have two things you don't that will make you lose, and it doesn't matter who wins this fight. I have two very important things in my defence against you. Do you want to know what those two things are?" she asked.

Zach looked back at Alex and Vic, who both shrugged in reply.

"One," Rachel continued. "I have Leo, a witness, who heard you say that you wanted this fight. Did I ask to fight you? No, I just agreed to it — there's a difference. Second, Leo will witness this whole thing, and he's able to *stretch the truth* a tad bit, so he's basically a big part of this, right Leo?"

"Yes!" Leo said, happy to help Rachel stand up to Zach.

"Exactly," she said. "So, it would be your word against ours."

Zach's confidence he'd felt when he had confronted Rachel had started to plummet from the sky down to Earth from the moment she'd started naming her advantages. Now his confidence hit the rocky surface and was plummeting down, deeper and deeper until it hit an unexpected core.

"So, I suggest you keep your mouth shut, or Leo over here will be very persuasive, understood?" Rachel said.

"Well," Zach said, "I say we fight."

Rachel snorted. "Hope there's a hospital around for you," she commented.

"I'm afraid that's where you'll be going," Zach shot.

"We'll see; now, fight!"

Rachel started with a punch to Zach's face, sending him to the ground. He quickly shot back up to his feet and responded to the blow with a kick to Rachel's shin; she returned with a hard kick to the groin, making him fall to his knees in pain. Before he could get up with his remaining strength, Rachel placed her foot on his chest and pushed him onto his back.

"For everything you do without mercy," Rachel said, and then she stomped hard on his stomach, making him spit blood. "For every time you hurt Leo," she said, and then she kicked him hard in the side. "For everything you do to everyone," she said loudly, and then she stomped on his lungs.

Zach gritted his teeth, waiting for the right moment to strike.

Rachel threateningly hovered her foot above Zach's throat. "Who do you think wins?" she asked.

"Me," Zach said. In a swift moment, he grabbed her by the foot and flung her across the hall and into the wall.

"There goes my tailbone," Rachel muttered to herself.

"Should we help?" Alex asked, gesturing to himself and Vic.

Zach looked at them and shook his head. "It's fine," he said. "Besides, I'm just about to finish her off." He got up to his feet with less force than before and walked towards Rachel with a limp.

"You're pretty good," Rachel said, slowly getting up to her feet.

"I will finish you," Zach said with a glare meaner than the Grim Reaper's.

Rachel rolled her eyes at his tasteless comment. "You wish," she said. With a leap, Rachel jumped up to her feet. "Like I said, you're pretty good, *but I'm better.*" She raised her foot high and kicked him back by his chest again.

"Impossible," Zach said. "How is a girl so strong?"

Now Rachel was mad. "Any girl can be as strong as me!" she roared as she lifted him up by the collar. "Don't make that mistake again." Rachel pressed her forehead to his and gritted her teeth.

Zach looked genuinely terrified of Rachel, as though he thought she would kill him without a second thought. He swore he saw her eyes turn red as she went for the final blow.

"Goodnight," Rachel said, and then she rammed her fist into his stomach. He fell to the solid ground, unconscious. Rachel looked at Leo with a smile. "Let's go to Neverland," she said, not knowing of the boys creeping in behind her.

"Rachel, behind you!" Leo said. He tried to dive for Rachel but was too late; she was gripped by the neck and suspended in the air by Alex as Vic ran to Leo and held him tight by the arms.

"Watch as she dies," he whispered into Leo's ear.

"We agreed to play fair!" Rachel wheezed.

"When did Zach say that? I'm pretty sure he didn't," Alex said, scratching the back of his head with his free hand, eyeing Leo.

Rachel felt Alex's thumb crush her windpipe. She gasped for air but none came, and all of the air she did have in her lungs left her body. She tried to lift her arm to punch Alex but she was too low on air to do that. She looked at Leo, who was frantically trying to escape Vic's grasp to save her. Rachel gave him a bittersweet smile and he stopped fighting, too shocked to continue.

"Tell Silas I—" Rachel gasped for enough air to finish her sentence. "Tell him I love him, bury me in *Snow White*, and ask him to put me in a glass coffin with gems and rubies and all of that." Her smile slowly faded before she remembered she had something else to say to her friend. "Leo, I—" she ran out of air and she couldn't finish her sentence.

"Rachel!" Leo screamed, tears springing to his eyes. He found the strength he needed and fought out of Vic's grip, pushing him against the wall. With one good punch, he knocked him out.

Shocked at this turn of events, Alex dropped Rachel's lifeless body and attempted to fight Leo, though there was no point because of the rush of adrenaline zooming through him. He beat Alex just as fast as Vic, and then he left them both on the ground. Leo ran to Rachel's lifeless body and put her head in his lap. Her skin was paler than snow, her lips weren't their natural pink hue, and she was awfully light.

"Rachel," Leo said, and he shook her lightly. "Come on; you've survived a lot of stuff that is worse than this," he pleaded.

Rachel remained the same.

"This really doesn't suit you," Leo continued, shaking her a bit more roughly now. "You look like one of those really expensive dolls you find in an antique shop. You look like an angel, so carefree. Honestly, this really doesn't suit you. Please go back to your regular self, the one that would slap me when I said something you didn't like. Come on,"

Tears flowed from his eyes more rapidly. When there still wasn't a reaction coming from Rachel, his sadness turned to anger. Leo wiped away his tears. "I swear on my life that one day I'll kill Vic, Zach, and Alex, especially Alex, for killing one of the only people who I care about in this miserable world!" he held her body tightly and cried into her shoulder.

He didn't notice the rising of her chest, her small gasps, and her drift off to what seemed like a peaceful sleep. He brought his head up from her shoulder and dried his tears.

"Leo," Rachel muttered.

Leo's gaze shot to her blissful smile and his eyes grew wide in pure relief. "Rachel," he said, shaking her. "Rachel, wake up, come on, we have to go to Neverland!"

"Silas," Rachel continued.

"Huh?" Leo wondered, listening to what she had to say. He leaned closer to her to try to hear what she said next—

No words came, Rachel just sat straight up, her forehead knocking into Leo's, sending her back to the floor.

"Ugh!" Rachel said, clutching her forehead in pain. "Bloody maples!" she cursed. "Why does this always happen?!"

"Because you always almost die!" Leo said, clutching his own forehead.

Rachel looked around. "What happened to these guys?" she asked, gesturing to Alex, Vic, and Zach.

"I beat them up so I could try to save you," Leo said.

Rachel's eyes widened at what he said. "I was almost dead; that means I wasn't breathing…" she trailed off and she gasped loudly at the realization. Quickly, she took her hands and rubbed her lips furiously.

Leo noticed her frantic movements. "What are you doing?" he asked.

"You said you saved me, and if I was almost dead, that means I wasn't breathing, so for you to save me, you'd have to *thoroughly* help me breathe, right? Which means you did either the kiss of life or CPR, right? Which means you had to touch me in ways that I prefer you didn't," she said, still rubbing her lips.

"I didn't save you that way," Leo said and rolled his eyes.

Rachel stopped her hand movements. "Then how did you save me?" she asked.

"I made Alex let go of you because he was strangling you, and now here we are," he explained.

Rachel breathed out a long sigh of relief. "Okay, that's good," she said. "We should go now."

"And leave the brats behind?"

"Remember? You're still my witness." Rachel got up to her feet.

"Well, to *Neverland*?" Leo asked.

"To *Neverland*!" Rachel proclaimed.

They ran to Sir Evergreen's office, which was vacant as usual.

"Man, this guy is never here," Rachel noted. "That's pretty irresponsible."

They went into the secret room. Rachel wrote **Neverland** on the blank chalkboard and jumped in after placing her hand on the glass.

"One day I'll tell her," Leo said, and then he jumped in after her.

CHAPTER TWENTY

SECOND STAR TO THE RIGHT

𝓡 achel and Leo stumbled out of the portal and landed in the middle of the road in what seemed like London, from the time the story *Neverland* took place. Cars honked and they quickly rushed to the curb.

"What now?" Leo asked Rachel impatiently.

"We wait for Peter Pan, obviously. When he goes to, I'm guessing, that house," she explained, pointing to huge, beautiful house in front of them. The walls were of a dark red brick, the windows had clear glass with pure white windowsills, and the front door was of a rich dark wood. "Then I yell out his name. He'll wonder why I know his name and come down here; I'll just say that I thought he was someone I knew and take it from there."

"So, we just wait for him?" Leo asked, as if doubting her plan.

"No, look, there he is!" Rachel said, pointing at one of the highest windows of the house she'd suspected Peter Pan would fly to.

"What are you talking about?" Leo asked. "There's nothing there—" but then he saw a silhouette, camouflaged in the darkness of the night.

"Hey, Peter!" Rachel said loudly, waving at the window like a maniac.

The boy looked down at them and flew down to their level. "Hello," he said. "Do I know you?"

Rachel feigned a surprised reaction. "Oh, sorry, I thought you were someone else."

"It's okay, but who are you?" the boy asked. Upon further examination, you could see he had messy dark brown hair, emerald green eyes, and an adventurous grin. He wore clothes made entirely of vines and other plants.

"I'm Rachel," Rachel replied, smiling.

"You're a girl?" the flying boy asked.

Rachel suddenly remembered that her hair was short and she still wore the school uniform; she silently cursed herself. "Oh, yes," she said innocently. "A pirate had my hair cut short and sent me away, and in the streets a young and polite couple gave me this outfit."

"Which pirate?" he asked.

"Blackbeard," she lied. "And your name is?"

"Peter Pan of Neverland!" he replied, his fist against his chest, over his heart. "Would you like me to take you to a beautiful island far, far away?"

"Yes," Rachel said.

"Would you like to see fairies?" he questioned.

"Of course," she said happily.

"Perhaps some mermaids?"

"Obviously."

Peter Pan was about to ask another question when he finally noticed Leo. "Who's he?" the boy asked.

"Oh," Rachel said, "he's just Leo, a good friend of mine, could he come?"

Just a what? Leo thought. *I have helped you, saved your life countless times, travelled through life-threatening fairy tales, been beat up for your sake, had to put on a jester's outfit while I* waited *for you, which took a while, I could go on for hours and hours. But the point is that we've been through so much and you call me a what?*

Peter Pan looked Leo up and down, not seeming to notice he wore the same outfit as Rachel, before he looked back at her and nodded with his charming, adventurous smile.

"Well," Rachel said, "how do we get there?"

"You see the bright star over there?" Peter Pan asked, letting his feet touch the ground. He leaned down to Rachel's height and pointed over to a bright star.

"Yeah, I see it," she replied.

"Well, do you see the one directly next to it? That's *Neverland*," he said. "*That's* where I'm taking you."

Rachel's smile grew wider. "But how?"

"Easy, with fairy dust," Peter Pan said. He whistled and a small bright light zoomed towards him, stopping a few inches from his nose. Looking closely, Rachel noticed that this small light was a fairy in a green dress. Rachel held back a gasp. This was Tinker Bell, *the* Tinker Bell that every five-year-old girl knew so well.

"What's she going to do?" Leo asked.

Rachel shot him a glare, noticing he didn't know who Tinker Bell was.

"This is how I'm going to take you to Neverland," Peter said, ignoring Leo's question. "With her fairy dust."

"Are you sure such a small fairy can have enough fairy dust to bring all three of us to *Neverland*?" Rachel asked, playing dumb.

"Just watch," Peter said. Against the small fairy's will, he grabbed her and shook her above Rachel's head, above his own head, and, reluctantly, above Leo's head. "Now think happy thoughts; they will lift you in the air!" With that last note, Peter bent down and pushed off, his thoughts lifting him up like he had said they would.

Rachel thought about the day she would be married and rose up from the ground. Leo just had to think of Rachel's sweet smile and attitude and he rose five feet above her. Rachel scowled at Leo and thought about food in general, she rose at least thirty feet above him; she smirked down at Leo, content with herself.

"Now come!" Peter instructed and started flying away.

Rachel gasped and followed quickly; Leo flew after her.

Rachel felt so free in the dark night sky, the stars twinkling not that far above her. She had never believed the dream she had as a small child would eventually come true. She used to dream that one day she would fly above the clouds and buildings, looking at everything below her, but this was such a long time ago. She'd entirely forgotten about that childhood dream. Rachel was so happy at this moment.

Peter guided Rachel and Leo to the height of the stars. At one point, he yelled back at Rachel, "Rachel, grab my ankle!"

Rachel gave him a peculiar look before she obeyed.

"Make sure he does it to you!" Peter instructed, referring to Leo.

Rachel shrugged and turned to Leo. "Grab my ankle!" she yelled at him. Leo gave her a strange look before she yelled at him, "Just trust me on this!"

Reluctantly, Leo grabbed onto Rachel's ankle.

"Hold on tight!" Peter yelled at the top of his lungs; this time, both Leo and Rachel heard him. They both tightened their grip. It's a good thing they did, for the stars seemed to zoom right past them, though it was them zooming past each star, faster and faster. The wind felt like it was stretching their faces, ripping past them continuously.

"Here we go!" Peter screamed.

Somehow, they got faster and crashed into the second star to the right.

Rachel expected to feel hurt, pain, and just fall. But as she slowly opened her eyes, she saw a bright blue sky around her. The clouds looked like cotton candy and her mouth watered, and then she started to fall. "Why am I falling?!" she screamed, her arms flailing wildly.

"You're not thinking happy thoughts!" Peter yelled down at her.

"Happy thoughts, happy thoughts," Rachel muttered to herself. "Silas!"

Nope, nothing, she was still falling towards the lake. Like lightning, she was struck with the memory of Hannah telling her she should learn how to swim; she needed to think happy thoughts! Then she realized the memory had a purpose. "Hannah!" she yelled. Rachel stopped falling and she rocketed back up towards Leo and Peter as if gravity had been reversed. She smiled, happy with herself, until she crashed into Leo, her forehead hitting him hard in the chest, which just ended up looking wrong.

Rachel flew away from Leo and behind a cloud, burning red with embarrassment. "Sorry!" she shrieked.

"It's fine," Leo said, also turning as bright red as though he'd just eaten a jalapeno.

"We should go to *Neverland*," Peter said awkwardly, trying to forget what he just saw.

"Please," Leo and Rachel squeaked in unison.

"Just think *down* and that's where you'll go," Peter explained, and then he descended, leaving them behind. Leo quickly followed and Rachel floated down after them.

Rachel was still trying to recover from her crash into Leo when a bullet flew past her head and she screamed.

"PIRATES!" Peter roared. And he wasn't just yelling that for the twisted pleasure of it. Below them in the open ocean was a huge pirate ship filled to the brink with ugly, misshapen men, each more revolting than the last. Rachel spotted one pirate in particular who didn't look like the rest. He had a revolver pointed at Peter, long curly black hair, a greasy black mustache, and evil blue eyes. On his head was a captain's hat with a large mauve feather. Beside him was another ugly pirate who wore a black bandana, a blue and white striped shirt that let out part of his fat belly, and black jeans. Rachel squinted to get a closer view of what was on his feet. She was shocked to see the obese pirate wearing two red flip-flops.

"Captain Hook and Smee," Peter said through a clenched scowl.

Rachel whipped her attention back to the tall pirate with the captain's hat and saw that instead of a right hand, he had a deadly sharp hook.

"What do we do?" Rachel asked Peter.

"You and *him* fly into the jungle," Peter instructed, referring to Leo once again.

"Got it," Rachel said. She turned to Leo and asked, "Did you hear that?" Leo nodded.

"Okay, I'll see you in the jungle. As for me, I'll go have some fun with these pirates. Now, think the saddest, most horrible thoughts." With that said, Peter flew over to the pirate ship where cannons were immediately aimed at him.

Rachel and Leo let themselves think of the possibility of death and they shot down to Neverland's trees. On the way down, Rachel eyed Peter and saw him fly in the distance at the exact same height she was. She knew what would happen, and she tried to go down faster, but before she could, a bullet grazed her leg as Peter flew away. Rachel crashed through the trees and bushes in shock at the bloody scratch on her leg before she hit the ground; the impact caused her vision to blur. The last thing she heard was Leo yell at her in a worried tone, "Rachel!" The last thing she saw was Leo dodge bullets and fly down to her before she blacked out completely.

Peter had heard the scream; he'd quickly looked back to see Rachel fall down, blood spreading across her leg. But what could he do? Flying to save her would be suicide, so he decided to continue with his original plan and fly in circles around Hook's ship. "Hello, Hook!" he said.

"Aim and fire!" Hook ordered. His crew frantically reloaded their cannons and aimed for Peter, only to shoot away parts of their ship, for Peter would fly behind the ship's pillars holding up the sails and dodge at the last moment.

Once Peter was satisfied with the amount of destruction, he flew away with a nod to where he estimated Rachel would be.

"I will get you next time!" Hook roared in rage, waging his silver hook in the boy's direction. Peter ignored him completely. He flew over to Rachel and Leo and watched as Leo wrapped Rachel's leg in her pant leg that he'd ripped off.

"What in *Neverland* are you doing?" Peter asked.

"Helping her, duh," Leo said, still wrapping the bullet wound.

Suddenly, Rachel awoke with a jolt that made Leo fall on her leg, putting pressure on her wound. Rachel yelped in pain and Leo quickly got off of her, for more reasons than one.

"Are you going to be fine?" Peter asked Rachel, his face an inch from hers.

Rachel nodded painfully, eyeing the deep cut.

"Come on, I know where we can go," Peter said, and then he carefully picked Rachel up. Holding her with one hand, Peter reached into his pocket and pulled out a handful of fairy dust. He threw it over himself and Rachel, and Leo of course, and they flew away.

Peter brought them to a tree with swings hanging off branches, a huge door placed in the middle of the trunk, and boys *everywhere*.

"Where are we?" Rachel wheezed.

"The lost boys' tree," Peter said as though she should know.

"Hello, Peter!" said a boy hanging upside down from the tree. He had bright green eyes, curly hair, and a crooked smile. He wore an outfit similar to Peter's, but instead of being made of vines and leaves, his was made of feathers of different sizes and animal skins.

"Hello, Curly," Peter said.

"Who are they?" another boy asked, hanging from a tree branch by his hands. He had dirt-brown eyes and extremely pale skin. He wore the exact same outfit as Curly, though he'd added a couple of leaves for uniqueness.

"This is Rachel," Peter said and nodded at Rachel. "And this is Reo, Tootles," Peter said.

"Leo," Leo muttered.

"Why are they here?" another boy asked, jumping down to the ground from a branch. His limbs were thin and bony and his ginger hair looked dull.

"Because they are my special guests, Nibs," Peter said, and he tried to walk towards the door. Before he could turn the handle, two identical boys stepped in front of them.

"Hello, Peter," they said in perfect unison. The two boys were obviously twins; they shared the same facial features and frail body type. They wore the same outfit as Curly.

"Hello, Lost Twins," Peter said urgently. "I would love to stay and talk, but I have to go inside and treat my special guest."

Finally, Leo thought, glancing at Rachel who looked like she was on the verge of passing out because of the pain.

The twins and the other boys in their way moved, and before Peter opened the door, it swung open to reveal yet another boy with teeth pointing out at awkward angles. He wore the same outfit as the twins, although he had some type of blanket over him.

"Hello, Slightly," Peter said.

"Hello, Peter," Slightly returned. He saw Rachel in Peter's arms and he stepped out of the way, letting the three people pass by him.

Peter carried Rachel to a bed made of wood with the same sort of blanket Slightly had draping over his shoulders. Leo peeled back the blanket and Peter carefully put Rachel down on the wood, as though she were an infant. When Rachel was comfortable, Leo put the blanket over her shoulders. He then sat on the opposite side of the bed in pure loneliness. Peter got down on one knee, pulled back the comforter on Rachel's leg, and examined the wound closely.

"It's not as bad as it could be," he noted.

"Good, now I'm going to go to the *Jolly Roger* and shove Hook's pistol up his—"

"Rachel," Leo reasoned, interrupting her, "you are in no shape to walk, let alone fight."

"Watch me," Rachel challenged and stood up out of bed. Peter stood up and watched as Rachel yelped in pain and sat back down. "Ouch," she said in almost a whisper.

"Told you," Leo said. "But oh ho ho, nobody dares ever listen to me, right?"

"What's up with the attitude?" Rachel asked.

"Nothing," Leo said and looked away from her, though what was in his head was definitely different. *'What's up with the attitude?' Is that really a question? You treat me like garbage!* he thought. *I help you on a daily basis and you ignore me every time I have something to say. I swear, you are lucky I love you!*

"I'm just going to wait a bit," Rachel decided, forgetting Leo had said anything. And so, they waited for a long while before Rachel decided that she would try to stand. "Nothing to it but to do it," she muttered before she shot up to her feet, the pain just a slight pinch. "Peter," she said, "give me some fairy dust."

Peter quickly obeyed and poured a handful of it in her hand.

"Thank you," Rachel said. She poured the fairy dust over her head, and within moments she flew out of the tree and out of the jungle.

"We should follow her," Leo said.

"Yep," Peter agreed. He and Leo sprinkled the magical dust over themselves and flew out after Rachel.

It had taken some time, but Rachel eventually found the *Jolly Roger* in the ocean, the crew repairing the ship. She took in the beautiful scene, the clear blue water, the bright fish underneath the clear surface, and the sandy beach without a footprint in sight.

She looked back at the ocean. "Water," she said. "The thing that could've saved Mom." The memories instantly flooded back and she replayed each scene over and over again: her mother being burned alive, her horrible friendship, and her father slowly dying because of her mother's death. It was all her fault, every tiny bit of it, all of it. She remembered the field trip to a fire department she'd gone on when she'd been nine. She remembered screaming at the men who worked there, cursing them for not making it in time, before her teacher controlled her and apologized. The feelings overwhelmed her and the spirit that had been placed in her soul started to take control...

CHAPTER TWENTY-ONE

SORCERESS

$\mathcal{P}$eter and Leo found Rachel rather quickly, but they were shocked to see her state. Peter's eyes doubled in size and Leo's jaw dropped.

There was Rachel, flying towards the *Jolly Roger* as a sorceress. Though Leo realized her sorceress self had changed, he figured it was just because the spirit possessing her wanted to up its game after what had happened last time. Her water dress was now flames, somehow not burning her; her gloves had changed from frost to a light purplish-pink frostbite; her once ice shoes were frozen blood, the soles dripping; her hair was knee-long and floated behind her like a cape. The last change was that the tiara on her head from her previous sorceress experience was now a large golden crown with a huge ruby in the middle.

"Does this usually happen?" Peter asked Leo.

"You'd be surprised," Leo replied.

Rachel wanted to burn Hook to the ground, or at least that's what she thought for sure she wanted. Either way, there was no stopping now. She made a flaming fireball appear in each of her hands as she floated down to the pirate ship.

The ugly pirates started to notice. They aimed their revolvers at her and shoot bullet after bullet, only stopping to reload on ammo.

Rachel wasn't fazed by this. Whenever a bullet came close to her, she just blew in its direction until it dissolved into ashes and fell down into the clear ocean water. As she got closer, panic grew on the ship until at last the hideous men were running around in circles, screaming for their captain.

Eventually, Captain Hook walked out of a cabin and roared, "What in the blasted hells do you want?!"

"Captain," Smee shrieked, "a strange woman is approaching our ship and nothing we do will stop her!"

"Waste of my time," the captain sneered. "Just shoot her down."

"We tried, Sir," the pirate apologized.

"Useless imbeciles!" Hook yelled. He took out his revolver, aimed it at Rachel's heart, pulled the trigger, and the bullet flew.

Rachel laughed at the pirates' sad attempts to kill her. Suddenly, a pain surged through her and she stopped her cackling; she slowly looked down at the source of pain and saw a bullet hole in her shoulder. She looked back at the ship and saw Hook's aimed revolver.

"There," the captain said, tucking the gun back into his belt. "And she'll probably die now." He turned around to walk back to the captain's quarters but was stopped by a hand. "Oh bloody hell, what is it now?"

"Captain," Smee said fearfully.

Hook turned to see the fireballs in the woman's hands double in size. He looked at Smee angrily and said, "We're in an *ocean*, Smee; I'm sure fire won't be such a problem—" He was cut off by a bloodcurdling scream of rage; he turned his head and saw Rachel fly towards the ship at full speed.

"Come on!" Leo urged, flying as fast as he could. "We need to stop her before she does something completely insane!"

"How long has she been like this for?" Peter asked.

"Not the time!" he yelled. Then he noticed something and he stopped mid-flight, causing Peter to ram like a bull into his back.

"Seriously?" Peter said, frustrated. "Why would you—" he stopped because he saw where Leo was looking, at a bloody patch on Rachel's shoulder.

"Rachel!" Leo yelled.

Rachel flew pretty close to the ship and started throwing fireballs at the wood. Some parts burned immediately and shrivelled up before dissolving into ashes, while others burned slowly. Captain Hook looked around worriedly before he saw a hole in the wood from the side of his ship; he jumped over the flames and dove out the hole.

"Captain—" Smee stopped because he saw what Hook was doing. He watched as his captain dove out of the ship. He tried to follow, but the flames spread in front of him.

Rachel turned around, satisfied, before she started flying away. When she saw Leo flying towards her, yelling her name, it broke her trance and she turned back to normal. The pixie dust was gone and her uniform was already dissolving; she started falling into the jungle, flapping her arms around uselessly.

"Peter!" Leo yelled. The boy who'd never grown up flew over to him.

"Where did she go?" Peter asked.

"She's falling to her death, dumbass!" Leo said loudly.

"Huh?" he asked.

"*Come on!*" Leo yelled before he started flying down after Rachel.

Rachel screamed as she fell, trying to grasp anything that she fell by, though at this speed she couldn't even grasp herself. She fell through branches, getting small scrapes all over her bare body before crashing to the ground on her tailbone. She wanted Leo and Peter to come swoop down and save her. The jungle was actually cold, mostly because of her situation. Yet Rachel also didn't want them to save her; these were boys she was thinking about. And she lacked clothing, which was *very* important. Slowly, she scrambled up to her feet, and miraculously, none of her bones felt broken.

"Rachel!" she heard Leo yell. Rachel's cheeks immediately flushed red. Spotting a way to hide herself from Peter and Leo, she jumped behind a tree with large leaves, well, behind one of the lower leaves, leaving only her head, shoulders, and feet visible.

Soon enough, Peter and Leo flew down, their feet colliding with the ground. "Ow," Leo said quickly before he spotted her and his cheeks burned bright pink.

"Um," was all Rachel could manage, looking at the ground.

"Rachel—" Leo said quickly. "So um, do you, maybe, perhaps, possibly, um, need anything?" Leo asked, rubbing the back of his head as he looked away.

Peter said nothing and flew above the trees.

"Um," Rachel said awkwardly, not able to look Leo in the eye, "could you maybe wait up above the trees while I wrap some leaves around myself? Just for, well, obvious reasons, and then can we go back to the tree? And I can make something wearable?"

"Sure," Leo said quickly and flew above the trees as though he were lightning — gone in a flash. Rachel was partially shocked to see him fly away so quickly but she wouldn't criticize. She ripped off five fuzzy leaves from the tree and wrapped them all around herself, one atop the other. She made sure each was secure before she called Leo's name.

Leo quickly flew down to her and let his feet slowly touch the ground. "Are you sure they're secure?" he asked.

"Yes," Rachel replied, rolling her eyes as though he'd asked if murder was legal. Reluctantly, Leo picked Rachel up and flew behind Peter to the large tree with all the boys. Gently, Leo placed Rachel down onto her two bare feet, careful not to rip the leaves covering her.

Holding the leaves around her, Rachel ran into the tree and shooed all the boys out before she slowly took off one leaf at a time, leaving one. She looked around and soon found a needle and thread underneath the wooden bed. Quickly, she ripped the leaves along her hand for the shapes she needed and sewed together each part.

"Is there something you know of that could maybe help Rachel with her leg injury?" Leo questioned Peter. "Like to make her fall asleep for a little while? She does need her rest."

"Sure, I know of a concoction; it would put her to sleep for thirty minutes," Peter said. "You're coming with me, though, and you'll need more fairy dust." He swiftly sprinkled the powdery dust over Leo's head and started leading the way through the jungle.

Together, Peter and Leo flew to a large murky lagoon where they collected a mermaid's fingernail. Then, they moved on to a filthy creek where they did a little digging before finding a brownish-yellow alligator's tooth covered in blood (Leo gagged at the sight). Peter tucked both objects into a small pouch in his outfit before he told Leo to follow him to a specific tree where he picked off three leaves.

"That's it," Peter said. He tucked the leaves into the same pocket as the tooth and fingernail before flying back to the large tree; Leo quickly followed.

"Rachel?" Leo asked, lightly knocking on the door to the large tree.

"Come in!" he heard Rachel call. Slowly, Leo opened the door and Peter flew in over his head. He saw Rachel sitting on the bed; she'd turned the leaves into small shorts and a shirt that stopped before the middle of her stomach. Leo drooled slightly at the exposing sight; he hadn't seen this much of her since—

"Hey guys," Rachel said while she waved, snapping Leo out of his disgusting thoughts.

"Hi," Leo squeaked, awestruck.

"Hello," Peter said. "We have something for you,"

"Really?" Rachel asked. "That's really sweet of you." She smiled largely.

Leo immediately noticed how he was acting and brushed it off.

"It's a concoction so you can sleep while you recover from the events of today," Peter said.

"For how long?" she asked, sounding fearful.

"Just half an hour," said the boy who never grew up. He took out the ingredients from his pocket and gave them to

Leo, who almost gagged. Peter picked a flower from a vine hanging down from the hollow tree trunk. He then brought the beautiful flower to a branch growing on the other side of the tree's interior where he snapped off a little bit of it and let the tree drip sap into the flower. He brought it back to the bed and placed it gently on the nightstand. "Drink this *after* you have your medicine," he instructed.

"You never said it was medicine," Rachel said, scrunching up her nose as though she smelled something horrid.

"Don't worry, it'll taste good," Peter assured.

"Okay," she said warily.

"I'll just make the medicine quickly," he said. He snatched the ingredients from Leo and started making something out of them.

"Was that a fingernail?" Rachel asked, worried.

"Unfortunately," Leo muttered.

"Who did it belong to?" she questioned, now disgusted.

"A mermaid," he replied quietly.

"You saw mermaids?"

"No, we just took the fingernail from the shore. Apparently, when mermaids make bets, the stakes can be as high as losing body parts, so don't ask about that."

"Here we go!" Peter said, returning with a green substance in a vial. He put it on the nightstand and reminded her, "Remember, you drink the medicine before the sap."

"I know, I know," Rachel said, as if Peter were Hannah telling her not to fight people who didn't let her have her way.

"We'll be back in a little while," Leo said.

"Sweet dreams," Peter said sweetly before he and Leo flew out of the tree.

Rachel sat in the bed and thought about the events of that day. Peter now knew that she could turn into a sorceress, but he still treated her the same. He was supposed to be the nice, clingy boy who'd just given her medicine. She sighed; that was the way Peter was supposed to be, nice, well, except for the one time he'd snapped at Wendy in the 2003 movie. But then there was Leo, who was his own character: not something made up of words, but an actual person. Leonardo Dash, that's who he was, someone who knew of her bad side, the side of her that she never had full control over, the side of her that had almost killed three boys at their school. He also knew that she had killed her own mother, which led her father to his grave when he should've lived for much longer, though, even knowing the flaws, Leo still somehow decided, 'Yep, it's a good idea to be this girl's friend.' And it surprised her. She wondered how other people would react if she told them the truth, but she didn't bother thinking about the possible outcomes.

Rachel sighed loudly and decided that she needed a nap. She took the vial and flower and was about to instinctively drink from the vial when she questioned, "Which one was I supposed to drink first?" She looked at the bottles and considered asking Leo or Peter which one to drink, but she was just too stuck up for that. She decided that if she did get it wrong, nothing bad would happen, so she drank the sap from the flower first and later proceeded to drink from the vial. She shrugged at the relief of feeling no pain, though she still felt wide awake. Rachel was about to question Peter's concoction skills but was interrupted by stabbing pain in her throat, suffocating her. Before she could cry out for help, she passed out cold.

Rachel's dreams were bizarre and terrifying, for her at least. She started the dream-turned-nightmare in Silas' castle walking down an aisle; shiny wooden pews were on either side of her. On the very end of every pew hung a bouquet of flowers with white and gold flowers. The carpet was white, with a line of gold sewn into the edges. At the end of the aisle was a priest wearing a white and gold robe; diagonal from him was Silas, who wore a suit that matched the carpet. Rachel looked up and gasped at how high the ceiling was. Along the clear white walls were stained glass windows showing past rulers and saints. Rachel looked down at herself. She was still the same girl, the same person, but today, she looked and felt like a queen. The dress she wore was exactly how she'd imagined it to be: it had no sleeves nor collar, it was fairly tight until it reached down at her waist where it poofed out, and around the top was lacy edging. She wore the accessories she'd requested: on her hands were white gloves and on her feet were white shoes with one-inch heels. There were even extra bride accessories she hadn't requested, like the white veil that flowed down her face with the top attached to a silver diamond tiara, a diamond necklace that matched her head piece, and two diamond earrings hanging gracefully from her ears, moving back and forth as she walked. But that wasn't all she wore. Even though Rachel couldn't see it, she felt makeup on her face; she knew without a doubt that deep red lipstick had been spread across her lips, a light coat of pink blush had been patted onto her cheeks, pink eye shadow lightly covered her eyelids, and mascara had been put on her eyelashes. One thing Rachel knew for sure was that her hair looked stunning. Even though she didn't see it at all, she knew two braids on the sides of her head were pulled back along with the rest of her hair into a bun, a little loose but just secure enough to stay in place and look stunning.

She continued her walk down the aisle holding a bouquet of gold and white flowers, just like the ones on the pews. The more she walked, the more uncertain she felt about this entire arrangement, as though marrying Silas would be a mistake, and a horrible one at that. Rachel pushed the thoughts aside; she knew what she wanted, and some feeling wasn't going to change that. She urged herself forward, but the sickening feeling was growing larger and larger with each step she took.

Something above the altar caught Rachel's eye. She looked up at a banner, white and gold of course, and it spelled Congratulations! But the letters were slowly disappearing, as though being peeled off. Rachel ignored it and continued forward. How long had she been walking? She looked at Silas' smile as she walked. Was the aisle getting longer? Another question popped into her mind. She continued walking. This was going to be the happiest day of her life, the one she'd tell her children about and then later on their children; she wasn't going to be second-guessing herself at this time, not now, not after all Silas had done for her by letting her borrow his army to save Leo, coming to the dwarves' cottage every day when she was first in *Snow White*, and, most importantly, loving her.

The congratulatory message on the banner was gone, replaced with a chilling red one instead. The new message read Avoid Temptations in blood-red letters. This sent a quick chill down her spine and she hurried to get this wedding over with. She glanced at the people in the pews and was shocked to see them all as still as dolls, lifeless. Their eyes were glossy and they stared forward, blankly. Rachel didn't even think they *breathed*. Rachel looked at Silas, plastered on a fake smile, and marched down the aisle. It seemed that she was advancing normally now. She made her smile larger with each step until every trace of uncertainty was gone and her foot splashed into water. She slowly looked down and had to stifle a scream at what she saw...

Blood.

Blood was underneath her feet, seeping into her white shoes, and slowly making its way to the top of her feet. Her feet were sinking into the liquid as the bottom of her dress floated lightly on the surface. Then the blood started seeping up her dress like gravity had been reversed and it made its way to the top in no time at all. Rachel looked around for somebody to notice her, or to notice their own feet being submerged in blood. But no, nobody did. Silas stayed at the altar with his large smile, but now she realized that his eyes were black, solid black. Nobody moved. The people in the pews stayed still. Nobody moved. The priest stayed diagonal from Silas with his blank expression. Nobody moved.

Rachel bolted for the doors. Through the blood she ran, splashing all the way, the thick substance flying up and landing on her face.

The large doors slammed shut the minute she was about to leap through them. Her fists pounded on them with all her might. She tried to make the doors budge, but they didn't. The wedding guests stood up and started walking towards her at a slow and unnatural pace, as though they were undead. Rachel grabbed hold of the handles and shook them but her hands slid off; she quickly looked down and saw blood on the door handles and now on her hands as well. She didn't care; all she needed was to get out of this hell of a wedding. Rachel grabbed hold of the handles and shook the doors with much more force than before. She felt like they would break off, but the doors didn't move, so she continued.

Suddenly, two hands grabbed her arms in a comforting manner, but when she turned, she saw a small girl with black eyes and blood seeping from her eye sockets. Rachel immediately punched the girl in the face with all her force.

"Rachel!" a familiar voice groaned in pain.

Rachel's eyes flew open and she sat up, looking around. Leo was next to her, clutching his right eye.

"Sorry," she said apologetically. She had her right hand still extended from the punch, which she slowly lowered while Peter gently let her left arm down and backed away.

Rachel felt a sudden strange sensation before her mind stopped all at once.

"What happened?" Leo asked, his hands falling to his side, looking Rachel, who was now slumped over, her eyes closed.

Rachel's mind slowly filled with thoughts based on the same thing: *Leo.* She sat back up and in a swift motion grabbed his shirt collar and brought his body close to hers. She kissed his cheek gently and smiled sweetly.

Peter flew out of the tree immediately.

Leo was shocked. When Rachel had grabbed his shirt, he thought she'd sucker punch him in the nose for no reason — that was something Rachel would do. But to pull him in *this* close to her? And then give him a peck on the cheek? When Rachel let go of him, he had a million questions formed up and ready to ask. First, he asked the one that she'd ask if she were in his shoes.

"What about Silas?" Leo asked.

Rachel tilted her head like a confused puppy. "What about him?" she questioned.

"You're going to *marry* him," Leo tried.

"So?" she asked.

Leo soon noticed her eyes weren't brown: they were *pink*, a bright, hot pink. He didn't know what had happened, but he needed to get out of this situation.

"You look a lot better, anyway," Rachel said.

Leo's cheeks turned as pink as Rachel's eyes at that compliment. She'd just compared him to a *prince* and he won the beauty contest? *Why am I thinking of that at this time?!*

Rachel threw her arm around his neck, pulled him closer to her, and pressed his nose with the index finger of her free hand. "I really like you," she said with a wink.

Leo's eyes grew wide. "What's wrong with you?" he asked, looking into her pink eyes.

"Nothing, I just really like you, problem?"

The truth was that this was the best day of Leo's life; Rachel was doing what she did in his favourite dreams. But he had at least a little decency and knew that if he let this go on any further, Rachel would regret it deeply.

"Speechless?" Rachel asked mischievously. "Aww, I didn't know I took your words away."

Leo fearfully looked into Rachel's eyes as she leaned forward for a kiss. He caught a glimpse of her eyes and saw them turn back to brown.

Just as Rachel's lips grazed Leo's, she fully returned to herself and jumped away from him like a spooked cat. "You tried to *kiss* me?" Rachel yelled, appalled.

Leo looked at her with wide eyes. "You tried to kiss me!" he retorted, regaining his senses.

"Why would I have kissed you?" she asked.

"I don't know!" he said loudly.

"I must've been under a spell or something, if what you said is true, because we both know I would never intentionally kiss you. The last thing I remember is drinking the sap and then the medicine—"

"You were supposed to have the medicine and then the damned sap!" Leo slapped his open palm against his forehead.

"Well, sorry," Rachel said sarcastically. "But maybe Peter has something he can make to stop this unfortunate turn of events," she said and rolled her eyes.

"Hopefully," Leo said, though secretly, in the deepest depths of his soul, he wished the complete opposite; this was his chance to get Silas out of the picture forever, but he squashed the thought under his dignity.

"Well, let's ask him," Rachel said, and she ran out of the tree with almost inhuman speed.

Leo followed along like he always did.

Peter flew down from a branch when he heard Rachel call his name. "Yeah?" he asked.

"Well, Leo and I were thinking that I was the way I was because I may have, um," Rachel gulped before continuing, "I-may-have-drank-the-sap-before-the-medicine, but it's fine, *right?*" she sped through the part where she told him the mistake she'd made.

"Oh, that's what happened?" Peter asked, floating up a bit and sitting on the nearest branch. "Well, that's simple: we just have to go to mermaid lagoon, get a vial full of the water there, wait two weeks, then you have to drink it, and then you will be fine, simple!"

"Two weeks?!" she croaked, her clenched fingers twitching. Leo smiled at this, then he stopped.

"I'm sorry, but that's how it is," said the boy who never grew up.

"Is there a way to know when the next time I'll be like this will be?" she asked, hopeful for something good.

"Every day at the same time as today until you get cured, so at lunch," Peter said.

Rachel fainted. Luckily for her, Leo caught her, as always, and before long, he had one arm under her knees and the other around her shoulders.

"Does that usually happen?" Peter asked.

"You'd be surprised," Leo said with a shrug. He carried Rachel into the tree and placed her down gently on the bed, as though she were an antique doll that he didn't want to break. "See you later," he said, and then he gently kissed her forehead before leaving. He left the tree and closed the wooden door behind him. "We can wake her up a little bit later," Leo decided.

"What's for lunch?" he asked Peter.

"Fish, berries, and fruit," Peter replied.

Leo sighed in disappointment.

Rachel woke after a blissful dream of her marriage to Silas. She called Leo in and he came right away, as though he had been waiting outside for her.

"So, are we going to get the lagoon water?" she asked.

"Actually, Peter and I already got that," Leo said apologetically.

"Seriously?" she asked.

"You were sleeping," he reasoned.

"Fine, but we need to go home. I just want to sleep in a real bed that isn't in the jungle and has a mattress," she said with a sigh.

"Thought you'd never say so."

"Come on, you enjoy going through fairy tales; admit it," Rachel said.

"Honestly, seeing your smile is the only part I like," Leo said.

"Did you get line that from some cheap movie or something?" she asked.

"Um yeah, just wanted to see your reaction," he answered, and then he silently cursed himself.

Rachel looked at him as though he had two heads.

"Oh, and I found the portal."

"You leave nothing to me," Rachel said, and then she stuck out her bottom lip in a pouty face.

"Do you want me to take you there and let you find it?" Leo asked.

"How dare you treat me like some child!" she said loudly, appalled.

"Sorry?" he asked.

"Don't *sorry* me! Just tell me where it is."

"But you said you wanted to do something."

"Forget what I said; just tell me where it is," Rachel said.

"Mermaid lagoon," Leo replied with a shrug. "Come on." With that all said and done, he left the tree, Rachel following behind.

"Peter," Leo said, "Rachel and I need fairy dust."

"Why?" Peter asked skeptically.

"We just need it; deal with that," Leo shot. "Oh right, silly me, I forgot you're too immature to deal with anything."

Before Peter could bury his fist into Leo's nose, Rachel stepped in between them. "Please, Peter," she said.

Reluctantly, Peter lowered his fist and reached into his pouch of fairy dust. Leo and Rachel smiled, but their smiles quickly faded when Peter added, "I'm coming with you."

"Really?" Rachel asked through clenched teeth. "That would be *wonderful*."

"Yes, wonderful," Leo said. He quickly pulled Rachel aside. "We can drown him in the lake," he whispered into her ear.

"Oh, hush," Rachel whispered back. "When he gives us the dust, we'll fly away as fast as possible to the lagoon and dive in without him seeing us. Oh, and you said lake, it's lagoon," she whispered.

"Whatever," Leo muttered under his breath before he and Rachel turned back to Peter.

"Here we go!" Peter said happily, and then he threw his fairy dust over himself, Rachel, and Leo. Rachel thought of her wedding day whilst Leo thought of bringing Peter to Earth and bashing his face in the pavement. They both rose ten feet above the ground.

"Now!" Rachel yelled and she and Leo flew away at lightning speed.

"Hey!" Peter yelled and flew after them.

Leo led Rachel back to the lagoon and they dove in, without Peter seeing them, as planned.

CHAPTER TWENTY-TWO

DEAD BOY

$\mathcal{L}$eo and Rachel fell into Sir Evergreen's secret room.

"To *Oz*?" Leo asked.

"No, we're going to figure out what happened to Nicolas," Rachel said in a serious tone. "He would be around your age now."

"What was his full name?" Leo asked.

"Nicolas Campbell," she replied.

Leo turned as white as a ghost. "Rachel," he said quietly.

"What, you gotta pee? Find a bathroom, dude."

"No, it's about Nicolas."

"What is it?" Rachel asked.

"I knew him," Leo answered.

"He did go to this school!" she realized, still happy as ever.

"He was my best friend... until last year," he said, taking a sad stroll down memory lane.

"Why the past tense; what happened?"

"Nicolas... Nicolas died last year."

"What? How?" Rachael demanded.

"Sir Evergreen said he'd gotten sick," Leo said.

"No, he always pulled through sickness!" she reprimanded.

"That's what everyone thought," he said in a sad tone.

"That's a lie!"

"His parents were devastated."

"Stop it!"

"His grave is near the school; if you want, I can take you there."

"It can't be," she said, nearing acceptance.

"I'm sorry but it's the truth," he said.

"You know what," Rachel said, "I bet Sir Evergreen said that to cover up a lie, a big, bad lie, and I'm going to find out what that lie is." She walked quietly past Leo and into Sir Evergreen's office, which was empty as usual, and started looking through one of the two filing cabinets.

"Aren't you going to help?" she said at a gawking Leo, who quickly scrambled up to his feet and started searching through the other cabinet.

Rachel noticed that the names were placed alphabetically by first name, so she quickly rushed over to the Ns and looked through them all. "Nicolas Jacks, Nicola Search, Nicolas Topper..." she trailed off until she spotted 'Nicolas Campbell' written in messy handwriting. She took out the file. She went back into Sir Evergreen's secret room, sat on the floor, and opened the file. Leo followed her and sat down in front of her.

"Idiot," Rachel said. "You forgot to close the door."

"Sorry," Leo said. He quickly got back up to his feet and closed the door before sitting back down, closer to Rachel this time.

Rachel looked at the amount of papers in the folder: newspaper articles, contracts, pages with his information, and more. She gave Leo one of the newspaper articles about his death:

PARENTS DEVASTATED BY NICOLAS CAMPBELL'S MYSTERIOUS DEATH

Nicolas Campbell was a student at the Immature Boys to Great Men Learning Academy. The school master of the academy, Sir Evergreen, reports that Nicolas was feeling odd and sick for two weeks before his death. Evergreen suspects mysterious food poisoning and will further inspect the food served at the academy as well as question his chefs. Nicolas' parents are devastated by his death and have sued the school for their beloved son's tragic passing.

Leo put the paper down and looked at Rachel, who was holding a small payment bill. Her hands trembled as she read. Leo leaned closely to her so he could read it as well.

Poison Payment
Total due: $30.00 Store: none - bought in alleyway. Use: Nicolas Campbell

Rachel dropped the piece of shrivelled paper and cried. "It can't be!" she said. "He was poisoned, by Sir Evergreen, *poisoned*."

Leo hugged Rachel tightly and she cried into his shoulder, he held back tears, knowing that he had to be the strong one.

"Sir Evergreen will pay," Rachel said, her sadness turning to anger. "I will have him executed." She stood up, making Leo let go of her, and stomped up to the mirror. She replaced **Neverland** with *Oz*, placed her hands on her reflection, and stomped through the rippling glass.

"Rachel," Leo said worriedly before walking in after her, leaving the folder behind. Before he went through the mirror, he caught a slight glimpse of water, ice, and fire. A scary sensation formed in the pit of his stomach before he followed after her.

CHAPTER TWENTY-THREE

KANSAS BECOMES HELL, YAY

Leo fell into the middle of a wheat field, though he noticed it was a light grey, and all around him everything was in either black, grey, or white.

"Kansas," Leo muttered sarcastically. "How cheerful." He got up and walked out of the field, prepared to look for Rachel. "Where in the universe — *what the heck?*" Leo stopped in his tracks because of what he saw: Rachel, as a sorceress, was burning down everything she saw then making an ice barrier around the infernos. She was also making ivy shoot up from the ground and entangling animals and objects to keep them in place. Only one word could describe the way Leo felt at the moment: shocked.

"Rachel!" Leo yelled, yet he regretted it once the words fully left his mouth. Rachel turned around with a look of pure evil; the look in her eyes was the definition of rage.

"Rachel?" Leo asked cautiously, afraid he'd make her even angrier.

"Rachel is gone," Rachel said in her sorceress voice. "She has been replaced by the all-powerful Cleverly!"

"Cleverly, what the..." Leo was utterly confused.

"Now die!" Cleverly yelled, and then she threw a fireball at him. Luckily, Leo dodged the fire and it disintegrated the wheat behind him.

"So much for harvest season," he muttered.

"What was that?" Cleverly yelled. "You'll have to speak up!"

Leo dodged a spiked ice ball thrown by the sorceress. "Who are you?" he demanded.

"You don't listen well, do you?" Cleverly asked. "I am Cleverly the Sorceress!"

"What have you done to Rachel?" he asked.

"I've taken over her body!" she declared. "Now she belongs to me!"

"She will never belong to you!"

"And why is that?"

"Because her heart is strong and pure, just like a bar of gold! She would never let her body be taken over by such a pitiful being!" Leo roared.

"On the contrary, she is rather easy to take over," Cleverly said, falling for his stalling trap. "Whenever she is hurt or upset or has a strong feeling that is negative, I make a small deal with her and offer to make all her dreams come true if she lets me take over — though this time I'm not letting her return to her regular self."

"She will find a way to defeat you!" he yelled. "Or I will, but either way she will make it through!"

In the nearby distance a cyclone was approaching.

"Almost time to go," Cleverly said. "But you'll be long gone before then."

"You know," Leo said, "one thing kids at school hate about me is that I don't go away easily."

"Well, let's change that!" she yelled. She then threw three fireballs at him; Leo ran in circles to dodge the fire.

"Told you I don't go away easily!" Leo said loudly. Saying this aggravated Cleverly more than words could describe and she scowled deeply.

While Leo eyed the nearing cyclone, Cleverly took this as an opening and threw another fireball at him. Thankfully for Leo, the sorceress' anger was affecting her aim and she just barely missed him, singeing his hair instead of burning him alive.

A light breeze filled the air and Leo breathed it in for all it was worth. His relaxation soon came to a halt when the breeze turned to high winds and knocked him down to his knees.

Cleverly's scowl suddenly turned upside down. "Almost time," she said.

"You're going to *Oz* and are going to destroy the place?" Leo asked.

"Well, what better way to restart my reputation?" Cleverly said. "Destroy every fairy tale until those damned characters don't know the meaning of happily ever after, then go after your world, only leaving the strongest and baddest to survive."

"But why?" he questioned.

"You see, child, this universe had me locked away for many centuries before my dear great-great-granddaughter set me free in this girl's body," she explained.

"Is this all you can do? Manipulate your victims?"

"No, of course not! I am an all-powerful sorceress; that would just be pitiful!"

"Then prove it to me," Leo challenged her.

"I know what you're trying to do: get me to leave this girl's body and then show you something cool. Well, news flash, it won't work on me," Cleverly snapped.

"You're smarter than you look, *Grandma*," he said.

"Excuse me?!" she roared.

"Sorry, I meant *Great-great-great-grandma*."

"It's only two greats! And don't worry; you will see my full power! This isn't over!" Cleverly watched as the cyclone neared and she flew up to it. "Goodbye!" she roared in rage.

"Now I need to find the portal," Leo said. "But first I'll wait for that to go away." He walked into the nearby forest and slept on the ground to wait out the tornado.

As soon as his dream started, Leo wanted to wake up; the first thing he saw was Rachel with blood all over her body. Her eyes were closed and her body was lifeless. Vines were wrapped around her wrists, hanging her in the air.

Suddenly, a whip came out of nowhere and lashed itself against Rachel's bare belly, causing her skin to slice and blood to spill. She let out a scream of pain as Leo's vision cleared. He saw that she wore cloth around her chest. Another piece of cloth was tied low on her waist, reaching her mid-thigh. He looked down and realized that he stood on a cliff; he looked down farther and couldn't see the bottom of this nightmare, for there was thick black fog blocking his view.

"Rachel," Leo said.

"Leo?" Rachel questioned quietly, her eyes still closed.

"Rachel, it's me, Leo," he tried. The more he spoke, the farther away Rachel seemed.

Rachel slowly opened her eyes one at a time. "Leo," she whispered.

"Rachel, it's me!"

"Leo, I have to tell you—" she was interrupted by a knife, and just like the whip, it came out of nowhere before stabbing into her foot; she screamed in pain.

"Rachel!" Leo yelled. "I-I promise to save you! I promise!"

Rachel was let free and she fell to her death, her screams echoing all the way down. Leo woke with a jolt before his memories cleared. "Portal," he muttered. He stood up and looked around; the cyclone was gone, but everywhere around him was chaotic. Everything was burned to a crisp and the animals she'd wrapped in vines were gone: all you saw was half the vine, the other half ripped away. "Cleverly will pay," Leo said in a murderous tone. Determination and anger bubbled in his blood.

Though it took him almost an hour, Leo eventually found the portal. He charged into the pig pen and found himself in Sir Evergreen's room. He erased *Oz* and replaced it with Snow White before putting his hands on the glass and jumping through the mirror.

Leo appeared in front of the famous princess' castle.

"Which way was it?" he asked himself. "Maybe somebody around here knows."

Leo failed his first three attempts to find out the castle's location. When he asked a mother and her child, they ran off. Leo then asked a shopkeeper, but she just told him that the prince would never take a second glance at him. When he tried to speak to a lonely man wandering in the streets, the man completely ignored him.

"Do you know where the castle is?" Leo asked a dog near a tall oak tree, growing desperate.

He hadn't expected the dog to reply, but through his snout the dog said, "Go east from here and take a right in two miles, then stay on that route for ten minutes, and then you will arrive at Prince Silas' castle."

"Um," Leo said, unsure if he was hearing things or not, "thank you."

"No problem," the canine replied.

Leo ran off to a shop, flirted with the female shopkeeper until she gave him a map, and then went east, stayed on the route for two miles, took a right, and stayed on the route until he arrived at Silas' castle as a sweaty mess.

"I need to see Silas!" Leo yelled at the guards who wouldn't let him pass.

"I've told you: you can't see the prince unless he wants to see you!" one of the two guards said.

"What's all the fuss about?" a voice behind the guards asked.

The two guards turned and were shocked to see Silas. "Uh, Silas," one of the guards said.

"Leave," the prince said and the guards fled immediately.

"Silas, I need to talk to you!" Leo said instantly.

"Who are you?" the prince asked, playing dumb. "Oh right, you're that useless mutt from the cottage where I first met Rachel; you're her friend, correct?"

"Yes," Leo said. "This is really important."

"You've come here to tell me to leave Rachel, haven't you, disgusting mutt?"

"No, even though I'd love to," Leo said, getting frustrated. "But Rachel's in danger and I came here to recruit you to help me save her."

"Lies!" Silas reprimanded. "You dare lie to a prince!"

"Look, prince-boy-pain-in-the-butt, we can fight later to give me something to look forward to, but right now, Rachel needs us."

"Where is she?" Silas asked, not letting his guard down.

"You wouldn't believe me if I told you, but follow me; I can show you and take you there," Leo said.

"Take me there immediately!" the prince demanded.

"That was the whole point of me coming here," he said.

CHAPTER TWENTY-FOUR

TWO BOYS VERSUS CLEVERLY
THE SORCERESS

"So, how do we get there?" Silas asked Leo impatiently, tapping his foot on the ground repeatedly.

"Good question," Leo said with a sigh, looking at the clear skies of Kansas.

Without warning, winds picked up and a cyclone appeared in the distance.

"What the? How?" Leo asked gratefully.

"Miracle?" Silas suggested.

"In that case, thank God," Leo said. He started running towards the cyclone with Silas sprinting behind; obviously, he didn't run that much.

"Hey, why do you trust me?" Leo yelled at Silas.

"Because I can tell you love Rachel as much as I do, and I know well as hell that you know she loves me, so I know you wouldn't kill me because she'd cry!" Silas hollered.

"I do not love Rachel!" Leo bellowed.

"Then why are your cheeks red?" Silas shouted.

"Shut up!"

"You should tell her sometime!"

"I told you, I don't love her!"

The cyclone was fifty feet away.

"How do you explain your blood-red cheeks?" Silas yelled.

"I'm allergic to your stupidity!" Leo sneered. "I'm afraid I might die!"

At thirty feet away, the prince yelled, "Red-cheeked lover!"

"Prince dummy!" Leo shouted.

"Screwed up psycho!"

"Psychopath!"

At ten feet away, Silas added, "Must be getting it from you!"

"I know Rachel's deepest secret and you don't!" Leo bellowed.

Silas was going to shout another insult but instead, he just questioned, "Wait, what?"

The tornado hit them.

Silas' head was spinning with questions while Leo covered his mouth to keep himself from vomiting. They caught a glimpse of each other for a quick second before being separated by the high winds that would hopefully carry them to Oz.

Eventually, after spinning like a toy top for what felt like hours, the cyclone spat Leo and Silas out into a forest.

"Where are we?" Silas asked as Leo threw up behind a bush.

Leo finished what he was doing before he replied, "The forest that Dorothy falls into." He looked at Silas and remembered the prince knew nothing of the tale. "It's part of the story; you wouldn't understand."

They walked around aimlessly for a total of three hours, sometimes passing by burned trees covered in ice with a thick coat of ivy which told them they were going the right way.

Eventually, they saw water magically floating in the sky.

"There's Rachel," Leo said. "We have to save her. Go talk to her; it might snap her out of it."

"It *might*?" Silas said. "No, it *will*." He walked confidently towards Rachel and she flew down to meet his eyes.

"Hello, Rachel," Silas said in an unsteady tone.

"*Who are you?*" Cleverly asked. "*Oh, you were one of the girl's friends.*"

"*Were?!*" Silas yelled, enraged. "I *am*!"

"*Sorry to say,*" the sorceress said, "*but she's as good as dead.*"

"So, you just took over her body?" the prince asked.

"*Precisely,*" she replied heartlessly.

Silas drew his sword, ready to strike—

"*I wouldn't do that if I were you,*" Cleverly said in a warning tone.

"Why shouldn't I? Are you threatened by my glory?" Silas asked.

"*No, it's just that this is her body, so it wouldn't have any effect on me.*"

"That's cowardice!" Silas yelled. "You will be defeated!"

"By us both!" Leo yelled, running towards them.

"*Ugh,*" Cleverly said. "*The pesky little fly who won't go away.*"

"That's the only thing we agree on," Silas said. Leo punched him and he shut up.

"Say goodnight, because Rachel will find a way to defeat you," Leo sneered.

"*Goodnight,*" Cleverly said as a fireball formed in her hand.

"Rachel," Leo said, "I don't know if you can hear me or not, but you need to fight this horrible spirit! To come back, to marry Silas, and to have your Happily Ever After, just like you always wanted! That was the whole point of going through fairy tales!"

"*Shut up!*" Cleverly yelled.

"For the risk, for the adventure, and most of all, for the love of it all!" Leo said loudly, ignoring Cleverly. "We went through fairy tales to have our own special story!"

"Yes, Rachel," Silas joined in. "We all need you, come back, for me, for Leo, and for everyone else you love in this world. Our lives wouldn't be the same without you!"

"*You fools!*" Cleverly said, regaining the situation's power. "*Nothing you say will help! It won't change your fate; you will die by my hand! Here and now!*"

"Please, Rachel!" Leo and Silas yelled together.

The fireball in Cleverly's hand grew. "*Any last words?*" she sneered.

"Yes," Silas said. "You will be stopped."

"You will be defeated," Leo said.

"And die unknown!"

"Goodbye!"

A fire-breathing dragon would've looked harmless compared to the way Cleverly glared at Silas and Leo. "*Goodbye indeed,*" she said. She extended her arm back, ready to give the blow.

"If it isn't us, it will be somebody else who will kill you," Leo said.

"For once I agree," Silas added.

"*Die!*" Cleverly yelled as she threw the fireball—

Suddenly, the sorceress fell to her knees with a scream of pain.

Leo and Silas looked at each other, confused.

"Nobody hurts my friends!" Cleverly yelled, though it was Rachel's voice that was doing the talking.

"*Stupid child!*" Cleverly yelled in outrage.

"No," Rachel said. "You're the stupid one for taking over my body — big mistake!"

"*No, hands off me! This can't be the end; I refuse to believe it!*" Cleverly made Rachel's body stand back up and fly high above the trees.

"What the—" Rachel's voice tried.

"*I will die here; I know that much!*" Cleverly roared, flying higher and higher. "*But when I leave your body, you will fall to your death!*"

"Get out of my body, you wench!" Rachel yelled.

"*Fine!*" Cleverly yelled and Rachel turned back to normal; her clothes started turning to ash.

"Not good! Not good! Not good!" Rachel yelled, her arms flailing.

"We need to catch her!" Silas yelled, running around like a headless chicken.

"Wow, you think I didn't know that?" Leo asked.

"I'll do it, I've been in this situation before!" the prince said, running underneath the spot where Rachel would fall. "It's a long story for later, so don't ask!"

Rachel needed clothes, not a *boy* catching her. But it was either that or death, and so she slowly closed her eyes, accepting her sad fate, and fell into Silas' waiting arms.

"Hello, princess—" Silas started.

"Cover your eyes!" Rachel yelled and slapped her palm to Silas' face. She saw Leo gaping at her and she yelled, "You too!"

"Right, sorry!" Leo said, and he immediately covered his eyes with his hand.

Rachel slowly climbed out of Silas' grip and slowly exchanged her hand with his so he was covering his eyes, making sure he still couldn't see her. "I'll be back in half an hour!" she yelled and ran into the forest.

"So," Silas said, slowly removing his hand from his eyes.

"So," Leo repeated, doing the same as the prince.

"We'll wait for her," Silas said, sitting on the ground.

"How much do you love Rachel?" Leo asked immediately.

Silas just stared at Leo before responding, "With all my heart."

"I will believe you," Leo said. "But if you ever hurt her in any way, I will try to kill you."

"Got it," Silas said, lying down on his back and looking at the sky. "Look, there's a ring-shaped cloud."

"Look, right beside it," Leo said, laying down opposite from Silas. "It's a girl rejecting a guy."

"Those are fighting words!" the prince said and shot up to his feet, fists raised.

"Give me all you've got!" Leo said loudly, copying Silas' position.

Silas charged at Leo and tackled him, Leo punched the prince in the jaw, Silas kicked Leo in the stomach, Leo poked Silas in the eye...

Their fight escalated to the two of them shoving each other violently into trees, taking small animals and throwing them at each other, and taking sticks and fencing.

Soon Rachel came back, adjusting her leafy dress so it would stay up. "Ta-da!" she said loudly. When she got no reply she yelled, "Hello?" Without any reply to any of her statements, Rachel grabbed a stick and hit them both on the head. "Ta-da!" she exclaimed once again.

"You look great, Rachel," Leo and Silas said in perfect unison.

Rachel rolled her eyes. "Seriously?" she asked.

"What?" the boys said.

"My two favourite boys in the entire universe can't get along?" she said overdramatically. "Can't you two at least try?"

"Fine," Leo and Silas said, eyeing each other, ready to fight if the other showed any indication of doing the same.

Eventually, Leo broke the awkward silence. "So, how did you defeat Cleverly?"

"Well," Rachel said, sitting down between Leo and Silas, "I could hear you two talking to me, though at first I thought it was all just some weird dream, but when I realized it wasn't after I'd pinched my wrist a dozen times, I knew I had to do something. So, before everything clarified it was pitch-black, but far away I could see the faintest light. It took me only five minutes to get to the light and that's when I saw Cleverly's true form: an old hag. I kicked her in the back and she fell. Then I saw through my own eyes again the world around me, *Oz*, and I saw you two as well, working together, and that really made me happy. So, I fought Cleverly like you two told me to do, and I eventually got my body back."

"Wait, you said the light was far away but it only took you five minutes," Leo said, confused.

"Well, either I can run really fast or it just looked far away," she said.

"So, is this the last of your voyages?" Silas asked.

"Yes," Rachel said, smiling. "But I just need to do one last thing before the wedding."

"That is?" the prince asked.

"My friend, she's my guest, I just need to fetch her, and then I'll stay at your castle until the wedding."

Leo winced every time she said 'wedding.'

"I just need two things for that last voyage," she continued. "An invisibility spell and a counterspell for that."

"I can have my personal wizard make those for you," Silas said.

"Perfect," Rachel said. "How long do you estimate it will take?"

"At most, a day," the prince said.

"Okay," Leo said, needing to speak. "Let's go!"

"I know where the portal is!" Rachel announced.

"Is it in Kansas?" Leo asked.

"No, it's near here," Rachel said.

"So that means there can be more than one portal back home," Leo said.

"Well, that's pretty good, I guess," Rachel said before she stood up and helped Silas to his feet.

"But if the one you found is a lake, Silas over here will have a fit," Leo said whilst he got up to his feet.

"I didn't trust you, okay?" Silas said in his defence.

"It's okay," Rachel said, helping Leo up. "It isn't a lake; it's a tree, and Cleverly marked it, and I know the way." She led them to a large tree with a huge snowflake floating above it. "Here," she said.

Leo immediately ran through the tree after Rachel said it was safe; Silas followed. And Rachel came in behind them.

"Time to go to *Snow White*," Rachel said, getting up off the floor in Sir Evergreen's secret room. She replaced Oz with **Snow White** before putting her hand on the glass and jumping through the mirror.

"You next, pretty boy," Leo said, gesturing to the mirror.

Silas punched Leo's shoulder before walking through the rippling glass.

"Ow," Leo muttered before slowly walking through the mirror.

CHAPTER TWENTY-FIVE

ELISHA TOO?!

$\mathcal{T}$he three of them appeared in front of Silas' castle.

"*Home sweet home!*" Silas exclaimed.

"I am going to *love* this," Leo said, glancing over at the prince.

After three hours, Rachel was fully convinced Silas would have a heart attack.

"Why did I agree to this?" Silas yelled in his room, sitting on his king-sized bed. Rachel was sitting beside him, lovingly stroking his knee to calm his nerves, though it was not helping.

"It's for another twenty-one hours," Rachel said. "Just think: it'll eventually be over."

"Can I just go to sleep and wake up when he's gone?" the prince asked desperately.

"What did Leo ever do to you?" she asked.

"Exist," he mumbled.

Rachel laughed.

"He annoys me!"

She laughed even harder.

"Is something the matter?"

Rachel was clutching her stomach now.

"Rachel, are you fine?" Silas asked, genuinely concerned. Rachel eventually calmed herself down. "Sorry, I just find it hilarious how much you and Leo have in common, but then you guys both hate each other."

"We have stuff in common?" he asked, disgusted.

"Yes," Rachel said. "Of course."

"Like what?"

"Oh, wouldn't you like to know," Rachel pressed her forehead against his.

"The wedding is really soon," Silas said.

"I can't wait," she said. "I bet you it'll look amazing."

"Yes, it will, but not as good as you will," he said sweetly.

"I love you."

"I love you, too," Silas said, and then he kissed her lips passionately.

Leo was enjoying himself quite a bit; he could go wherever he pleased at any time he wanted, well, thanks to Rachel. At first, he was afraid that if Rachel went to the bathroom and he was left alone with the prince, Silas would beat him half to death, but instead, he was free to do whatever he wanted.

The first thing Leo did was go to the large kitchen and request a five-course meal, which took some time for him to fully consume. Afterwards, for the following hour he explored the castle. He found the servants' quarters, a large hall used for ceremonies and events, fancy lavatories, and to complete his day he found a room filled with cakes. He ate one before he looked at the clock hanging from the wall and decided he should find himself a guest bedroom to stay in. He walked back to the hall filled with guest bedrooms that he'd found earlier, chose a random one, and quickly fell asleep once his body made contact with the bed.

Rachel whispered a soft goodnight to Silas. They fell asleep in each other's arms, but little did they know their problems were far from over.

Early in the morning, Rachel felt something nibbling at her neck. She giggled lightly. "Silas," she said quietly.

"Yes?" Silas asked, still half-asleep.

"Stop it," she said in between giggles.

"Stop what?" he questioned.

"Stop what you're doing; it tickles."

"I'm not doing anything."

Rachel suddenly opened her eyes and saw black hair. She then realized what was happening: it was Night, sipping away at her blood. She screamed and kicked him off of her.

Silas sat up and saw a petrified Rachel, blood dripping from two holes in her neck. "Rachel," he said worriedly.

"It's him," Rachel said, pointing at Night.

"Who are you?" Silas demanded.

Night didn't waste any time and quickly jumped out of the open window.

Silas turned back to Rachel and hugged her to his chest. "It's going to be fine," he said.

"V-v-vampire," Rachel stuttered. "It's been three vampires that have drunk my blood, th-three."

Now the prince was ghostly white. "What was that?" he asked.

"Three vampires, then this," Rachel said, slowly shaking her head. "Why?"

"Wait, three vampires have drunk your blood, and then today?" Silas asked, worried.

"Yes," Rachel said.

"Rachel," the prince said, his voice shaky, "if you get bitten by three different vampires and then get bitten again, regardless of whether or not it's one of the vampires' second encounter with you, you will become a vampire."

Rachel shook her head faster. "No, tell me that you're just joking, please."

"I'm sorry," Silas said and hugged Rachel tightly.

"No, no, no; I can't become one of them," Rachel said as the tears started flowing down her cheeks. Silas slowly let go of her and she curled up into a little ball, still facing him. "It can't come to this," she said. "Yesterday it was fine, but today I'm going to become a—" she choked on her breath and pain suddenly started surging through her neck. Rachel let out one of the loudest screams she had ever made and clutched her throat. She felt the two holes in her neck clear and heal.

"Rachel!" Silas gasped, not sure what to do. He looked around and eventually spotted the glass lamp. "I'm sorry," he said. He took the glass lamp and smashed her in the forehead, and then she passed out cold.

Suddenly, Leo burst into the room in his pajamas. "I heard Rachel scream!" he exclaimed. Then he took in the scene: Silas holding a shattered lamp above Rachel's head, Rachel unconscious with tears flowing from her eyes, and the large bedroom window open.

"You *ass!*" Leo roared and punched Silas in the face, causing the prince to throw the remainder of the lamp directly next to Rachel's head.

"Look at what you could've done!" Silas yelled and punched Leo in the gut, even though his nose was already bleeding.

"What were you going to do?!" Leo screamed, his voice cracking. "Kill her and then throw her out the window?!"

"No!" Silas shot back. "I love her!"

"Well, I do too!"

"Too bad for you; she's mine!"

Rachel felt pain, then it went dark. She heard the sounds of glass shattering and furious yelling but it all felt so far away. She opened her tired eyes to see red on white, perhaps blood on a floor? The red spelled out the message: Avoid Temptations. Where had she seen those two words before? Oh yes, in every dream she'd ever had, for her entire life. Rachel now knew for sure that she was dreaming, for those words only made themselves present in her sleep. She continued to gaze at those words until they melted away and the surface beneath her feet caved in until there was just a tube. Gravity pulled her and she fell down the dirt hole; she then realized it was a rabbit hole. Then suddenly the walls around her turned to wind that spun her around. A beautiful tiled floor formed beneath her feet and the wind cleared; Rachel danced peacefully until fairy dust was sprinkled above her head. She rose high above the tiles, and then she saw a window roughly the shape of a door. She felt the urge to jump from it, and jump she did. She was high up, but the fall down was quick and she landed on a soft bed. Rachel pretended to sleep and waited for her one true love to come and wake her. She felt someone pick her up and gently kiss her cheek. When Rachel was put down, she saw Silas standing alongside Leo, both having blank stares across their faces, waiting for something.

"What do you want?" Rachel asked, though her voice made no sound.

Silas and Leo faded away and Rachel's outfit changed into the ballgown she'd worn at the first ball when she had danced with Jonathan. Then it changed to the light blue nightgown she'd worn at Rapunzel's tower, then to the dress when she'd faked her sleep at Sleeping Beauty's castle. This quickly changed to the natural outfit she'd made for herself in *Neverland*. The clothes she'd borrowed from the old woman in *Wonderland* formed onto her but quickly turned into the leaf dress she had crafted in *Oz*. But the next outfit was her favourite: a simple brown dress with a white apron, the outfit she'd worn when she first met Silas. She smiled, but that quickly faded when her dress and apron turned into a dress made of water. Frost quickly crawled up from her fingertips and faded away at her elbows, her eyes glowed gold, and Rachel was terrified of herself. She could see what she'd looked like in her monstrous stage and this sight almost brought tears to her eyes.

"Sorceress," Rachel whispered.

Then everything went dark. Rachel slowly opened her eyes. The pain was gone, but what creeped her out was Silas and Leo looking down on her. The two boys quickly stood straight up, avoiding her peculiar glances.

"Are you okay?" Leo asked immediately.

"Yeah, just fell asleep," Rachel said, rubbing her head.

Leo gave Silas a dirty look. "Actually, you didn't fall asleep; Silas knocked you out with a lamp," he said, crossing his arms.

Rachel looked at Silas. "Is that true?" she asked.

Leo smiled, ready to see Rachel dump Silas.

"It is true indeed," Silas said. "But only because you were in horrible pain and I couldn't bear to see you like that, so I let you sleep."

Leo's smile disappeared.

"Well, thank you, I guess," Rachel said, and then she smiled.

Leo and Silas looked at each other before swivelling back to Rachel, unsure if they were seeing things or not.

"What?" Rachel asked.

Silas opened the drawer of his nightstand, pulled out a mirror, and gave it to Rachel. "Angle it to your mouth," he instructed.

Rachel didn't know why he was acting this way, but she did as he said.

"Open your mouth," Leo said fearfully, realizing that there was a reason Silas had knocked her out, and he figured that was her transformation.

Rachel slowly opened her mouth and dropped the mirror at what she saw: her two top canine teeth were gone, replaced by two deadly sharp ones that were perfect for piercing skin. She slammed her mouth shut and turned to Silas. "What time is it?" she asked.

"Almost noon, why?" the prince replied.

Rachel blinked. "I have to go. Leo, come on."

Leo looked startled before he quickly nodded his head and followed Rachel out of the room, leaving Silas alone and dumbfounded.

"Where are we going?" Leo asked Rachel as she pulled him along down a set of hallways.

"To a guest room," Rachel replied simply, as though this answered all of his questions. After several minutes of running, Rachel brought Leo into a guest bedroom with a large red bed, two bathrooms, and many cabinets.

Leo looked fearful. "Why are we here?"

"You know why; now lock me in the bathroom!" Rachel said quickly after locking the entrance to the bedroom.

"I-I wouldn't do that to you," he said.

"Not a choice," Rachel snapped. "Once I pass out, I'll wake up and be all lovey-dovey mode on you, remember?"

"Oh, right," Leo said, recalling what had happened at the tree in *Neverland*.

Rachel suddenly passed out and fell onto the floor.

"Dear Lord, Rachel?" Leo asked. He knew that at any second she would wake up and love him, but he wouldn't literally drag her into the bathroom, and if he carried her it would take too long, so he stayed by her side and waited for her to awake. The sooner it started, the sooner it would be over.

Not many seconds passed before Rachel sat up with pink irises.

"Hey Lee Lo," she said sweetly, placing her hand on Leo's cheek.

"Just thirty more seconds, that's all," Leo said.

"Yeah, only a little thirty seconds," Rachel said, sticking her bottom lip out in a pouty face.

Leo eyed Rachel's hand before looking back at her.

"Rachel doesn't love me; snap out of it."

"But I know you love her. Admit it: you love these moments," she said.

Leo was shocked. He was frozen and immobilized and Rachel took this as an opening; she grabbed him by the collar and pulled him into her kiss.

Leo heard keys inside the lock outside of the guest room but thought it was only his imagination; he was wrong. The door burst open and in came Silas. "Rachel, what's the matter?" he asked. Though he didn't continue his questioning after what he saw.

Rachel suddenly turned back to normal and she pushed Leo away. "You know what happens!" she said loudly. "That I'm cursed to love you for a minute! Why didn't you lock me in the bathroom?!"

"Rachel," Leo said quietly.

"No excuses!" Rachel yelled. "You let me *kiss* you! That's outrageous!"

"Rachel," Leo peeped.

"WHAT?!" Rachel roared.

"Silas is over there," Leo squeaked, pointing at Silas, who just stared in shock.

Rachel turned swiftly. "Silas, look," she started.

"It's okay," Silas said, raising his hand to stop her. "I heard everything you just said. I heard that you're cursed to love Leo for a minute, and that's why you," loud cough, "kissed him."

"Look, you see this *idiot* over here?" Rachel said, gesturing to Leo. "Didn't lock me in the bathroom like I told him to."

"She had fainted and was lying unconscious on the floor; what was I supposed to do?" Leo said in his defence.

"I understand," the prince said. "I just want to know if it's permanent."

"No!" Rachel said before quickly adding, "just for two weeks. It started a couple days ago. The cure will be ready by the end of those two weeks, thank God." She looked at Leo. "No offence."

"None taken," Leo said with a shrug.

"Well, I'm going to the kitchen to get some food," Rachel said. She stood up and was about to leave when Leo grabbed her ankle like a small child.

"Please don't leave me with him," Leo pleaded.

"You'll be fine," Rachel said with a smile before she left.

"No!" Leo yelped and still held on to her.

Rachel lightly kicked him off before leaving the room, closing the door behind her. Leo stood up and was about to walk away when Silas punched him square in the face.

"Why?!" Leo yelled.

"You let my fiancée kiss you!" Silas raged.

"She was on the floor because she had fainted, okay?"

"Do what she wants you to do!"

"Would you have dragged her across the floor?" Leo yelled, throwing another punch.

"If that's what she really wanted!" Silas shot, dodging Leo's punch.

"You're such a spoiled brat!"

"Yeah, right; if I were spoiled, I would've chosen a rich girl as my wife! But if I could, I would run you through with my sword!"

"Why wouldn't you?!"

"Because I know Rachel cares for you, and if you were dead, she would be furious with me, and that's the last thing I want!"

Leo calmed down and so did Silas.

"Thanks for caring for her; you have no idea how much she loves you," Leo said.

"She really cares for you as well, I can tell," Silas said. "Now, I'm going to go check to see if my personal wizard has prepared the potions I need."

The prince left the room and realization struck down on Leo. "Wait," he said, disgusted. "Did me and Silas just get along?"

Rachel had just finished her dinner when Silas ran into the dining hall, calling her name out loud. She looked up from her plate. "Yes?" she asked.

"The potions are ready!" Silas exclaimed happily.

"Okay," Rachel said, wiping the corners of her mouth before standing up. "I'll drink the invisibility potion and leave the counterspell with you. If Leo asks, could you just tell him I'm sleeping?"

"Got it," Silas said. He took out two glass vials from his pocket and gave one to Rachel.

"Here we go," Rachel said before she popped off the cork and gulped down the concoction. Before long, her nose started disappearing, then it spread across her body until you could see right through her. "And it makes your clothes invisible!" she exclaimed.

"Be safe," Silas said as Rachel gave him back the vial.

"I will," Rachel said before walking away.

"I'll be waiting here for you!" Silas called.

Rachel walked out of the castle and to the lake in front of Snow White's palace. She jumped in and appeared in Sir Evergreen's office. She saw Nicolas' file still on the floor so she put the papers back into the folder and hid the file behind one of the sacks of cold coins. Rachel then rushed out of the academy and to the all girls' school.

After sevon hours, Rachel walked into the girls' academy. She opened the school doors and walked inside, careful to not make a sound. *Where would Hannah be?* she asked herself as she crept around the academy. *Oh, in her room,* she decided. Rachel ran to her and Hannah's dorm and opened the door slowly, surprised to see Hannah laughing alongside Elisha Bright, the person she despised the most.

"Wind?" Elisha asked Hannah.

"Probably," Hannah said, though she didn't finish her thought for Rachel interrupted,

"Hannah," she said. "I'm right here, in front of you!"

"Did you hear that?" Elisha asked.

"Yeah," Hannah replied.

"Look, I'm Rachel, remember? Your best friend?" Rachel said. "Here," she slapped both Elisha and Hannah across their faces.

"Ow!" they said together.

"Hannah, you're coming to my wedding!" Rachel said, grabbing Hannah's hand.

"Rachel left," Hannah said.

"I'm really her," Rachel said.

"No, she left in the middle of the night; I haven't seen her since."

Rachel rolled her eyes, leaned close to Hannah, and breathed out of her mouth. Hannah immediately scrunched up her nose. "Never mind; it's definitely Rachel," she said and waved her hand around the air in front of her face, accidentally slapping Rachel.

"Wow, thanks," Rachel said.

"I don't know how you're invisible, but I'll go with you," Hannah said. "But Elisha is coming with us."

"What?" Elisha and Rachel said together.

"Elisha too?!" Rachel said, outraged. "She is not coming with us to my fairy tale!"

"Hannah, I told you, Rachel hates me forever; there's no use," Elisha said.

"Rachel, just give her a chance. Elisha deserves a fresh start, just like you. Maybe a fairy tale is all she needs," Hannah tried.

Rachel moaned in annoyance. "One chance. Now follow my voice out of here."

Rachel led Hannah and Elisha to the front doors of the school without them being detected.

"That was easy," Elisha said.

"Zip it," Rachel snapped.

"Yes, ma'am," Elisha teased.

"Don't get on my nerves," Rachel warned.

"Sorry," Elisha said quietly.

Rachel then brought the two girls to the boys' school where she snuck them into Sir Evergreen's secret room and the mirror.

"Why wasn't anybody in the office?" Hannah asked Rachel.

"Because the headmaster of this place is an irresponsible twit," Rachel replied. "Now jump through the mirror."

"Rachel, have they been giving you alcohol?" Hannah asked, concerned.

"Oh, for crying out loud," Rachel said, and then she pushed Hannah and Elisha through the mirror. "There, actions always work." She jumped in.

The three girls appeared in front of Silas' castle and Rachel told them it was fine.

"Silas!" Rachel called and ran towards the prince who sat on the stairs in front of his castle. He heard her call, and then he tossed the vial over to her. Rachel barely managed to catch it and then she quickly poured the counterspell down her throat. Her nose was soon visible, then it spread, and before long, she was completely in view.

"Much better," Rachel said happily as she looked down at herself. She gave the vial back to Silas before she swivelled back to Elisha and Hannah. "Elisha, Hannah, this is my fiancé, Silas," Rachel said. She turned back to Silas. "Silas," she gestured to Hannah, "this is my best and only friend, Hannah." She cleared her throat and quickly added, "And the other person is Elisha."

Elisha and Hannah waved awkwardly while Silas bowed with one hand over his heart.

"Silas, do you know where Leo is?" Rachel asked the prince once he straightened from his bowing position.

"I think he's in the kitchen being a pig," Silas replied.

"Cool, give these two guest rooms and I'll go get Leo to meet them." With that said, Rachel rushed off to find Leo.

Silas turned back to Elisha and Hannah. "What does *cool* mean?" he asked.

Rachel rushed into the kitchen to see Leo eating chocolate cake. "Leo!" she called.

Leo looked up from his chocolate cake with frosting on his chin. "Where were you?" he asked.

"I brought over Hannah and her friend," Rachel said casually.

"You went to get them on your own?" Leo asked.

"Well, you have an icing goatee, but I can't take a picture of it, so I think we're even."

Leo immediately took a napkin and wiped the icing off of his chin. "What goatee?" he asked.

"Whatever," Rachel muttered before she cleared her throat and said, "Come and meet them; we'll be waiting in the hall with all the guest bedrooms. But not for long because I need to take them to Little Miss Maid Martha and have their dresses designed for the wedding." Rachel then rushed out of the kitchen.

"Well," Leo said, looking down at his unfinished piece of cake, "I will miss you, but I must go now."

Rachel met up with Silas, Hannah, and Elisha in the guest room hallway.

"Now," Rachel said to Elisha and Hannah, "there's someone else I want you two to meet; he should be here any second."

With perfect timing, Leo came running towards them immediately after Rachel finished her sentence.

"Hey," Leo said. "You wanted me to meet someone?"

"Yeah," Rachel said. "This one over here with the blond hair is Hannah, and the one over there with the black hair is Elisha." She turned around to face her two guests. "Hannah, Elisha, this is Leo, one of my only friends, right after Hannah."

"Nice to meet you," Leo said, and he shook their hands as though there was actually something professional about him.

"Okay," Rachel continued, "now that you've met, Silas, could you call Martha, you know, the maid that helped with my wedding dress?"

"Sure," Silas said calmly before he shouted, "*Martha!*" Instantaneously, Martha came running towards them at full speed, stopping perfectly in front of Silas before curtseying and standing straight back up. "Yes, Sir?" she asked.

"First of all," the prince said, "is Rachel's wedding dress ready?"

"Yes, Sir," Martha replied quickly. "It's in the future queen's chambers."

"I have chambers?" Rachel whispered to Silas.

"Yes," Silas whispered back before he diverted his attention back to his maid. "These two guests need dresses for the wedding. They will design them, of course. Now, go off with them."

"Understood," Martha said. She turned to Elisha and Hannah. "Please come with me." Without giving them a second to take a step, the maid grabbed the two guests by their hands and dragged them away.

"Silas," Rachel said, "could you maybe come with me to arrest some very bad people?"

"Who?" Silas asked as Leo walked into his guest bedroom, ready to take a nap.

"Well, one of them killed a boy who was my friend, and the other three tried to kill me, several times," Rachel said.

"I'll have the army ready in less than an hour," Silas said firmly and quickly rushed off.

"I wonder if Leo's doing anything important," Rachel whispered to herself when Silas was out of view. She walked into Leo's guest room to see him lying in his bed.

"Yeah?" Leo asked.

"You're going back home to live there, right?" Rachel asked.

"Mmhmm," Leo said, nodding his head.

"Could you do me a favour?" she asked.

"Yeah totally, what?" he questioned.

"Could you perhaps break the mirror?"

Leo sat straight up. "Rachel, if I broke the mirror, then I wouldn't ever be able to talk to you again."

"I know," she said. "But it's for the safety of both worlds, so nobody ends up like Sir Evergreen, or at least not with a mirror. Just for the peace of these worlds."

Leo slowly shook his head. "I'll break the mirror, if you promise it'll make you happy."

"Thanks, Leo," Rachel said sleepily, not answering his question. "It means a lot. Now scooch over; I'm tired."

"Didn't you say you'd never sleep with a boy?" Leo asked as he scooted over.

"You're no boy; you're one of my best friends," she said, pulling the comforter and sheets back.

"If I'm not a boy, then what am I?" he questioned.

"You're a human."

"But if I'm not a boy, but I *am* a human, does that make me a girl?"

"You would be a weird girl."

"So, I'm a boy?"

"No, you're a," yawn, "human."

"But every human has a gender," Leo said.

"Hmmm," Rachel said. "You figure it out." With that said, Rachel fell asleep with her head in Leo's lap.

Leo looked at Rachel who slept peacefully using his lap as a pillow. He yawned and fell asleep.

"Rachel," Rachel felt someone nudge her.

"Hmm?" she mumbled.

"Why are you here?" the voice asked.

"Because I want to be here," Rachel replied.

"Why are you sleeping with Leo?"

"Because he's my best friend."

"Rachel, open your eyes."

Rachel slowly opened her eyes and saw Silas staring down at her, his arms crossed. She sat straight up and looked around. Leo lay passed out beside her with a temporary dent in his thigh.

"The army is ready," Silas said.

"Okay," Rachel said, pulled the comforter back.

"Hannah and Elisha are in the kitchen," he said.

"Good," she said, getting out of bed.

"Why were you sleeping with Leo?"

"Because I was talking to him and I guess we both just fell asleep."

"Okay, well, like I said, the army is ready."

"Well, let's go!" Rachel said excitedly and ran out of the room.

Silas eyed Leo with hatred before running off after Rachel.

Before long, Rachel was helping royal soldiers jump into the pond in front of Snow White's palace.

"Silas," Rachel said at one point, "I think we should leave fifty soldiers here because honestly, I don't think we need that many men to join us. Three more would be enough."

"Yes," Silas agreed. "From what you've told me, they don't have much of a defence system."

Rachel let only three more soldiers jump into the pond. Afterwards, Silas gave his army specific orders to stay at the pond. Rachel then took Silas' hand and they jumped into the pond.

CHAPTER TWENTY-SIX

YOU'RE UNDER ARREST

$\mathcal{R}$achel and Silas appeared in Sir Evergreen's secret room along with the ten soldiers.

"Rachel," the prince said, "you lead the way."

Rachel nodded. She then opened the door to Sir Evergreen's office, and for once, he was there. "Hello?" the headmaster said, trying to seem innocent.

"You have committed so many crimes," Rachel said firmly. "You are guilty of stealing from the universe inside the mirror numerous times, and you are guilty for the murder of Nicolas Campbell."

Sir Evergreen immediately stood up and ran out of his office. The soldiers looked at Rachel and she nodded; the men under her control then ran out of the office.

By the time Rachel and Silas made it to their soldiers, Sir Evergreen was tied up and had two soldiers holding him from behind.

"Where are the other three?" Silas asked Rachel.

"I'm pretty sure I know," Rachel said, and then she led Silas and the remaining soldiers to the hallway where

Zach, Vic, and Alex had almost killed her. Just as she had guessed, the three boys were lying on the floor.

"Arrest them," Rachel commanded.

The soldiers had already tied up Vic and Zach when Alex found his last bit of strength. He bolted to Rachel and in a swift motion grabbed her by the throat and rose her above the ground.

"I'm telling you," Alex said, "I will kill you."

"Get away from her!" Silas yelled. "Guards, seize him!"

But as the soldiers tried to pry Alex away from Rachel, he held his grip on her neck. "I will ruin your life, scar you," Alex said. "And then I'll kill you so brutally that nobody will be able to tell the corpse is you!"

One of the guards punched him in the face and Alex finally lost his grip on Rachel. Together the soldiers tied him up and Silas hugged Rachel tightly. "He will never do that to you," Silas whispered into Rachel's ear.

"I know," Rachel said as Alex's words rang in her ears.

"Take them back to the mirror," Silas said firmly and his soldiers quickly obeyed.

The soldiers, the soon-to-be prisoners, Silas, and Rachel went back to Sir Evergreen's secret room.

"Okay, we just need to go back through the mirror," Rachel instructed.

The soldiers all nodded. "Yes, future queen," they said in unison before they marched one at a time through the rippling glass.

When the soldiers and prisoners were gone, Rachel asked Silas, "Did you tell them to call me that?"

"Maybe," Silas replied with a smug smirk.

Rachel playfully punched Silas, who scooped her up in his arms and walked through the mirror, turning sideways so Rachel wouldn't collide with the mirror's frame.

"Can you believe that Rachel's getting *married?*" Hannah asked Elisha as they were being fitted for their dresses.

"Well she *is* allowed to grow up, and I think that marriage is a big part of growing up," Elisha replied. "And I'm really happy for her."

"Me too, but I really can't wait to see her in a wedding dress," Hannah said with a few snickers.

"Do you think there will be any objections?" Elisha questioned.

"No, I don't think so; why would you ask such a ridiculous question?"

"I don't know. I guess I just wanted to see what you'd say."

Rachel and Silas appeared in front of his castle along with the soldiers and prisoners.

"Put me down," Rachel said.

"Yes, future queen," Silas said smugly whilst he gently let her feet touch the ground.

"Don't call me that," Rachel said. "I'll be in my chambers." With that said, she ran off into the castle.

Silas smiled as she ran through the door. When she was out of his view, he turned back to his soldiers. "Put these disgusting criminals inside the dungeons and throw away the key!"

"Yes, Sir!" the soldiers replied before taking the four prisoners inside the castle.

When his soldiers were out of his view, Silas walked over to the maze of roses and walked in, planning to get lost.

Not finding his way back was *not* part of Silas' plan. But then again, he did want to get lost in the maze.

"Great, just great," he muttered to himself as he found himself at another dead end.

Silas eventually gave up on the idea of finding his way out and climbed up onto the wall of roses. He saw his castle about ten walls away and he jumped to the next wall. "Just about ten more of those," he said under his breath.

Rachel eventually found her chambers in the huge castle. She kicked open the doors and gasped at how amazing it was. Her bed was just over the size of a king bed, and the actual room was the size of a quarter of a football stadium. Rachel walked over to her bed and spotted her wedding dress: it was gorgeous and just how she wanted it to look. She went over to her bathroom and looked at the sparkling sink, the smooth walls, and the perfection of it all. Rachel walked over to her closet and just laughed at the enormous size; it could've easily been mistaken for two bedrooms missing a wall. Shelves and racks lined the walls, and there were actual mirrors. In the centre of her closet was a huge bench.

Rachel suddenly heard a knock at the door. "Yes?" she called.

"It's Martha."

Rachel rushed over to the door and opened it. "Hello, Martha."

"How do you like the dress?" the maid asked.

"It is the definition of gorgeous," Rachel said.

Martha smiled at this. "Good to know," she said.

Rachel noticed Martha was carrying a cauldron. "What's that for?" the future queen asked.

"To give you warm water," the maid replied simply.

"Oh, yes, but what's going to heat it up?"

"The fireplace."

Rachel turned around and noticed a large fireplace with a stack of chopped wood beside it. She quickly turned her attention back to Martha. "I can take the cauldron from here," she said.

"It is really heavy," Martha warned.

"Come on, don't doubt me." Rachel took the cauldron from Martha and immediately regretted it. "Dear Lord, what's in this thing? Bricks?"

Martha calmly took the cauldron back and brought it to the fireplace. "Just water," she said.

"Anyway, I'm going to change into something nice and then head out to find Silas," Rachel said, walking into her large closet and closing the doors behind her.

Martha shrugged her shoulders and walked out of the room after hanging the cauldron on the hook above the firewood in the fireplace.

Rachel chose to wear a simple purple dress with matching shoes and her hair in two braids. She looked fairly good.

Leo held his stomach as he looked for Rachel's chambers, feeling like he was going to explode because of the amount of food he'd eaten. "Do you know where the queen's chambers are?" he asked a random guard who nodded.

"Just go down this hallway and you'll eventually see them," the guard replied.

"Thank you," Leo said before continuing to walk. He eventually found Rachel's chambers and knocked at the door.

"Come in!" Leo heard Rachel's voice call. He opened the door and Rachel ran out of her closet wearing blue jean overalls and a white T-shirt. She grabbed Leo by the wrist and pulled him onto her bed. "How do I look?" she asked.

"You look fine, why?" Leo said.

Rachel rolled her eyes and ran back into her closet, coming back out several minutes later wearing a blue knee-length dress. "How do I look?" she asked.

"Really, really good," Leo said with big eyes, standing up to get closer to her.

Rachel smiled and started, "I'm going to miss you. I don't know how to say this." She looked down at her hands as she fiddled with the fabric of her dress. She looked up nervously then quickly back down.

"Rachel," Leo said. "Are you alright?"

Rachel took a strong step forward and basically jumped into his arms, hugging him tightly, she gripped his back as if her life depended on it. Leo's breath hitched quickly, but he hugged back, holding her tightly in his arms.

"I'm going to miss you," Rachel said into Leo's chest. "You better not die or something, got it?"

"Got it," Leo said. "Now I just need to go back home, and then I can break the mirror."

"Yeah," Rachel said. She walked out of the room, then she walked back in and looked through the drawers in her nightstand. "You need something to break the mirror with," she said as she pulled out a deadly sharp knife.

Leo gulped as he carefully took the knife from Rachel's hands.

"Now let's go," Rachel said, and she walked back out of her chambers. Leo followed like he always did. She led him out of the castle and in the direction of Snow White's palace.

Eventually, Leo asked her, "Why do you want me to break the mirror?"

Rachel stopped in her tracks for a moment before continuing. She did not look back. "I told you," she said, "I don't want anybody to follow in Sir Evergreen's footsteps."

"Why can't you come home, though?" he asked.

"Because Silas is here, and Silas is my happily ever after."

"If Silas really loved you, he would come with you to where you would want to be."

"Leo, don't you understand Silas' position? He's a prince, which means he's going to eventually be king, which means he can't just abandon his kingdom for me, and besides, I like it here." She turned around and hugged Leo for the last time. "We're inside a fairy tale, but not everything can be achieved or altered," she said quietly.

"Fine," Leo said as Rachel let go of him.

"Okay," Rachel said and Leo could've sworn he saw a tear roll down her cheek as she turned around. He said nothing, like a dog following its owner.

If only that owner wasn't leaving the dog.

Forever.

"Here we are," Rachel said as she and Leo stood in front of the pond in front of Snow White's palace.

"Ladies first," Leo said.

"If you say so," Rachel said before jumping into the pond.

"I'm going to tell her," Leo muttered before jumping in after her.

They appeared in Sir Evergreen's secret room.

"Are you ready?" Rachel asked.

"Yes," Leo said, even though he was terrified of saying goodbye. He took out the knife from his pocket and stared at it for a moment before he looked back into Rachel's eyes. "The antidote for the love thing is on your nightstand."

"Thanks," Rachel said. "I'll miss you." She gave him a tight hug. "So, you'll just have to erase **Snow White** and then stab the mirror and chalkboard; the chalkboard is just to be safe, but yeah, just in case."

"Rachel," Leo said, putting the knife down beside the mirror.

"Yeah?" Rachel asked.

"Remember at the dwarves' cottage when I kissed you, pretending to be Silas? You asked me why, but we were interrupted by the dwarves?"

"Oh yeah," Rachel said, recalling the memory.

"You said we would get back to it." He grabbed her shoulders. "Let's get back to it now, right now, without any interruptions this time."

"Leo, you're acting weird—" Rachel said.

"Look, Rachel," Leo said, interrupting her. "I kissed you because—" he took in a deep breath. "Because I love you!" He kissed Rachel once on her soft lips before pushing her back through the mirror. He erased **Snow White** from the chalkboard and stabbed the solidified mirror and chalkboard with his knife. Shattered glass and charcoal fell around him and he exhaled the deep breath he'd taken in.

Rachel appeared in front of Silas' castle, flustered. She didn't know how to react or what to think of it, but she pushed it to the back of her mind, remembering that she was going to be married in less than two weeks.

CHAPTER TWENTY-SEVEN

LEARN YOUR VOWS

$\mathscr{R}$achel tried to keep Leo out of her mind the best she could, but he was on her mind from dusk till dawn, every day. And every day at noon she'd lock herself in her closet with chocolate cake to calm the feelings down.

Luckily, Silas unintentionally gave her something to keep her away from her thoughts. He'd said it was tradition for the bride and groom to prepare vows for the wedding. So, in all her spare time, Rachel worked on that. It was seven days to the wedding and she had to memorize her vows. Pretty simple, right?

Easier said than done. It had been six days and the next day would be her wedding, though she didn't know where it would take place. On that night she worked extra hard to memorize her vows. She repeated each word of every phrase to herself in order over and over again until it was stuck solid in her memory. Before she jumped into bed, she said her vows aloud: "Meeting you could only be described as fate; becoming your friend was the best choice of my life;

but falling in love with you I had absolutely no control over. I love you more than my life. I promise with all my loving heart to rule by your side until the day we must part. But even after death, my feelings for you won't change, not even in the slightest. I will watch down on you until you join me, and even then, I will love you eternally." Rachel exhaled and popped the cork off the vial of lagoon water. She swallowed it all down in one gulp and jumped into bed, and before even a minute had passed, she fell into the most blissful sleep she'd ever had.

Morning sun woke Rachel and the maids came running in, ready to get Rachel ready for the most important day of her life.

As Martha helped Rachel with her wedding dress, the future queen recited her vows, though it was all just a blur.

"You'll be fine," Martha reassured her. "It's just the pressure getting to you."

"At least one of us thinks so," Rachel muttered under her breath.

Rachel attempted to recite her vows as she ate breakfast, but nothing came out right.

"They'll come flowing back the minute you need them," Martha said as she secured Rachel's veil, though her voice was slightly uneasy.

As Martha put all of Rachel's jewellery on, Rachel again tried to recite her vows, but like all of her other tries, nothing came out correctly.

"You'll remember them," Martha said, sounding desperate.

"Who do you want to walk down the aisle with you?" Martha asked Rachel before they had to leave for the wedding.

"Hannah," Rachel replied quickly before going back to attempting to recite her vows.

Twenty minutes later, Rachel stood inside the dwarves' cottage. Apparently, Silas wanted their wedding to be special, and so he had made arrangement for the wedding to take place where they first met. It made Rachel's heart smile as she stood next to her best friend on the happiest day of her life.

"The doors will open and you'll see blue petals leading you to where you're supposed to be," Martha said to Rachel before she ran off.

Rachel stared at the door as she recited what she hoped were her vows.

"What's on your mind?" Hannah asked.

"I can't remember my vows, but I'm hoping they'll come back to me when the time comes," Rachel said. Rachel turned to look at Hannah for the first time all day, and when she did, her jaw dropped. Hannah had her hair done up gorgeously, her dress was silver without any sleeves, around her neck hung a diamond necklace, on her feet were glass shoes, and on her face was the perfect amount of makeup.

"Hannah," Rachel said, "you look stunning."

"You look better," Hannah said, blushing.

"I can't believe this day is actually happening," Rachel said and smiled. "If someone told me over a year ago that I'd be marrying a prince, I would have called the local asylum and have that person locked up — but look at me now!"

Slowly, the doors opened and Rachel gasped at the sight. In the daisy field in front of the dwarves' cottage on either side of the makeshift aisle were wooden pews, perfectly placed. She looked at the end of the aisle and saw Silas wearing a white suit. A small boy was beside him holding a pillow with two rings on it. Diagonally behind Silas was a priest reading through his book of lines. Rachel grabbed Hannah's arm in shock and wonder as they slowly walked down the aisle. Music started playing and Rachel saw Doc, one of the dwarves, playing the piano that had been set up beside the cottage. The people in the pews stood and turned to look at Rachel; their huge smiles, especially those on Silas' parents' faces, only made Rachel's smile grow larger. And even better, her vows were starting to come back to her.

Rachel and Hannah made it to the first row of pews. Hannah left Rachel and sat next to Elisha, who wore a beautiful blue dress that made Rachel self-conscious of her own clothing. She would've definitely punched Elisha for wearing something that made her look plain, but this was her wedding, and she wouldn't let anything ruin it. She walked up beside Silas and turned to face him.

The guests in the pews sat down and smiled at the soon-to-be married couple.

"You look amazing," Silas mouthed to Rachel.

"You, too," Rachel mouthed right back.

"Today we are here to see the binding of these two souls," the priest started. "The binding of Prince Silas Charming and Miss Rachel Free Angel."

Rachel smiled, but then suddenly her vows disappeared as quickly as they had returned, and she frantically tried to remember them.

"Please join hands," the priest said. Rachel and Silas held each other's hands in love. "As tradition," the priest continued, "the groom will start by saying his vows followed by his future queen. Please start."

"Like the sun, water, and food, I need you to live happily and healthily. Without you, I'm empty inside. Today, you will be mine forever, officially. When you are sick, I will do everything in my power to help. When something troubles you, I will eliminate your worries. I will love and comfort you so you never feel alone. I love you with all my heart and I ask that you agree to be mine," Silas said lovingly.

"Now the future queen," the priest said.

"Um," Rachel said, "meeting you could only be described as... love. Becoming your friend... uh, good choice. But, um, falling in love with you, I couldn't control. I like you more than life. I promise to rule by your side until I die. And my feelings for you won't change."

"Um," the priest said, cringing, "Prince Silas Charming, do you promise to love Rachel Free Angel eternally for the rest of your lives, until death shall you part?"

"I do," Silas said with a smile, ignoring Rachel's sad excuse for vows.

"Miss Rachel Free Angel, do you take Silas as your husband, through sickness and health, until death shall you part?"

"I... um," Rachel said. "I—"

"Excuse me," Elisha said. She stood in the aisle and flashed a wicked smile at Rachel. "I forgot to say, *I object.*"

Rachel let go of Silas' hands and glared at Elisha. "Why you little—"

"Angel?" Elisha said. She looked down at herself. "I know; I look fabulous today."

Hannah swirled to Elisha in shock. "Elisha, you — you tricked me! You made me think you'd changed! You lied! About our friendship, about *everything!*"

"No," Elisha said calmly, "the friendship was very true, the one between Rachel and I; *tell her. Rachel.*"

Hannah spun to Rachel for an explanation. "Was it?" she demanded.

Rachel glanced between her best friend and her greatest nemesis and grunted in frustration. "Yes, we were friends. But that, but whatever that sad excuse was, is as dead as my parents."

"Rachel," Hannah said, calming down, "you never told me about your parents."

"Well, what was I supposed to say?" Rachel roared. "'Hey Hannah, by the way, my mom was burned alive and my father died of an alcohol addiction.' Come on! My mom, one of the most important people in a child's life, died when I was two years old, and my dad died when I was five! My relatives took everything we owned, everything, and either kept it or threw it out! On top of it all, remember that bruise I had on my hip for a while? Well, *deary*, that was because my abusive uncle literally threw me into his truck before bringing me to the girls' school! That hell! And I didn't tell you because you'd go all 'oh poor sweetie' mode on me and that was the *last* thing I needed!"

"I-I'm so sorry," Hannah said, tearing up. "I-I never knew."

"And to make things worse," Rachel continued, pointing at Elisha, "this brat went to the same school to be with me like some stalker! And after that, until I left, every damned girl in the school despised me, and they probably still do."

Silas, the priest, and everyone else stayed quiet, unsure of what to say.

"Well, sorry about your life," Elisha cut in, "but this little chat answered my question about why you're so messed up, and I wouldn't be surprised if it ran in the family, oh, your poor relatives."

Rachel looked at Elisha as though she wanted to kill her, which she did. "Like you're one to talk," she sneered. "You're the one who went to the same school as me just so you could be with me, and then there's your persisting insanity."

"You're the one who won't come and actually fight me."

"Gladly!" Rachel yelled and ran over to Elisha. "Ever smell knuckles?" Before Elisha could reply, Rachel rammed her fist into her nose. When she withdrew, blood ran down Rachel's fingers and dripped onto the floor.

"I hate you!" Elisha yelled with a bloody nose.

"Likewise."

Elisha kicked Rachel in the stomach so hard that she stumbled back into the altar.

"Stop this madness immediately!" the priest demanded.

Ignoring the priest and the pain in her back, Rachel shot back up to her feet and was about to run back to Elisha—

Silas wrapped his arms around Rachel, keeping her in place. "She is no threat to us," Silas whispered in her ear from behind. "We can lock her away in the dungeon as soon as we're married."

Rachel looked up at his reassuring smile and let the matter go. He was right; what could *Elisha* do to a *king* and *queen*? "Can't wait," she said, settling down. She stood up to her full height. "And I remember my vows now."

"But—" Elisha started.

"Zip it, child," the priest snapped. "Haven't you caused enough trouble?"

Elisha dropped down onto the pew, crossed her arms, and put on a pouty face.

Rachel took a deep breath and restarted, "Meeting you could only be described as fate; becoming your friend was the best choice of my life, but in falling in love with you, fate took the reins and I'm so glad they did. I love you more than life itself. I promise to rule by your side until the day I die. But even beyond the grave, my feelings for you won't dull. I will watch down on you until you join me, and even then, my love for you won't change, not even in the slightest." She took in a deep breath. "I love you."

"I love you, too," Silas said.

"You may kiss the bride," the priest said.

Silas placed a hand behind Rachel's back and the other on the back of her head and dipped her whilst kissing her passionately, making the crowd cheer wildly.

Once Rachel and Silas parted, the priest continued, "And now that the prince is married, he will be king, and his wife shall be queen." He whistled and two small girls wearing identical knee-length white lace dresses walked down the aisle, each carrying a purple pillow with a crown resting on top.

"Fudgeball donuts, those are gorgeous," Rachel said in awe.

"It'll look even better on you," Silas whispered into her ear.

The girls carrying the crowns arrived at the altar and the priest continued once again. "First, we will crown the prince, for he is the heir to the throne; then, we will proceed to his wife." He took the crown from the girl on the left and turned to Silas, who bowed down. "Prince Silas, will you lead this kingdom justly and never betray it?"

"Yes," Silas said without hesitation.

"Hereafter, people will now know you as *King* Silas," the priest said, and he placed the crown atop the new king's head. He took the other crown and turned to Rachel. "Rachel," he said, "do you promise to lead this kingdom justly and never betray it?"

"Yes," Rachel said, bowing down just like Silas had done.

"Hereafter, you shall now be known as *Queen* Rachel." He placed the crown on top of Rachel's veil and she slowly stood up, not used to how this new weight on her head felt. Silas looked at Rachel and smiled at her lovingly. "I'm a queen," she said, almost in a squeak.

The priest cleared his throat before continuing, "We will all return to the castle to celebrate in the ballroom; invitations are necessary to be let in." He walked away from Rachel and Silas and in the direction of the village near the castle.

"Guards," Silas said immediately, addressing the soldiers behind the pews, "arrest Elisha, here, in the front row, and put her in the dungeons."

Elisha gasped. "You can't!" she shrieked.

Rachel walked up to her nemesis and smirked. "He just did," she whispered before walking to Silas and linking her arm in his.

The soldiers grabbed Elisha by either arm and started marching her towards the castle.

Rachel and Silas took their seats in a beautiful carriage to go back to the castle while the king's parents were put in another carriage. They set course as everyone from the pews followed behind.

Upon their arrival in the village, the two carriages were bombarded with cheers from the crowds along the streets leading up to the castle.

Silas opened the carriage door for Rachel whilst his father did the same for his mother and they hurried into the castle, along with the many invited guests.

"Where's the ballroom?" Rachel whispered to Silas, who let out a small chuckle.

"It's right down this hallway, actually," Silas whispered back.

"Gotcha," she said.

They walked down the remainder of the hallway, took a quick turn, and arrived in an extraordinary ballroom with a smooth wooden floor. Gold chandeliers with at least twenty candles were hanging from the ceiling. Beside the doorway on the other end of the room was an orchestra, ready to play at any moment.

"And here's the ballroom," Silas said happily, leading Rachel to the middle of the dance floor as the guests flooded in.

Once everyone had arrived, the orchestra started playing a glorious symphony perfect for Valentine's Day.

"Ready to dance?" Silas asked his queen.

Rachel snapped to attention. "What? I can't dance," she said quickly.

"Don't worry," the king said. "I figured that would be the case. I had my shoes made out of solid wood, so if you stepped on my foot it wouldn't hurt."

"I don't know about this," Rachel said quietly.

"Just try." Silas placed his right hand on her waist and the other on her shoulder. "Now you put your hands on my shoulders," he explained. Rachel quickly did so and he continued, "Now, when I step back with my right foot you step forward with my left, and vice versa. As for the parts that only look difficult, it's just us waltzing around the dance floor. To put it simply, it's the same thing over and over again, occasionally moving about."

"Okay, seems simple," Rachel said.

"Ready?" Silas asked.

"No," she replied.

"*Now*," the king said and started stepping back. Rachel quickly stumbled forward, barely missing Silas' toes, and they continued, back and forth, until Silas slightly pulled her back, forcing her to move along the dance floor with him. At one point, when she needed to step back with her right foot, she stepped on the bottom of her dress and tripped. Luckily, Silas tightened his grip on her and made it look like her small trip was planned.

"Thanks," Rachel whispered.

"No problem," Silas answered. "Wouldn't want our queen to get hurt, now, would we?" He took his right hand off of her waist and grabbed her hand. He reached out, still holding onto her, and they glided blissfully across the smooth floor. At one point, Silas twirled her away from him and quickly brought her back, planting his left hand on her back. With the speed and dizziness, Rachel fell back, depending on Silas' hand.

"How much more of this?" the queen asked, standing back up.

"Well, after this there's cake," Silas said.

"Cake?" Rachel asked and her eyes lit up with joy.

"Over at the table in the far corner," Silas said, and he nodded to the part of the ballroom he was referring to.

Rachel traced his gaze to a table with a large five-layered cake on top.

"Oh, dear Lord," Rachel gasped and accidentally stepped on Silas' foot.

"Do you want some?" the king asked.

Rachel quickly nodded, her eyes never leaving the cake. "What flavour is it?"

"Marble," he replied.

"I need it," she rasped.

"Three more minutes then we can have it, and maybe some of the marshmallows dipped in chocolate."

Rachel turned to him quickly. "What?"

"Look, on the table beside the cake."

And there it was, beside the majestic cake was a chocolate fountain, and alongside it was a plate holding large marshmallows. Beside the plate was a cup with skewers so you wouldn't get your fingers covered in chocolate.

"Two minutes," Rachel protested.

"Okay, my queen."

They waltzed around the ballroom, Rachel counting down the seconds until she could get a taste of the precious cake.

"One hundred and fifteen," she said. "One hundred and fourteen, one hundred and thirteen..."

"Fifty, forty-nine, forty-eight, forty-seven..."

"Twenty, nineteen, eighteen..."

"Three, two, *one.*" Rachel quickly grabbed Silas' hand and brought him to the cake.

"Since we are done dancing we will move on to the food!" Silas called out for every guest to hear.

At these words, the guests cheered.

"Ready?" Silas asked as he picked up the large knife that was beside the cake.

"Don't swing the knife around!" Rachel joked and laughed. "But yeah, slice this baby open." She licked her lips. She then noticed what she had said and her eyes widened. "I didn't mean for it to sound like that."

Silas chuckled and nodded. "It's okay; it was funny."

Rachel smiled at his remark.

As Silas was about to slice into the cake, he somehow, as though he'd never held a knife in his life, let the knife slip and it cut his index finger, drawing blood.

"Are you okay?" Rachel asked. She leaned down to get a closer look, but suddenly, a scent filled her nose and she gasped. The smell was sweet and something she wanted to smell forever. She stood straight back up, ignoring the smell and her sudden dizziness. Rachel grabbed a napkin and the knife. "Here," she said, giving Silas the napkin. "Are you going to be okay?" she asked.

"Yeah," the king said. "And look, I wrapped the napkin around the cut and folded it in the corner so it won't come off."

"Okay," Rachel said. She took a plate from beside the cake, quickly cut two slits into the pastry, and served the slice onto the plate. "Hungry?" she asked.

"You bet," Silas said, and then he smiled. He cleared his throat and called out, "*Martha!*"

Martha immediately ran into the ballroom, closed the door behind her, and stopped directly in front of Silas. "Yes, Sir?" she asked.

"I want you to make sure every guest in this room gets a slice of cake," Silas instructed.

"Yes, King Silas," the maid said, and then she stood in front of the cake, already cutting out slices.

Rachel turned to Silas, holding two forks. "Dig in," she said, smiling widely.

"Wouldn't have it any other way," Silas said, taking one of the forks from her.

Rachel noticed that the blood from the cut was starting to seep through the napkin and she had a sudden wave of nausea flow over her. She handed the plate over to Silas and covered her mouth and nose.

"Rachel, are you okay?" Silas asked, concerned.

"Just a little bit dizzy," Rachel answered, unsure of what was happening. "I need to rest."

"Why don't you go to my chambers to rest?" he suggested.

"Okay," she accepted. She put her fork back on the table and stumbled through the crowd of guests, feeling overwhelmed.

"Rachel, are you okay?" Hannah asked her best friend as she passed.

Rachel turned. "Yeah," she replied. "Just a little bit tired; I'm going to rest and stuff."

"Uh huh," Hannah said, unconvinced.

"The queen is going to her chambers to rest, but let the party go on!" Silas called out loudly.

The crowd of guests cheered as they ate their cake.

Rachel opened the doors to Silas' chambers and sluggishly stumbled inside. "Spotless," she said. "Not surprising." She looked around the large room and saw an open window, the curtains blowing because of the wind. *Weird,* she thought. She walked around the bed and was about to close the window when she noticed Night crouched down on the floor. "*You!*" she yelled. "You're the reason I'm a vampire!"

Night shot up to his feet and clutched her throat. "Let me tell you what's going to happen," he said strictly. "I'm going to put you down, leave, and you're going to forget I was here. Or, if you want to be stubborn, I'll drink every drop of your blood until you die, understand?"

Rachel slowly nodded her head, even though she had another idea in mind.

Night put her down. "Stay," he instructed as though she were a dog.

Rachel waited until he turned around, ready to leave, and then she jumped on his back and buried her fangs into his neck.

"Get off!" Night roared, but Rachel stayed, her legs wrapped tightly around his waist, her arms gripping his chest, her mouth filling up with blood. "Do you know what happens when a vampire drinks another vampire's blood?"

But Rachel wasn't listening to a word he said, engulfed in the taste and smell of his sweet blood. Her eyes glowed a deep blood red, and she consumed his bodily fluids.

Eventually, Night dropped to the floor, dead, but Rachel continued consuming his blood, not letting a single drop go to waste.

Rachel slurped up the last of Night's blood and she exhaled slowly, taking in the delicious taste. She let go of the vampire and looked down at her bloody wedding dress. "Great," she said. "I look like a murderer... wait," she looked at Night's corpse, "I-I *am* a murderer," she gasped as she stumbled up to her feet and sat on the bed. "I'm a murderer," she said to herself once again before she broke down into sobs.

Silas thought of Rachel until the party died down, and eventually ended. He imagined her resting in a nightdress under the comforter of his bed, waiting for him.

The guests left and Hannah was shown to her own special chambers.

Once he was cleared for the night, Silas rushed to his chambers, expecting to see Rachel asleep, but he was instead welcomed by the sight of his wife crying hysterically. "Rachel?" he asked.

The queen turned and the king saw blood on the corners of her mouth and all over the top of her white wedding dress. Rachel's makeup was smeared and her eyes were red from crying.

"Rachel?" Silas asked. "What happened?"

"I couldn't help it!" Rachel sobbed.

"Couldn't help what?" he questioned.

She pointed at Night's lifeless body, lying face down on the floor. He was obviously dead.

"I-I killed him," she cried.

Silas took a step back for his own protection.

"He threatened to kill me; I didn't have a choice. I'm sorry, but-but please don't leave me here."

Cautiously, Silas walked over to his wife and hugged her, letting her tears soak his shoulder. "It's all alright," he said. "We would've had him executed anyway."

Rachel looked up at him and licked the blood from her lips. "R-really?" she asked.

"Yeah, we just need to take care of your dress and his body."

"Before I killed him," she continued, looking away, "he said something to me."

"What did he say?"

"He asked if I knew what would happen if a vampire drinks another vampire's blood."

"He probably just wanted to catch you off guard," Silas said.

"You have a library here, right?" Rachel asked.

"Of course," he replied. "Why?"

"I just want to do some research on some fun topics," she answered.

"Okay."

"I should probably get changed out of this bloody-once-beautiful dress," she choked back a sob.

"Yeah, I'll get a maid to give me a really big bag to put him in," Silas said, trying not to gag at Night's bloody corpse.

"And put him in the trash?" Rachel suggested.

"Yep," he replied with a gulp.

"Yeah, I'll go and change," she said, and then she quickly ran out of her husband's chambers.

Silas looked down at Night once Rachel had closed the door behind her. "You know, you brought this on yourself, buddy."

Rachel rushed down the hallway to her chambers, avoiding everything. Whenever she saw a shadow, she'd run into the closest closet.

Rachel finally closed the doors to her chambers and exhaled in relief. She changed from her bloody wedding dress into one of the many lace nightgowns hanging in her large walk-in closet.

Rachel looked at herself in the mirror and started talking to her reflection.

"Why am I such a monster?"

"I don't know," came a deep, feminine voice.

Rachel looked around. "Who's there?"

"I'm right in front of you, silly," the voice said again.

The young queen looked at her reflection in the mirror and waited a moment.

"Hello, there," said her reflection.

"Oh my God," Rachel gasped.

"Don't be surprised, I'm technically you—"

"I'm delusional."

Her reflection rolled its eyes. "Vampires have a bunch of powers, you know, and since they don't have a reflection, they make one that's identical to them."

"I'm going insane," Rachel muttered to herself.

"Look, you vampiric freak," her reflection snapped, "I'm you, you're me, okay? Deal with it."

"Prove it," Rachel said, glaring into her own eyes.

Her reflection rolled its eyes again. "How am I supposed to prove that? It's a fact. Anyway, read it in your thick book; it'll tell you at some page."

"Why are you only talking to me now? I've been a vampire for more than a week," Rachel demanded.

"Because there's always a curse made, and humans shouldn't see what I'm going to show you because they would call you a witch, and blah blah blah. Your vampire instincts or whatever made me care for you."

"What is it?"

"I can show you someone you desperately want to see, whether you think you want to or not."

Rachel scoffed. "Oh please, that's a load of crap."

"I know it's complicated, but being a vampire isn't that bad, and the reason why it's not that bad is because of all the powers."

"No, it's horrible," she said firmly. "And that's why I'm looking for a cure."

"Get an exorcist!"

"Ha ha, so funny."

"It's so obvious, though," her reflection muttered.

Rachel's eyes immediately widened. "You know the cure?"

"Cure, *cure*, you act like being a vampire is a disease."

"It might as well be; look at the facts!"

"Isn't that something you should be doing?"

Rachel glared at her reflection. "Tell me the cure. Now," she demanded.

"Ooh, look who's getting feisty; and didn't you say all I have said is a load of crap?"

"I'm sorry," Rachel said, relaxing.

"Next time, I have to go be another vampire's reflection." With that said, Rachel stared at a blank mirror.

Although the objects behind her started showing up. Rachel didn't.

CHAPTER TWENTY-EIGHT

MONTHLY MEAL

*R*achel knocked quietly on Silas' door before creaking it open and taking a step inside. "Hi," she said quickly.

"Hello, Queen," Silas said with a smile.

"Don't call me that," Rachel said, cracking her own smile.

"It suits you," Silas reprimanded.

"Doesn't mean I like it," she muttered.

"You know," he said, changing the topic, "you need your own maid, someone to look after you while I'm away and help with your, ah, *vampire instincts*." Rachel sat on the bed alongside him and rested her head on his shoulder.

"But how do we know she'll keep that secret safe? What will she think of you when she finds out that the king is married to a-a-a," she tried to find the right word, "that the king's married to a *monster* in a human's body?"

"We'll find the right person, and nobody thinks you're a monster in a human's body."

"I do."

Silas ran his fingers through her hair and sighed. "You're not; you're just someone who was unfortunate enough to turn into a vampire."

"And isn't a vampire a beast? Just some monster," she choked on her breath. "And that's what I am now."

"Sometimes," he said. "Some vampires are beasts, a monster in a human's body, but not you: you're Rachel Free Angel, the bravest, most beautiful woman I've ever met. Nothing will ever change the way I think. I vowed to stay by your side, remember?"

"But things have changed. What if, over time, I get worse, and truly become a monster?" she said as tears started running down her cheeks.

"Then I will help you return to who you are now."

"But what if I'm like glass? And once I'm shattered you can glue me back together but you'll still always see the cracks?"

"That's why you sand things down; you do whatever you can to fix what's broken."

"But it'll never be the same as it was before, no matter what you do. There'll always be the scars of what has happened."

"I'll try my best," Silas assured her.

"*We'll* try our best," Rachel said.

Silas scooted aside and held her face in his hands. "But no matter what—"

"I'll love you," Rachel finished and pulled him into a loving kiss.

Silas slowly pulled away and used his thumb to wipe away her tears. "Yeah, forever."

"So," Rachel said, "how will this maid thing work?"

"Well," Silas said, a bit shocked she had changed the subject so easily. "There's auditions with the best maids in the country. The auditions themselves will be held in the ballroom. You will choose who will be your maid."

"Can I get a list of all the names?" she asked.

"Fair enough. When do you want them to audition?" he questioned.

Rachel pondered the question for a few moments before she decided. "Three days from now."

"I'll let Martha know," he yawned. "Are you tired? Or am I the only one who's exhausted?"

"You are definitely not the only one," Rachel replied with a yawn. Silas stood up and pulled back the heavy comforter on his large bed. Rachel met his gaze and she realized what he meant.

"Oh," she said. "Um, I'm going to sleep on my own for a little while longer."

"Oh," Silas said, a bit surprised. "Sure, sweet dreams, my queen."

"Oh my God," Rachel said as she walked out of Silas' chambers. "Sweet dreams to you as well," she added as she closed the doors behind her.

As Rachel walked, Leo stepped back into her thoughts. Did he think she was a monster like she did?

A random maid opened a door and Rachel, not looking where she was going, smacked into it and fell on her behind.

The maid must've heard the sound because she ran out of the room to Rachel's aid. "Oh, my goodness, my queen; I am so terribly sorry," she apologized frantically.

"It's fine," Rachel said, rubbing her sore forehead. "I wasn't looking where I was going."

"Are you sure?" the maid asked.

"Yes," she assured her. "Have a good night." With that said, Rachel walked off to her chambers with her thoughts of Leo.

Rachel opened the doors to her chambers and closed them behind her before flopping herself onto her bed and falling asleep instantaneously.

Rachel dreamed of her last moment with Leo before he pushed her back through the mirror and shattered it.

"Rachel, I love you," Leo said. He shoved Rachel through the glass but she held onto his arms tightly.

"You're not getting rid of me that easily," she said firmly.

With a shocked expression, Leo tried to shove her through the rippling glass again. She held her grip. "Rachel, you need to go back to Silas; you love him."

"I thought I did," Rachel said, stepping out of the mirror. "But I was wrong." She erased the words **Snow White** and looked back at Leo. "I never loved Silas at all." She took the knife from his hand. "Instead, I've always loved you, right from the beginning." She stabbed the knife into the solid glass and the mirror shattered. "I was just too blind to see it." She dropped the knife and kissed Leo passionately, glass shards falling around them.

Leo was surprised but eventually grew into the kiss, loving every passionate second of it. He pulled away and breathed. "I never thought this day would come."

"Same here," Rachel said, and then he pulled his face back to hers.

Rachel woke up with beads of sweat flooding her forehead. "What did my imagination just conjure?" she breathed.

Rachel stayed in bed for a moment, staring at the ceiling, her dream relentlessly replaying itself in her mind over and over again.

There was a sudden knock at the door and Rachel bolted upright. "Yes?" she asked.

"It's your morning maid," a voice said.

"Martha?" Rachel asked, recognizing the insecure voice.

The door opened and Martha walked in, holding fresh sheets. "Hi."

Martha helped Rachel out of bed and into a beautiful purple dress. Afterwards, while Rachel brushed her hair, she redid the bed with the warm sheets.

"Goodbye, Martha," Rachel said as she walked out of her chambers, proudly wearing her crown.

"Goodbye, Queen," Martha replied quickly.

Rachel made her way to the large library on the third floor of the large castle after a steady search. She scanned the aisles before realizing that the books weren't organized in any way whatsoever. "Guess we're doing this the hard way," she muttered to herself.

As Rachel looked through the books, she realized that most were spell books and others were about monsters of all sorts. Just before she lost all hope, a blood-red book caught her eye. She slipped the book off the shelf and read the scripted title: *All you need to know about Vampires and their Beastly Tendencies.* She took off her crown and traced her finger across the detail. She glanced at the librarian and at her crown. Back at the librarian who was reading a book and back at the glistening crystals on her crown. Back at the shrivelled old woman at the counter who was reading a recipe book and back at the many diamonds on her large crown. Rachel glanced back and forth between the librarian and the crown for several more minutes before she decided to sneak out of the library. She did not want the librarian to suspect anything about her, considering the book she was taking. She slipped off her knee-high boots and tiptoed out of the library, gently closing the large wooden door behind her. Rachel slipped her boots back on and walked to her chambers.

The queen sat on her bed and opened the large book. The first page contained the following information:

Vampires have been around since the dawning of time. They await in hiding, preparing for the perfect time to strike. These beasts feed on human blood. They need the amount of blood a single person has in their entire body at least once a month to stay sane or else they will lose all proper functioning and devour anything that comes in their way. If deprived of blood, after a certain amount of time their body will shrivel up and turn to dust. Once these monsters are on the verge of losing sanity, they use the last of what thinking process they have left and drink whatever blood comes their way, no matter how much they try to stop, even if it's the one they love most. Vampires need blood because they lose a fair amount.

What is most dangerous about these monsters is that they fit in perfectly with humankind, but at any time they can pierce a neck with their vampire fangs.

We should pity vampires who were once human but are now beasts. These unfortunate souls have been bitten by three different vampires. Be careful not to be bitten by three different vampires because you will be transformed into these—

Rachel slammed the book shut and put in on her nightstand as tears stung her eyes. "I-I am a beast, I was right, and that's how the world sees me." She looked out her window at the kingdom she ruled. "They all think vampires are monsters."

"Rachel," Silas said with a knock at the door. He heard sobs and quickly opened the door. "Rachel," he gasped and quickly sat beside her. "What happened?"

"I-I told you," she cried.

"What?" he questioned.

"I'm a monster and the entire world knows it."

"You are not a monster, or a beast, or anything of the sort," Silas said firmly and held her face in his hands.

"You're probably the only person who thinks that," Rachel said.

"You are Rachel Free Angel, your own person, and nothing will ever change that," he said as he wiped away her tears with his thumb.

"But I am a crybaby," she chuckled.

"If you are then I will always be here to wipe away your tears."

"Anyway, now that you're here and have made me feel better, I'm going to explain what I just read."

CHAPTER TWENTY-NINE

RESOLUTION

"So, basically what you're saying is that you need to have the amount of blood that an average human being has in a month, or else you'll go haywire, and that vampires drink blood because they lose blood?" Silas asked.

"Yes, exactly," Rachel said.

"But how do you lose blood?" he questioned.

"I'm not entirely sure," she answered. "Maybe by vomiting? Maybe when I go to the bathroom."

"Perhaps."

"Do you know of anyone who might have a cure?"

"I know Jack, my personal wizard; I would bet on my life that he does."

"Well then, let's go to Jack."

"I promise you he will have a cure," Silas said. "He is Jack, after all."

"Sorry, my boy," Jack said apologetically. "I wish I had a cure for vampires, but why do you need such a thing?"

Rachel and Silas tensed. "Oh nothing," the king said. "Just curious."

"Well, have a good day," the wizard said.

The king and queen walked out of Jack's den and Rachel broke down.

"What if I'm stuck like this forever? I'll end up killing every being in the entire world, or worlds if we're counting mine, and Lord knows how many more."

"Rachel," Silas said, placing his hands on her shaking shoulders. "We will find something; that I can promise with certainty."

"But what are we going to do for now?"

Silas looked at his feet for a moment before his eyes lit up like firecrackers. "I have an idea," he said.

Rachel was scared of his enthusiasm. "What is it?" she asked fearfully.

"I have around a dozen prisoners in the dungeon due for execution; we can cancel the execution and let you have them."

"Dungeons aren't just a single cell where nobody can see through the bars, smarty pants," she added, relieved she found a way around his murderous plan.

"We have a torture room — several, actually," he mentioned.

Rachel gawped at him. "You just want to bring the prisoners to the torture room and let me—" she gulped, "let me *murder* them ruthlessly?"

Silas hugged her tightly. "I know you don't want to. I know it's a psychotic plan. But it's only temporary and these people have been locked away for years; very few of them have visitors and even fewer are remembered."

"Okay," Rachel said. "Let's say I go along with your plan… how will you explain to the guards why the prisoners are being taken to torture rooms and not returning?"

"I'll tell them it was a private execution."

"So, they are going to have an execution, like planned, but what if we run out of those prisoners?"

"By then we'll have a long-lasting solution that will work for sure," Silas assured her.

"I'm sorry, I can't," Rachel said, and then she turned around to leave.

"Rachel," he pleaded and grabbed her by the hand, "just hear me out."

"Well, Silas, what am I supposed to do in the torture room?" she roared. "It's not like most of them will willingly give up their lives. And what am I supposed to say? *Oh, hello there, mind if I just murder you mercilessly?* Seriously, Silas, I love you but I can't possibly murder people."

"Rachel, vampire kisses put people to sleep, remember? You can kill them painlessly."

"Silas, I said I would not kill anybody." Rachel ripped her hand from Silas' grip and stormed off to her chambers.

"Just sleep on it, okay?" Silas called after her.

That night, Rachel vomited up blood along with her dinner before a restless sleep. Her dreams didn't help.

Rachel dreamed that she was on the verge of losing her sanity. She was in Silas' chambers and they were both sitting on his large bed. Rachel's eyes flickered from brown to red, though her husband didn't notice.

"Silas, I've been really thirsty lately," the queen said, licking her lips lustfully.

"We still have the prisoners, remember?" the king replied, picking at his sock.

"I'm not — I'm going to murder people," she said.

"You've finally agreed to my plan, eh?" he asked.

"Yeah — no — yes of course."

"I can tell you who you can start with."

"Don't worry; I've already decided," Rachel said, licking her vampire fangs.

"Who?" Silas asked, moving on to the next sock.

"*You*," she said.

Silas turned to her at lightning speed and noticed her red eyes, her sharp fangs, and her sadistic grin. He let out a scream as Rachel tackled him to the ground and bit into his neck.

"Rachel! Stop! Rachel!" Silas screamed.

Rachel sat up and covered his mouth with her palm before diving back down for more blood. She drank and drank Silas' blood until she no longer had to muffle his screams, or groans, or any noise whatsoever.

The king lay still on the ground as Rachel satisfied her hunger.

Rachel sat awake and immediately started crying. "No, I would never!" she said to herself.

Once these monsters are on the verge of losing sanity, they use the last of what thinking process they have left and drink whatever blood comes their way, no matter how much they try to stop, even if it's the one they love most. Rachel remembered.

This can be prevented with a simple 'yes,' a voice in her head rang.

No, Rachel said to the voice.

It's those prisoners or Silas: pick one. The prisoners would be a wise choice, though.

Rachel made a difficult decision and hoped Silas would agree with it.

Rachel walked along the hallways to Silas' chambers, contemplating her decision and how she would tell Silas.

Her time to contemplate was over; she walked in front of the doors to her husband's chambers and knocked lightly with a shaky hand.

"Come on in," she heard Silas' loving voice call from inside.

Slowly, Rachel creaked open the doors and closed them silently behind her. "Silas, I-I made a choice about me needing human—" she choked on her breath quickly, "blood," she rasped.

"Yes?" Silas questioned, looking up from his desk in the corner.

"It's not one of the options we talked about," she said quickly.

Silas placed his quill down in his small jar of ink. "Yes?"

"But I think we could make it work," she added.

Silas stood from his cushioned chair with a raised eyebrow.

"And it could work well."

The king took smooth steps towards his queen.

"But I won't force it upon you."

"Just tell me what it is," he said.

"Vampires only lose their sanity if they don't drink blood for a month, so if I have a little every day, then I'll be fine."

"Yes, that is correct."

"Have you ever been bitten by a vampire?" Rachel asked.

Silas slowly put the pieces together and a look of terror clouded over his beautiful eyes. "I'm guessing you want to ask if I'll let you drink a little bit of my blood every day. Of course, with the knowledge that people can only turn into a vampire after three bites from different vampires, and one more bite to trigger the transformation, I'll be fine. But then there's blood loss."

"I've looked into that," Rachel said, ashamed she would burden her true love with such a thing. "And if I take a small amount every other day, we'll be completely fine, the both of us. And we'll have found a cure before anybody has to find out about this."

"I agree," Silas said.

Rachel looked up and saw every trace of terror gone from his eyes. "Thank you," she choked out. A tear escaped her eye and she ran to Silas, who hugged her tightly as soon as she collided with his chest.

"I'm so sorry I'm this way," she cried. "It's my fault in the first place. I should've been more careful. I should've—"

"None of this is your fault in the slightest," Silas said as he ran his fingers through her hair.

That day and the next went by quickly, though the nights were filled with nightmares for Rachel. She tried to distract her vampiric thoughts with the list of maids.

-Edith
-Crystalis
-Shirley
-Beverly
-Beatrice
-Eloise

Rachel scanned the list, her finger running along the names. She stopped cold when she read a name that brought back memories too painful to forget. "Bring in Rose!" she called to no one specific.

"What is it?" Silas asked, sitting alongside her.

"I want to see her *now*," she ordered and slammed her hand down on the table, barely missing the porcelain cookie platter.

Silas was shocked by her stern expression but quickly overcame it. "You heard the queen; bring Rose!"

A small girl no older than fourteen ran in front of them and bowed quickly. "Yes?" she asked in a squeak. The maid looked around anxiously, hearing the other maid candidates murmur about why the queen would request such a pathetic girl.

"Come closer," Rachel demanded in a soft but commanding voice.

Rose walked up to the table where the king and queen sat.

In a flash, Rachel was leaning over the table to get a closer view of Rose, her chair on the floor because of the swift motion. The maid had a striking resemblance to her old doll.

"Can I touch your hair?" Rachel asked the maid.

Wide-eyed, Silas looked at his wife, wondering what would possess her to ask that question.

"Y-yes," the maid replied.

Rachel stroked her fingers gently through the maid's coffee-coloured hair. She then ran her thumb lightly along Rose's cheek before gazing into the girl's deep ocean blue eyes.

Silas gulped down a thick ball of saliva.

Rachel looked at Rose from head to toe in amazement, as if witnessing a ghost. "A-are you real?" she asked.

"Y-yes," Rose stuttered, surprised by the queen's reaction to her.

"You will be my maid," Rachel said softly, slowly taking her hands away from the maid.

"Uh, are you sure?" Silas questioned.

Rachel picked up her chair and sat down. "Yes, and nothing in the universe will change my mind in the slightest. Where's Martha?"

"I'm not sure—" the king said.

"*Martha!*" Rachel hollered.

Without a second to lose, Martha ran into the room and stopped in front of Rachel. She took a quick bow before standing up straight like a soldier. "You called?"

"Yes," the queen said. "Send the rest of the maids home, and as for Rose, get her a maid's dress in different shades of violet, as well as a paper rose for her to wear in her hair, on the right side of her head. Give her black shoes with white gloves and stockings. And all of these will be given to her by the end of the week, understood?"

"Yes," Martha said quickly, making a mental note of everything that needed to be given to the new maid.

In the queen's chambers, Silas and Rachel sat beside each other on the large bed.

"So why did you choose Rose?" Silas questioned inquisitively.

"She reminds me of someone I knew, someone who was very dear to me. Though unfortunately, I'll never see her again," Rachel replied.

"Who?" he asked.

"Well, she isn't exactly a person," she answered.

"What was she?"

"A doll my mother gave to me on my first birthday, my best friend, until my father died and my relatives took Rose."

"That's horrible."

"That experience made me stronger, though, and it helped make me the person I am today." She glanced away quickly. "Anyway, let's change the subject."

Silas quickly said, "I forgot to tell you that you'll be getting a butler."

Rachel stared at him for a moment.

"Yeah right, ha ha, real funny."

Silas kept a straight face.

"You are joking, right?" she asked.

Silas hadn't been joking. Over lunch she sat with her butler, a boy no older than sixteen with auburn-coloured hair and sea-green eyes. He looked as though he only ate once a day. He wore a tight black suit with matching gloves and black shoes. The boy looked more like an undertaker than a butler.

"What did you say your name was?" Rachel asked awkwardly.

"Frederic Hazenvow," the butler said sternly.

"Where did you say you were from?" she questioned.

"The Northern Hills Village," Frederic replied in a sharp manner. "Also, I have to mention that you look especially gorgeous today."

"Thank you," Rachel said, and then she glanced down quickly at her purple gown that Silas insisted she wear.

Frederic looked down at his plate of food and said nothing for a short while, sitting like a robot.

"You can eat, for crying out loud," Rachel said sternly, her mouth now full of food.

"Uh, yes." The butler started cutting into his lamb.

"Is there anything you would like to share?" Rachel asked after she forcefully swallowed her food.

"My mother is healing from a horrible sickness and my father is coming back from the war soon."

"Fascinating."

"It was so awkward!" Rachel complained to Silas, who was biting his fist in an attempt not to laugh. "I mean he just sits there like some robot!"

The queen heard small chuckling from outside the closet in her chambers. She stuck her head out of the closet to see

Silas coughing. She glared at him silently for a moment. "Trying to cover up your snickers?"

Silas looked away. "Maybe."

"But honestly, he has no emotion," she said, and then she ducked back into the large walk-in closet.

"So, would he be a good butler?" the king questioned.

"Yes," the queen replied honestly. "But like I said, he's basically a robot."

"Every butler is trained to be like that."

"Good Lord."

"Are you almost done?"

"Yes, I'm finished; it's just that these dresses are so hard to get on, considering how tight they are."

"Come on out, then; I would like to see your beautiful face."

Rachel walked slowly out of the closet, holding two parts on her dress on either side and doing a small curtsey.

"Gorgeous," Silas said, and he stood up.

"Thank you," Rachel said with a large smile. "Anyway, I'm going to read about vampires."

"Enjoy your lecture," he said. He left the room, closing the door behind him.

Rachel sat on her bed alone in her chambers and opened up her book about vampires. She found a page entitled Vampire's Kiss. The page read:

A vampire's kiss is a kiss given by a vampire, obviously, though the effect of the kiss is far different than a kiss shared by two humans. The victim of a vampire's kiss will fall unconscious, giving the vampire easy access to their blood. However, if two vampires share a kiss, nothing will happen. Only a small percentage (5%) of vampire-kiss victims ever wake up.

She flipped to another page:

Vampire Blood

When a vampire drinks another vampire's blood, their fangs grow slightly, making them even more dangerous than they already are. In a vampire's blood there is always a small dose of poison circulating throughout their body. Vampires aren't affected by this poison, but if a human even touches vampire blood, the part of their body that touched it will burn and the skin in that area will peel off the bone, leaving tissue exposed. Over time, if the burn isn't treated, it will spread. And before three months, the entire body will have no skin and will start decomposing at a faster rate.

Rachel flipped through more pages, searching for the cure to being a vampire, but nothing came up.

CHAPTER THIRTY

ELLIS

$\mathcal{L}$eo took out his buzzing phone out of his bag with an irritated facial expression. He saw messages popping up on the screen from the anonymous sender again:

M.M.
Are you in Italy yet?
M.M.
Tell me when you land.
M.M.
Are you aboard the plane yet?
    Leo let out a frustrated sigh and replied quickly:
Leonardo Dash
Stop texting; my plane ride isn't leaving for another half hour.
M.M.
Tell me when you get on.
Leonardo Dash
I'll text you when I land, and you haven't even told me your name yet.

M.M.

You don't need to know that yet.

Leonardo Dash

If you don't tell me now, I'll go straight back home away from you.

M.M.

Why do you want to know my name?

Leonardo Dash

Because I only know you as "M.M." which isn't a name. Besides, you already know mine; somehow, you always knew.

M.M.

Do you want my full name or just first?

Leonardo Dash

You know I want this to be fair, and you know my full name.

M.M.

Ellis Evergreen, and I should probably tell you my gender because yours is obvious by your name.

Leonardo Dash

What do you mean?

M.M.

Ellis is mostly known as a male's name, but I'm a female.

Leo then realized her last name was awfully familiar. He quickly sent:

Leonardo Dash

How are you related to Sir Evergreen?

M.M.

That's why I didn't want to tell you my name. Everybody always makes the connection to my father.

Leonardo Dash

I'm guessing you're one of Lucy's sisters?

M.M.

Yes.

Leonardo Dash
I have more questions.

    He didn't get any other replies after that. He left the bathroom and boarded his nine-hour flight without a hitch.

    After an hour of staring out his window, Leo's phone started buzzing again. He checked the messages. The first one that popped up was from his mother, making sure he'd gotten on the plane without any problems. He sighed and scrolled down the list of unread texts. He came across several other messages from Ellis:

M.M.
Hello, sorry for not replying sooner, I had some business that I had to attend to. But no more questions, please; we can talk over everything in Italy. And I'm not talking to you for the pleasure of it; we both know that.

Leonardo Dash
How do you know about it though?

M.M.
We can discuss that in Italy. Now, are you on the plane yet?

Leonardo Dash
It seems unfair that you are allowed to ask questions.

M.M.
For crying out loud, this question isn't personal. That's what I mean: no PERSONAL questions.

Leonardo Dash
Fine, yes, I'm on the plane. Also, can you pick me up when I land, at the Italy International Airport, at nine p.m.?

M.M.
Alright, but I have to go. I'll see you in person for the first time when you land, well, outside the front doors.

Leonardo Dash
I'll see you then.

M.M.

Bye.

Leonardo Dash

Bye.

Leo put his phone back in his small bag and slept peacefully.

He was awoken by the sound of buzzing. Another text from his mom asking if he was alright. He quickly replied and reread some of his and Ellis' first texts. 'I know who you are, Leonardo Dash' was the first text he'd received from her. He replied a startled 'How did you get my number?' All he got in reply was something that startled him even more. He remembered thinking that he was one of the only ones that knew, nobody else. And the following texts only brought further surprises.

Leo closed his eyes and erased all thoughts of Ellis; he didn't want to think about her right now. They were only meeting for one specific reason, that was all this trip was about: the meeting. He could do a little bit of sightseeing, considering he was going to be in Italy for ten days. Leo breathed out slowly and let himself fall asleep.

Rachel immediately took hold of his mind. "I miss you, Leo," she whispered gently. "Please come back; I can't do this without your love and support."

"I know this isn't real," Leo muttered to himself.

"I miss you," she continued. "I can feel myself losing more control day after day; I need you."

"Rachel, you don't mean that, and we broke the mirror, remember? I can't go back, even if I tried," he said to her.

"What if there are more?" she said to him softly. "We can be together, just like we're supposed to."

Leo looked into Rachel's eyes for the first time in his entire dream. "This is just my imagination humouring my inner hopes," he said sternly to her.

"Don't you trust me?" Rachel said to him, caressing his face in her hands. "Look at this place. Maybe around us is your blank imagination, but am I?"

Leo glanced around him, at the whiteness surrounding him and Rachel. He looked back at Rachel, into the deep russet pools of her eyes, at her rosy cheeks, at her small button nose, and at her lacking feminine physique. "Maybe," he said softly, almost to himself.

"Exactly," Rachel said, pulling his face closer to hers. "I'm not just here because you're imagining me; I'm here because I belong near you. I belong closer to you than words could ever possibly describe. I'm *part* of you."

Suddenly, a buzzing sound rang in Leo's ears and he sat up, awake. He checked his phone and saw another text from Ellis.

M.M.

How much longer until you land?

Leonardo Dash

About an hour or so. You just woke me up, by the way. I must've slept for a while.

M.M

Oh, okay.

Leo looked around and saw the two passengers on either side of him fast asleep. He sighed and stuffed his phone back into his small bag and let himself sleep for the rest of the plane ride.

"*All passengers please make your way to the exit,*" the flight attendant's voice rang through Leo's ears. "*I repeat, all passengers please make your way to the exit.*"

Leo snapped awake and stood up along with every other passenger. He quickly joined the applause for the safe flight before grabbing his bag and making his way to the exit.

As he waited in line for his passport to be checked, Leo texted Ellis:

Leonardo Dash

Come and pick me up please.

M.M.

On my way, I'll be there in twenty minutes.

Leonardo Dash

Thanks.

Leo put his phone in his pocket and made his way through the airport security.

As he headed for the doors to leave the building, a young woman caught his eye. Her back was turned to him, her hair was identical to Rachel's, and she wore small jean shorts with a white T-shirt, something random and casual. He took a step towards the young woman but caught himself. Rachel was in a castle in another universe, far away from him. He'd pushed her through the glass of Sir Evergreen's magic mirror and shattered it. He remembered how reluctant he had been, afraid he'd never see Rachel again, though she convinced him with the truth that the mirror had been around for long enough. He made his way out of the front doors, lugging his suitcase behind him. He texted Ellis:

Leonardo Dash

I just got outside, where are you?

M.M

The black car in front of you; I just opened the door to the front seat.

Leo looked in front of him and saw a black Volvo with the front door open, revealing an empty seat. He put his phone in his pocket and walked towards the car. The trunk popped open and he lifted his suitcase into the large space before walking to the front of the car and taking a seat inside, slamming the door shut behind him.

"Thank you for meeting me here," Leo said.

"No problem," said the person beside him.

Leo put his hand out to shake hers. "Leonardo Dash, so nice to meet you in person."

Ellis turned and Leo could immediately tell she was Sir Evergreen's daughter. She had the same chestnut brown hair, though in full colour as opposed to his headmaster's greying hair, and the same piercing parakeet-green eyes.

"Ellis Evergreen," she said kindly and shook his hand. "It's a real pleasure to meet you as well."

"You don't have the same accent as your father," Leo said, surprised as he let go of her hand.

Ellis frowned slightly as she took hold of the steering wheel. "My mother raised me and my older sister, leaving Lucy with Robert."

"Robert?" Leo asked, putting on his seat belt.

"My father's name."

"Oh right, I forgot he had a name."

Ellis chuckled. "So why did we have to meet up here in Italy again?"

"Because I couldn't just ask my mom to let me go to a random place where I have no family to protect me," he said sarcastically. "I'm Italian, I think I forgot to mention."

"So that's why you have an Italian name," she said. "Ready to go?"

"We're going to your place, right?"

Ellis froze and slowly turned to him. "You didn't book yourself a hotel room? All I have is a small condo that I'm renting for ten days!"

Leo gulped down his saliva and peeped out a small, "No." He didn't know why, but Ellis gave off a threatening vibe.

She let out a disappointed sigh and turned back to the windshield. "You're sleeping on the couch."

"Thank you," Leo said thankfully.

"It's fine," she said in a grunt. "And I can reply to your questions while we drive, so ask away." She pressed her foot down on the gas pedal and they sped out of the airport parking lot.

"Who's your mother?" Leo asked immediately.

"Viola Anastas," Ellis replied quickly.

"That's a beautiful name," he said.

"She's Greek, and my grandparents liked Viola, so yeah," she said.

"Can you speak Greek?"

"*Fysiká kai boró*; of course I can,"

"Wow," Leo said, mystified. "How did Viola and Robert meet?"

"My mother travelled to the United States for business, where she met Robert. They *fell in love*, the classic term of stupidity. But Robert only wanted my mother for her powers of time travel, weather, and mind manipulation. By the way, this is going to answer your question as to why I know about my father's mirror, the first question you ever asked me.

"Oh, where do I begin in this story that has intertwined our souls? Well, my mother's family has magical powers, like I just said. Robert learned about this and seduced her into loving him. She used her powers to please him so he would be happy, something the old twit didn't deserve in the slightest. Robert got so obsessed with the power that he married my mom. Then they had my sisters and I. My mother found out about his greed for power and divorced him, thankfully, though in the lawsuit she only got her two older children, while Robert got Lucy. Lucy was only an infant at the time. She probably doesn't even remember what Mother looks like. But unbeknownst to my father at the time, Lucy doesn't have any powers. He was hoping he could manipulate her into using her powers for his own cruel needs." She grinned. "Instead, he has had to raise her like a regular daughter. And don't ask 'why doesn't she have powers?' because it's obvious. With Robert having no powers, it was a fifty-fifty chance. I can only imagine how furious he was when he found out she's a regular human, like him."

"Do you have powers?"

Ellis snorted, "What do you think 'M.M.' stands for?"

Leo took a moment to find an answer, "Magical Mage?"

"Try again," she said.

"Magic Manufacturer?" he tried.

"No."

"Magic Mirror?"

Ellis rolled her eyes. "Mirror *Maker.*"

Leo's eyes grew wide. "You made Sir Evergreen's magic mirror?"

"Yes," she replied. Ellis took one hand off the steering wheel and twirled her fingers around. Slowly, glass started to form, then a frame grew around it, and on top a small chalkboard. The small mirror dropped into her hand and she gave it to him. "A small hand mirror," she said. "Though you can't really use a mirror of that size to travel. Of course, it could be used for other things that Robert never knew about. Like I can make a mirror with a soul inside that can show the mirror's owner the world around it in detail."

"Like Snow White's stepmother's mirror," Leo said in awe.

"Where do you think she got that mirror?" she asked. "I was maybe six years old at the time, my parents were still together, Lucy wasn't born. I had made Robert's magic mirror two years before and he loved going to *Snow White.* Oh, and another thing he liked was money, and in *Snow White* the evil wench was willing to pay him a lot of gold coins for something very magical. So, he brought me to the witch's large mansion and I made the mirror. Of course, this was before the witch married Snow White's father and all of that. I've made several magic mirrors for people, my father leading me to the magic mirror owners of course, and he would get paid every time."

"What other mirrors did you make?" Leo asked, now gaping at the magical woman beside him.

"Hmm, the Beast's mirror, you know from *Beauty and the Beast*. Another memorable one was the Snow Queen's magic mirror; I almost froze to death while I made her mirror. I've made several other mirrors, actually, but those three are the ones I remember the most."

"Do you have any other magical powers?" he questioned.

"There's a power my mom doesn't have but her parents have that was passed down to me," she said.

"Which is?"

"It's one of the most powerful magics of all; it's life and death bending. Which means I can bend someone's life force or their life itself and make them stay alive longer or shorten their life. Same thing with any other species: I can make a plant die with a snap of my fingers. That's why my mom never had to call pest control; I weakened the rodents that would sneak into our garage at night, and then we would bring them somewhere far away. And death bending is kind of the same thing. I have the power to visit the underworld at will, though it takes up so much of my energy that I can only do it once every several weeks and only for a week at most. What's weird is that it's very rare for someone to have both life and death bending. My grandmother had life bending and my grandfather has death bending. It's rare to have both for two reasons. First, that amount of power usually can't fit inside a human's body; and second, usually it's only females who have the power of life bending while men usually have the power of death bending, but yet, here I am, with three powers. And here we are." She parked her car in the parking lot of a red brick condominium.

"You're just renting this place?" Leo asked, bewildered at the beautiful sight. "Who would want to rent this out?"

"That's what I said when I saw it online," Ellis said with a large smile as she unbuckled her seat belt.

They exited the car and Ellis led Leo inside the condominium to her apartment. There she unlocked the door and walked inside, Leo trailing behind her like a dog.

"Take your shoes off and put them in the closet," Ellis instructed as she did so herself.

Leo took off his shoes, put them in the closet, and had a look around. In front of him was the sitting room where a large patterned vintage couch sat against the wall. In front of the couch was an oval-shaped table with coasters and napkins on it. Diagonal to the couch was a small sofa facing the door; behind the sofa were doors to an open balcony. Beside the door was a doorway to the dining room, which led to the kitchen. Leo turned to his left from the entrance and saw a door to a small bedroom. He turned to his right and saw a door leading to the bathroom.

"This is really nice," he muttered.

Ellis came up behind him and breathed down his neck. He jumped three feet in the air and turned back to her, clutching the area behind his neck. Leo saw Ellis chuckling.

"Why would you do that?" he asked, cheeks red.

"Because," Ellis explained through chuckles, "you looked so tense and focused, I couldn't help it."

"Never do that again," he said sternly.

"I'll try," she said, and then she went into her bedroom.

"Are you getting a taser?"

"No, I'm getting you a blanket."

"Are there bugs on it?"

"It was a small prank; get over it."

Leo sat on the sofa and sighed loudly.

"What is it?" Ellis asked as she came out of the bedroom with a thick yellow blanket.

"It's just so overwhelming, a thirty-year-old woman makes magic mirrors and—" Leo said with hand gestures.

"I'm actually older than thirty, so thank you for the compliment," she said.

"No problem," he said, and then he continued, "and there's a whole bloodline of magic, and well, there are vampires inside the mirror—"

"Wait, what? Fairy tales don't have vampires in them, not a single one."

"Well, there are three vampires that I know of that turned my dear friend into a vampire, and now I bet she's looking for a cure."

"It must've been that stupid wench that my father made deals with. She had vampire children, and vampires have no limits. Those vampires that were *siblings* had children together," Ellis said.

"Excuse me, what does that have to do with the vampires inside the mirror?" Leo asked.

"My father — I mean Robert made deals with a woman, a vampire with several children, all vampires. The deals were that she gave him money and could use the mirror freely, come and go in our house as she pleased. Mother was furious but kept a tight lip; she was mostly furious because those little monstrosities were violent as hell. I swear to the Lord, the wench would always bring over her children and let them roam free as if it were her house while she and Robert went to the study, where he kept his mirror. The little satanic brats tried to bite me."

"So again, what does this have to do with the vampires in the mirror?" Leo asked once again.

"I'm getting there," said Ellis. "The hag probably let her brats go into different fairy tales, probably around three per tale, so they could make more vampires. I mean who wouldn't want to get rid of those sad excuses of children? But into *fairy tales* of all the places?"

Suddenly an idea struck Leo like lightning. "You can make magic mirrors, so could you make another one to transport me into fairy tales?"

"Not at the moment," Ellis said simply.

"Why not?" Leo asked, suddenly frantic.

"I made one for a client three weeks ago. It takes a month to replenish my magic power, especially for such a large task. Why?" she asked calmly.

"What do you mean by client?" he questioned.

"The people who know about magic mirrors want them, obviously. I have a good price, especially for such a magical thing. They tell me where to meet them and at the requested location I make the mirror; afterwards, they give me the money. The price varies from different type and size of mirror. So, for your mirror, how much would you give for it?"

Leo's face went blank. "You can keep the mirror; I just want to use it."

"Then let me rephrase this: what amount of money are you willing to give for my magic? Because as I mentioned, it takes a month to fully regain all of my magical power."

"Don't you have a magic mirror of your own?"

"Yes," she turned to him, "in Greece."

Leo sighed in frustration. "What time is it?" he asked, aggravated.

Ellis checked her phone. "Almost one a.m., why?"

"Goodnight," he said. He took the blanket from her arms, lay down the couch, and threw the blanket over him.

"Aren't you going to change?" Ellis asked.

Leo glared silently at her. "No," he muttered, before turning on his side, facing the wall, and letting himself sleep.

Ellis shook her head in disappointment before walking into her bedroom.

CHAPTER THIRTY-ONE

VAMPIRE'S CURE

$\mathcal{R}$achel pleaded with her mirror for her reflection to come back, but it didn't.

"I'm sorry. Just let me have the cure, tell me what it is, then you can leave forever!" she begged.

Suddenly, her reflection appeared, arms crossed. "It's funny how you're only apologizing to me when you want something in return."

"I didn't mean it," Rachel said.

"Didn't sound like that."

"I swear, just put me out of my misery, please."

"Do you really want the cure?"

"Yes, I can't even stand the thought of drinking Silas' blood."

"Fine," her reflection said.

Rachel looked up with hope in her eyes.

"The cure is absolutely none of your business; try again some other day."

Rachel turned beet red. "I thought you cared for me!" she roared. "You said so yourself, that my vampiric instincts were making you like me! Just tell me what's the cure, what can turn me human…"

Her reflection looked away. "I'm sorry, but I can't tell you."

"Of course you can tell me!" she yelled loudly. "You have a mouth; use it!"

Her reflection stared back at her; slowly, she morphed into a grey-coloured demon, like a gargoyle. Fangs grew from her mouth, larger and larger until they curled underneath her chin. Horns sprouted from her forehead, longer and longer. Suddenly, her skin cracked, her horns and fangs chipped away, until she was a scared little girl with deathly pale skin, warm red eyes, and glistening tears streaming down her cheeks. Then she turned back into the grey-coloured demon, and slowly morphed back into the little girl, though the girl had vampire fangs and small horns and the same grey skin. She looked into Rachel's eyes and let her tears fall. "Don't you see?" the small child asked. "No matter what happens, no matter what you do to fix something, you'll always see the scars. It doesn't matter. Like what I just showed you, the creature, then the child, then the child becomes the demon. But I didn't show you the last stage, after she gets *cured*."

"Show me," Rachel said, mystified.

The small girl was about to protest but closed her mouth. Slowly, she dried her tears and looked away. The grey of her skin turned to pale beige, her small horns shrank back into her head, and her fangs turned back into regular canines.

Rachel breathed out in relief. Nothing bad had happened; her reflection was just bluffing.

Then she started shrieking in pain. The girl's skin chipped away, revealing solidified blood which glistened like ice. Her bones turned blue before cracking and snapping. Her teeth fell out and were replaced with deadly sharp teeth, like a rabid beast. She continued shrieking until at last, her eyes turned to blue and ice crawled around her body. She turned and looked into Rachel's eyes and rang out in a deep tone, "*It never gets better. Even if you try to fool yourself and say it's okay, the scars will be there, some even worse than the cut itself.*"

Rachel stumbled back from the mirror, terrified of what she saw. "B-but what if I don't turn out a monster?"

"I never said what the scar was, specifically, did I? But you will regret it if you become human again. If you play against fate," her reflection warned, turning back into the young queen's reflection.

"I will make my way out of it," Rachel said sternly.

"I'll tell you what the cure is when you're mature and strong enough to face the consequences and overcome them," her reflection said wisely.

"Excuse me?" Rachel said. "I'm the queen here, you are but a reflection, and I'm strong and mature enough. Tell me the cure right now."

Her reflection looked into her eyes. "I will give you the information when you prove to me that you are responsible enough to withhold the information."

"No—"

Her reflection flashed the small demon child and Rachel stumbled back.

"Do you want that to happen to you?" her reflection warned. "Do you want to become a rabid creature that can't be tamed? An unloved, horrid, hideous *beast?*"

Rachel pursed her lips.

"That's what I thought," she said, and then she slowly dissolved into nothingness.

"But how am I supposed to prove to you that I'm responsible?" the queen asked, suddenly frantic.

"That's for you to figure out." Only her reflection's eyes remained.

"But—"

The reflection was gone.

"But how am I supposed to prove that to you?"

"It's a test for you to pass," echoed her reflection's voice.

"Wait!" Rachel pleaded. "I need to become human again! No matter the price!"

There wasn't a reply after that.

Rachel crumpled to the floor, defeated. She started sobbing.

"Already, you can't even hold yourself together after I specifically told you what to do. Honestly, if you're going to be human, stop replacing moments of your life with pointless crying," came her reflection's voice.

Rachel looked up, hoping to see herself in the mirror; there was nothing. She quickly dried her tears; the reflection was right. She wasn't ever going to accomplish anything by sitting on the floor and sobbing. She looked at the book on her nightstand and took a seat at the foot of her bed, book in hand. She flipped through the pages, absorbing the words. If she wasn't going to be responsible at the drop of a hat, then she would start slowly. Though first things first, she needed to understand all the power she had in her blood, mind, and heart as a vampire, and more importantly, how to control it.

She spent the rest of the day searching through every nook and cranny of the library for books about vampires.

At the end of her search, Rachel carried to her chambers seven thick books to hopefully help her fully comprehend what being a vampire meant, what she had to do to survive (other than the obvious), and especially the cure. She finally took a seat on the edge of her bed and flipped open one of the seven books—

There was a knock at the door.

"Yes?" Rachel asked, standing up and walking in front of her nightstand, obscuring her books.

Silas stepped into her chambers, and Rachel let out a sigh of relief. She sat back down on her bed, moving the book to her pillow.

"Hello, darling," Silas said.

Rachel cringed at the word 'darling.' "Please don't call me that," she said.

"Sorry," he apologized. "Anyway, what were you doing in here, all alone?"

"I'm reading about vampires, because I can't find the cure without learning a single thing about what I've become."

"I suppose that's true."

"Now, the reason you came here? I would like to get back to my reading."

"Right, dinner is going to be in twenty minutes, just wanted to let you know."

"Oh, okay," Rachel said. "Though I think I'll have to miss it, considering how much research I'll be doing. Keep in mind that I would like to be human."

"Well, um," Silas said, unsure of what to say, "I'll tell the chef to put your food away for later." The king walked out of the bedroom and closed the door silently behind him.

"I said you had to be responsible, not starve yourself," a voice came from behind Rachel.

The vampire turned in a swift motion to see her reflection in the mirror above her nightstand with arms crossed.

"I need to put things aside to learn more about vampires!" Rachel exclaimed with hand gestures.

"Vampires can starve just like humans, for food or blood, understand? You can't go slowly killing yourself and make up stupid excuses; that's being childish!"

Rachel scowled deeply at her reflection.

"You want to prove to me you're responsible? That you're *mature*? Then take care of yourself properly, choose wisely when it comes to anything, and most of all, don't lose control like you did with Night, and yes, I know about that."

Rachel gaped at her reflection.

"And close your mouth, for God's sake." With that said and done, her reflection melted away.

Rachel closed her book, left it on her nightstand, and ran after Silas.

The dining room was serving delicious food, as well as awkwardness. Silas' parents weren't there; apparently, they had eaten their dinner earlier.

"So," Rachel said from beside Silas as she slowly swallowed a chunk of lettuce. "How was your day?"

"It was pretty good," Silas replied slowly, cutting a cherry tomato in half. "What made you come down to eat?"

Rachel was tempted to tell him the truth but she decided that it could wait. "I was just hungry," she lied.

"Oh, but I guess that's a good reason to eat," he said.

"Yeah," she said with a light chuckle. She looked down at her bowl of salad and saw that the cheese at the side was tinted red because of the beets. She gazed at the dark red beets, so red, like blood. Rachel caught herself drooling and she snapped her mouth closed, licking away the saliva from the corners of her mouth.

"Is tonight *blood night?*" Silas asked randomly, obviously aware of her drooling over beets.

Rachel gulped down a small piece of cucumber. "I think we could start tonight, skip tomorrow, and then the next night do it—" she managed.

"And so on and so forth," he finished her sentence.

"Yeah."

"We can do it after dinner."

"But remember to push me off if I lose control, no matter how much you love me. Use violence if necessary; I don't want you to end up like Night," Rachel said, finishing her salad.

Silas looked at the beets she'd left aside. He could only imagine the pain being a vampire caused her, drooling over anything a deep-red colour. How did she feel when she ate bloody meat? How did she survive on the daily? Was that the reason why she was always cooped up in her room now? Or perhaps it was his suggestion to murder prisoners... His thoughts trailed off and he glanced at Rachel, who was waiting for an answer. He forcefully swallowed the rest of his salad, and then he cleared his throat.

"Only if necessary," he said.

Chefs ran to the table and took away their bowls, replacing the appetizer with the main course: a juicy, bloody steak with steamed broccoli on the side, two spoonfuls of buttery mashed potatoes, and the perfect amount of salt.

Rachel's eyes widened at the sight of blood directly in front of her. She covered her mouth and cupped her stomach for she felt her appetizer already crawling up her throat.

"I-I can't eat this," she said, standing up. "I'll be in your chambers; meet me there after you eat."

Silas stood up to go after her but heard the small sound of grunting, as though she was urging to throw up. Nobody wants to be seen throwing up, especially not people full of pride like Rachel. He sat back down and stared at his bloody steak, the very thing that had made his wife sick to her stomach. He called in the head chef. "Nothing bloody from now on, understood? Not a trace of any red liquid," he ordered firmly.

The chef nodded frantically and took the two dishes away.

Silas stood up and started the long walk to his chambers. Rachel was probably there by now and she was hopefully feeling better. He knocked lightly on the door, and when he didn't hear a reply, he opened it. He immediately gasped at the sight of Rachel biting her wrist and drinking her own blood.

"Rachel, what are you doing?" he asked.

Rachel spun towards him with red eyes and bloody fangs. "It keeps healing," she said. She showed him her wrist and he saw the two holes her fangs had caused close.

"But how?" Silas asked.

"Vampires have many powers; we just need to figure them all out," she said, remembering what her reflection had told her.

"What other powers do you have?" he questioned.

"I'm not sure, though I want to find them all out."

"Now, for the reason you're here."

Rachel gulped and wiped the blood from the corners of her mouth. She sat with her legs crossed on the middle of his large bed, and he carefully took a seat beside her.

The king smiled a fake smile at her and slowly gave away to her cold touch holding his chin up and keeping his head back. "Are you ready?" Rachel asked him.

Silas glanced at her red eyes before closing his, and then he let out a faint, "Yes."

With a quiet cry of despair, Rachel sank her fangs deep into his neck and she could feel him tensing in her grip. She gulped down blood until she felt full for the night and let him go.

Silas sat straight up and looked at her eyes that were back to their regular brown. He felt blood trickling down his neck and wiped it away with his hand.

"Thank you," Rachel rasped, looking away as guilt flooded into her heart.

"As long as it's for you, I'll do anything you could possibly want or need," he said softly, standing up.

"Soon we won't have to do this anymore; I promise," Rachel said.

"I know," Silas said, walking into his bathroom. "Don't worry about it. We'll get there on our own time, right?"

"Well, I guess," she shrugged.

"Anyway, I'm going to have a bath; I'll see you later?"

"Alright," Rachel stood up and walked out of his chambers. "See you later," she said before closing the door.

"What do I need to do to prove I'm responsible?" Rachel demanded her mirror like she did every night.

Her reflection appeared, unlike every time Rachel asked. "Ask me something else," she said with crossed arms.

"Can you please answer my question?"

Her reflection rolled her eyes, already starting to disappear.

"Fine!" Rachel said, suddenly frantic.

Her reflection's bottom half reappeared.

"You'll tell me anything other than the cure and how to act responsible, right?"

Her reflection nodded.

"Well then, tell me all the powers a vampire has," she demanded.

Her reflection shrugged. "You haven't been a vampire for too long, so I'm not entirely sure what powers you've developed, or if you've developed any at all yet."

Rachel frowned.

"But I have something that you might want to know."
The vampire looked at her reflection expectantly.

"Remember the demon that possessed you?" her reflection asked.

"She was a sorceress, not a demon, smarty pants," Rachel scoffed.

"She was delusional."

"How would you know?"

"Do you want to know or not?"

Rachel pursed her lips.

"She's a demon," her reflection continued. "And she isn't gone yet, and the fact that you're a vampire doesn't help. Do you remember that thing I showed you, of the girl and the demon? That demon is Cleverly. She's harvesting her magic bit by bit; she will come back soon, and this time she won't give you any mercy whatsoever."

"H-how do I get rid of her?" Rachel asked, suddenly afraid.

"It'll happen when you become human again."

"How long does it take for me to get responsible?"

"I can't tell you because you might get cocky and it will ruin everything." Her reflection glanced down. "You should get some sleep. Goodnight."

"Goodnight," Rachel said with a smile. "And thank you, for everything you've told me."

Her reflection smiled back before fully vanishing.

Rachel stared at her bed and then at the door.

She needed to find the cure soon, before she lost control and Cleverly took control of her. The young queen bolted out of her chambers and ran to the library. She looked through the high shelves until she found what she was looking for: a book of cures for magical mishaps. This would at least give her somewhere to look, or better yet, the cure itself. The vampire sat at a table and looked through the table of contents. She remembered her sixth-grade teacher telling her that if you needed something at a specific page, to always look thoroughly through the table of contents.

With her finger, Rachel read each title carefully, looking for any hints of the vampire cure. She came to a title: Vampire's Cure - Page 389. She immediately flipped to the page and realized that this book only showed where you could get information. She read the text expectantly, knowing that there would be information to where she could be cured:

The vampire's cure is something that many people desire, sometimes to blackmail others who want it, or for themselves to become human again, yet this book doesn't have that specific information you want. You are a vampire reading this, I'm assuming. Just read further and you'll know the key information to becoming human.

There is an old shopkeeper who goes by the name Joe Stock. He lives several towns away from the Royal Charming castle. Go to him with this book and fifty gold coins and he'll tell you everything.

Rachel looked behind her and saw the time; it was almost seven and she was getting quite hungry.

The queen brought the book to her room, put it underneath the covers, and went back to the dining hall to eat.

CHAPTER THIRTY-TWO

ELLIS REVEALS

$\mathcal{L}$eo spent the day at Ellis' rented apartment, sitting on the couch and doing research on her computer.

"What are you looking for?" Ellis asked, walking out of the kitchen with a cup of coffee in hand.

"How many of those are you going to have?" he asked, referring to her coffee.

Ellis quickly glanced down at the steam rising from the liquid, and then she snapped, "You answer my question first."

Leo sighed loudly. "Just looking for magical sightings; I don't know. I mean there's magic everywhere, and you and your family prove that."

"Any luck so far?" she questioned.

"No," he replied grimly.

She sipped loudly on her coffee.

"Could you not do that again? With your *sixth* cup of coffee?"

"I should dump this on you," she muttered. "Now scooch over, I want to see what you're looking at."

Leo moved aside and Ellis plopped herself down beside him. She looked at the screen and put her coffee down on the table. "Give me my computer," she said sternly. "You're looking this up with the wrong words." She quickly typed a different phrase into the search bar: vampire sightings by Evergreen family tree. What looked like thousands of sites popped up. "And besides, why do you want to know about sightings?"

"Because I was hoping it would lead me to vampires."

"Didn't you try to search up something for vampires?" she asked, closing her computer.

"Of course I tried, but only vampire romance novels and T.V. series showed up, nothing real."

"Well, let's get our mind off this magic stuff and do some sightseeing; the fresh air will clear our minds, right?" Ellis suggested.

"I guess," Leo said softly, standing up and stretching his back.

"Now go get changed in the bathroom; you've been in those clothes for a day and a half," she said.

"I haven't had lunch or breakfast," he noted.

"We can eat somewhere while we're out."

"Alright." Leo opened his suitcase, got out a new outfit, and went into the bathroom to change.

Ellis glanced at his suitcase and saw he had barely packed anything. "Men," she sighed.

The first place Ellis and Leo went to was a diner with the smell of fresh food leading them to the open glass doors. They waited patiently for a waiter to see them before being brought to a table for two.

After observing the menu carefully, they both ordered drinks and a meal.

"You seriously ordered coffee?" Leo said to Ellis as the server took their menus.

Ellis shrugged. "I'm feeling tired and lazy; I need around eight cups to feel even slightly motivated," she reasoned.

"And how did that happen? How are you *immune* to the power of coffee?"

"First of all, I'm not fully immune; it just takes a lot of coffee goodness," she said, raising her index finger. She raised a second finger. "And second, I drank so much coffee when I was first allowed that its effect was dulled."

"I guess that is a good reason," Leo shrugged. He spaced out and looked around the restaurant. There were many perfectly spaced tables. People were talking intently while they either ate their breakfast or lunch. Different smells filled his nose and he closed his eyes just to relax. He would find a cure for Rachel so she could turn back into a human. He was going to go back to her and tell her what he'd learned, and then she'd finally give him the appreciation he deserved. He wasn't doing this for the appreciation; this was just so she could be happy. A strong aroma of pancakes with a side of eggs filled his nose.

"Leo, come back to Earth," Ellis said, snapping her fingers in front of his face.

Leo's eyes shot open and he saw his breakfast in front of him. He immediately started ripping the pancakes apart and shoving them down his throat, bite by bite. The maple syrup mixed with the rest of the flavours flawlessly, then he started scarfing down his eggs.

"Never forget to feed a man," Ellis said, one hand supporting her head as she bit into her buttered toast.

Leo stabbed his fork down to get more without looking at the plate, and instead of hearing nothing, he heard a scrape. He looked at his food and realized he'd eaten it all.

Ellis gaped at him. "Do you want my eggs too?" she asked.

"No, that was enough," he said, patting his belly.

"You finished all of that in a matter of seconds, definitely less than a minute at least."

"Now, I need to ask you something I forgot to ask earlier," Leo said, wiping his hands with his napkin.

"Ya?" Ellis asked, mouth full.

"Do you know the cure for being a vampire? The thing that will turn vampires into humans?"

"Yeah, of course," she said as though he had asked if she were human.

Now it was Leo's turn to gape at her. "What is it?" he asked.

Ellis' next words made Leo's eyes grow wide.

"I need to get to Rachel *now*," he said.

CHAPTER THIRTY-THREE

THE CURE'S TRUTH

$\mathcal{R}$ achel woke happily the next morning, ready to go on her journey to find the cure to being a vampire. The first thing she did after eating breakfast was tell Silas her plans to go and travel for the vampire cure. He hugged her tightly and told her that he should come, though she protested. She needed to get the cure on her own, to take responsibility for not being smart enough to fend off the vampires who were the cause of this situation. He told her that he would get a carriage ready, though she disagreed; this was her mission and she would do it without the help of anyone else.

The king let go of her and helped her pack for a short journey, giving her a map as well so she could easily navigate the lands. Rachel meanwhile just made sure she had a mirror, so that she could talk to her reflection and know if she was doing anything drastically wrong.

With a loving kiss goodbye, Rachel left the safe castle and journeyed out into the world of *Snow White*, map and mirror in hand.

After almost an hour, Rachel felt like giving up. She looked at her reflection in the mirror, mimicking her like a reflection should.

"Talk, please," Rachel pleaded to the mirror, though her reflection still mimicked her. "Tell me if I'm doing this all wrong."

Her reflection rolled her eyes quickly, and then she went back to mimicking.

"At least tell me more about Cleverly," the queen pleaded, looking ahead at the path she was following.

Her reflection started talking. "Cleverly is a demon, as you already know. She is not a spirit, or a sorceress, or an enchantress, as you've made the mistake of thinking. She is very much alive, and enjoys taking over bodies, and if it's a good body, she'll stay; if not, she'll leave. When she was younger, she conquered all the elements: Earth, Water, Fire, Wind, Life, and Death. To make her victims lose control, somewhat, she'll make sure they're at a weak point, filled with a negative emotion, and make a deal with them. She'll then take over their body entirely and wreak havoc, which is why you need to find the cure soon to get her out of your soul. Once she's out she'll be in her original demon form, with less power because she doesn't have a human body. Instead, she'll be a greyish-blue-coloured demon, with horns and everything. Then we can kill her once and for all, so she never even tries to take over anything ever again. Understand?"

"Well, of course, but why hasn't she been acting up?" Rachel said.

"Because she's had no reason to make a deal with you," her reflection explained.

"You mean when she says she'll give you power to cause chaos and get what you want? Then she takes over and you're stuck on the sidelines? I remember that vividly."

"Well, she's stuck in your body right now, and she can hear everything we're saying, every single word."

"What do you mean *stuck*?" the queen questioned.

"I mean she's stuck in your soul because a strong, huge chunk has been added. Do you know what it is?"

Rachel stopped walking and stared at her reflection for a moment.

Her reflection rolled her eyes. "*Responsibility.* You're not losing control at all, not with your emotions, and you're not letting your vampire instincts take over at all. Aren't you proud of yourself?"

Rachel continued walking after glancing down at the map to make sure she was going in the right direction. "Two more towns left to pass then we'll be there," she said. "And I am proud of myself; I've never been able to control my temper in the slightest."

"That's kind of sad, considering half of the people in the universe know how to control their temper at age ten or eleven, at most twelve. Here you are, fifteen, just learning how to do that."

Rachel frowned. "I can walk the rest of the way in silence."

"Say no more," her reflection said, and then she vanished.

Rachel tucked the hand mirror in her woven sack and continued on.

Two more small towns passed by before she finally spotted her destination. She started following signs that pointed towards *Joe's Shop of Books*. She imagined a small shop with bright fairy tale-worthy walls. This made her remember the time she and Leo went to *Brandy's Books*, where she got her diary. She pushed the thought away and looked at her surroundings. She saw more and more signs pointing to the bookstore, and then she found it at last: a small shop on top of a hill with bright green grass. The cheerful sight made her smile. She took her book and sack of coins out of her large bag and held them tightly to her chest.

Rachel opened the door and walked inside.

A cloud of dust attacked her and she coughed loudly.

"Who is it?" a man's voice came from nearby.

"A customer of sorts," Rachel said, and stopped her coughing.

A gruff old man came out from behind a shelf and smiled warmly at her. "Hello, there; what kind of book would you like?"

"It's not a book I'm looking for, and I'm assuming you're Joe?" she said.

"That's me, Joe, the owner of this delightful little bookstore. Anyway, what do you mean it's not a book you're looking for?"

"It's an answer, well, information that I need."

Then he saw the book and sack she held tightly.

"Oh," he said. "That's why."

Rachel looked down. She showed him the book, and then she handed him the sack full of coins.

"Come to the counter," Joe said, and he led her to the side of the shop. He walked behind the counter and poured out the coins, each one making a loud *clink*. Quickly, he counted them. "You want the vampire's cure, isn't that it?"

"Yes," Rachel said firmly, gripping the book tighter.

"It's simple, really," he started. "You talk to Death himself about getting your vampire side removed, along with any other curse or what have you, then he'll let you live freely as a cleansed human, well, not exactly *cleansed*."

"How do I talk to Death? Is there some type of communication device?" she questioned.

Joe looked at her with eyes of coal. "*You die*."

TO BE CONTINUED...

386

ACKNOWLEDGMENTS

To my parents, friends, and family for their undying support. A big thank you to my grade school teacher, Mme Francine, for letting me write most of my book during her class. And I am thankful, of course, to Mme Lynda, my sixth-grade teacher, for her ongoing encouragement, and for asking me for a signed copy, because that meant the whole world to me.

Thank you to my friends who have been there to comfort me when I've been sad, especially to Chrystle for being my closest friend for the past three years. To Emilia, for being my first actual friend. To Makayla for always putting a smile on my face. To Lauren, for geeking out with me. To Gabby, for your sarcastic attitude. For Sophie, who's been friends with me for so long. I appreciate every single one of you, and also to Freckle Face, who will probably never be reading this, but thank you for being one of my closest friends throughout most of my life. Thank you to Vicky, Nico, and Freckle Face for the use of your names in this book; I am deeply appreciative. You all mean so much to me, so much more than words could ever possibly hope to describe. Thank you for existing.

Made in the USA
Monee, IL
05 January 2020